*# I read this book ② times*

## Praise for Arlene James and her novels

"A wonderful story of God's care."
—*RT Book Reviews* on *Baby Makes a Match*

"Another entertaining Chatam House story."
—*RT Book Reviews* on *An Unlikely Match*

"A unique plot with likeable characters creates an engaging combination."
—*RT Book Reviews* on *The Heart's Voice*

"Arlene James has an exquisite way with words and emotions in *To Heal a Heart*. The characters and intricate plot will resonate long after the last page is turned."

—*RT Book Reviews*

# ARLENE JAMES

## Baby Makes a Match
### &
## An Unlikely Match

◆ **HARLEQUIN**® LOVE INSPIRED®CLASSICS

Recycling programs
for this product may
not exist in your area.

First published as Baby Makes a Match by Harlequin Books in 2010 and An Unlikely Match by Harlequin Books in 2011.

ISBN-13: 978-0-373-20853-1

Baby Makes a Match & An Unlikely Match

Copyright © 2017 by Harlequin Books S.A.

The publisher acknowledges the copyright holder of the individual works as follows:

Baby Makes a Match
Copyright © 2010 by Deborah Rather

An Unlikely Match
Copyright © 2011 by Deborah Rather

**Printed in U.S.A.**

**HARLEQUIN®**
www.Harlequin.com

# CONTENTS

**Arlene James** has been publishing steadily for nearly four decades and is a charter member of RWA. She is married to an acclaimed artist, and together they have traveled extensively. After growing up in Oklahoma, Arlene lived thirty-four years in Texas and now abides in beautiful northwest Arkansas, near two of the world's three loveliest, smartest, most talented granddaughters. She is heavily involved in her family, church and community.

## Books by Arlene James

### Love Inspired

#### The Prodigal Ranch

*The Rancher's Homecoming*
*Her Single Dad Hero*
*Her Cowboy Boss*

#### Chatam House

*Anna Meets Her Match*
*A Match Made in Texas*
*Baby Makes a Match*
*An Unlikely Match*
*Second Chance Match*
*Building a Perfect Match*
*His Ideal Match*
*The Bachelor Meets His Match*
*The Doctor's Perfect Match*

# BABY MAKES A MATCH

Then Jesus lifted up His eyes, and seeing a great multitude coming toward Him, He said to Philip, "Where shall we buy bread, that these may eat?" But this He said to test him, for He Himself knew what He would do.
—*John* 6:5–6

For Lisa Onvani,
friend, artist, beautiful soul.
Thank you,
DAR

## Chapter One

"**S**ix hundred dollars?" Bethany gaped at the mechanic. The man was unknown to her, just the first possible help that she had found along the road to Dallas after steam had started pouring out from under the hood of her pathetic little heap. "You've got to be kidding. The car wasn't worth six hundred bucks when I started out in it!"

The hulking fellow wiped grease from his hands with a grimy red cloth. "Can't argue with that," he agreed, eyeing the offending vehicle.

"Look, I'm not even going as far as Dallas," she pleaded, clutching the thin cotton skirt of her empire-style, ankle-length blue-and-white-flowered sundress, inadvertently pulling the fabric taut across her distended belly. Her slenderness made her look further along in her pregnancy than she actually was, but she didn't think about that now. "Isn't there something you can do to get me to Buffalo Creek?"

He scratched his bald head. "Tell you what, I'll give you three hundred cash for it as is. Maybe I can part it out, get my money back that way."

"Three hundred?" Bethany repeated in dismay.

Making three hundred dollars beat shelling out six hundred that she did not even have, but how was she to make it to Buffalo Creek if she sold her car? The baby moved, producing an odd fluttering sensation inside her abdomen, as if to say she might as well get on with it. She wasn't going anywhere in a broken-down car that she couldn't fix, anyway, so she really had no choice here. That didn't solve the problem, though. She shook her head, trying to see another way.

The tubby, middle-aged man spread his hands, displaying sweat stains on his coveralls. Bethany didn't know how he managed to work in this old garage in the stifling July heat.

"Sorry. Best I can do," he said. "You can always get a bus ticket at the diner next door."

Well, that was better than nothing, she supposed. Sighing, she shook back her dark hair and smoothed her hands over her mounded belly, feeling a cramp building.

The cramps had started a couple of weeks ago, at only five months into her pregnancy. She had attributed them to stress. Lately, her life had consisted of reeling blow after reeling blow. This was just one more.

Trying to look on the bright side, she reminded herself that three hundred bucks would more than double her pathetic bankroll. Besides, it was really her only option. She could take the money and buy a bus ticket or sit beside the road until she grew roots here, just a couple of hours from her brother.

"Thank you very much," she said quietly, accepting the offer. "I appreciate your help."

"I'll get your cash."

While the mechanic went for the money, Bethany

opened the trunk on her old car, lifting out the smaller of her two suitcases. Thankfully, she'd had sense enough to pack up her important papers, including the title to the car, which she'd bought used way back in high school.

Eight years later, she was afoot again, but she didn't suppose she could complain about that. The car had been far more dependable and serviceable than anything or anyone else in her life. She was sorry to see it go, sorry enough to feel tears gathering.

So, what else was new? She'd cried so much lately that it would have been easier to count the minutes she *hadn't* wept.

The mechanic returned with a receipt and a stack of bills. Bethany signed over the title before going back to the car for the remainder of her belongings. He helped her wrestle the larger suitcase out of the trunk. Stacking the smaller piece of luggage atop the larger one, she pulled up the handle, unlocked the wheels and rolled the lot out into the sweltering Texas sunshine.

Squinting, she slung her handbag over one shoulder, gathered up her hair in her free hand and trudged toward the diner. Not ten months ago, she'd chopped off her dark, sleek locks at her chin, but since she'd gotten pregnant, it now brushed her shoulders again. Thankfully, with the sun hanging low in a white-hot sky, the distance was short. She silently prayed that the wait would be also.

*Lord, please, I don't want to be stranded here in this dot on the map for hours on end. Can't You help me out? I mean, after everything else that's happened, can't I get a break here? I just want to get to my brother safely. And soon.*

Absently, she noticed a somewhat battered, dirty white double-cab pickup truck, towing a large horse trailer behind, on the feeder road that ran along Highway 45. The rig slowed and turned into the eatery's parking lot. The driver obviously knew what he was doing. Plodding along, Bethany watched as he expertly maneuvered the rig into the shade of the only tree within sight, drawing up mere inches from the portable sign at the edge of the lot.

A tall, slim-hipped, light-haired cowboy with broad shoulders got out and fitted a pale high-crowned hat onto his head before moving down the side of the trailer. She couldn't see what he was doing, but it was none of her concern. She had enough concerns of her own.

Somehow, she had to get to her brother. She didn't have anywhere to go except back to Buffalo Creek and Garrett. Her brother was the only family she had and the only person on the face of the earth who would undoubtedly help her.

The cramp suddenly seized her, radiating from her navel outward, not really painful but worrisome. She gasped, then walked on, wishing that she had called Garrett to let him know that she was coming. She hadn't thought of it in her rush to get away, and she was probably the last person in the civilized world who didn't own a cell phone. There was a phone at the convenience store where she'd worked nights and a phone in the modest little house in Humble where she had lived for the past seven years. She had reasoned that she could navigate the few blocks between them without an expensive cell phone.

Bethany staggered into the relative cool of the diner, clutching her belly through the cheap sundress with one hand. Every booth in the small, narrow building was occupied and only three of seats at the counter were vacant. She maneuvered her bags to an out-of-the-way spot near the cash register and hitched up onto the stool next to them at the near end of the counter.

A waitress, with improbably red hair coiled into a frothy bun atop her head, placed a glass of iced water in front of Bethany, who seized it gratefully and drank it straight down. Smiling wryly, the waitress refilled the glass. Slender and hard-looking, her wrinkles had wrinkles.

"What can I get you, hon?"

It occurred to Bethany that she hadn't eaten all day. That couldn't be good for the baby. Her cramp easing, Bethany heard the door open behind her as she glanced at the menu on the wall. "What's the bean burger?"

"A joke. And a bad one. Ain't nobody ordered one of them things since I been here, and I been here since the doors opened. You one of them vegetarians, are you?"

"Uh, no."

"Regular burger, then?"

"Sure. No fries."

The waitress, whose name tag identified her as Shug, yelled over her shoulder, "One favorite, minus the spuds!" She immediately turned a smile upward, looking past Bethany. "Well, hello, sugar. Make yourself at home."

"Thanks," said a man's deep voice.

Boots clumped on the floor, then the cowboy from the parking lot slid onto a stool to Bethany's right, placing his hat, brim up, on the vacant seat between them. The waitress plunked down another glass of water and leaned on the counter. "You look like a hungry man. What'll you have?"

He waved a big, long-fingered hand. Bethany noticed from the corner of her eye that his hair was blond with a touch of tawny red to it. She looked away as he turned his head toward her.

"I'll have the favorite, with the fries," he said in that deep, slightly amused voice. "To go. And the biggest iced tea you can manage."

"A favorite with the works!" Shug shouted, reaching for a forty-four-ounce disposable cup.

Bethany shook her head, remembering fondly the days when she could have downed the same without thinking about it. She'd spend all day trotting to the bathroom if she tried that now. The waitress delivered the iced tea, flirting mildly all the while, before turning back to Bethany.

"Anything to drink 'cept water for you, hon?"

"The water's fine. I was told that I could get a bus ticket here, though."

"Yes, ma'am." Shug stuck her pencil into the wild bun atop her head and reached under the counter, coming up with a big, hardbound book. "Where you headed, hon?"

"Buffalo Creek."

Beside her, the tall cowboy shifted, as if his interest had been stirred.

Shug consulted some sort of schedule and shook her head. "The nine-twenty-two goes right past there, but it don't stop 'til Dallas. Gets in there around midnight."

Dallas. "You've got to be kidding me," Bethany murmured, dropping her forehead into her upturned palm. That was at least forty miles too far, and how was she to get back to Buffalo Creek? Garrett had written that he'd bought a used motorcycle for transportation. Even if they could somehow manage her luggage, she wasn't stupid enough to climb onto the back of that in her condition. Besides, he had no idea that she was coming—or even that she was pregnant.

"You wouldn't know how much a taxi might cost from Dallas to Buffalo Creek, would you?" she asked Shug.

"Honey," the other woman said drily, "this right here is as close as I've ever been to either place. Or anywhere else for that matter."

"I see." Gulping, Bethany swept a hand over her bulging stomach.

"Well, you think on it," Shug said, stowing the book again. "You got nearly five hours before that bus gets here."

Bethany suppressed a sigh and offered up a wan smile. God, as usual, did not seem to be listening to her. Someone else clearly was, though.

"Did I hear someone mention Buffalo Creek?" the cowboy interjected, swiveling on his stool.

Shug immediately drifted his way, saying, "Little mama here is trying to get there. You know it?"

"Yep," he said. "Headed that direction myself."

Bethany finally turned to look at him. She didn't generally find light-haired men attractive, but this was a shockingly handsome man with smiling, cinnamon-brown eyes and dimples that cut grooves into his lean cheeks and a made a cleft in his strong, square chin. His neatly sculpted lips curled up at the corners, a lock of tawny hair falling rakishly across a high brow.

His gaze dropped to her protruding belly, then slid

to the luggage stacked beside her. He turned away the next moment, but then he seemed to make a decision.

"I can give you a ride, if you like."

"There you go!" Shug crowed, throwing a hand at Bethany even as she addressed the cowboy. "I knew you was a gentleman."

The cowboy winked at her, and she laughed. The woman must live to flirt. "What do you think, hon?" she asked Bethany. "This your lucky day or what?"

"Oh. Uh…" Bethany stalled, waiting for the alarms to go off in her brain. Everyone knew that accepting rides from strangers was a dangerous proposition. Even if she was hopelessly stranded. She shook her head. "Th-that's very kind, but I wouldn't want to impose."

"No imposition," he said, "and I don't blame you for being wary. I just thought…" He shrugged, propped his elbows on the counter and turned his head to look at her. "You seem to be traveling alone."

Bethany lifted her chin. "I am."

"The Dallas bus station is right downtown," he went on, nodding. "I wouldn't want anyone I know stepping down there alone at midnight with no idea how to get where she needs to go next."

Bethany gulped. "I see."

A bell dinged. Shug whirled away and back again, sliding a plate onto the counter in front of Bethany.

"Want I should write down his tag number and take a picture of him with my cell phone?" she asked. "Just in case he ain't the gentleman he sizes up to be." She grinned at the cowboy, adding, "Just 'cause you're good-looking don't mean a girl hadn't ought to protect herself. In fact, it probably means she should!"

He chuckled. "Hey, I'm harmless, just trying to do a

good turn." He reached into his back pocket and pulled out his wallet. "You can take a photo of my driver's license if that makes everyone feel better."

"That'd come in handy in case I feel the need to call the law," Shug said bluntly, pulling her phone out of her apron pocket.

He slapped his license onto the counter, and Shug took a photo of it.

"How about your phone number, too? In case I feel the need to call *you*." She waggled her eyebrows. "Maybe I need a ride to Buffalo Creek."

He laughed, and that bell dinged again. A white sack appeared in the kitchen window, and the cowboy got to his feet, reaching for his license as Shug carried the sack to the cash register.

"Better make up your mind," he said to Bethany, "because I can't leave those horses sitting out there in the heat any longer." He looked down at her then, saying, "I'm harmless, I promise, but it's up to you."

Suddenly, she remembered what she'd been doing when she'd first caught sight of his rig. She'd been praying for a safe way to get to her brother, with a minimum of delay and hassle. Maybe, she thought, God *had* actually listened this time.

"I ought to call first and let someone know I'm coming."

"Go ahead."

Making her decision, she got to her feet. "Ma'am, Shug, could I use your phone?"

"Why, sure, hon." The waitress handed it over, reaching for Bethany's untouched plate with the other hand. "I'll just wrap this up for you."

The cowboy put out his hand. "Name's Chandler."

"Bethany," she said, placing her hand in his. "Bethany Ca—" She stumbled over the surname. "Willows. Bethany Willows." She still couldn't help thinking of herself as Bethany Carter. That, however, was behind her now, and all that really mattered was getting to Garrett and finding a way to make a life for herself and her child.

Stepping away, she called for the first time the cellphone number that Garrett had sent in his letter. She had not dared call before, with all that had been going on in her life and his, and she dared not bring it up now, for both their sakes.

After only a few seconds, he answered. Relieved to hear the sound of her beloved brother's voice, she mentioned tentatively that she was coming to see him. He sounded elated and assured her that it would be no problem. She almost told him about the cowboy, but in the end, she decided against it.

Why worry him when he could do nothing about it, having only a motorcycle as transportation and a workday to get through? She wouldn't impose on him too much or jeopardize the life he'd managed to put together for himself. Besides, she felt no threat from this Mr. Chandler. Maybe it was because he was so handsome, but if he'd meant her ill, why would he have let Shug take a photo of his license? Garrett, however, wasn't likely to see it that way. Prison, she had heard, made a man suspicious.

Getting off the phone as quickly as she could, she passed it back to its owner, smiled her thanks and squared her shoulders before facing the stranger who had offered her a ride.

"I'm ready."

"Let's get on the road. Next stop Buffalo Creek."

"Uh, no," she muttered, patting her belly, "I think we'll be stopping before then."

He just laughed and pointed her out the door.

Biting off a huge chunk of burger, Chandler chewed a few times and swallowed without ever taking his eyes off the road. He'd already made short work of the fries, preferring to eat them while they were hot.

"I guess Shug was right," his passenger commented. "You were a hungry man."

"Not really."

He glanced in Bethany's direction and again felt the jolt of her beauty. God had blessed this Bethany Willows with sleek brown-black hair, pale pink skin as smooth as porcelain and a startlingly piquant face. Broad at the brow and cheek but with an adorably pointed chin, it put him in mind of a drawing of a fairy princess in a children's book. Her delicate nose and brows offset huge, tilted eyes of cornflower blue, rimmed with dark lashes, and wide, plump lips of a rich, dusky rose.

She shifted in her seat, crossing her legs beneath the full skirt of her flower-print sundress. The straps of the elasticized bodice tied at the shoulders, emphasizing the delicate line of her collarbone. She seemed petite but was, in fact, taller than average. He judged her to stand at least seven inches over five feet, which still left her a good eight inches shorter than his own six-foot-three-inch height. The pregnancy bump merely called attention to her long, slender limbs and lithe dancer's body.

"So you stopped to eat but you weren't hungry?" Those big blue eyes looked a question at him, her fairy face tilting to one side.

He tried hard to marshal his thoughts. Aiming his gaze straight ahead, he formulated an explanation. "When you rodeo for a living, you learn to eat on the move and whenever it's convenient. I saw a good place to park the trailer, it was getting on to the dinner hour, so I pulled over."

A big part of what he did for a living was just getting him, his horses and his gear from one place to the next. It was a logistical nightmare sometimes, and took careful planning. He and his partner, Pat Kreger, sat down every few weeks and worked out a schedule, deciding which contests made the most sense. They'd managed to improve their standings year by year and had hoped that this year they might make the national finals in team roping, which was why Chandler was alarmed and somewhat irritated by Kreger's failure to show up in Georgia this past weekend.

The Fourth of July holiday offered up some of the richest rodeos of the summer, and Kreger should have been there, but he hadn't showed, and his phone went straight to voice mail every time Chandler called. No one Chandler had spoken to had any idea where Kreger might be, and that was decidedly odd, for Pat was a particularly sociable fellow. Chandler supposed that his partner could be ill and holed up in the little house they shared on the small ranch that they co-owned, but it was more likely that he'd merely given in to some wild impulse and hared off in a different direction. It had happened before, though not often.

If his sister, Kaylie, a nurse, had been in town instead of gallivanting around Europe on her honeymoon, Chandler would have asked her to go out to the ranch and check. As it was, he could only hope and pray that Kreger was well and could offer up some clever excuse.

"So you're a rodeo cowboy, are you?" Bethany Willows asked, pulling his thoughts back to the moment.

"That's right."

"What events?"

"Tie-down roping, steer wrestling, team roping."

"No bull riding or bronc busting?"

Chandler grimaced mentally. Those were the glamorous events. Bull riders and bronc busters were tough, skillful *hombres,* but the most successful ones were compact men with low centers of gravity. Chandler's size and skill set partly dictated the events in which he competed, but he wouldn't have had it any other way. He loved working with a rope. Still, he wanted to impress this woman, silly as that seemed.

"Nope, and no barrel racing, either," he answered flippantly.

She laughed at that, barrel racing usually being a female event, and he cut her a glance that became a stare when he caught sight of that beaming smile. It knocked the breath right out of him and left his chest hurting. He stared until she lifted her burger in both hands and nipped off a small bite with her even, white teeth. Freshly jolted, he jerked his gaze back to the highway and gobbled down the last of his own meal. Wadding up the wrapper, he dropped the paper into the bag standing open on the console between the seats, doing his best to forget what he'd seen. Or rather, what he had not seen.

He had not seen a wedding ring on her long, tapered, slender finger.

# Chapter Two

"So where can I drop you?" the cowboy asked, carefully checking both of his sideview mirrors as he clicked on the rig's right signal.

They had driven in silence for the better part of the trip, though he had stopped when she'd asked him to, without complaint. The silence had been protracted during this last leg of the journey, however, so much so that Bethany had closed her eyes and pretended to sleep for part of the time. Now, she waited to reply until the truck and trailer had exited the highway.

She gave him the address. He gaped at her, his reddish-brown eyes popping wide.

"That's Chatam House!"

"Yes, do you know it?"

He studied her as if trying to decide whether she was serious. "How do *you* know it?"

"Oh, I grew up around here," she answered airily, not about to tell him the whole of that story.

He gave her an odd look. "That makes two of us. Actually, I still live here, and I almost always have, except for when I was away at college. I have a little ranch out west of town now."

"I left Buffalo Creek as soon as I graduated high school," she said. She had literally walked out of the graduation ceremony, gotten into Jay Carter's car and driven straight to the airport, where they'd hopped on a plane to Vegas. Two days later, he'd carried her over the threshold of the house in Humble and left her there while he raced off on business.

"That's probably part of it," the cowboy mused. "What year was that?"

She told him, and he nodded. "I graduated from college that same year. That would make you about twenty-four. Right?"

"Exactly twenty-four."

"I'm twenty-nine. Guess we just moved in different circles back then. My sister, Kaylie, is about your age, though."

Bethany shook her head, trying to remember any Chandlers she might have known. "I don't recall her." That wasn't surprising. She hadn't had many friends. Her stepfather hadn't liked anyone coming around the house to witness his abusive behavior.

"I guess Buffalo Creek's not as small as it feels sometimes," Chandler murmured.

"What is it, about thirty thousand people now?"

"Something like that," he said, nodding. He made a careful left turn and eased over a pair of railroad tracks.

Those old tracks, leftover from the days when Buffalo Creek had been a major transportation center for the cotton growers in the area, crisscrossed the town. The cotton was long gone now, but the trains still rattled through town several times a day. Oddly enough, Bethany had missed them when she'd first moved to Humble. The trains were all she had missed, though. Garrett had already been sent to prison, and their mother had been a different person by then. After their mother's death, Bethany would never have considered coming back if Garrett had not returned here. She still didn't understand why he had, really. Maybe the parole board had dictated where he had to go.

As the city rolled past, one graceful street after another, excitement built in Bethany. Her hands skimmed over her belly. Her pregnancy was going to be a shock to Garrett. She probably should have told him, but they'd been out of touch when she'd first realized that she was pregnant. He'd just gotten out of prison, and she'd had no idea where he was headed or how to reach him. Then her world had begun to dissolve, and she'd judged it wiser, all things considered, not to tell her brother about it.

She'd never dreamed how it would all turn out. How could she?

Obviously, Chandler mused, he needed a refresher course in the basics of introductions. Somehow, he hadn't managed to get his last name out there at the diner, and Bethany had apparently assumed that his given name was his surname. Or had she? He tried to remember if she had glanced at his driver's license as it had lain there on the counter, but he just didn't know.

Thinking of that bare ring finger on her left hand, Chandler took his eyes off the road long enough to glance at her pretty face, and a shiver of *something* crawled right up his spine to the top of his head.

What, he had to ask himself, were the odds that he'd

just accidentally run into a pregnant stranger on the side of the road who was headed not only for his hometown of Buffalo Creek, Texas, but right to his family home? The aunties, no doubt, had something to do with this.

His aunts, maiden triplets in their seventies, might be a tad on the eccentric side, but they were good women. Even more than his retired minister father, they epitomized Christianity for Chandler. They lived to serve a greater cause, dedicating their time, talent, money and even their home, the antebellum mansion known as Chatam House, to the needs of others. They weren't perfect, of course.

Hypatia, the undisputed head of the household, could be a bit prim. She wore her dignity, along with her pearls, like a protective cloak. Magnolia, or Mags, on the other hand, couldn't have been any more down-to-earth if she was covered in it, which she often was, being a master gardener much more concerned with the appearance of her roses than herself. It wasn't unusual, in fact, to find Aunt Mags in a dress and rubber boots decorated with mud. Odelia, bless her, was sweetness personified, sweetness with a heavy dose of silliness. He, along with his cousins, secretly but fondly referred to her as Auntie Od and chuckled about the weird clothing and oversize jewelry that she wore. She especially had a thing for earrings and lace hankies, so much so that the rest of the family routinely speculated about how many of each she might actually possess.

Chandler smiled. No, not perfect but very dear, and as generous and loving as it was possible for three human beings to be. Why, last winter they'd opened their home to his cousin Reeves and Reeves's little girl, Gillian, and just recently, they'd taken in an in-

jured professional hockey player, who just happened to
be Chandler's new brother-in-law. Yes, whatever had
brought pretty, pregnant Bethany Willows here to Chatam House, the aunties almost surely had a hand in it.
He supposed he'd find out what that was soon, as they
had just passed the brick column at the eastern edge of
the fifteen-acre estate.

He slowed the rig, braking carefully so as not to
stress the quartet of horses riding in the trailer. Those
animals, each one trained to a specific task, were essential to his livelihood and constituted a significant
financial investment, besides being as dear to him as
any pet. As the rig slowed, Bethany sat up very straight,
her hands clasping her belly, her gaze trained out the
window at the shoulder-high yew hedge that flanked
the wrought-iron fence.

They came to the gate, which stood open, as usual,
its elaborate scrolls and bars culminating in a large
brass-plated *C,* and there, on a slight rise, stood the
grand old house. Two stories of whitewashed, hand-
hewn stone blocks, it featured half a dozen Doric col-
umns across the veranda and a substantial porte cochere
on the west end. The black trim around the windows
and doors echoed the color of the black slate roof, just as
the redbrick walkways and steps, flanked by a colorful
profusion of flowers, reflected that of the tall chimneys.
Dead center of the veranda stood a bright yellow door
framed by narrow leaded-glass windows on the sides
and an elaborate fan-shaped one on top.

Chandler eased the rig between the brick gate col-
umns and aimed it up the deeply graveled drive that
swept over the easy, green-blanketed hill and circled
back onto itself, branching off at the top to pass be-

neath the porte cochere and on past the carriage house, erected at right angles behind the mansion. The staff, Chester and Hilda Worth and Hilda's sister, Carol Petty, lived in rooms above the carriage house bays, as did Magnolia's mysterious new gardener, Garrett somebody.

Garrett, a tall, dark-haired man in jeans and a snugly fitted T-shirt, strode across the lawn at that very moment, apparently heading toward the enormous old magnolia tree on the west lawn. Bethany swiftly released her safety belt with one hand and slapped the button to roll down the window with the other.

"Garrett! Garrett!"

Her hands fumbled for the door handle and the lock. Alarmed, Chandler braked to a stop. She grabbed her handbag and literally baled out, sobbing and laughing.

"Garrett!"

The muscular, dark-haired man lifted a hand to shade his eyes from the sun as he looked in her direction, then he took off running toward her. Just before he got there, she turned to hold out a hand, yelling to Chandler, "Wait! Just wait!"

Garrett Whatever-His-Last-Name-Was threw his arms around Bethany, lifting her off her feet. The pair embraced tightly for several moments, so wrapped up in each other that they didn't have eyes for anyone or anything else, their dark heads bent close. Chandler put the truck in Park, set the brake and got out. Still the two clung together.

Not quite able to look away from what he knew to be a very emotionally charged moment, Chandler pulled Bethany's luggage from the backseat of the truck and set it on the brick walkway before ambling toward the house. He'd reached the steps up to the porch before Garrett the gardener set Bethany back on her feet, his hands going to her distended belly. Chandler saw Bethany duck her head and had the distinct impression that Garrett hadn't known about the child. He did not look displeased, however, just the opposite. In fact, he and Bethany seemed to care deeply for each other.

Shaking his head wryly, Chandler stepped up into the shadows of the deep veranda. Looked like the aunties' new gardener had a family in the making. Chandler was more than a little envious. One day he would like to have a beautiful wife like her and a couple of kids. But first, he had to get his financial house in order.

If he and Kreger continued to finish in the money for the rest of the year, Chandler could finally pay off his share of the ranch and think about building his own house on the place. That would leave Pat in full possession of his childhood home and allow both of them to start new phases in their lives. Right now, though, that gardener out there was in a better position to support a wife and child than Chandler was.

Not bothering to knock or ring the bell, he did what most of the family would do; he opened the door and walked in, knowing well that the house was rarely locked until the last person retired for the night. He'd been in that marble-floored foyer a thousand times, but still he measured with his eyes the sweep of the magnificent staircase that curved up to the second floor and lifted his gaze past the sparkling chandelier to the ceiling, where some unknown artist had painted blue sky, gauzy clouds and wafting white feathers. He'd never understand how that person had managed to give the impression of sunshine and magnificence. It left the viewer with the feeling that God looked down from Heaven upon the Chatam household. Chandler had always found that a particularly comforting thought, almost as comforting as the aunties themselves, whom he was suddenly anxious to see.

"Hello!" he called. "Where is everyone?"

A frothy white head appeared around the edge of the library door on his right. It was topped by a big, floppy bow of pale pink and anchored by big, butterfly-shaped earrings colored in variegated shades of pink, purple, yellow and blue. A bright pink smile broke across a rounded, drooping face with the Chatam cleft chin. Amber eyes twinkling, Odelia stepped into the foyer in a swirl of multicolored gossamer layers.

"Chandler, dear! There you are!"

The ubiquitous lace hanky appeared, beckoning him to follow. Smiling broadly, he strolled into what was one of his very favorite rooms in the big old house, but he didn't get far, his way blocked by a head-high stack of cardboard boxes.

Hypatia came from behind the stack to kiss his cheek, her silver hair twisted into a smooth figure eight at the nape of her slender neck, pearls in place. She wore a crisp, collarless linen suit of khaki tan with elbow-length sleeves and a pleated skirt.

"We've been expecting you," she said in indulgent tones.

"Expecting me?" He remembered suddenly that Bethany had called ahead. No, that couldn't be right. Bethany hadn't known who he was, so she wouldn't have told Garrett to expect him, Chandler Chatam, to be with her, and even if she had, it wasn't as if he and the gardener had ever officially met. He'd only glimpsed the man from a distance and heard him mentioned. Chandler shifted his weight, one booted foot placed forward, his hands at his belt. "What do you mean, you were expecting me?"

"Well, when that nice Mr. Kreger dropped off your things for you," Odelia trilled, "he said you'd be along." She waved her hanky at the stack of boxes.

Shock rolled over Chandler in waves. "Kreger, P-Pat Kreger, brought this stuff over here?"

"Just a little while ago," Hypatia confirmed.

Chandler thumped himself in the chest, asking stupidly, "For me?"

"Of course, dear," Hypatia said. "We hung your clothing in the cloakroom until you decide which suite you want."

Chandler turned around and walked out into the foyer again. He stalked past the staircase and partway down what was referred to as the "east" hall to the first door on the left. Chandler opened the door and stepped inside the cluttered space. There, along one wall, hung a dozen pairs of neatly pressed jeans and almost twice that many shirts, all his.

Shock morphed into a confused, unwieldy amalgamation of emotions, the only one he could identify being anger. Whirling, he stepped back into the hall. And nearly bowled over Mags. She shoved her thick iron-gray braid off her shoulder and folded her arms, making the short sleeves of her dark plaid shirtwaist dress cut into her surprisingly pronounced biceps. She looked up at him, a frown on her wrinkled, work-hewn face, her cleft chin thrust forward mulishly.

"What's going on, Chandler?" she demanded.

"I don't...I..."

Her expression softened, and she clamped a spotted, surprisingly strong hand onto his forearm. "You can tell us, dear," she said. "Obviously, since you had Kreger bring your things here, you know we'll help in any way we can, though hopefully it won't mean choosing sides between you and your father."

His father. Chandler pushed away any consideration of that situation and focused on the part that had to do with his supposed partner.

"I'm sorry, Aunt Mags, but I have to find Kreger." He looked past her toward the foyer, determination hardening his jaw. "Right now."

He sidestepped around her and strode to the front door, which he went through without a word of farewell. Whatever Kreger was up to, Chandler told himself, the explanation had better be a good one. He saw nothing of Bethany and the gardener, but at the moment his thoughts were centered on his own problems. Bethany Willows and Garrett could take care of themselves.

The rumble of the engine preceded the sound of tires on gravel by less than two seconds. Bethany rose from her seat on the brick steps at the side of the house beneath the carport, or porte cochere, as Garrett called it, and hurried toward the front drive. She arrived just in time to see Chandler's rig completing the loop as it headed for the street. She glanced to the side and saw that her luggage waited for her on the front walk. The truck turned right onto the street and accelerated. Unaccountably deflated, Bethany sighed.

"Guess he got tired of waiting." She turned back and retraced her steps, dragging her toes in the gravel.

"Is that a problem?" Garrett asked. "You said he's not your husband."

"I said I don't have a husband," Bethany corrected softly.

"Actually," Garrett pointed out, his gaze skimming over her distended belly, "I think you said that you've *never* had a husband."

Bethany stepped up next to him, turned and sat on the rough edge of the brick. "That's right." She repositioned her handbag on the step, keeping her gaze averted.

"So when you wrote me to say you'd eloped to Las Vegas…" Garrett prodded.

"Wasn't true," she admitted tersely, propping her elbows on her knees and resting her chin in the cradle of her upturned palms. She'd only thought it true at the time, but Garrett didn't need to know that. No one did.

"And this Jay Carter?"

"Never existed." True again, as far as it went.

"Then why," Garrett demanded, spreading his hands, "did you let me believe all this time that he did?"

Bethany bowed her head, debating with herself. If she told Garrett the truth, he'd want to go after Jay, just the way he'd gone after their stepfather for hurting their mom; yet she couldn't quite bring herself to outright lie to him. Closing her eyes, she whispered another part of the truth, "I didn't want you to worry about me."

When she turned her head, she found his piercing blue gaze trained on her from beneath his dark brows. He shoved both hands through his dark spiky hair. Like her, he had a bit of a pointed chin, but his strong, square jaw was perpetually shadowed with the soot of a heavy beard that he'd struggled to keep cleanly shaved since the age of fourteen. At six-one, he wasn't as tall as the cowboy, she mused, but Garrett was a bit more bulky. He'd muscled up in prison, but he'd always been stronger than average and of a protective nature.

"If I hadn't been in prison, you wouldn't have had to lie to me," he muttered.

Bethany groaned, feeling lower than dirt. "You've got to be kidding! My situation is not your fault. How could you even think it?"

Garrett came up off the steps. Whirling to face her, he thumped himself in the chest. "I was the one in prison! I should have been here for you—and Mom."

Bethany stood and went to him, placing her hands on the hard bulges of his biceps. "You went to prison because you tried to help Mom."

Their father had died in a ditch collapse when Garrett was seven years old and Bethany four. Ten years later their mom, Shirley, had remarried. Doyle turned out to be a controlling, abusive brute who regularly beat their mother. Three years into the marriage, he had beat Shirley so severely that she'd been hospitalized for nearly a week. The day that Doyle had gotten out of jail on bail, Garrett had gone after him, giving the brute a taste of his own medicine. The result had been Garrett's own arrest. Unable to make his bail for himself, Garrett had languished in jail for several months. During that time, Doyle convinced Shirley to forgive him and drop all charges. In frustration, Garrett had pleaded guilty to a reduced charge and gone to prison, telling Bethany that they were all better off that way, for Doyle would surely beat Shirley again and it would be safer if Garrett couldn't get his hands on the man.

He was too right. Not two years later, Doyle had beat their mother to death.

"That doesn't change the fact that I wasn't here for you," Garrett insisted.

"You couldn't help Mom or me," Bethany insisted, "and I'm glad you were out of it." She herself had escaped as soon as she could. Pushing away thoughts of the past, she looked to her brother. "I'm so glad to be with you again."

He hugged her. "Ditto." After a moment, he went on nonchalantly, "So, is the cowboy the baby's father?"

Stunned, Bethany pulled back. Denial leaped to the tip of her tongue, but for some reason she clamped her lips against it. Maybe because she wished the cowboy was the father. At least he was kind to her and true to his word. Better him than a scheming liar and cheat. Besides, it was best to say nothing at all about the baby's father.

*"Tell and I'll take that kid you want so much. Don't think I can't."*

Shivering, she said, "It doesn't matter who the father is. This is my baby, mine alone."

"Why'd you break up with him?"

She looked down at her toes. "He doesn't want to be a father."

Garrett shifted his weight, his feet scuffing in the gravel. "That why you came here, Bethy?" he asked, using her childhood nickname.

She turned back to him, her eyes filling with tears. "I came because I wanted to see you, and because I didn't have anywhere else to go. I don't have enough money to get my own place or any way to pay the rent just now. I hoped you'd be able to help us out until the baby comes."

Nodding, he asked, "When is that?"

"Middle of October."

"So about three and a half months."

"Yes."

"I think we can work out something." He slipped an arm about her shoulders and walked her across the redbrick stoop and through a bright yellow door into a long dark hallway.

"The misses will probably be in the front parlor waiting for dinner," he told her. They walked on to the end of the hall past a TV room on one side and a kitchen on the other, according to the aromas emanating from that room. "Food's great here," Garrett told her with a smile. "This is the west hall," Garrett informed her as they turned right. "There's a real ballroom off the east hall, along with a music room, library and study. Dining room's on this side." He waved a hand.

They came to the end of a broad, sweeping staircase in what was obviously the front foyer of the house. They stopped, and Garrett turned his gaze upward, pointing toward the ceiling. Bethany gasped at the mural overhead and took in the sparkling crystal chandelier. Garrett ushered her through the wide door of a large room crammed with antiques and flowers.

An older woman rose from an armchair placed at a right angle to them. Short and sturdy, she wore a dark shirtwaist dress with penny loafers. Her gray hair hung across one shoulder in a thick braid, the tip brushing a pair of reading glasses in her breast pocket. Her oval face, while wrinkled and sagging a bit, showed a lean strength. She regarded Bethany with bright amber eyes, tilting her cleft chin to one side.

"Hello," she said, curiosity ringing in her voice.

"Bethany," Garrett said, "I'd like to introduce you to Miss Magnolia Faye Chatam. Miss Magnolia, this is my sister."

"Oh, my dear!" Magnolia exclaimed. "What a surprise!" She hurried forward, reaching out for Bethany's hand and clasping it firmly. "You are as pretty as your brother is handsome."

Bethany smiled. "Thank you. He says you've been very kind to him."

Magnolia waved that away. "He's been a great help to me."

"Ma'am, I already owe y'all more than I can ever repay," Garrett said solemnly, "but I hope you don't mind if I ask a favor of you. My sister needs a place to stay. I'd like her to stay with me for a while, if you and the other misses don't mind."

Magnolia seemed slightly taken aback. "In that tiny attic room?"

"We can manage," Garrett insisted. He clasped a hand onto Bethany's shoulder. "She doesn't have anywhere else to go, ma'am."

Two new heads popped up then, and two more pairs of amber eyes turned Bethany's way. Another woman rose from another wing chair. She turned fully to face them, her manner almost regal. Despite her leaner, paler face, she looked very like Magnolia, her silver hair coiled in a heavy figure-eight chignon at the nape of her neck. Her collarless tan suit called attention to the strand of pearls at her throat, and she held in one hand a pair of gold-rimmed half-glasses.

The third sister wore a flutter of rainbow organza. Plumper than the other two, she wore her stark white hair in short, fluffy curls with a big, floppy, soft pink bow tied atop her head and a pair of large, brightly colored organza butterflies affixed to her earlobes. It was all Bethany could do not to laugh with delight.

Tearing her gaze away from the butterfly lady, Bethany looked to Magnolia.

"My sisters," she said. "Miss Odelia Mae Chatam and Miss Hypatia Kay Chatam." Bethany nodded at each in turn.

"Sisters," Magnolia said, "I have the privilege of introducing Garrett's sister, Bethany…" Her voice trailed off.

The moment of truth had arrived, the moment when they would know what a fool she had been. Would they look down on her? Would they judge? She gulped and lifted her chin.

"Bethany Sue. Bethany Sue Willows."

Not a Mrs. Nor a Miss. Just Bethany Sue Willows. And more pain and shame than she knew how to bear.

## Chapter Three

The sisters traded looks.

"Ms. Willows," Hypatia said, inclining her head. "Welcome to Chatam House."

Bethany nearly collapsed with relief. "Thank you, but won't you please call me Bethany?"

Hypatia Chatam smiled serenely. "Thank you. Given names are always easier with three Miss Chatams about." She beckoned them closer with a wave of one hand, saying, "Join us, please."

Magnolia crossed over and took a seat next to Odelia on an elaborately carved settee upholstered in a lush floral damask. Hypatia returned to the gold-striped wingback and nodded Bethany toward its twin. Garrett stood beside her, his arm stretched across the chair back.

"When is the baby due?" Odelia warbled eagerly, butterflies dancing.

"Eighteenth of October," Bethany answered cautiously.

"So," Magnolia said to her sisters, "the master suite, do you think?"

"What?" Garrett exclaimed. "No, no, that's not necessary."

They blithely ignored him.

"Hmm, yes, I think that would be best," Hypatia mused.

Odelia clapped her hands again. "Room for the two of you and the baby!"

Without warning, Bethany burst into tears. "I'm sorry! Garrett said you were kind, but I never dreamed… I never expected…"

"Now, now," Hypatia said calmly.

"It has become clear to us," Magnolia put in, "that the good Lord has ordained Chatam House as a place of sanctuary for those in need. We are only following His dictates, dear."

"And babies are such fun!" Odelia chirruped.

Bethany laughed, blinking away her tears. "I don't know how to thank you. I promise I won't abuse your hospitality. I intend to look for a job right away."

"Is that wise in your condition?" Odelia worried aloud.

"I was working until I came here," Bethany told her staunchly. "I can certainly continue."

"That might not be so easy," Garrett warned. "It's one thing to continue working at a job after you become pregnant. It's another to get someone to hire you when you're almost six months along."

"Well, it's a matter for prayer," Hypatia said in a tone that clearly indicated the subject was closed for the moment. "Bethany, I'm sure you'd like to freshen up before dinner. Garrett, will you show her the retiring room, then ask Carol to set two extra places at the dining table."

Garrett nodded. "I'll get your bags in, too, sis."

"Chester will help you both settle into your new space later," Hypatia decreed.

"Father would be so tickled, don't you think?" Odelia said as Bethany rose and hurried from the room at Garrett's side.

"The master suite was old Mr. Chatam's room," Garrett whispered to Bethany. "He died at the age of ninety-two in nineteen-ninety-nine, and they still speak as if it was yesterday."

"I don't care if they set a place for him at the dinner table!" Bethany whispered back.

"They're not *that* eccentric, and they're sharp as razors, believe me."

"Oh, Garrett," Bethany cried, laying her head on his shoulder, "I'm so glad I came!"

Maybe, she told herself, the Willows family was finally going to come right.

"Well, my dears," Hypatia said, keeping her voice low, "it looks as though we're going to have a full house."

Magnolia nodded, oddly satisfied. She'd known Garrett as a child. After his father had died, Garrett had come around occasionally asking to mow the yard. She'd let him mow for an hour or so, paid him and sent him on his way. After his mother had remarried, he'd started showing up with bruises, but he would never answer Magnolia's questions about how he'd obtained them. She'd heard rumors, but once she'd asked outright if his stepfather had hit him, Garrett had stopped visiting. Later, when she'd learned that Mrs. Benjamin had been hospitalized and Garrett had assaulted his stepfather, she'd expected the boy to get off with a reprimand. Instead, he'd gone to prison. She had always considered that a grave miscarriage of justice, so when he had approached her in the yard just over two months ago, Magnolia had hired him on the spot. Garrett had quickly become a household favorite. Now, his pregnant sister, Bethany, had come to them. Magnolia definitely felt the hand of God at work.

"Even with Chandler here," she said, "I don't see what else we could have done."

"Oh, of course Bethany has to stay!" Odelia gushed. She bit her lip. "But I know I heard Kaylie say that Garrett's sister was married."

Hypatia nodded. "Yes. I recall the same thing."

"Perhaps they've divorced," Magnolia suggested.

"Perhaps," Hypatia murmured. "I confess to some curiosity, but all will undoubtedly become clear in time."

"What God wishes us to know, He will reveal," Magnolia added with a nod.

"I'm more concerned about Chandler, frankly," Hypatia went on.

Magnolia, too, was concerned about their nephew. They had hoped at first that his moving in here had signaled a compromise of sorts with his father, who disapproved of both Chandler's occupation and his partner, Kreger, but something else was obviously afoot, and Chandler hadn't seemed to know what that was.

"We've prayed a long time for him to make certain things right in his life," Magnolia pointed out. "Maybe the good Lord is forcing his hand a bit."

"True," Hypatia agreed.

"Or," Odelia exclaimed, hunching her shoulders with

excitement, "we could have another romance brewing! Wouldn't that be lovely? Chandler and Bethany and a baby! What fun that would be!"

Magnolia rolled her eyes at her sister. "That's a stretch."

"Why? Don't you think she'll like Chandler?"

"That's not the point."

"I'm sure he'll like her, and they'll be living in the same house, after all. Once they get to know each other, anything could happen."

"Now, now," Hypatia cautioned sternly, holding up a hand. "We're getting just a bit carried away here, don't you think?"

Odelia turned a vexed gaze on her. "You're the one who always says that God has a reason for everything."

"Those reasons don't have to be romantic, though," Magnolia interjected.

Odelia blinked. "But they could be."

Hypatia sighed. "Let us leave this subject, please. We don't want to be assigning motives to God now, do we?"

"I suppose not," Odelia mumbled. Then she brightened. "But it will still be fun to have a baby in the house. Maybe we can babysit!"

Nodding, Magnolia shared a look with Hypatia, whose lips firmed against obvious laughter. Bowing her head to hide her own smile, Magnolia rolled her eyes again. Oh, to be as joyful as her dear, frothy-headed sister! On the other hand, Mags was supremely satisfied with her own life. The lives of her and her sisters had been, from the shared day of their birth, a life of privilege, which just meant, as Mama and Daddy had always said, that they were obliged by God to do as much good as they possibly could for others.

Lately, God seemed to be bringing those opportunities to do good right to their doorstep. The outcome thus far had been quite rewarding, resulting in two weddings.

While a romance seemed unlikely in this case, whatever God had in mind, Magnolia was sure that it would be, at the least, very interesting.

Sighing wearily, Chandler turned the rig between the gateposts and aimed it up the rise toward Chatam House. He'd spent the last thirty-six hours fruitlessly trying to catch up with his old buddy and erstwhile partner, Patrick Kreger.

His very first course of action had been to drive straight out to the ranch, where he'd found a family by the name of Cantu in residence. Mr. Cantu had proudly claimed to have purchased the ranch only days earlier. A broken-down old piebald had snuffled around the corral next to the barn, the corral where Chandler had intended to off-load his own horses. Instead, after examining the loan closing papers that Cantu had graciously provided and recognizing Kreger's signature, Chandler had turned around and hit the road again, managing to keep his temper in check until he was away.

After he'd calmed down, he'd made two phone calls. The first was to his cousin Asher, an attorney, who agreed to see him Monday morning. The second call went to an old friend, Dovey Crawlick, who ran a shoe-string animal rescue operation a mile or so southeast of town. She had kindly given Chandler space for his horses at a more-than-reasonable rent and told him that she'd heard Kreger was staying in the Maypearl area.

After following rumors across the state, Chandler

eventually wound up calling on Kreger's elderly great-uncle, from whom Pat had recently requested a large loan and been refused.

"Don't hold with gambling," the old man had said morosely, "but he said they'd break his legs if he didn't come up with the cash."

Chandler had to conclude that Kreger had sold the ranch to cover his gambling debts. That was when Chandler had given up the chase. He'd known, of course, that Kreger was apt to wager a bit here and there, but it hadn't seemed to be a serious problem. Until now.

In a foul mood, Chandler made his way back to Chatam House in the wee hours of the morning. He couldn't help thinking about Bethany. Had the aunties allowed her to move into the carriage house with Garrett? He rather doubted that, unless of course the two were married. If they weren't, they probably soon would be. Then he'd have to see her, them, on a daily basis. With everything that had gone wrong in his life lately, that seemed like adding insult to injury.

Not wanting to rouse the household, he decided to sleep in his truck. It would not be the first time that he'd sacked out in the backseat. He needed to hide his trailer, though. Dovey hadn't had room for it at her place, but the aunties would not appreciate having a dirty horse hauler parked within sight of the street. Moving mechanically, he backed the trailer through the porte cochere, past the carriage house and around the corner of the building out of sight.

After rolling down all the windows to take advantage of the slight breeze, he crawled into the back cab. He set aside his hat, tugged off his belt and boots and curled up on the seat, his head pillowed on his folded forearms. But peace proved elusive as his mind played restlessly over all he'd learned.

That Pat had sold the ranch out from under Chandler hurt, but the reason hurt just as much. He'd trusted Pat Kreger. He had defended Pat staunchly against his father for years. In the end, however, Hub had been proved right about Kreger, and eventually Chandler would have to deal with that. Just then, though, he was trying to wrap his mind around the fifty-thousand-plus dollars that he'd apparently poured down a bottomless hole.

The thought made him physically ill, his disappointment so deep that it was a constant ache. His whole future had just disappeared! Why hadn't he known that Pat was out of control? Why had he made so many excuses for his old buddy?

Feeling brainless and foolish, Chandler did the only thing he knew to do. He prayed.

*Lord, I need Your help here,* he began. *I've been stubborn and stupid and, boy, am I paying for it. I'll be paying for some time to come, too. But I deserve it. So I guess first of all I need to ask for Your forgiveness. I really want to do better from now on, to let You guide me. Meanwhile, I'm in a fix. I can't live off my old aunts. I need some real cash. To get that, I need a new partner, but how do I find a new partner when I'm not even sure I can trust my own judgment anymore? Please give me some real direction here, Lord.*

Chandler went on, pouring out his troubles and concerns, facing his deepest fears and failures and beseeching his Lord for aid. He thought of Bethany again. By all appearances, things had turned out well for her, at least. He felt a prick of envy, but whether for her or Garrett, he didn't know. A little of both, maybe. He drifted into a place of comfort before he could figure it out, and rest found him at last. He slept deeply and completely, his mind a blank, despite the heat and cramped quarters.

Suddenly, bright daylight blinded him. He thought that he must be dreaming, for hands seemed to grapple about his shoulders. Fists closed in the fabric of his shirt, and he instinctively stiffened. The next instant he was being pulled bodily through the open window of the truck cab.

Panicked, he brought his feet up onto the seat and pushed, angling his shoulders through the window, until he could get his hands on the roof of the truck and haul out the rest of the way. He barely got a foot on the ground when a fist slammed into his shoulder. It would have hit his jaw if he hadn't been in the process of bringing down his second foot.

"Hey!"

He let the blow turn him, his hands coming up defensively, and glimpsed a dark head before a second fist flew his way. Ducking left, he felt knuckles clip his ear. Tucking his chin, Chandler threw a hard right, glancing a blow off his opponent's ribs. After an answering pop high on the left side of his chest, he started slugging madly. A savvy fighter, the other guy stepped in close, wrapped his arms around Chandler's shoulders and threw him onto the ground. Chandler made sure that they both went down, twisting to land on his side rather than his back.

"Can't leave her alone, can you?" a voice growled in his ear as the two wrestled.

"What?" Chandler squawked.

"You're not going to bounce in and out of her life!"

"Who?"

"Don't want the kid, but you want her, don't you?"

"What're you tal—"

Something hit Chandler on the side of the face and shoulder, something prickly and stiff.

"Ow!"

"Ouch!" yelped the other guy.

Chandler rolled away, becoming aware of a great din, something more than his own grunts and groans and the scrabble of gravel. One sound stood out among the others, the sound of his aunt's voice.

"Stop that! Stop it right now!"

Realizing that the blows had ceased, Chandler looked up. Magnolia glared down at him, a broom in her hands.

"Aunt Mags?"

"What on earth do you think you're doing, Chandler Chatam?"

"Defending myself!" Chandler exclaimed.

At the same time, his opponent barked, "Chatam?"

She switched her gaze in that direction. "And you, Garrett Willows! Why are you fighting with my nephew?"

Garrett rocketed to his feet. "He's your nephew?"

Chandler sat up, trying to catch his breath. Garrett the gardener had attacked him? He glared up at the dark-haired man towering uncertainly over him. Willows. Garrett Willows. Wasn't that what Magnolia had said? Was he Bethany's husband, then? The idea seriously rankled.

Chandler shoved up to his feet and pointed a finger. "*He* attacked *me*!"

"Chandler?"

Hearing Bethany's voice, Chandler whirled. She

stood beneath the porte cochere with Hypatia and Odelia, her cornflower blue eyes wide.

"Why are you fighting with my brother?"

Brother. He glanced at Garrett Willows. His aunts' gardener was Bethany's *brother*?

She looked as stunned as Chandler felt—and stunning. In dark brown leggings and a long pink top with tiny puffed sleeves, her dark hair a silken fall to her shoulders, she looked wholesome and healthy and radiant. And pregnant, he reminded himself. And the *sister* of Garrett Willows, *not* the wife.

Chandler folded his arms and glared at his opponent. It wouldn't do to smile at such a moment. It wouldn't do at all.

Only a few moments earlier, in company with Hypatia and Odelia, Bethany had been on her way to the sunroom for breakfast. Then a grim-lipped Magnolia had emerged from the kitchen with a broom in hand, exclaiming that she had seen "them" fighting when she'd gone out to water the pot plants on the stoop. She'd stomped off toward the side door; Hypatia and Odelia had promptly followed, leaving a curious Bethany to bring up the rear. Bursting from the house, she'd seen two men rolling around on the ground and hitting each other. Magnolia had surged forward and smacked them both with her broom. When they'd fallen apart, Bethany had been shocked to see that one of them was her brother! And the other…Chandler! Chandler *Chatam*?

She shook her head. "I—I don't understand."

Her brother cast her a hooded glance and started to beat the dust from his jeans and bright blue T-shirt.

"Well, that makes two of us," Chandler said, glaring at Garrett. "What possessed you to come after me like that?"

Garrett ducked his head, muttering sullenly, "I saw you hiding in your truck around the corner of the building, and—"

"I wasn't hiding!" Chandler interrupted. "I was sleeping. I got back late and didn't want to wake anyone. I parked back there because I knew my aunts wouldn't want the horse trailer sitting where it could be seen from the street."

"Well, how was I supposed to know that?" Garrett snapped. To Bethany's shock, Garrett turned on her, demanding, "How on earth did you get involved with a Chatam, anyway?"

Before Bethany could answer, Hypatia stepped up and asked, "Do you two know each other?"

"No!" Bethany exclaimed.

At the same time, Chandler said, "Yes."

Odelia giggled and clapped a lace hanky between her hands, looking from one of her sisters to the other. "Didn't I tell you?"

Bethany had no idea what she was talking about, but it was difficult to take her seriously when she wore vivid yellow-and-white awning stripes, culminating with earrings fashioned to resemble stylized suns. They were almost as large as the visible ball in the sky overhead.

Hypatia made an exasperated sound and looked from Bethany to Chandler. "It can't be both."

"He told me his name was Chandler," Bethany blurted defensively.

"And it is," he drawled. "Hubner Chandler Chatam the third."

"You never said Chatam!" Bethany insisted.

"Oh, my word," Magnolia muttered.

Chandler sighed. "Look, it's just one of those crazy coincidences. I picked her up alongside the road about halfway between here and Houston."

"You were hitchhiking?" Garrett roared at her.

"No! I was trying to buy a bus ticket in a diner."

"But he said he picked you up alongside the road."

"The *diner* was alongside the road," Chandler stated pointedly.

"I don't care how you met him!" Garrett bawled. "What matters is that he's the father of your baby!"

There were audible gasps. Bethany gulped. Oh, how had this all gotten so muddled?

Chandler glared at her. "Did you tell him that *I* was the father?"

"No! I just didn't say that you *aren't* the father."

He parked his hands at his waist. "Come again?"

She opened her mouth to explain, heat burning her cheeks, when a pain seized her, so unexpected that she doubled over. "Ow!"

Both men rushed forward. Four strong arms surrounded her.

"Sis!"

"Bethany!"

"Ohhh," she moaned. "I-It's just a c-cramp."

"Bring her inside," Hypatia instructed smartly.

Chandler stepped back so Garrett could sweep her up in his arms, but the cramp was already waning.

"It's all right," she gasped. "Really. I—I can walk."

Everyone ignored her, moving en masse toward the house. Chandler leaped ahead and held open the bright yellow door as the sisters swept through. On their heels,

Garrett carried Bethany inside, striding swiftly down the shadowy back hall to the family room.

"Honestly," she protested. "You don't have to carry me."

"It's either him or me," Chandler growled.

Bethany glanced over Garrett's shoulder at him. Despite needing a shave and looking somewhat haggard, the man was handsome enough to make a girl's heart go pitter-patter. And a Chatam! Her mind whirling, she quickly looked away.

Garrett carried her to a plush love seat, which matched the oversize sofa in the center of the room, where he at last set her on her feet. Stalling for time, Bethany tugged at the hem of her tunic and adjusted the tiny puffed sleeves before smoothing her hands across the thighs of her brown knit leggings before sitting down. The Chatam sisters primly seated themselves on the full-length sofa. The men stood opposite each other, arms folded.

"Now, then," Hypatia said calmly, "I think we all need to know just who the father of this child is."

Bethany bowed her head. Could the situation be any more mortifying? It wasn't just embarrassing, though; it was dangerous, and she had to think of her child first.

She gulped and mumbled, "I can't tell you."

"But it's not Chandler?" Hypatia pressed.

Bethany shook her head, gaze averted.

"Satisfied?" Chandler asked, glaring at Garrett.

"How was I to know?" Garrett demanded. "She shows up, pregnant and unmarried, with you." Bethany flinched, hearing it stated so baldly. "All she'll say is that the father doesn't want the kid," he barreled on, "and you take off without even bothering to meet me!"

"I had important business! And why would I bother meeting you? I didn't know you were her brother. All I knew was that you're the gardener here, and I don't report to the gardener!"

"Stop it!" Bethany cried, shocking even herself. "Just stop snarling at each other. Neither of you has any reason."

"No reason?" Chandler demanded. "He hit me!"

"You hit me back," Garrett grumbled, rubbing his ribs.

Bethany sighed. Her eyes filled, and she bit her lip, but then she managed to say softly, "I don't want to talk about who the father of this baby is anymore."

Garrett shifted. "But—"

"You heard her," Chandler snapped. Bethany glanced up, straight into his warm brown gaze. "It's her business," he muttered, glancing away.

"Of course," Hypatia said, as if that settled the matter.

"You're right," Magnolia agreed at the same time. Garrett looked like he might explode for a moment, but then he gave his head a sharp nod.

"Well, that's that, then," Odelia announced with some satisfaction. "And now we're all friends."

Bethany choked back a startled laugh. Then a weight seemed to descend on her shoulders. These were good people, every one of them. Her brother had offered her support when she needed it most. The Chatam triplets had taken her into their home without a moment's hesitation. Chandler had offered her a ride when she was nothing more than a desperate stranger stranded beside the road. Good people, indeed, and good people deserved the truth.

But she couldn't give it to them. Not now. Not ever.

She gulped and closed her eyes, remembering the look on Jay's face when he'd learned that she was pregnant. He didn't want this child, but he would take it from her if she ever told anyone what he'd done. With her family history and his resources, that would be too difficult.

Silence reigned for a long moment, then Garrett turned to face Chandler and squared his shoulders. They were both beginning to show a few scrapes and bruises but nothing that wouldn't be gone by morning.

"I apologize," he said. "I have a history of overreacting where the women in my family are concerned."

Chandler shrugged, his gaze skimming over Bethany. "No real harm done, I guess."

Garrett nodded curtly and moved to stand at her side, saying, "You have to admit that it's a lulu of a coincidence, my sister stumbling into your path."

"No kidding," Bethany murmured. Even Chandler lifted his eyebrows and nodded in agreement. Not so the triplets.

Hypatia shared an amused look with her sisters and calmly said, "Oh, my dears, do you not realize that for God's children, there are no coincidences? Only plans."

# Chapter Four

Straightening, Chandler felt an eerie feeling skitter up his spine.

No coincidences for God's children.

Chandler knew that God had plans for the lives of believers, but he'd never before thought of it in quite that way. He suddenly remembered his father speaking from the pulpit.

*"God allows nothing into our lives without a reason."*

As a teenager, Chandler hadn't paid much attention, already at odds with his dad over his friendship with Kreger. Both he and Kreger had been horse-mad and dreaming of careers in rodeo. Pat's grandfather had encouraged their interest, but Hub believed that sports were frivolous, mere hobbies, certainly not occupations fit for Chandler men. Only lately, since Chandler's sister, Kaylie, had married a pro hockey goalie, had Hub rethought his prejudice somewhat.

Now, suddenly, Chandler heard his father's long-ago words with a different ear and applied that new interpretation to his meeting Bethany.

If Kreger had flown in to compete as they'd planned, he'd have been riding with Chandler back to Buffalo Creek. They wouldn't have left for home early that morning because Pat never hauled himself out of bed before he had to, which meant they'd have stopped for dinner long before they'd have reached that little diner. The only reasonable conclusion was that Chandler would have missed Bethany completely if things had gone as *he* had planned. No telling where she'd have wound up then.

A fresh chill ran up his spine, and he found himself wholly identifying with Garrett's impulses. If Bethany was his sister... But she was not his sister. She was, instead, a very attractive, *single* woman.

A single *expectant mother*, he reminded himself.

No, Chandler didn't blame Garrett for wanting to pound someone.

His ears perked up when Magnolia asked Bethany if she still intended to look for a job. Putting aside his thoughts, he listened to Bethany reply, "As quickly as possible."

"Sis, do you really think anyone is going to hire a woman as pregnant as you are?" Garrett asked, looking down at her.

Bethany sighed but otherwise did not answer.

"It is a problem," Hypatia agreed gently.

"I can't just live off your generosity and my brother's until the baby comes," Bethany pointed out.

Chandler surprised himself by speaking the instant the thought entered his mind.

"Dad might be willing to hire her."

Five pairs of eyes turned to him. Well, it only seemed logical. In fact, he was surprised that his aunts hadn't thought of it themselves. He cleared his throat and said, "Dad is about to open the new Single Parents Ministry to the public, isn't he?"

Hypatia brightened. "That's right. He's been talking about hiring a receptionist."

"That would be perfect," Bethany said, sitting forward. "What do they do there?"

"Offer parenting classes, support groups, Bible studies," Hypatia said. "They've also put together a panel of advisers, attorneys, mental health professionals, charities, anyone who can help lighten the load of a single parent."

"It sounds wonderful!" Bethany gushed.

"It's part-time, so the pay wouldn't be much," Magnolia warned.

"Still, it's something," Bethany pointed out.

"And of course you'll stay here until after the baby comes and you're on your feet again," Odelia put in.

For the second time that morning, Chandler watched Bethany's eyes fill with tears. She reached a hand up to her brother, who pressed her fingers with his, smiling.

"Looks like God brought both of us to the right place," she noted in a shaky voice.

"You'd think I'd learn to let Him handle things, wouldn't you?" Garrett said with a guilty glance in Chandler's direction.

Bethany chuckled and wiped tears from her cheeks. "That's something I guess we both have to work on."

Watching those slender fingertips swipe at the moisture on her ivory cheeks, Chandler felt a lump rise in his own throat and shifted uncomfortably. He realized suddenly that it was past time for him to be about his own business, even if he was tired due to lack of sleep.

That, he told himself stoutly, was what was behind this sudden emotionalism, surely.

"How soon do you think I can speak to your father about the job?" Bethany asked him.

Chandler opened his mouth, but Hypatia spoke first.

"Chandler, dear," she said, "might you take Bethany to meet your father Monday?"

"Me?"

"That will give us time to speak to Hubner about it beforehand," Hypatia said to Bethany.

"Grease the skids, in other words," Garrett said wryly.

Magnolia laughed and quipped, "I'll get out the oil can."

Meanwhile, Hypatia answered Chandler. "Of course *you*, dear. You're the perfect person to do it."

Chandler flung a hand at Garrett. "Why not him?"

"On the back of my motorcyle?" Garrett retorted, shaking his head. "Not in her condition."

"And Chester is busy," Odelia informed him helpfully, "especially Monday. It's Hilda's shopping day, you know."

The aunties themselves did not drive. Chandler thought of his appointment with his cousin, the attorney, on Monday and a hundred and one other things he needed to get done as quickly as possible, but he knew that he had to do this. Talking to his dad about a job had been his idea in the first place, and Bethany was not getting on the back of that motorcycle if he could prevent it.

"Yeah, okay, fine," he said with less grace than he might have. "Now if that's settled, I'm going to move most of my stuff into the attic."

"You're moving in here?" Garrett asked, his brows drawing together.

Chandler rose. "Yeah. You have a problem with that?"

"No, of course not. Just surprised."

"That makes two of us," Chandler muttered. He purposefully did not look at Bethany, but turned to dispense kisses to the papery cool cheeks of his aunties, thanking them for their hospitality.

"Don't worry," Hypatia said, beaming a smile. "It's a very big house."

"The east suite should suit," Magnolia began, but Chandler waved that away.

"Naw, I'll just take one of the big bedrooms."

"In that case," Odelia chirped, "perhaps the room behind the attic stairs? It has a window and is convenient to the attic."

Chandler shrugged. "Fine with me."

"Perfect!" Odelia exclaimed, clapping her hands. "That's right next to the master suite where Bethany and Garrett are staying."

Chandler raised his eyebrows. Evidently, the aunties were going all out in their support of the Willows siblings. Well, it was no skin off his nose, especially when they were willing to house him, too. But not for long, God willing, not for long. In fact, with single, pretty Bethany in residence, the sooner he got his business in order and moved out of Chatam House, the better.

It was all he could do to keep from looking at her one more time before he stepped out into the corridor and strode toward the library.

"I'll give you a hand."

Chandler glanced over his shoulder at Bethany's brother.

"That's not necessary."

"No, I insist."

*O-o-o-kay,* Chandler thought, wondering if Garrett was about to warn him away from his sister. Not that Garrett had anything to worry about. The very last thing Chandler needed in his life right now was a woman, especially a pregnant woman.

"Your breakfast will be waiting in the kitchen when you're done," Hypatia called.

Chandler brightened, thinking of Hilda's excellent cooking. "A ray of light in an otherwise dim world," he retorted drolly.

"If that means Hilda's cooking is the best, I couldn't agree more," Garrett said, lengthening his stride to bring himself even with Chandler.

Chandler shook his head. "First you try to beat me down and then you jump over into the amen corner."

"For the record," Garrett retorted, keeping pace with Chandler, "I *did* beat you down."

"In your dreams, brother."

"I'm not *your* brother."

Chandler snorted. "You could be. Neither of them can throw a decent punch, either."

"Now you've gone from dreaming to sheer insanity," Garrett said drily, and for some reason they were both suddenly grinning. "You handle yourself pretty well, too, though."

"Thanks," Chandler drawled.

"So where'd you learn to fight like that, anyway?"

"I rodeo for a living," Chandler replied. "There's always some drunk cowboy wanting to take you down a peg." The truth was that he hadn't been in a real fight in ages, but early on the occasional fracas into which Kreger had dragged him had almost seemed, well, fun. "How about you?"

Garrett paused just outside the library door and met Chandler's gaze. "Prison," he answered grimly.

Chandler rocked back. "Yeah? How come?"

Garrett sighed. "Like I said, I've been known to be a little overprotective of the women in my family."

"Do my aunts know about this?"

"Absolutely. I just thought you should know, too."

Chandler folded his arms. "Suppose you clue me in, then."

"Okay, but let's do it while we're working. Breakfast is calling me."

Chandler could find no argument against that, and later, having heard the full story, he could find no quarrel with Garrett's presence in the household, either. In fact, in his opinion, though he didn't know Bethany's story, the Willows siblings appeared to have gotten a pretty raw deal in life so far.

*"God allows nothing into our lives without a reason,"* whispered his father's voice then, and right behind it came Hypatia's. *"Do you not realize that for God's children, there are no coincidences? Only plans."*

Chandler supposed that one's actions and decisions played into what God allowed and planned for a believer. Everyone had free will, after all. Still, a loving, omniscient God could be trusted to have reasons and plans, which meant that whatever was going on with him now, God had allowed for His own purposes. Chandler believed that those purposes would ultimately work for his benefit, for God did not curse His own children;

He blessed them. Chandler knew that his life had been greatly blessed, especially compared to the lives of Garrett and Bethany Willows.

As he sat down with Garrett at the battered table in the warm, spacious kitchen to eat Hilda's fluffy scrambled eggs and crisp bacon, his situation suddenly looked a lot better than it had only last night, and Chandler determined to move forward prayerfully. With that in mind, he took the time to give silent thanks.

*For this food and all the blessings in my life, Lord, I give You thanks, especially for the fresh perspective. Guess I needed that, and whatever else You will also surely provide. Seems like I forgot that. I'm sorry. Won't happen again. But if You could speed things up so I can get out on my own again, I'd sure appreciate it.* He chuckled. *And a little patience on my part wouldn't hurt, either.*

When he looked up, he found Garrett Willows watching him. Chandler smiled. "Trying to turn over a new leaf."

Garrett arched a dark eyebrow at that, muttering, "Lot of that going on here."

Chandler glanced around the homey, old-fashioned, redbrick and stainless-steel kitchen. Where better to get a fresh start, he asked himself, than here at Chatam House?

Now if only he could find a new partner and win some money… That, too, he decided he would leave in God's hands. Surely, with a little prayer and patience, it would all work out. After all, for God's children, there were no coincidences, only plans. And God's plans, he finally realized, had to be far superior to his own.

They could hardly be worse!

\* \* \*

Fitting his left boot into the stirrup, Chandler grasped the horn with his left hand and swung up into the saddle. He shook out his loop. Sensing that they were about to go to work, the big bay, named Red Rover, danced until Chandler reined him to a standstill.

A good night's rest had cleared Chandler's mind. He'd spent the previous day making phone calls and settling into his room. Immediately after an excellent dinner, he'd turned in, as much to escape Bethany's unsettling presence as to be well rested for today's activity. She was a complication he didn't need, and now she was there in the house with him. Sure, it was a big house. He just hoped it was big enough. He needed all of his concentration if he was going to make this work; his very future depended on it.

He'd been surprised and pleased yesterday to find that Drew Shaw, a saddle bronc rider and one the finest heelers that rodeo had ever known, was on the lookout for a new partner, his previous header having retired. Chandler had eagerly made this appointment and driven to Stephenville, some two hours east of Buffalo Creek, and this modest private arena on the edge of town. This, he mused, might be the most important Saturday morning of his entire career.

Feeling as nervous as the quivering horse, he backed the big bay into place. They had been practicing for nearly an hour now, but this would be for time. Drew and his mount, a beautiful chestnut sorrel, already waited in their box. Chandler looked at Drew, who sat poised with lasso in hand, and signaled the chute man.

An instant later, the yearling steer shot past. The penalty line broke from the steer's neck and the barrier rope dropped away. Chandler spurred the bay, who leaped into action, instantly matching stride with the steer. Operating on practice and instinct, Chandler felt the loop leave his hand, saw it drop around the steer's horns. Perhaps two seconds later, Drew threw down his own loop and closed it. Chandler turned his bay, and in a blink, the steer was immobilized.

"Time!" shouted Drew's wife, Cindy.

She stood on the second-from-the-bottom rung of the metal-rod arena fence, her belly protruding between rods, a stopwatch in one hand. Chandler had been secretly amused to arrive and find the statuesque blonde pregnant. Seemed like pregnant women were becoming the norm in his life. Maybe he should've brought Bethany along today. She might have enjoyed the outing.

Then again, maybe not. The last thing he needed just now was a distraction, and Bethany Willows was proving to be just that. He couldn't seem to stop thinking about her, wondering why God had placed her in his path that day.

Drew loosed the steer, coiled his rope and rode over to the fence to take a look at the stopwatch. He then turned and rode toward Chandler, who hung his coiled rope on the saddle horn. A smile split Drew's round, freckled face.

"Pretty good. Let's take three or four runs at it and get an average. What do you say?"

"Sure thing."

After another hour, they called a halt, walking their horses to cool them down. As Chandler took care of his bay, he ran over the morning's work in his mind. In all honesty, Drew's technique was technically perfect but not nearly as showy as Kreger's. Chandler missed that flamboyance and enthusiasm, but he was smart enough to know that Drew's businesslike approach could be the competitive edge that would put them on top as a team. Drew, in fact, was not the one whose skills were on trial here.

*Lord,* he prayed silently, as he strolled over to Drew's rig, *let me measure up.*

"So what do you think?" he asked. His heart was beating like a big brass drum.

Leaning against the fender of his pristine, late-model dualie, Drew removed his pale straw hat, revealing thin, light brown hair, and refit it to his head. His wife stood next to him, her arms folded. Just a few inches shorter than Drew, she wore a T-shirt that didn't quite cover the elastic inset in her jeans and big, white-framed sunshades, her streaky gold hair pulled back into a short ponytail.

"Looks like we might fit," Drew said.

"In the arena, anyway," Cindy put in.

Chandler said nothing to that, knowing that it had portent he didn't quite understand. Drew's pleasant expression never altered, but the pale hazel eyes that met Chandler's were blatantly measuring. "We're not party folk," he said. "We don't go to the bars and lay out at night."

"I don't, either," Chandler told him, "not as a habit."

"That's not what we heard," Cindy said bluntly.

Chandler felt his stomach drop. It was true that he'd waded through more than his fair share of dives, but only to haul Kreger out of one jamb or another. He wouldn't use Pat as an excuse, though. In all truth, he had *chosen* to become Pat Kreger's keeper, and now he was paying for it.

"I don't know what you've heard," he said, "but frankly I'll be happy if I never have to walk into another bar."

A long look passed between husband and wife before Drew nodded at Chandler and said, "We'll pray on it and get back to you."

A relieved smile pushed up from Chandler's chest. "And I'll do the same. Can't make a mistake that way, can we?"

"Not if we're letting the Lord lead," Drew said with a grin. The two men shook hands, and Chandler took his leave.

"Okay, Lord," he said from behind the wheel of his truck as he headed back to Buffalo Creek, "it's all up to You now. If nothing else, You've shown me a better way of doing things, and I can see that I need to make some adjustments."

He'd start with regularly attending worship services, he decided. He often attended Cowboy Church when he was competing, but not every rodeo boasted a Cowboy Church pastor. On those weekends when he was home, he avoided church. More accurately, he avoided his father by staying home, but he knew that had to change, starting tomorrow.

The thought flitted through his mind that at some point he'd have to choke down his pride and admit to his dad that he was right about Kreger, but Chandler let that notion go on its way. He had enough to think about already. More than enough. If one of the things occupying his mind lately was pretty, dark-haired and pregnant, well, better her than his ongoing battle with his father. Wasn't like he had much choice about it, anyway. She was in his head whether he wanted her to be or not.

* * *

"Garrett? Bethany? Are you riding with us?"

Magnolia's voice came to Chandler through his bedroom door. Mechanically looping his tie and fashioning
a knot, he wandered over and shouldered the door open.
Magnolia stood in front of the sitting room of the master
suite. Bethany appeared from inside, holding closed her
faded cotton bathrobe at the throat. It would not close
over her distended belly or the knit shorts and top that
she wore beneath it. She smiled sleepily at Magnolia.

"Good morning. Garrett's already gone down."

"Bethany," Magnolia said, "you're not dressed.
Aren't you going to church, dear?"

"Oh, I—I'm moving slowly this morning," she answered, shrugging.

Chandler spoke up before he even knew that he was
going to. "She can ride with me. I'm not going to Sunday School, just worship."

"How thoughtful," Magnolia said, glancing toward
him.

Leaning forward, Bethany followed Magnolia's line
of sight. Letting his gaze roam over her, Chandler adjusted the knot of his tie and turned down the collar
of the white shirt that he wore with a pair of dark blue
jeans and his best ostrich quill boots. He realized that
he was smiling and quickly looked away, but he couldn't
help thinking that in addition to that pretty face and
beautiful hair, Bethany had really nice legs. In fact, with
her rumpled hair, bare feet and pregnant belly, she was
the most feminine thing he'd ever seen.

Bethany shook her head at him. "Thank you, but I'm
not feeling all that well this morning." She lifted a hand
to her temple as if to say that her head hurt.

"Oh, I'm so sorry," Magnolia crooned. "Are you sure you'll be all right here alone? Would you like me to stay with you?"

"No, no," Bethany insisted. "I'll be fine. I'm going to get something to eat and rest a little more. You go on with the others, and I'll see you later."

"I'm not sure you should be alone," Magnolia said worriedly.

"I wouldn't let Garrett stay. I'm certainly not going to let you," Bethany told her firmly. "Besides, I have a phone here. I'll be fine."

"Well, if you're sure," Magnolia murmured.

"Go," Bethany ordered, smiling.

Magnolia nodded and hurried off, tossing a speaking look in Chandler's direction. He wasn't sure why or how Bethany Willows had suddenly become his responsibility, but God knew the woman needed someone to look out for her and since her brother wasn't around, he supposed he was elected. He ambled down the short hall and leaned a shoulder against the doorjamb of the sitting room door.

"You know that the staff have Sundays off, don't you?"

"Yes, Garrett told me."

"I was going to grab a bite to eat on my way to church. I can bring something back for you, if you like. Won't take long."

Bethany smiled. "Thanks but that's not necessary. I'll go down and rummage around the kitchen in a little while, toast an English muffin or something. Garrett says Hilda makes her own."

"She does," Chandler confirmed, straightening away from the door frame.

"Great! Well, I won't keep you." With that, Bethany backed into the room and closed the door.

Chandler stood for a moment, telling himself that she was an adult fully capable of making her own breakfast. On the other hand, if she was feeling unwell, it wouldn't hurt him to toast an English muffin. Aunt Mags would undoubtedly expect it of him. He headed down to the kitchen.

Listening to the sounds of Chandler's footsteps as he moved away, Bethany let out a sigh of relief. Then she pushed away from the door, turned and caught sight of herself in the mirror over the sitting room mantel. Groaning, she stared at her rumpled hair and pale face, recalling how handsome he'd looked in his Sunday best, his face cleanly shaven, blond hair neatly combed. She looked as if she'd passed a rough night, when in fact the opposite was true.

She'd slept soundly, but she'd awakened in a panic, knowing that if she went to church this morning, she was bound to run into someone who'd known her back in high school, someone who remembered her elopement, someone who would undoubtedly ask about her obviously absent husband. She just couldn't face that yet. It was simply too embarrassing, especially while she was carrying this belly around.

Walking over to the Victorian sofa, she plopped down, frowning. What did she say when, inevitably, someone asked about her husband? That she was unmarried, never married, divorced, perhaps? She didn't want to lie, but she didn't want the truth out there, either, for numerous reasons. She slumped back against the sofa cushion, telling herself that she couldn't hide forever. Sooner or later, she would have to face this dilemma.

She mulled the problem but had found no solution when someone tapped on her door again a few moments later. Wondering who that could be now, she got up to answer, only to find Chandler Chatam standing there, a china plate in one hand and a glass of orange juice in another.

He thrust the plate and juice at her, saying, "You can stick those in the dumbwaiter when you're through with them." As he sauntered off toward his own room, he nodded toward the tiny elevator set into the wall at the end of the hallway. It came out downstairs in the butler's pantry, as she had discovered on her first day here.

Bethany looked down at the plate in her hand. It contained an unpeeled banana, a toasted English muffin and generous dollops of butter and some sort of jam. For a moment, she couldn't do anything more than stand there and stare, but then her stomach rumbled hungrily. Suddenly she realized that he'd made her breakfast.

Galvanized, she called out, "Thank you!"

"You're welcome," came the disembodied reply.

Carefully closing the door, Bethany let her smile grow. Setting the glass of orange juice onto a small writing desk, she reached for the still-warm muffin and dipped it into the soft butter before biting into it. Slightly crunchy and dusted with cornmeal, it filled her mouth with delight. Chatam House, she decided, closing her eyes, was a very good place to be indeed. And these Chatams, they were something else. Chandler, for instance, was the very epitome of the man's man, yet he was very thoughtful, kind, not to mention forgiving, helpful, handsome…

Oh, why couldn't she have met a man like him instead of Jay Carter? But the past could not be changed, and her future no longer had room for a man. Besides, what on earth would a man like Chandler Chatam want with a fool like her? And a child. Not exactly every man's dream package.

Jay's insidious voice whispered through her head.

*"You think any other man is going to want you with your crazy background and a kid in tow?"*

No, even if she could bring herself to trust again, she couldn't believe that a good man like Chandler Chatam would ever want her. Better that she should just concentrate on being a good mother to her child and forget about him. If only she could figure out how to do it.

## Chapter Five

Shifting on the pew next to Odelia, Magnolia glanced up the broad central aisle of the sanctuary at Downtown Bible Church and noted that Garrett and Chandler were working their way through the throng together. One dark and one blond, they were the perfect foil for the coloring and good looks of the other. Magnolia knew that once Hubner laid eyes on Chandler, the current discussion would be at an end, and the sisters had not yet accomplished their purpose, which was to promote Bethany as a candidate for the job of receptionist at the Single Parents Ministry.

Looking back to her older brother, who stood in the aisle next to Hypatia, Magnolia tamped down her impatience. Hubner had been a wonderful pastor, and she was pleased that he'd taken on the administration of the Single Parents Ministry. Not too long ago, the Chatam sisters had feared that Hub had essentially checked out of his life. After being widowed for a second time, he had suffered a heart attack. His daughter, Kaylie, a nurse, had then moved in with him and nurtured him back to health, but no one had seemed able to coax him back into his life and ministry. Thankfully, God had accomplished that through Kaylie's marriage to Stephen Gallow, and no one was happier about it than Magnolia, but her brother could be unreasonable where his youngest son was concerned.

"So do you or do you not need a receptionist?" she demanded, ignoring the look of exasperation that Hypatia dropped on her.

"I will," Hubner hedged.

"The question," Hypatia said, "is not will you need a receptionist, but *when* will you need a receptionist."

Hubner shrugged and hitched his dress slacks up around his middle. It wasn't so much that Hub had a pot belly as that his already slender frame had more or less shrunk around it, making that a prominent feature, and his rigid, somewhat backward-leaning posture, an effect of his bifocal glasses, called attention to it.

"I suppose I'll have to start looking for someone soon," he said, lifting his cleft chin.

"Excellent," Magnolia replied. "We'll be sending over someone special for you to interview tomorrow."

Hubner shoved his glasses back up onto his nose and sighed. "This isn't one of your causes, is it, one of your lost sheep?"

"Not at all!" Odelia exclaimed. "Why, she's practically a member of the family. And who knows, if she and Chan—"

Magnolia elbowed her. Hypatia hastily spoke over the resulting yelp. "She's the sister of Garrett Willows, our gardener, and she's, er…"

"Going to have a baby!" Odelia whispered happily, loud enough to be heard yards away. She glared at Magnolia as if daring her to use the elbow again.

As if that would do any good. Magnolia rolled her eyes in exasperation.

Chandler and Garrett arrived just then, and Hypatia rushed to head off any awkwardness between father and son. "Hubner, you remember our gardener, Garrett Willows."

"Sir," Garrett said, shaking hands with the older man. "Nice to see you again."

Hubner smiled and nodded. His gaze then shifted to Chandler, whom he greeted with raised eyebrows. "Well, well," he said. "Will wonders never cease? It's Sunday, and my son is actually in church."

Magnolia sighed at the same time as Chandler. Why was it, she wondered, that Hubner could extend the hand of nonjudgmental fellowship to any stranger on the street and yet greet his own son with such barbed criticism? She supposed that it had something to do with a father's expectations of his son and the son's need to go his own way.

"Hello, Dad," Chandler said sarcastically. "Nice to see you, too."

Magnolia verbally jumped between them before things could get out of control. "We're so pleased to have Chandler living at Chatam House now."

Hubner blinked. "Living at Chatam House? With Patrick Kreger?"

"No, of course not with Kreger," Chandler snapped, "and it's only temporary."

Hypatia hastily changed the subject. "Have you heard from Kaylie and Stephen?"

Hub pursed his mouth and briefly bowed his head, but he surrendered to the change of subject. Smiling tightly, he replied, "She's anxious to get back here to oversee the construction of the new house. I think Stephen is less enthused about the house than about getting in condition for the hockey season."

"That's understandable," Magnolia said, "given what he's been through since his accident." That set Hub off on a long report on Stephen's current condition.

Stephen had accidentally driven his car through a garage wall and injured himself severely. Thanks to the influence of Dr. Brooks Leland, Stephen had wound up recuperating at Chatam House in an effort to avoid the press. There he had met Kaylie, who'd been hired to oversee his care. The two had quickly fallen in love and were now on an extended honeymoon. They had sold Stephen's Fort Worth house and were now building a beautiful new home on the east side of Buffalo Creek. When it was finished, Hub intended to move in with them, at Stephen's invitation. Magnolia and her sisters were grateful for that, as it meant that they did not have to worry about Hub being cared for as he aged. They themselves had cared for their widowed father until his passing, but Hub was only a few years older than them.

"All in all, he's doing very well," Hub said, winding up.

Thankfully, the service was starting by the time the subject had been exhausted, and Hypatia hurried everyone into seats. Chandler sank down between Magnolia and Garrett. She caught a look of sympathy on Garrett's face and told herself wryly that her nephew may have made a friend between blows. Stranger things, as she well knew, had happened. Why, they had happened to another of her nephews, Reeves Leland, who had met and married an old childhood nemesis, Anna Miranda Burdett, at Chatam House just this past winter.

Suddenly Magnolia wondered if Odelia might not be right after all. She thought of the way Chandler had stood up for Bethany when she'd refused to name her baby's father and how he'd proposed that his father should employ her. Magnolia remembered, too, how studiously he'd tried not to glance in Bethany's direction at dinner last night, then how he'd offered her a ride to church this morning. Could it be that Odelia was right and romance was blossoming at Chatam House again?

Stranger things indeed.

Magnolia smiled, wondering if it would be wrong to give God just a little bit of a helping hand.

Stepping up onto the low, concrete stoop of the 1960s-era, ranch-style brick house that was the head-quarters for the Single Parents Ministry, Chandler reached out to pull open the heavy, commercial-type glass door and held it wide for Bethany to pass through. She was looking as businesslike as it was possible for a woman in her condition. Her short-sleeved navy blue dress featured an empire waistline with a skinny yellow belt that perfectly matched the narrow band holding back her dark hair and the soft, flat shoes on her slender feet. Whatever had kept her out of church the day before seemed to have passed, but she betrayed a certain nervousness when she paused on the threshold and pulled in a deep breath.

Chuckling, Chandler said, "I know just how you feel."

"Do you?"

"I'm looking for a new partner, and I had a tryout of sorts just last Saturday. I haven't been that nervous since I passed a note to Mary Ann Catcher in third grade."

"Check one if you like me. Check two if you don't," Bethany teased, paraphrasing an old country song.

Chandler grinned. "Something like that."

"And of course she checked number one."

"Actually, she stuck out her tongue and threw a pencil at me. Good pencil. I used it for a couple weeks."

They both laughed as the door swung closed behind them. The laughter took the edge off the dread that he felt at facing his father. It wasn't enough that he should give Bethany a ride over here this morning. Oh, no, Magnolia had privately insisted that he personally introduce her to Hubner, as if that would endear her to the old man. Still, Chandler would do his best.

Standing in the tiny entry hall of the converted house, Chandler saw that straight ahead was what had obviously been the dining room, now fitted out with an old desk, a new computer and several thinly padded chairs to make a reception area. The living room, now a classroom, was on the right, with the kitchen tucked into the far corner next to the dining/reception space. Chandler imagined that the two or three rooms that opened off the hall to the left would be used for offices or storage.

His father came out of that hall, a smile on his face. "We're not officially open for another week," he was saying, "but if I can help you, I'll—" He stopped dead in his tracks, his jaw dropping.

Chandler hadn't expected quite that reaction. His father couldn't be *that* surprised to see him again so soon, and the aunts had surely mentioned Bethany to him the day before at church. Lifting a hand to the small of Bethany's back, he urged her forward, saying, "Dad, this is Bethany. She's looking for a job. The aunties thought I should introduce you to her myself."

Hub's face turned six shades of red. Confused by this reaction, Chandler shook his head, even as Hub bawled, "Chandler Chatam! Please tell me that you've married this girl!"

"Married!" Chandler echoed, knowing instantly what his father was thinking. So did Bethany.

"Not again," she moaned, casting Chandler an apologetic look. In high dudgeon, Hubner didn't even seem to notice.

"Odelia all but spilled it yesterday! Almost a member of the family! But I never dreamed that my own son would…" He shook a hand at Bethany, palm out, demanding of Chandler, "How could you?"

"But he didn't—" Bethany began.

Chandler grasped her wrist, squeezing hard enough to shut off the flow of her words. "No! Just forget it," he barked at her, glaring at Hub. "My father always knows best where I'm concerned. He knows all my thoughts, words and deeds. And each and every one is a disappointment to him. I've never done a right thing in my life so far as he's concerned! Don't even waste your breath. He's seen us together. He already knows everything he needs to know."

Bethany turned to him, lifting her hands to his chest, either to comfort or to calm him. "I'm sorry, Chandler," she whispered.

He shook his head. This was not her fault. "No, *I'm* sorry. I should have known better than to bring you to my father. Let's just go. You shouldn't be working, anyway." Hub always thought the worst of his youngest son, but this just plain hurt.

"Oh, no," she said. Pivoting on her heels, she fixed his father with a hard stare. "You go on to your appointment," she told Chandler firmly. "I'll be right here waiting when you get back."

"Bethany, this is not a good idea," Chandler argued. "He won't believe you."

"I'll be here when you get back," she stated again, meeting his gaze.

Those bright, cornflower-blue eyes left him no option. Glumly, Chandler nodded. Shooting his father a bitter glance, he spun and shoved through the door. Once outside, he hesitated, breathing heavily. The impulse to stride back inside and sweep Bethany out of there was strong, but she had told him to go, and he had no right to overrule her.

Besides, Ash was waiting, and Chandler needed legal advice. Over the years, he'd poured more than fifty thousand dollars into the ranch that Kreger had just sold out from under him, and he needed to know if he had any legal redress, any hope of recouping some portion of his investment. Even now, he'd hate to have to sue his former friend, but perhaps he could levy a lien against the ranch.

And to think that he'd felt guilty about not telling his father about Kreger's lies! He'd certainly be keeping that to himself now.

Heavy of heart, Chandler went to his truck and slid inside. He glanced at the door to the house, now the offices of Single Parent Ministries, as proclaimed by the sign in the yard, and inserted the key into the ignition. Pausing, he beat down the need to go back inside and drag Bethany out of there. Finally, he started up the truck and reluctantly drove away.

\* \* \*

The elderly man standing before her shifted his weight, his bushy eyebrows drawn together over the tops of his wire-rimmed glasses in a frown. All the Chatams, Bethany noted, seemed to have cleft chins. She brought her hands to her waist—or, rather, to where her waist had once been—and frowned right back at him.

"You are wrong about your son."

Dull red crept up Hub Chatam's throat from the open neck of his shirt collar, and he stuck out his chin. "My sister said yesterday that you were practically a member of the family. Then today he shows up here with you in that condition. What should I think?"

Bethany rolled her eyes. "My brother, Garrett, is the gardener at Chatam House. Your sisters treat him like he's a member of the family. I suppose that's what she meant. All I know is that they've been more than kind to me. They gave me a home when I had nowhere else to turn." She smoothed her hands over her belly as her muscles began to tighten.

"So you and Chandler both are living at Chatam House," Hubner said. "Well, that explains a good deal."

"Separately," Bethany pointed out. "We're not together. We moved in separately."

Hub scoffed at that. "I wouldn't expect anything else. But if you and Chandler aren't together, why did he leave the ranch?"

She could only shake his head. "I don't know. That's his business."

"I see."

She doubted that, but she didn't feel like arguing just then. Her stomach muscles clenched painfully. "Do you mind if I sit down?" she asked, trying to relax. "I feel like I'm carrying around an anvil in here."

"Of course, of course." He swept a hand toward the desk. "This way." He waited for her to walk over and sit down, then pulled a chair close and sat facing her. "I must say…Bethany, is it?" She nodded. "I must say, Bethany, it's rather unusual for a woman in your condition to be out looking for a job."

"I don't see why. A woman in my condition has to live just like everyone else. I was working as a clerk in a convenience store until a couple weeks ago, but it's too hard now for me to stand on my feet all day."

"Ah. Well, the standing would be at a minimum here." He folded his hands and regarded her thoughtfully for some time before quietly saying, "I'm sorry for what Chandler has done—"

"Chandler has been very good to me," she interrupted sharply. "We first met beside the road *a few days ago*, and he brought me to my brother at Chatam House."

"And my sisters believed that tale?" Hubner exclaimed.

Meaning that he obviously did not! Exasperated, she started to get to her feet. "I see that Chandler was right. I'll just wait outside for him to return."

"I didn't say I wouldn't hire you," Hubner quickly told her, lifting a hand.

She sat back once more, surprised. "I can have the job? But why, if you don't believe me?"

"I can't imagine anyone else would hire you in this condition, so, yes, you can have the job. It seems the best thing to do."

Bethany wasn't about to talk her way out of a paycheck by arguing further. Surely, in time, he would see that he was mistaken about her and his son.

"Thank you," she said.

"You're welcome, but there is a process to go through."

"Fine. No problem."

He rose then to go into his office for an application.

Bethany wondered what had occurred between father and son to foster such distrust on Hubner Chatam's part, but it was really none of her business. Besides, she needed this job, if only to pay her doctor bills. She knew that she had to have her cramps checked out, which meant that soon she had to find a doctor here in Buffalo Creek, and doctors expected payment.

Pastor Hub, as he told her to call him, went over a folder that outlined the ministry's objectives before leaving her to fill out the application. Bethany made short work of the form and eagerly scanned the list of programs and classes soon to be available.

"Oh, this is wonderful," she said when Hubner returned, "but you're open for business only three days a week?"

"Yes, that's right. Tuesday, Wednesday and Thursday. We have an emergency number that is answered through the church, and I don't mind telling you that I've been working much more than three days a week getting this off the ground. I hope to be able to cut back to that soon, and then eventually to hand off my duties to a younger person. I think perhaps I'll continue to teach some of the classes, though."

Part-time work was better than no work, Bethany mused. After the baby came, she could look for something better paying. Until then, this would have to do.

They agreed that she would start first thing the next morning, primarily to field calls from people wanting information. They discussed her other duties, which were minimal, and then Hub showed her around the place.

Their business concluded, they wandered back to the reception area to resume their seats.

"Would you be offended if I said that I would pray for you?" Hub asked after a moment.

"Not a bit." Especially, she thought, since God did not always seem to hear her own prayers.

"Good, because I sense that you have been deeply hurt."

She didn't deny it, but quickly qualified, "Not by Chandler."

"Then perhaps you will tell me who it is that has hurt you," Hubner urged.

She met his gaze, quipping, "You want the whole list? Or just the worst one?"

"Let's start with the worst one," he said gently.

Her answer didn't even require thought. "My step-father." Jay's perfidy barely even registered when compared with what Doyle Benjamin had done. "He murdered my mother."

Hub reared back in surprise, but then his expression softened into sympathy. "Oh, I remember now. A great tragedy."

She nodded, and they discussed that time in hushed tones, including how Garrett had gotten caught up in the fallout.

"I didn't realize that about your brother," Hub said, "but I'm glad you told me."

Chandler pushed through the door at that moment.

He glowered at his father in silence, then switched his gaze to Bethany. "Ready to go?"

"Yes." She slid to the edge of her seat and paused, hoping Hub would apologize for his earlier behavior, but instead he lifted his chin and looked away. Heart sinking, she rose to her feet.

Hub, too, stood. Never taking his eyes off Bethany, he said, "I'll expect to see you tomorrow morning promptly at eight o'clock."

"I'll see you then."

He patted her shoulder, saying, "Casual attire. We want a relaxed atmosphere. No need to drag out your Sunday best."

"That's good," she replied wryly, "because this dress is about the extent of it."

Hub chuckled, and she answered with a smile before turning toward Chandler. He nodded, a pleased gleam in his warm cinnamon eyes. Whatever his problem with his father, he wasn't bothered by the idea of her working with the man. Bethany allowed Chandler to sweep her back out into the July heat. The two men never spoke to one another, but she was too happy to worry about it just then. Only later, in the front seat of Chandler's pickup truck, did she stop to think about that and its implications.

"I'm sorry if I created problems between you and your dad," she told Chandler sincerely.

He lifted an eyebrow at that. "Hardly. My father and I have had problems since I was in high school." He shifted in his seat then, adding, "I had a particular friend my father did not approve of."

"Ah. But that was a while ago," she pointed out.

"Not long enough," Chandler drawled. Sighing, he

admitted, "The truth is, Dad was right about my friend. It just took me this long to find it out."

"He's not right about you, though," she said. Chandler shot her a surprised look. "I mean, he wasn't right about you today."

"Nope."

"So, what makes you think he's right about your friend?"

Chandler shrugged, and she thought for a moment that he would fob her off with some clever, muddled quip. But then he gripped the steering wheel with both hands and told her how his "friend" had betrayed him and how slim his chances were, according to his attorney, of ever receiving restitution.

"That's why you're looking for another partner," Bethany said.

"That's why."

"And all that money is just gone?"

He literally squirmed over that. "Yeah, according to my cousin, the attorney. I was too stupid to insist on drawing up a contract or having my name put on the deed, and Ash doubts a lawsuit would succeed because I was living there, working there and keeping my horses there while I was giving Pat money. Even though we had a verbal agreement that half of it would go toward a down payment on my share of the ranch, it would be his word against mine, or at the very best, an arbitrated settlement that I already know Kreger can't pay."

"I'm so sorry," she told him softly. "I know what it feels like to trust someone with your future and be betrayed."

Turning a grim face toward her, Chandler shook his

head. "It's nothing time and prayer can't resolve. Lots of time and prayer."

She couldn't help grinning at that. "You sound just like your father now."

He couldn't have looked more stunned if she'd belted him, but then he laughed. "Don't say any such thing to him. It's liable to give him another heart attack."

She gasped at that. "He has a bad heart?"

"No. He had a heart attack due to a blockage in one of his veins, but his heart is still strong. My sister, Kaylie, explained it all to us. She's a nurse."

"I see."

Bethany thought about what he'd told her. They had more in common than she could have imagined, and she wasn't so sure that what had been done to her was so much worse than what Chandler was dealing with. Betrayal was betrayal. But at least he still had one parent. How sad that they should be at such odds.

"So what are you going to do now?" she asked. "Any plans?"

Chandler nodded. "I've placed my horses with a friend, and I've already been to see another man about taking me on as his partner. As soon as I get some money in hand, I'll find a place of my own. Until then… thank God for my aunties and Chatam House."

"Amen!"

"It's humbling, though," he said, tossing a wry smile her way. "Starting all over when you thought you were on the right track to begin with."

"Humbling," she echoed, nodding.

"And a little scary," he added.

She rubbed her hand over her belly. "No kidding."

"But it's going to be okay," Chandler said, sounding as if he was trying to convince himself as much as her. "Right?"

She looked up to find him watching her, concern etching a line between his brows. It was the same expression that his father had worn earlier, but she doubted that he would care to know that, so she merely smiled and told him what he wanted to hear.

"Yes, we're all going to be fine."

Somehow. Eventually.

She hoped.


"See you soon," Chandler said, offering his hand to Drew Shaw.

"Sure thing, partner," Drew said, grasping Chandler's hand in a hearty shake.

Chandler had been pleased and hopeful when Drew had called Tuesday to suggest that he come to Stephenville a few more times to see how things went with the two of them. Anxious to devote as much time to fostering this partnership as possible, Chandler had toyed with the idea of finding someone else to get Bethany to and from work. With his father working feverishly to get the ministry offices ready to go public next week, his sister out of town and Chester busy with the aunties, however, Chandler didn't know of anyone on whom he could call to give Bethany a ride. Magnolia had suggested his brother Morgan, but Chandler had thought of Morgan's fast little sports car and nixed that idea. He'd just have to make it to Stephenville and back while she was working.

After meeting with Drew Wednesday, Chandler had decided to withdraw from the individual events that he had entered and concentrate on securing a partnership with Drew. That paid off Friday, when Drew and Cindy offered him partnership papers. He'd taken them to Asher, who'd found no fault with them, and had carried them back this bright Saturday morning, signed, sealed and now delivered.

"I'll get those entries in today," Cindy said as Chandler slid behind the wheel of his truck. "If there are any problems, I'll let you know."

They had agreed that she would be the manager in this newly formed partnership, but she would not take care of Chandler's individual entries. Chandler had acted informally as manager for both him and Kreger, and neither had worried overmuch about who paid what, which meant that Chandler had paid most of the entry fees for both of them. Drew, on the other hand, had already set up a special bank account to handle their fees and winnings and an agreement on payouts. Very businesslike. For his part, Chandler had written a check to cover his half of the first entry fee. Hopefully, the next one would come from their joint winnings.

As he drove toward Buffalo Creek, Chandler let his mind wander. Drew had suggested that they debut their team at a rodeo in Lawton, Oklahoma. The purse wasn't huge, but the stock provider was well-known and the location was about equidistant for both of them. Cindy had confirmed that slots were still available, so Chandler had agreed.

A forthright woman, Cindy made Chandler think that she might be uncomfortable to live with, unlike Bethany, who was sweetly willing to get along and go along. He didn't dislike Cindy, and Drew certainly seemed happy with her; Chandler just didn't think that he would be comfortable married to her.

Bethany, on the other hand, had an entirely different effect on him. She made him want things, a home and family of his own, someone to share his thoughts, concerns and joys with, someone who looked at him the way Cindy looked at Drew. It was nonsense, of course.

Chandler was in no position to offer Bethany, or any woman, anything, especially not the monetary kind. His rapidly dwindling bank account testified to that. He was happy to do what he could, of course, like driving her to and from work, and he was glad that the aunts had stepped up to provide a home for her, but Bethany's brother would have to manage the rest.

Chandler wondered idly just how much money Garrett made. The aunties were generous, but they couldn't be paying him much above minimum wage. Then again, they also provided housing and food. Still, he couldn't be taking in much, and working only three days a week, Bethany wouldn't be in a position to add to their joint coffers.

On the other hand, Chandler himself had nothing at all coming in just now and quite a lot going out, which meant that he had nothing to offer a woman at this point in his life. If things were different, though…

He mentally shook his head. Better not to even go there. The last thing any woman, even a pregnant and unmarried one, needed was a broke cowboy who couldn't even put a roof over his own head, let alone hers and her child's. Besides, Bethany didn't have any interest in him. Best he go about his own business and leave Bethany to God.

He was so distracted by his thoughts that he found himself pulling to a stop in front of the mansion rather than going on around to the side of the house. He decided to leave the truck right there for now, eager to share his good news with his aunts. Smiling to himself, he climbed up onto the porch and let himself in the front door.

Bethany practically fell into his arms, gasping, "I need a doctor!"

Barefoot and wearing only shorts and a T-shirt, she hunched over and grasped her belly, telling Chandler without words that the need was urgent. Scared half out of his boots, he swept her up into his arms, shouting for his aunts.

"They're at a meeting," she groaned. The aunties supported numerous causes, which meant that they could be anywhere in town, and wherever they were, Chester and the town car were with them.

Chandler didn't bother to suggest that they fetch her brother or wait for him to be informed. Instead, he practically ran across the porch with her, leaving the door standing wide open, and dropped her onto the backseat of his truck before sprinting around to jump beneath the steering wheel once more. Lights flashing, he drove her to the emergency room at Buffalo Creek Memorial Hospital as rapidly as possible, while she wept and moaned in obvious pain.

Terrified for her and the child, he went to the only place he knew to go to at such times, straight to the throne of God.

## Chapter Six

Chandler brought the truck to a stop at the curb in front of the emergency room door and hopped out. Bethany slid to the edge of the seat and let him gather her into his arms.

He carried her through the automatic doors into the crowded waiting area, calling out, "We need some help here!"

Immediately, the crowd parted, and Chandler rushed toward a cubicle that contained a registration desk.

"She's in pain," he said to the woman behind that desk. "It's too early."

Within moments Bethany was being whisked into the treatment area by a nurse pushing a wheelchair. Chandler fell into step with the chair. The nurse began shooting questions at them, questions only Bethany could answer. Chandler was horrified to hear that she had been feeling a regular "tightening" since rising from her bed that morning and that in the last hour the "cramps" had become increasingly painful.

The nurse delivered them to a curtained bed, but when Bethany made to rise, Chandler lifted her into his arms once more and placed her on the gurney. Another nurse swooped in to take her vitals, while the first promised that a doctor would be with her shortly. The new nurse took a hospital gown from a stack on a nearby counter and shook it out. Chandler immediately stepped outside the curtain. The clerk from the front desk was waiting for him with a clipboard and ink pen in hand.

"Name?"

He answered without thinking, "Chandler Chatam."

"*Her* name."

"Bethany—"

She interrupted him, asking for and jotting down an address before thrusting the clipboard at him. "Sign here. You can take care of the rest later."

His mind whirling, he took the pen and signed.

The other nurse shoved back the drape. He hurried back to Bethany's bedside and took her hand in his again. Tears rolled from her eyes and into the hair at her temples.

"I'm scared," she whispered in a trembling voice.

"Gonna be okay," he promised, silently adding, *Please, Lord. Please!*

Clasping his hand, she nodded, but her chin wobbled. He reached back and pulled a hard plastic chair close, so he could sit right next to the bed. Someone came in with a machine of some sort and peeled away the covers and gown to bare Bethany's stomach. Embarrassed, Chandler kept his gaze trained on Bethany's face as she maintained her crushing grip on his hand.

Finally, the doctor came in. Like the nurses, she was no one Chandler knew, no one his sister, the nurse, or his older brother Morgan's best friend, Dr. Brooks Leland, had ever introduced. Brisk and efficient, with a blond ponytail and a square, unadorned face, she identified herself as Dr. Andersen as she moved a rectangular instrument over Bethany's belly.

"Well, he's not in position," she noted after several moments of staring at a computer screen.

"He?" Bethany said, sniffing. "It's a boy?"

The doctor shot her a look. "Oh, did I spoil the surprise?"

Bethany shook her head. "No. They couldn't tell before." She looked at Chandler, whispering in a tone of wonder, "It's a boy."

A boy. Chandler gulped, his chest suddenly feeling as tight as a big brass drum. Bethany was going to have a son. Chandler wondered what he would look like and what his name would be. He wondered if he would ever have a son, and he knew that if he were ever so blessed he would storm the gates of heaven for that child.

He could do no less for Bethany's child. If he didn't, who would?

The doctor said that she needed to examine Bethany, so he hurriedly stepped outside the curtain once again. The examination seemed to take forever, but Chandler used every moment of it to silently plead for Bethany and her son, just as he would have if that little boy had been his own. He wished suddenly that this baby was his, and for the first time he felt the kind of paralyzing fear that Bethany must be feeling. It was not just sadness and pity, not just a detached sense of possible disaster, but a bone-deep terror that something too precious for words was at stake, something that could never be replaced and would forever be missed if God did not extend His great mercy at that very moment.

Closing his eyes, Chandler begged for that little life and the woman who carried it.

"What does it mean that he's not in position?" Bethany nervously asked the doctor.

"Means he's not ready to be born," the doctor told her, having finished her examination. "You're not ready, either."

One of the nurses opened the curtains and allowed Chandler back in. He came immediately to Bethany's side.

"You mean she's not in labor?" he asked, obviously having overheard.

"Not in real labor," the doctor said.

"Thank God!"

The doctor went on to explain about Braxton-Hicks, which she described as a sort of practice labor. Bethany breathed out a sigh of relief even as the doctor mentioned that stress often exacerbated the cramps. She'd had plenty of that lately, but Bethany determined not to waste one more moment worrying over the past.

"I'm going to order some meds, then if everything's okay in a couple hours, she can go home," the doctor said to Chandler. "Just make sure that she sees her ob-gyn as soon as possible."

Chandler opened his mouth, but then he closed it again and nodded. Bethany bit her lip. Obviously, the doctor thought Chandler was the father of her child. Bethany knew that she ought to correct that mistake, but she was too embarrassed to do so. Besides, what difference did it make when they might never see any of these people again? Chandler didn't speak up, so she reasoned that she should follow suit.

The doctor exited, leaving the curtains open. Nurses and techs came and went. After a while, the medicine did its stuff, and Bethany could finally relax.

She discussed with Chandler whether to call her brother and his aunts, and together they decided not to at this point. Why panic everyone when there was no crisis? She felt a little foolish about that, but Chandler insisted otherwise.

"Don't even go there. How were you supposed to know it was false labor? Even if you had suspected, you'd have had to be sure."

That was true. "You don't know how terrified I've been. Every time I'd get one of those cramps, I'd worry that something was wrong."

"This has been going on for some time, then?"

"A few weeks."

"Didn't you discuss it with your doctor back in Humble?"

She shook her head. "I thought they were just cramps, so I intended to bring it up at my next scheduled visit. Then everything blew up, and I hit the road."

"Blew up?" he echoed, and Bethany could have bitten off her own tongue. "What do you mean?"

"Chandler!"

Another nurse suddenly breezed in through the opening in the curtain. Young and attractive, she wore pink scrubs and a surprised expression.

"Oh, hey, Linda. How are you?" Even as she let out a relieved sigh, Bethany cringed inwardly. So much for never seeing these people again! He looked at Bethany and made the introductions. "Linda, this is Bethany. Bethany, this is Linda Shocklea, a friend of my sister's."

"Everything okay here?" Linda asked.

"Yeah, I think so," Chandler replied. He gave her a quick explanation.

"Ah," said Linda. "Glad it's nothing more serious." She beamed at Chandler, exclaiming, "I haven't seen you in forever! What do you hear from that sister of yours?"

"*Nada.* She and Stephen should be home from their honeymoon soon, though."

"I knew they were hung up on each other even before I heard about the engagement," the woman said, sweetly smug, "but no one said anything about you! I didn't even know you were married, let alone about to be a daddy."

Chandler looked at Bethany. And said nothing.

Linda chattered on for a few minutes before the doctor strolled in to announce that Bethany could go. Chandler turned a tight smile on Linda as he smoothly rose to his feet.

"Looks like they're kicking us out of here," he said needlessly. "Good to see you."

"You, too." She smiled at Bethany. "Nice to meet you."

Bethany nodded as the other woman turned away.

The nurse arrived as the doctor left and handed some papers to Chandler. He glanced over them and muttered, "Be right back."

Knowing that, at the very least, she owed him an apology, Bethany verbally reached out. "Chandler."

He turned back, glanced at the nurse, nodded grimly and slipped away before Bethany could say another word. She told herself that it would serve no purpose to blurt the truth now, but deep in her heart, she knew that she hadn't spoken because she was ashamed—and because she so desperately wished that Chandler *was* the father of her son.

Chandler knew that he should have set the record straight from the very beginning, but it hadn't occurred to him until it was too late, and now the whole hospital was going to think that he was married! That, however, was surely better than having everyone assume that he was about to become an unwed dad, as his very own father did. Besides, he couldn't bring himself to embarrass Bethany by blurting the truth of her situation, what he knew about it, anyway, which was that she was pregnant and unmarried. All in all, Chandler told himself, it might be easier just to marry the girl and forget about trying to explain this mess.

He carried the papers that the nurse had given him to the checkout desk and waited impatiently while a distraught woman argued with the implacable clerk. As he waited, he fished his wallet from his hip pocket. He wasn't responsible for the charges, of course, but Bethany certainly could not pay, and someone had to. Besides, as insane as it was, he *wanted* to pay. Or maybe what he wanted was to be what he was pretending to be, her husband and the father of her child. Like that could happen.

When his turn came, he laid down his debit card. He couldn't afford a family, he told himself, but he could manage this; then, when he saw the actual fee, his stomach dropped. This, he knew, was just the tip of a financial iceberg big enough, no doubt, to sink a battleship, let alone a struggling rodeo cowboy. She needed someone with a steady paycheck and a settled lifestyle. That being the case, he couldn't help wondering why God had allowed him to get caught up in this situation. God surely had a purpose, though, just as the aunts asserted. Maybe this was it, this one act, that and getting her to safety at Chatam House.

Stuffing the receipt into his pocket, he strode back toward the treatment area. Just as he was about to turn away, he caught sight of his truck still parked at the curb in front of the emergency room door. A yellow slip of paper fluttered in the breeze, caught between the wiper blade and the windshield. Groaning, Chandler rushed outside and snatched it free, knowing that he was going to find a parking ticket.

*Okay, God,* he prayed silently, *You've got my attention now. Big-time. Just tell me what You want, and You've got it. I've been stupid, and I've been foolish. Worse, I've been deaf, but I'm listening now. Just tell me what to do.*

On the trip home, Bethany apologized and apologized. Chandler shook his head, muttering about circumstances and misunderstandings, but Bethany felt awful about the whole thing, so awful that she didn't even think about the emergency room bill.

Garrett and the sisters had come in to find Bethany gone and were on the verge of calling 911 when she and Chandler arrived. After a rushed explanation, Bethany took a seat in one of the comfortable armchairs at the end of the room. No sooner had she relaxed than Garrett asked how she'd paid the bill.

Bethany slapped her palms to her cheeks and gasped. "I didn't! I—I guess they're going to bill me."

Chandler, who had been prowling around the front

parlor like a big, restless cougar ever since they'd come in, finally struck a pose, leaning against the ornate plaster mantel with his arms folded. "I took care of it."

While Bethany gaped, Garrett faced Chandler. "Why would you do that?"

Chandler shrugged. "Someone had to."

Garrett looked at him thoughtfully. "Thanks, man. I'll pay you back."

Chandler pushed away from the fireplace and strode toward the doorway, one hand reaching into his shirt pocket. He paused in front of Garrett and proffered a crumpled sheet of yellow paper. "Take care of this and we'll call it even," he said gruffly, walking out of the room.

Garrett smoothed the slip of paper against one palm, studying it, and turned a surprised expression on his sister. "It's a parking ticket. Illegal parking in an emergency zone."

The sisters traded looks before turning their gazes on Bethany. Magnolia tilted her head, saying, "Chandler seems awfully troubled over a simple parking ticket. Is there something you haven't told us, dear?"

Bethany couldn't bring herself to confess that Chandler had been mistaken for the father of her child. Again. Then she remembered the best news of all.

"I'm going to have a little boy!"

The sisters erupted with expressions of delight. Talk turned to such things as names. Bethany looked at Garrett and knew they were both thinking the same thing.

"Our father's name was Matthew," she noted softly.

Garrett smiled. "I'm sure Dad would have liked to have his grandson named after him."

Teary eyed, Bethany beamed. The baby moved,

seeming to roll from one side of her abdomen to the other. Grinning, she smoothed her hands over her distended middle. "I think he likes it, too!"

"Halfway there," Magnolia said approvingly. "Now all you need is a middle name."

"First, I need an ob-gyn," Bethany said. "I have to find a local doctor right away, but I've already called everyone in the phone book, and no one can see me."

"Time to call Brooks," Magnolia stated flatly. Rising, she went for the phone.

Ten minutes later, Bethany was speaking with Brooks Leland, general practitioner and Chatam family friend. After hearing what the emergency room physician had said, Dr. Leland promised to arrange an appointment for her with a colleague who was an ob-gyn, saying that his office would get back to her within forty-eight hours.

"Well," Hypatia declared after Bethany had ended the call, "we have much to give thanks for." She fixed Bethany with a regal eye, adding, "I'm sure you'll want to attend worship tomorrow in praise for today's blessings."

Smiling weakly, Bethany nodded, knowing that no excuse would be sufficient to keep her at home tomorrow. Accepting her fate, she tried not to dwell on the uncomfortable prospect of attending services at Downtown Bible Church. Perhaps everyone she had known had moved on by now. Perhaps she wouldn't even be recognized. Besides, Hypatia was right. She had too much to be thankful for *not* to attend worship.

Still, Bethany quailed at the thought of encountering old friends who would undoubtedly ask about her "husband." Some might even remember Jay attending her mother's funeral with her. She tried to convince herself that it would be okay to say that she was divorced, but she didn't know if she could get the words out of her mouth. Perhaps she could just say that she was no longer married and pretend not to hear any other questions. Faint hope, at best.

Chandler missed dinner that evening, which was just as well, and he was nowhere to be seen again on Sunday morning, either. Somewhat relieved, Bethany got ready for church, wearing the same navy-and-yellow outfit that she had worn to her job interview, and allowed herself to be bundled into the sisters' town car. She even meekly submitted to being included in their senior women's Bible class, deeming that safer than seeking out women of her own age. She balked only when she found herself herded ahead of Garrett through the great arched sanctuary and into the center of a long pew already occupied by none other than Chandler Chatam. Bethany could do nothing but drop down next to him, smiling weakly.

He nodded in greeting, but he could not seem to keep still during the service, as antsy as a puppy. Bethany tried to concentrate on the sermon but was too aware of him to do so. Deeply thankful when the service ended, she rose and pushed as close to Garrett as possible while she waited to exit the pew. The Chatam sisters were in no apparent hurry, however, and stood in the crowded, busy aisle, chatting with various individuals. One of them, a rather portly old gentleman with a bald head undisguised by a thin comb-over, a rakish bow tie and a brass-headed cane, had attached himself to Odelia and showed no sign of moving out of the way. Garrett finally managed to ease out into the aisle behind him. Bethany had a bit more difficulty.

The only way she could slip past the old fellow was to lean as far back as possible to get her belly out of the way. Unfortunately, at the last moment, she stepped on a hymnal that had fallen unnoticed to the floor. The book slipped, and with it went her foot. She'd have toppled backward over the pew if Chandler had not lunged forward and scooped her against him.

For a long moment, they stood there, staring into each other's eyes, until she became aware that the sisters were anxiously inquiring as to her well-being.

"I'm fine," she told them, pulling away to finally step out into the aisle. "No harm done."

Chandler edged past her and quickly cleared the way, sweeping his long arm in a broad arc. Bethany ducked her head and doggedly began to weave her way around one cluster of individuals after another to the double doors at the back of the sanctuary. The instant she passed through those massive doors, however, she found herself face-to-face with the dreaded past.

"Bethany!"

Cleo Ann Mathis had once been Bethany's best friend. As girls, they'd shared sleepovers, birthdays and childish dreams, but as Bethany's home life had deteriorated, so had their friendship. By high school, they'd been nothing more than nodding acquaintances. The intervening years had been good to Cleo Ann. A little heavier, she now wore her light brown hair short and spiky and bleached almost white, but the smile was quintessential Cleo Ann. Quaking inside, Bethany allowed herself to be embraced.

"Hello, Cleo Ann."

"I can't believe this! Just look at you. No one said a word."

Who would, Bethany asked herself, with her brother gone from town, too?

A number of other women had gathered around by now. They began shooting questions at Bethany.

Bethany tried to order the questions in her mind. "Uh, d-due date is mid-October. It's a boy, and yes, I've moved back here."

"Let us give you a shower, then," someone said. "We'd be glad to."

Before she could decide how to reply to that, Cleo Ann asked, "So how and when did you two meet?"

Bethany looked at her old friend helplessly. You two?

Suddenly, a hand gripped her arm and a familiar voice said, "Excuse us, ladies. Gotta run."

Bethany felt herself propelled forward. Cleo Ann and the others called farewells, to which Bethany replied with an apologetic wave. Hurrying to keep up with Chandler's long strides, she allowed him to guide her through the foyer, out the front doors, along the sidewalk and around the corner to his truck, which was parked parallel to the curb.

"First the whole hospital, now the whole church," he muttered.

She gasped, reality crashing down. "They think we're married!"

"Big surprise, right?" he said, handing her up into the passenger seat.

Moaning, Bethany dropped her head into her hands while he jogged around to the driver's side. "Oh, Chandler, I'm so sorry. I never meant for any of this to happen. I didn't even mean to sit next to you in church! Why didn't you say something this time?"

"You think I should've whistled everyone to attention and announced that I am not the father of your child? That would've gone over great." He started up the engine and pulled away from the curb.

"Why didn't you just walk away, then?" she asked, tears clogging her throat.

"So you could do what? Tell everyone that you're pregnant and unmarried?"

"That's better than them believing that we're married to each other!"

"Really? And who do you suppose they would think the father is, anyway? Especially after yesterday."

Bethany wept. This was even worse than her worst fears. "I don't mean to keep dragging you into this. Honestly, I don't."

Chandler sighed and pulled the truck over again to loop an arm loosely about her shoulders. "I know that, and I'm not mad, I'm just… I don't know what I am."

"You're too good, is what you are," Bethany managed, wiping her eyes. "You're just too good."

"All I am," he said, shaking his head ruefully, "is confused. I'm just trying to figure out what God is doing in my life. I just want to know what He wants of me."

"That makes two of us," she told him.

"Well," he said, "I expect we'll find out soon enough. Let's just hope it includes the whole town figuring out that they're wrong about us."

"No kidding," she muttered. They couldn't have been more wrong, in fact, no matter how much she might wish otherwise.

For some reason, he laughed. She didn't know why, but she smiled.

Nothing had changed. It was still the most awkward situation she could imagine, but for the moment, just being able to smile was enough.

## *Chapter Seven*

Wondering whose luxury sedan stood parked in front of the house, Chandler hopped out of the truck and followed Bethany up the brick walkway and onto the stoop beneath the porte cochere. He had forgone practice with Drew today to take Bethany to her doctor's appointment, which had apparently gone well. It seemed that a lot of first-time mothers had Braxton-Hicks contractions.

"And very few of them actually deliver early," Bethany was saying.

"That's a relief," he replied absently, reaching around her to pull open the bright yellow door.

She went before him into the darkened back hall, lighting it up with her sleeveless lime-green knit dress. Her sleek, dark hair bounced in a jaunty ponytail at the crown of her head.

"Plus," she went on blithely, "they'll let me prepay the fee."

"Excellent." He wondered silently how long that would take.

They came to the central hall and made the turn

that would take them to the foyer, but before they got that far, Magnolia appeared from the direction of the front parlor. He noticed her rigid posture and the grim line of her mouth, as well as a fearful hardness about her eyes. Even more worrisome, the loud, cheery tone with which she addressed them sounded patently false.

"Hello, dear ones! We've been waiting for you. You have a caller, Bethany dear, a Mr. Haddon." Chandler glanced at Bethany, who shook her head. Mags leaned closer and said, "He's an attorney."

Bethany's blue eyes widened. "An attorney? What does he want?"

"He wouldn't tell us," Magnolia hissed, "and I don't like it one bit."

Chandler could see the pulse leaping in the hollow of Bethany's throat and instinctively stepped closer to her. Gulping, she looked up into his eyes, and he saw at once that she was frightened, but she turned and stiffly followed Magnolia into the parlor. He went with her, determined not to let her out of his sight.

Defying habit, the aunties had parked their guest in the front section of the spacious room where three stiff, scroll-armed chairs, placed perpendicular to the front window, faced a hard-backed, carved oak settee. Perched on the settee was a tall, slender man in his forties with a beaked nose, freckles and an abundance of neatly trimmed cinnamon-and-sugar hair. His paleness, coupled with the pale natural linen suit that he wore with a white shirt and beige tie, made his obsidian eyes seem reptilian. He had evidently refused tea, a fact that could not have endeared him to the aunties.

As Magnolia hurried to reclaim her chair, the stranger rose, the handle of his briefcase clasped in one hand. "Clarence Haddon," he said tersely. "I must speak to you in private, Ms. Willows."

"Not happening," Chandler said flatly. The aunties signaled their approval with nods and taut smiles. Haddon did not so much as look at him.

"I—I think my brother should be here," Bethany said, lifting her chin. She glanced at the aunties, who rose as one. Nodding, they hurried from the room, ostensibly to notify Garrett. Chandler stayed right where he was.

The lawyer abruptly sat down again and brought his briefcase to his knees. Extracting a sheaf of papers, he thrust them at Bethany. She gingerly took them and scanned down the first page as Haddon smoothly stated, "As you can see, my client has empowered me to offer you a cash settlement in return for your, shall we say, discretion."

A dull red flush crept up Bethany's throat into her cheeks. To Chandler's shock, she tossed the papers in Haddon's face, exclaiming, "Ten thousand dollars not to name Jason Widener as the father of my child!"

Jason Widener. That name emblazoned itself on Chandler's mind.

Haddon flattened the papers against the top of his briefcase, saying, "Let me remind you that a father has certain rights."

"Let me remind you," Bethany snapped, "that bigamy is illegal!"

Chandler jerked. Bigamy? It didn't take a rocket scientist to figure out Bethany's situation at that point. The poor woman had obviously fallen prey to some slick scoundrel.

"I have seen no evidence of bigamy," Haddon said with smugness.

Bethany folded her arms. "I have a signed marriage license from the state of Nevada. How's that for evidence?"

"An unrecorded marriage license is a curiosity," Haddon told her, waving a hand, "nothing more."

"What do you mean, *unrecorded*?" Bethany demanded, dropping her arms. Chandler stepped closer.

"I assure you that there is no record of a duly executed marriage license with your name on it in the records of the state of Nevada."

"That's impossible!" Bethany exclaimed. "I have the license!"

"Signed by whom?"

"Myself and Jay Carter."

*Jay Carter?* Chandler thought. *Who was Jay Carter?*

"And did you receive that license in the mail or take it with you after the ceremony?" Haddon asked slyly.

Bethany frowned. "I think we took it with us."

"Then the license could not have been submitted for registration, could it?"

Chandler wanted to hit something. He had been surprised himself, upon signing as a witness for his sister and Stephen, to hear that the license had to be returned to the state. Only after it was recorded and stamped would it be surrendered to them. "Jay Carter obviously planned his scam very carefully."

"Perhaps," Haddon said. "I couldn't say. My client is Jason Widener."

"They're the same man!" Bethany exclaimed, tossing her arms wide.

Haddon looked her squarely in the eye. "Prove it."

The color drained from Bethany's face.

"If they weren't the same, Widener wouldn't be willing to pay her hush money," Chandler pointed out.

"Jason Widener is a wealthy, prominent man with the means to prevent unwarranted challenges to his reputation," Haddon said calmly. "It's done all the time."

"Unwarranted!" Bethany exclaimed.

"Were he the father of your child," Haddon continued, just as if she hadn't spoken, "he would certainly have the means to claim his full parental rights."

Chandler knew a threat when he heard one. So did Bethany. She stepped back as if from a coiled rattlesnake. Impotent anger filled him. He knew that she was weighing the threat that Jason Widener would attempt to take her child from her if she so much as whispered his name in public.

Just how much more would this villain take from her? He couldn't be satisfied with her heart, her self-respect, her dignity? He had to threaten her child, too?

*Oh, Lord, please help her,* he thought. And then it hit him. God had helped her. He'd sent her to the Chatams, to one Chatam in particular, to *him.*

While Chandler was grappling with that, Bethany softly said, "I have no intention of claiming that Jason Widener is the father of my child and never did."

Haddon lifted an eyebrow, as if to say that was not quite sufficient.

Bethany swallowed, dropped her gaze and said, "Because he is not the father of my child."

"So who is?" Haddon pressed, clearly intent on a complete denial. "This imaginary Jay Carter you speak of?"

Imaginary? Chandler felt his hands coil into fists,

but this snake was not the one that deserved the beating. Hurried footsteps sounded in the background, but Chandler was too angry to pay them much mind, too focused on Bethany and her misery.

She dropped her gaze, whispering, "I don't know who the father of my child is."

It was total humiliation, and Chandler could not bear it.

"That's a lie," he said, jolted by the sound of his own voice. The next words, however, were completely intentional. "*I* am the father of this child."

Oddly, it was a relief to say it, even if it wasn't, strictly speaking, true. A father could be a father by choice, though, he told himself.

It was impossible to say who was more startled, Haddon or Bethany.

Haddon blinked. "You're not Garrett Willows?"

"I'm Chandler Chatam," he said, "and you are leaving." Striding forward, he reached down and hauled Clarence Haddon to his feet.

"Ch-Chatam?"

"That's right." Chandler smiled, relishing the power of the Chatam name as never before. "You can tell your client that if he knows what's good for him he'll leave us alone. We don't ever want to hear from him—or you—again. Now, get out."

Clasping briefcase and papers to his chest, Haddon beat a hasty retreat.

Chandler sighed, feeling better than he had in some time, and turned to Bethany. She stood with both hands clasped to her head as if to prevent it from exploding. Beside her stood her brother, arms folded, rage snapping in his electric blue eyes.

"You're the father, after all?" he yelled, glaring at Chandler.

Chandler winced, realizing what Garrett must have heard—and, thankfully, what he hadn't heard. Suddenly, the aunts were in the room, and everyone was talking at once.

After several moments of chaos, Chandler roared, "We're getting married!"

It was like shutting off the radio. Instant silence.

Chandler parked his hands at his waist, defiantly adding, "That's all anyone needs to know."

Suddenly, Odelia rushed forward, hanky waving. "I told you! I told you! How wonderful!"

At the same time, Garrett's face cleared and his arms dropped. "Really?" he said to Bethany. "You're getting married?"

"Of course we are," Chandler replied for her, catching Odelia as she threw her arms around him in a congratulatory hug. "That's what people having babies do."

Hypatia beamed, her glowing amber eyes telling him that, while she didn't know the details, she knew exactly what he was doing and approved wholeheartedly. Mags just smiled, then broke out laughing in wonder.

Only Bethany stood like a statue, her mouth ajar. After a moment, she began to shake her head, but he knew that marrying her was the only thing to do, the right thing to do, and exactly what he wanted to do.

Now all he had to do was convince Bethany.

"You've got to be kidding." It came out as a mere whisper, her expression one of disbelief. He could not have meant what he'd said. Yes, everyone assumed that they were a couple, but… She shook her head. "You've got to be kidding me."

Taking her by the shoulders, he bodily turned her before wrapping his arm about her waist and walking her right past her brother and his aunts, through the foyer and into the library. It was one of Bethany's favorite places, a handsome, spacious room, with rich furnishings, a beverage bar and walls of books. She walked through it numbly. A lovely, quiet, very private study opened off the far corner, and that was where Chandler took her now, guiding her straight to the massive Victorian walnut partner's desk. Spinning her to face him, he placed his hands atop her shoulders and looked down into her face, his expression intense.

"This marriage is best for all of us. Think about it," he urged. "My own father believes that this child is mine. And he's not alone. Your brother even believes it now. The doctors and nurses at the hospital, everyone at church thinks that this child is mine. At least, they assume that we're married, too. So, okay. Maybe God is trying to tell us something here." He dropped a hand to the side of her stomach. It radiated warmth and strength. "Maybe I *should* be this little boy's father."

Bethany shook her head. He couldn't have thought this through. "Do you have any idea what you're saying?"

Chandler backed off a step then, his hand going to the back of his neck. "Oh, yeah." He huffed out a breath. "But, look, I've always wanted a son, and he needs a father, a real father. Seems like I'm elected." He spread his hands. "Okay, I'm not much of a bargain, I know, but better me than Jason 'Jay Carter' Widener. Bigamist."

"No kidding," she concurred, blushing to the roots

of her hair. She'd hoped that he would never know what a fool she'd been.

"Bethany, look," he said, moving closer again. "No one has to know that we haven't been married all along. Well, no one who doesn't already know."

And those few were not likely to say anything, Bethany realized. Still… "I won't ask anyone to lie for me."

"Of course not. I wouldn't suggest such a thing, but if we marry quietly and just don't broadcast the date…" He shrugged.

Bethany bit her lip, trying to think it through, but her mind was whirling like a tornado. She managed to snatch one thought out of the swirl, an important one.

"Chandler, do you *want* to marry me?"

He took his time formulating his reply. "Bethany, right now I can't afford a wife and child, frankly, but I think we're supposed to do this, and if we are supposed to do it, then God will work it out, and in the meantime, that little boy is safe from a man who is *not* his father and doesn't want to be. I at least want to be his dad."

"Matthew," she whispered, her throat clogged with disappointment. Oh, what a fool she truly was! "His name is Matthew."

Chandler's gaze dropped to her middle, and he swallowed. "Matthew," he said. "I like that."

"W-we still need a middle name," she told him inanely, blinking back tears.

"How about Chandler?" he suggested hopefully, lifting his gaze to hers. "Matthew Chandler Chatam. Has a nice ring to it."

That was when she began to cry, big splashy tears flooding her cheeks.

"Hey, look," he said quickly, "I get that your first stab

at marriage didn't turn out so well for you, but you know exactly what you're getting into here. This is to protect Matthew. All this means is that Widener will have to come through me to get to him. Not that he will. Why would he? He wants to keep you from naming him as the father. Okay. Name me. But for my sake, let me be Matthew's married dad, not his unmarried dad."

"So it would be a marriage in name only," she surmised dully. Of course. What else could it be?

Blinking, Chandler shifted his weight. After a moment, he said, "B-but not forever."

She sobbed, no longer sure why she was crying now. Her gratitude was all mixed up with her admiration of this man and her stupidly breaking heart. Had she really, in some secret part of her brain, thought he might come to care for her?

He rushed on. "What I mean is, we can separate quietly later when…" The words tailed off.

Feeling weak suddenly, Bethany sagged against the edge of the desk and tried to get hold of her rioting emotions.

What difference did it make that he didn't want her? He wanted her son, and she would be selfish beyond bearing if she didn't grab such a father for her little boy. God might well have brought them here for this very reason. Where was her faith?

Keeping her gaze averted, she began drying her cheeks. "All right. When d-do you w-want to do it?"

"You mean you'll marry me?"

She nodded, unable to say more.

He leaned forward at the waist and braced his hands on his thighs, gasping as if he'd just finished a footrace.

"Whew! Wild, huh?"

Watery laughter startled out of her. "No kidding."

He laughed. Laughed. Then he straightened and strode for the door, saying, "I'd better get on this. The sooner the better, right?"

"Guess so," Bethany murmured as he left the room.

She glanced around the study, taking in the warm oak paneling, the sheltered window seat, the lovely old paintings, the antique armchairs and handsome grandfather clock. All was exactly as it should be.

And yet, everything was different.

She was getting married. Again. This time for real. And yet, not.

She shook her head, tears starting again. That seemed to be her particular talent, making marriages that were not quite real. At least this time, she knew it up front.

They married the following Friday in the office of a Justice of the Peace in Lawton, Oklahoma. Chandler wore his best boots and a brown felt hat, his darkest blue jeans, a white shirt piped in navy and a brown tie and matching Western-styled sport coat. Bethany chose a knit jumper the same shade as her blue eyes and a ruffled white blouse with white sandals.

Chandler had called his cousin Asher for a legal opinion. After determining that Bethany's situation presented no impediment, Ash had advised that Oklahoma required no residency, no blood tests and no waiting period. Because Chandler had to be there anyway to compete, the situation seemed tailor-made. They slipped out of the house before daybreak, picked up the horses and made the four-hour drive up to Lawton. Along the way, they stopped off at a discount jeweler's and purchased matching gold wedding bands.

It wasn't much of a ceremony, just Chandler, Bethany, the JP and a doddering female clerk. Bethany's hands trembled so violently when she slipped his ring onto his finger that she almost dropped it, and then she flinched when he kissed her so that it wasn't a real kiss at all, landing as much on her cheek as her lips.

He told himself that he shouldn't have expected otherwise. She'd made her wishes concerning this marriage abundantly clear. Much to his disappointment. Nevertheless, he remained convinced that, even if temporary, this marriage was best for everyone, him, Bethany, the baby and their respective families.

It was just after two o'clock in the afternoon when Chandler helped his new wife up into the passenger seat of the truck. He loosened his tie as he slid behind the steering wheel, asking, "Hungry?"

"Starved, actually," she answered.

"We'll grab something on our way to the motel." He started the engine. "We should call my aunts as soon as we get there, though I imagine they've figured out what's going on by now."

"Yes, I imagine they have. Garrett, too."

Chandler nodded. "Once I eat, I've got to change and get to the arena to check on the horses and meet Drew." As soon as they'd arrived in Lawton, they'd gone to the arena and dropped off the horses and trailer. He'd arranged to meet Drew for check-in as close to three-thirty as he could manage. "You can relax at the motel until I get back," he told her.

"Could I come with you?" Bethany asked tentatively.

Chandler jerked a glance at her, surprised but pleased. He managed a nonchalant shrug. "Sure, if you want. Keep a lookout for Lee Boulevard, will you?"

Bethany nodded and dutifully began reading street signs. She spotted a drive-through that offered fried chicken dinners, so they carried that to the motel, then sat around a desk affixed to the wall in the crowded double room to eat. He made the call, speaking briefly to Hypatia, letting her know to expect them back Monday afternoon. He didn't see any reason to rush back to Buffalo Creek Sunday night. Might as well sleep in and take their time. It was their honeymoon, after all. Sort of.

He was just getting off the phone with the aunties when Bethany went into the tiny bathroom to change her clothes. While she did that, he removed his tie and coat and swapped out his boots and hat, rolling back the cuffs of his longs sleeves. Bethany emerged a few minutes later wearing a long red tunic and black leggings with tall red boots. Worn to a comfortable suppleness, they weren't cowboy boots, but they did have a Western heel.

"Is this okay? I can't get into my jeans."

"You look great," he told her honestly.

"Thanks." She wrinkled her nose and plucked at the tunic. "I used to wear this as a dress."

Chandler admitted to himself that he'd have liked to have seen that then cleared his throat and led her out of the room.

They met Drew and Cindy walking across a field where they'd parked, about a hundred yards away from the rodeo arena.

"Hey!" Chandler shook Drew's hand, smiling and nodding at Cindy, whose gaze boldly swept over Bethany.

"This is my wife, Bethany," he said, finding that

the words rolled off his tongue with surprising ease. "Honey, this is my new partner, Drew Shaw, and his wife, Cindy."

Drew's jaw was hanging open. He recovered and doffed his hat just as Cindy launched herself forward and dealt Chandler a stinging slap on the upper arm.

"You rat! You never said anything about being married and having a kid on the way! What's wrong with you?"

Before Chandler could stammer a reply to that, Bethany came to his rescue. "Men! They think we know everything that goes through their heads, even when they're as private as this one." She gave Chandler a little pat on the chest. He thought his shirt buttons might just pop, his heart swelled so.

Drew chuckled, shaking his head. "Man, you could've saved me a lot of headache if you'd just brought your woman around sooner."

"What do you mean?" Bethany asked.

"I mean, Cindy might not have worried so much about the two of us partnering up if she'd known he was married. In her words, she doesn't want me 'hanging around with some chick magnet' while she's stuck at home with the baby."

Chandler laughed. "No chance of that here."

"Oh, please," Bethany said in a scoffing tone. "If ever there was a chick magnet..." She broke off, color blooming in her cheeks.

Chandler grinned. He supposed he'd drawn his fair share of female attention, but he'd stopped paying attention to the buckle bunnies who came around a long time ago. Too many party girls more interested in the party than a guy holding out for something serious when the time was right.

The time wasn't right, not by Chandler's reckoning, but "something serious" had blindsided him anyway. He guessed it happened like that a lot. Too often, though, what blindsided a fellow turned into a hit-and-run. His heart didn't just slow at that thought, it all but stopped.

"That's what wives are for," Cindy was saying, "to keep the chicks away. Right?" She winked at Bethany, asking, "So when are you due?"

"October eighteenth."

Cindy patted her baby bump. "This one won't show up until the first of November."

"He," Drew said, grinning. "It's a boy."

"No kidding?" Chandler laughed at himself, that being one of Bethany's favorite phrases. She was rubbing off on him already, this new wife of his. "Ours, too."

"That's cool," Drew said. "Who knows? Maybe one day our sons will be roping partners."

Something lurched inside Chandler, and he felt the warm glow of fatherly pride. Whatever happened with him and Bethany, he told himself, he'd always have Matthew, at least. If that didn't seem like quite enough just now, well, he'd have to leave that to God.

# Chapter Eight

*Ours, too.*

Those simple words had echoed in Bethany's head from the instant that Chandler had spoken them. They raised goose bumps on her skin and plucked at her heartstrings.

*Our child. Mine and now Chandler's.*

The momentous ramifications weighed on her, filling her with equal parts joy and concern.

The air unit kicked on, filling the dark room with its rattling hum. Chandler rolled over again on the other bed. Apparently, he was having as much trouble getting to sleep as she was. She couldn't forget that this was their wedding night or that Chandler had offered to get separate rooms instead of just separate beds for them.

Knowing that money was a concern for him, she had insisted that this would be fine. Besides, if anyone should come looking for him, it would look decidedly odd if they weren't together. The main reason, however, was that she simply hadn't wanted to be alone on this of all nights. It didn't change anything, of course. This marriage was still a sham. At least it was a legal sham.

She told herself that was a step forward, but it didn't feel that way. It felt…lonely.

Chandler shifted again and punched his pillow into a more pleasing shape. She suspected that part of his restlessness had to do with the fact that he slept—or tried to sleep—fully clothed in jeans and a T-shirt. Another reason probably had to do with his performance that night.

He and Drew were leading the team roping, though two more go-rounds of competition remained before overall winners could be determined. Drew was in first place in his personal event, too, while Chandler had come in ahead in the steer wrestling and second in the tie down.

Bethany hadn't been able to watch the steer wrestling, not after the first competitor. If anyone had told her that she'd wind up married to a man who did something so dangerous as throw himself off a running horse onto the horns of a stampeding steer, she wouldn't have believed it, and she dared not dwell on it now.

To distract herself, she asked into the silence, "Do you ever hear the air conditioner at Chatam House?"

Chandler pushed up onto one elbow. From her bed, she could just make out the shape of his head in the darkened room. "Nope. Never do."

"Isn't it right above us in the attic there?" she mused. "I think that's what Magnolia said, that they put the central air units in the attic."

Chandler collapsed back onto his pillow. "Yep. Air units are in the attic."

"Thought so."

For a long moment, only the hum of the fan blowing cold air into the room filled the silence. It occurred to

Bethany that she had been remiss, and this was as good a time as any to say what should have been said earlier.

"Chandler."

"Hmm?"

"Thank you. For everything. For offering me a ride back there in that diner. For introducing me to your dad and driving me around. For rushing me to the emergency room and not embarrassing me that day in church. For throwing Jay's lawyer out of the house. Most of all, for claiming Matthew."

Matthew. Not her. He hadn't claimed her, even if she was his wife, but she couldn't let that matter.

She sat up, aware that her white sleep shirt and baggy shorts made her more visible than him.

"You'll be an awesome dad," she said, knowing in her heart that it was true.

Chandler slid his hands behind his head. "I did this as much for me as anyone else," he muttered at the ceiling.

She was glad that his reputation was safe now, glad that she could do that much for him, at least. God above knew that he deserved it, that and more.

"You don't owe me any thanks, Bethany," he went on. "You're sharing your son with me. There's not much greater gift than that."

Bethany smiled, feeling as though her heart smiled, too. "I prayed that my child would have an awesome dad, you know. I just didn't think it would be you."

"Who would?" he retorted wryly.

She could have argued that point but feared giving away too much of her feelings. Instead, she changed the subject.

"Speaking of awesome," she said, injecting a note

of fun into her voice. "I have never seen anything like what you did today. I had no idea anyone could move that fast or that accurately. And the horses! Oh, my goodness. How long did you have to train them? Cindy says you're a 'dab hand,' by the way."

Chandler chuckled. "Not sure what that means, frankly, but I've been working with this bunch for years."

He talked about the horses for a while. Ginger Boy was eight years old and had been with him almost the whole time. He'd had Red Rover, a nine-year-old, for only five years.

"Arroyo," he went on, "is the old man, nearly seventeen. We've been together the better part of a decade. He was the first horse I bought on my own. As for Ébano, he's the youngster at six, and I've only worked with him about a year. He'd been through a few hands before I got him, and nobody had really pegged him as a roping horse, but I think we can win together. He's got good bloodlines and a natural talent, even if he is a bit high-strung, which is why I got him at a good price of ten thousand."

"Ten thousand dollars?" she exclaimed.

He turned his head, targeting her form in the dark. "That's a tenth of what a good roping horse can cost. I figure he's really worth seven or eight times that. Like I said, he's got fine bloodlines."

"Kind of like you," she mumbled around a yawn, stretching out on her bed again.

"Can't take any credit for that," Chandler said softly. "That's just pure blessing, being a Chatam."

"Yes, I know." She yawned again, feeling pleasantly tired now. "Thank you," she said again some minutes later, thinking that she and Matthew were Chatams now, too. The words whispered out on a sigh.

*Pure blessing,* he'd said, and he was certainly right about that.

It was her last thought before sleep finally claimed her.

Listening to the soft, even breathing of his wife, Chandler rolled onto his side and stared through the darkness at the white figure on the other bed.

*Some wedding night,* he mused. Some wedding. Come to that, it was some marriage.

At least it was legal.

He couldn't help wondering now what it was going to cost him, though. He'd been so worried about finances that he hadn't stopped to worry about any other sort of cost. Now, he knew that he was in serious danger of losing his heart.

Being with her tonight, introducing her as his wife, knowing she was up there in the stands watching him, it had all felt so right. She had even cemented his partnership with Drew, which felt more like friendship now, rather than just a business arrangement. It would likely be more permanent than this marriage.

He wished that their marriage was more than just a convenient, temporary agreement, but it did have its benefits. Having Bethany on his arm would make any man proud. And how many men could choose their sons? Funny, though, that his reputation didn't seem so important now. Why should it? He'd been letting Kreger drag it through the mud for years, after all. Still, he didn't want to be thought of as the sort of man who would impregnate a woman outside the bonds of marriage, especially not as the sort of man who would do that and then abandon the mother of his child, not to mention the child himself. Yes, this marriage did have benefits for him.

His main concerns were Bethany and Matthew, however. Maybe it wasn't much of a marriage, but it was a marriage to a Chatam. He had given them both that much.

Chatams were godly, loving people, and they took care of their own. He had no doubt that his father, sister, brothers, aunts, uncles, cousins, every last member of the family would accept and love his wife and son, even if some of them would be less than pleased with him once word of this marriage got out.

The aunts would stand by him, though. He had no doubt of that. He smiled, grateful and glad.

Bethany was right. He did have an excellent pedigree. That, he realized, was one of the greatest blessings of his life. It was about time that he started living up to those bloodlines.

*Thank You, Lord,* he began in silence, *for letting me be born a Chatam.*

He had much else for which to be thankful, too, so much that he felt himself sinking into sleep before he could get through the mental list. He struggled to stay with it, but sleep finally pulled him into dreams. Even from there, he reached out instinctively to God, until he at last knew peace.


"My sister's here," Chandler announced as soon as the truck turned up the drive early that next Monday afternoon. He nodded toward a small red convertible parked in front of the mansion.

Bethany sat up a little straighter, one hand going to her hair, which she'd slapped up in a messy ponytail bun. She felt tired and grimy after the trip back from Lawton this morning and all that went with dropping off the horses again, not that Chandler had let her help with that. He wouldn't even let her get out of the truck for fear that the horses would bump into her. She supposed he was right about that, but she so wanted to be as much a partner to him as Drew was, as much a partner as Cindy was to her husband.

Of course, the Shaws' marriage was real.

The rodeo had fascinated and frightened her, though she'd done her best to hide the latter from Chandler. The roping was all skill, but the steer wrestling… Chandler was bummed because he'd finished out of the money in his personal events that weekend, but at least he and Drew had taken second place in the team roping, which seemed to please Drew. Chandler, however, appeared to feel that he'd somehow let down the team. Bethany hoped that seeing his sister would perk him up.

The aunts had told her a lot about Kaylie and her husband, Stephen. Chandler had also spoken of his younger sister with great affection, which Bethany felt was surely mutual. Whether that affection would extend to the pregnant woman who was now his wife, Bethany didn't know. In truth, she couldn't think of any reason why it should.

Chandler brought the truck to a stop in front of the house and came around to take Bethany's arm as she slid out on her side. He escorted her up the steps and across the porch to the door, where he paused, lifted his eyebrows and said, "Here we go."

They'd already discussed what sort of reception they

could expect from his aunts and her brother. Kaylie presented a complete unknown. Bethany sucked in a deep breath, and Chandler opened the door.

"Surprise!"

Odelia rushed forward, waving her hankie wildly. She wore tiers of bloodred lace and rubies the size of robin eggs on her earlobes, hopefully fake ones. A petite, big-eyed young woman with long, soft sandy-red hair watched calmly from the center of the foyer as Odelia hugged first Bethany and then Chandler, babbling about shopping and cakes and honeymoons.

"And look!" she exclaimed, waving her hankie at the young woman, who wore a chic sleeveless sheath of crisp lilac linen, her hair held back by a matching headband. "Look who just showed up!"

Bethany shrank inwardly, rooted to the floor in her flip-flops, bagged out navy leggings and a clownish polka-dotted top that she'd found on clearance at the discount store. She had never felt less attractive.

"Kaylie," Chandler said, slipping away from Bethany to hug his sister. "Welcome home. Is Stephen here?"

"No. And don't change the subject."

"Which is?"

Drawing back from the embrace, Kaylie tilted her head and lifted her eyebrows at her brother before looking pointedly to Bethany. Then she balled up her fist and punched him in the gut. The blow didn't so much as rock him, but he caved belatedly and let out a long-suffering sigh. Odelia giggled uncertainly.

"You could've told me," Kaylie accused before abruptly shooting Bethany an apologetic glance. "I didn't even know he was seeing anyone, let alone married!"

Chandler seemed to struggle for an explanation before he finally said, "We decided for our own reasons to keep it quiet."

Kaylie turned to Bethany, saying sweetly, "Hello. I'm Kaylie."

Bethany trilled her fingers in a hesitant wave. "Bethany. Pleased to meet you."

"Come, come!" tittered Odelia, waving them all toward the parlor. "Come and see!"

Kaylie tossed a look at Chandler as she moved to follow her aunt, muttering, "You're lucky that was my fist and not Stephen's."

Chandler sighed again and rolled his eyes, holding out his hand to Bethany. She went to him gratefully. Together they entered the parlor.

"Surprise!"

This time it was a group effort. The aunties stood around a tea trolley laden with a white cake decorated with spun sugar roses and the words "Congratulations, Bethany and Chandler." It looked for all the world like a single-layer wedding cake. Thankfully, it bore nothing so incriminating as bells or a tiny statue of a bride and groom. The cake in itself would have been surprise enough; add Garrett and the rest of the staff along with an entire shop full of baby goods, and the effect was simply stunning.

Beside her, Chandler seemed every bit as staggered as Bethany was by the goods crammed into the room. He lifted his hands, palms out, as if to say, "What happened?"

With a glance in Kaylie's direction, Hypatia answered the unasked question. "We went shopping for the baby. The, ah, cake was Hilda's idea."

"Oooh," Bethany said, spying a beautiful spooled crib. That was for her baby? She rushed toward it, unable to help herself.

The aunts had outfitted the antique reproduction with a blue, yellow and green patchwork quilt, pale blue sheets and matching tailored bed skirt. In addition, it was filled with stuffed animals and tiny clothes.

"Oh, look!" There was a neat little sailor suit spread across a teensy pillow and next to that a wee pair of blue jeans and color-blocked Western-style shirt.

Chandler nudged a stuffed horse on wheels with one booted toe. "First mount," he said with a chuckle.

All in all, there was more paraphernalia than Bethany could ever have imagined. She'd pictured a second-hand bassinet, a few glass bottles and a small layette, and here was everything they could possibly need!

Chandler stood in the midst of it all and spread his arms, saying to his aunts, "You know you've gone way overboard."

"Oh, but we had such fun," Hypatia said dismissively, waving them over to the tea cart with a regal roll of her hand. "Come now and cut the cake."

Hilda, her thin, straight gray-and-gold hair tucked behind her ears, produced an elegant silver server, smiling so widely that her double chins almost wreathed her face. Her husband, Chester, dressed in his usual short-sleeved white shirt and black slacks with black suspenders, produced a camera and focused it at the tea trolley, while Hilda's sister Carol, her dull blond hair wrapped around her head in a thin braid, hurried to take small china dessert plates from beneath the cart.

Chandler looked at Bethany and held out his hand, one eyebrow arched. Smiling, she went to him and together they moved behind the tea trolley. Hilda turned over the silver cake server. Bethany gripped it. Grinning, Chandler wrapped his big hand around hers, and they posed for the camera. They cut the first piece of the single layer, then laughingly carved out two more while Chester continued to snap photos. These first pieces were served to the aunties. A piece for Kaylie followed, then those for Garrett and the staff. Finally, they cut a piece to share.

Carol handed them two forks, and for a moment, they stood there staring at each other. Chandler's gaze slid to his sister. Then he looked back to Bethany, cut off a bite and fed it to her. With Kaylie there it was foolish, but Bethany couldn't resist indulging in this one minor wedding ritual. She mirrored Chandler's actions. He was smiling when he started to chew. Then suddenly he snatched the plate from Bethany's hand and pretended to hold her off while gobbling it down. Everyone laughed. Immediately, Hilda took up the server to plop another piece onto an empty china plate and shove it into Bethany's hands.

She no longer cared what she looked like in her well-worn clothes and messy bun with her pregnant belly sticking out. She was at her husband's side, celebrating their marriage and coming child among friends and family. It occurred to her suddenly that these dear old ladies were now her aunts as well as Chandler's and, by extension, Matthew's. That, too, was reason to celebrate.

When Kaylie sought her out a little later, Bethany allowed herself to be pulled aside with only a hint of trepidation.

"It's belated, but welcome to the family," she said.

"Thank you."

"I'm stunned, of course. This is so unlike Chandler. I mean, to marry in secret without telling anyone, and then to present us with baby and bride at once."

"I-It's not what you think," Bethany began, swamped with guilt, but Chandler was suddenly at her side, his arm sliding about her shoulders.

"It is what it is," he stated defensively. "It's not like I need the family's approval to marry."

"Of course not," Kaylie said. "But what about Dad? He's going to be hurt because you didn't let him perform the ceremony and because you didn't tell him the truth when you first introduced him to Bethany."

Chandler bowed his head. "It wasn't my intention to hurt Dad, and he didn't exactly give me a chance to explain anything. He just jumped to the worst possible conclusions about me."

Kaylie threw up her hands. "So you didn't tell him that you were married? Yeah, that makes perfect sense."

"This is ridiculous," Bethany muttered. Surely, they could trust his sister and the rest of the family with the truth. "We were only ma—"

"Doing what was best for us," Chandler interrupted, clamping her tightly against his side. "If Dad can't accept that, it's his problem."

Kaylie sighed. "I'm not saying he was right to jump to conclusions, but it wouldn't have killed you to do the right thing even if he didn't."

"Chandler *always* does the right thing," Bethany declared, frowning. "You should know that."

Kaylie blinked at her. And then she beamed. "Yes. You're right." She turned her smile on her brother. "He does always do the right thing. Eventually."

"You three come have some tea," Hypatia called just then, having seated herself in her favorite chair.

"Yes, ma'am," Kaylie replied. She quickly leaned in and kissed Bethany's cheek, then patted her brother's and walked back to join the party, smiling.

Chandler kept his arm about Bethany's shoulders until his sister was out of earshot. Then he put his forehead to Bethany's, lifted a hand to her belly and softly said, "This is my son, mine and yours. That's what we agreed and that's all anyone needs to know. Right? When and where we married is no one else's business."

"You can't blame me for not wanting her to think badly of you," Bethany argued softly. "She thinks you lied to your father about being married!"

"All that matters is that you're now my wife," he whispered, "the mother of *my* child, and what's best for the two of you takes precedent over everything else. Besides, Kaylie's too sweet to think badly of anyone, least of all one of her brothers."

Bethany sighed. She hated that no one else really knew what a selfless, caring thing he had done. He wrapped his arms around her and hugged her tight. Bethany closed her eyes, wishing that this marriage wasn't just a convenient arrangement. She wanted a real marriage and real love with a real man. Like Chandler.

Hypatia called them again, and they broke apart to eat more cake and drink cups of tea, herbal in Bethany's case, in secret celebration of a marriage that really wasn't. Why, Bethany wondered, did that always seem to be the case where she was concerned?

*A wedding,* Chandler told himself again, *deserved to be celebrated, even if it had to be celebrated in se-*

*cret,* and he blessed the aunties for seeing to it. He was glad that his sister had wandered into the midst of the thing, too, even if it had caused some uncomfortable moments. He hated not telling her the whole truth, especially because it seemed to pain Bethany, but the more people who knew, the greater the chance that Matthew's parentage would be questioned. Chandler wasn't worried about Widener. The man would be a fool to inject himself into the situation at this point. Bethany, on the other hand, could be publicly embarrassed without the names Widener or Carter ever coming into it, and that Chandler could not abide.

Still, Kaylie was his sister, one of the people who loved him most in this world, and she would never knowingly do anything to hurt him or anyone else. That was the very thought in his mind when Bethany yawned behind her hand and excused herself before heading upstairs for a nap.

"I'll bring all this stuff up later," Chandler told her, and Garrett promised to help.

"I should be going, too," Kaylie said, getting to her feet. "Stephen and Dad will be wondering what happened to me. Walk me out," she said to Chandler.

He cast a glance at the aunties before following his sister out into the foyer. She turned on him at once, whispering, "You don't fool me, Chandler Chatam."

Alarmed, he took her arm and steered her into the library, closing the door behind them.

"You just married that girl," she went on. "I don't know why you waited. Maybe you didn't know about the baby until recently. Maybe you had to be sure that you were the father."

He looked her straight in the eye and said, "I *am*

that baby's father, and I don't want anyone thinking otherwise."

"Oh, Chandler." She hugged him. "Of course you're the baby's father." She pulled back and framed his face with her hands. "And you obviously adore Bethany and your son."

He didn't know what to say to that, except, "I—I just want to do what's best for them."

"Naturally. Whatever held you two back, I'm glad you worked it out because she's obviously head over heels for you, too."

He'd have laughed at that—if it hadn't hurt so unexpectedly to know that Kaylie was wrong about Bethany's feelings.

"'Chandler *always* does the right thing,'" Kaylie mimicked dreamily. "No wonder you love her so much. She thinks you hung the moon."

Love Bethany? Even as his heart clunked inside his chest, he opened his mouth to deny it, but then he clamped his lips shut again. What kind of an idiot denied loving his own wife? Besides, he wasn't entirely sure that he didn't love Bethany. On some level.

Oh, who was he kidding. He was crazy about her. Not that it made one whit of difference. The marriage was what it was, what they had agreed to.

"I—I'm sorry about Dad," he said truthfully, turning the conversation away from his feelings for Bethany and hers for him, or her lack of them.

"I know," Kaylie said, "and don't worry. Your secret's safe with me. You've done the right thing, and that's what matters most."

"I'm not asking you to lie to anyone," he pointed out, mentally squirming.

She waved a hand as she got to her feet. "Of course not, but whenever anyone asks me when and where you got married, I'll simply say that I'm not sure of the date, which is the absolute truth. You eloped, with none of the family the wiser. I'll have to tell the rest of the family that you and Bethany are married, though, especially Dad."

Chandler shrugged. "I never intended to keep them in the dark indefinitely."

"Dad's going to be upset."

"So what else is new?"

She shook her head. "Chandler, you've got to make your peace with him."

"I know, I know, and I will. When the time is right."

Kaylie sighed. "I guess that will have to do. Now, I have to get home before Stephen and Dad run out of polite conversation." She promised to tell Chandler all about the trip later and hurried off saying that she was looking for a larger house to lease for the three of them while her and Stephen's new house was being built. "A *much* larger house," she said with a cheeky grin.

"Thankfully we're here with the aunties," Chandler told her with heartfelt sincerity.

She went out, chuckling. Chandler walked into the foyer to find Magnolia there, obviously waiting for him.

"I just wanted to let you know that we moved your things into the master suite," she said softly.

Chandler's eyebrows jumped up into his hairline. "What about Garrett?" How was he to share a suite with Bethany *and* her brother without letting the latter know that this marriage was not all it seemed?

"Garrett's moved back into the carriage house,"

Mags told Chandler. "That leaves plenty of room for the baby."

Relieved, Chandler blurted, "Thanks, but I hope we're in our own place before he's born."

"Oh, what a shame that would be," Magnolia said, all but pouting. Chandler's jaw dropped. Mags was the last one he'd have expected this from! She quickly recovered and lifted her chin, adding, "Odelia will be so disappointed."

Laughing, Chandler hugged her. "You don't fool me, you old softie."

Magnolia gave him a sheepish grin. "Having a baby around could be fun."

Chandler headed for the stairs. "I'll remind you of that when he's waking up the whole household night after night." Suddenly he wondered if he'd lost his ever-loving mind. What did he really know about being a father or a husband? Why hadn't he just walked away? He could have at any juncture. He still could.

"I have earplugs!" Mags called after him.

He just laughed. He didn't believe for a moment that she'd use them. No more than he believed that he could ever walk away from Bethany and her, *their*, son.

## Chapter Nine

Staring at the hat atop the highboy dresser and the boots arranged neatly on the floor beside it, Bethany hugged herself. Why hadn't she thought of this? Of course, the aunties and Garrett would assume that a husband and wife would share a bedroom. As far as they were concerned, this was a real marriage, a whole marriage, so naturally they'd moved Chandler's things into the master bedroom of the three-bedroom suite. Perhaps, she thought wistfully, they ought to just forget this marriage-in-name-only business and do their best to make this work, not that she had anything to say about it. This was Chandler's choice, and she had agreed. It wasn't fair to try to change things now.

She heard his footsteps in the sitting room. Funny how quickly she'd come to recognize his particular long, sure gait. Garrett's steps were quieter, quicker. *Must be the boots,* she thought, smiling.

"Don't worry," he said from the open doorway. "I'll move into one of the other bedrooms."

She turned to find him leaning a shoulder against the doorjamb. "Garrett—"

"Has moved back into the carriage house," he said quickly.

That made sense. Still…

"If you move, everyone in the house will know that we're not, um, together."

He shrugged and shook his head. "My aunts won't say anything. Not to either of us. Maybe not even to each other. Certainly not to anyone else."

She doubted that Garrett would say anything, either. The sleeping arrangements between a husband and wife were a private, matter after all.

Straightening, Chandler gave his head a jerk as he asked, "Which of the other rooms do you want to use as the nursery?"

Her hand resting automatically atop her belly, she said, "The closest one, I guess."

He looked behind him as if judging the distance between doors and nodded before moving forward into the room. Bethany stood awkwardly where she was. He came to a stop mere inches from her. Lungs seizing, she looked up hopefully. For several heartbeats, his warm brown gaze held hers. Words that she longed to say sprang to her tongue.

*I don't want another sham marriage. Can't we try to make this real? Give me a chance to be the wife of your heart.*

But then Chandler lifted his eyes and carefully reached around her for the hat atop the highboy. Abruptly, Jay's acidic warning drowned out her longings.

*"You think any other man is going to want you with your crazy background and a kid in tow?"*

Feeling foolish, she quickly moved aside.

"Only be a minute," Chandler said, bending to pick up the boots.

Nodding, she hurried out into the sitting room, leaving him to rummage through drawers in search of his things. He came out a few moments later, his arms full, and clumped across to the room Garrett had occupied. It took several more trips, but eventually he had all of his things out of her room.

"That's it," he said, disappearing through his door once more. He was back in an instant, his arms empty. "You can take your nap now."

"Thanks," she said, smiling wanly. "I will."

"I just might have a nap, too," he told her, "once I get all this stuff put away. Busy day."

She nodded. He stood there for a few moments longer, then he returned her nod, stepped back and closed his door. Bethany went into her room and did the same. It was, perhaps, the loneliest moment of her life.

After moving his things from Bethany's bedroom, Chandler virtually hid in his room. He told himself that this was far more comfortable than sharing a motel room with separate beds, but it somehow felt more private. Worse, he knew that everyone in the house thought they would be sharing that one bed and that, to his shock, embarrassed him. They were adults, after all, and she was his wife, for pity's sake. Except that she wasn't, not in every way. And she never would be.

He didn't even go down to dinner, letting everyone think that he was sleeping when what he was really doing was worrying. The cowardice of that shamed him, as it left Bethany to explain his absence. He'd heard her pause outside his door moments after Chester called them down for the evening meal, but she hadn't knocked, so he'd let her go on her way while he stayed behind to stew about things he couldn't control.

He worried about how Bethany truly felt about this marriage, if his presence in the suite would make her uncomfortable and whether he'd be able to provide her with her own home before the baby came. He pondered failure as a husband and a father, as well as in his chosen career, basically second-guessing everything in his life. Eventually, before he could drive himself completely mad, he went to his knees and found a measure of peace.

It did not come soon enough to keep him from oversleeping the next morning.

Bethany woke him at only the last possible moment. As a result, he had to dash out of the house without breakfast or a shave to get her to work on time. On the way, they briefly discussed how they were going to handle Hub and decided that they would simply present a unified front and apologize for any hurt feelings.

They barely got through the door, however, when Hubner attacked.

"You lied to me!"

Tired, heartsick and starving, Chandler felt his own temper spike, but he bit his tongue. At first.

"You *both* lied to me!" Hubner accused. "I expect it from you," he snapped at Chandler. Then he glared accusingly at Bethany. "But you, Bethany?"

"Now, wait a minute!" Chandler interrupted angrily. "Bethany did what she had to do, and you didn't believe her anyway, so what difference does it make?"

"What difference? That's my grandchild she's carrying, and she denied it to my face! How can I ever trust either of you again?"

"Think what you will of me, Dad," Chandler said, more wounded than he'd expected to be and downright furious at this criticism of Bethany. "I've made my share of mistakes. But Bethany has done nothing wrong."

Quite the opposite, in fact. She had been wronged. Even if Hubner didn't know that, this was unfair, so far as Chandler was concerned.

"Nothing?" Hub scoffed, raking her with a scathing glance.

Chandler lost it. "How dare you judge her!" he shouted. "Don't think I'll let you get away with jumping to conclusions about her! You've done that with me time and again, and I've put up with it because you're my father, but she's off-limits!"

"Okay, that's enough," Bethany interjected calmly. "I'll take it from here, thank you." Going up on tiptoe, she kissed Chandler on the cheek. Then she lifted both hands and literally shoved him backward out the door, which she pulled closed firmly behind him.

That kiss threw him off balance to the point that a long moment passed before he fully realized what had happened.

He was reaching for the handle to go right back inside when he heard Hub say, "Bethany, I did not mean to imply... I don't know any of the details, but i-it was not my intention to insult you."

Bethany folded her arms. "No. Only to insult your son."

Chandler stepped to the side, out of sight of the glass door, curious as to what she would say next.

"You don't understand," Hub said in a morose voice.

"Somehow I failed that boy. He's always done the very thing that I don't want him to do."

"He's not a disobedient boy!" Bethany pointed out. "He's a man, a very fine man, a far better man than you seem to know. Maybe he's not perfect, but who is? At least he always does what he believes best, though no one seems to give him credit for that."

"What he thinks best is too often *not*!" Hub argued.

"In your opinion. Okay, so you sometimes disagree. So what? Why can't you see past that to the man he is? Sure, he's made some mistakes. Everyone does. But you have no reason to be disappointed with the man he has become."

"You say that because you're in love with him," Hub grumbled.

Chandler didn't realize that he was holding his breath until Bethany quietly said, "I say that because I know him."

Chandler dropped his head.

No matter what Kaylie thought, Bethany clearly was not in love with him. Why would she be? If not for the aunties, he wouldn't even be able to house and feed her. He'd let Kreger lead him around by the nose for so long that he'd completely lost his way. And he'd called that loyalty!

"He's just doing what he always does," Bethany went on, showing him real loyalty. "He's doing his best for everyone. You may not believe that, but it's the truth."

"I don't know what to believe," Hub muttered. "I just don't understand any of this."

"You could give your son the benefit of the doubt, though," Bethany told him gently. "You do everyone else."

Chandler smiled wanly. She didn't love him as he wanted her to, the way a wife usually loved her husband, but she was a good friend, good enough to defend him.

For a moment, Hub said nothing, but then he muttered, "Everyone else isn't my son."

"And that's the real problem, isn't it?" Bethany said quietly. "You judge him more harshly because he is your son."

What Hub replied, Chandler couldn't quite make out. It didn't matter, anyway. Hub would always think the worst of him. Chandler accepted that.

As for Bethany, he expected nothing more than the respect and friendship that she'd already shown him. She might have settled temporarily for a marriage with a man whom she couldn't love, but that wouldn't last. As loyal and sweet and considerate as she was, sooner or later, she'd want her freedom.

When that time came, he was honor-bound to let her go. He'd agreed to that, and he would keep his word.

But somehow, he had to manage to keep his heart in the process—even if it meant keeping his distance from this lovely and lovable wife of his.


"I'm worried about you," Garrett said, more than a week later. "I thought when you married Chandler that things would change."

Leaning forward, he braced his elbows on his knees, sitting opposite Bethany in one of a pair of antique armchairs that matched the sofa upon which she sat. Bethany leaned back into one corner of the sofa, hitched her leg up onto the seat and went about tying the shoestrings of her cheap, bright yellow tennis shoes.

"Things have changed," she told him.

Not as much as she would like, perhaps, but things had changed, and for the better. She no longer had to worry about Jay or, rather, Jason. She need not fear being thought of as an unwed mother and all that implied. As Mrs. Chandler Chatam, she could hold her head up high and finally put the past behind her. Best of all, Matthew had a father who wanted him. How could she complain about any of that—or expect more? So what if her husband had ignored her for the past week and more?

It hurt, that was what, and she had to do something to change it.

"You shouldn't be working," Garrett said. "You're not well."

"I'm fine," she told him, keeping her gaze averted as she shifted sides and hitched up the other leg. "Pregnancy is not a disease, you know, and I like my job."

In truth, the work did not overtire her, but her cramps had gradually returned. Still, that didn't bother her nearly as much as Chandler did.

He had barely spoken to her lately. Even when he'd driven her to and from work, he hadn't really been there, and now he was heading out to another rodeo without even telling her goodbye. She'd heard him head downstairs just moments ago, and she wanted to catch up with him before he left.

Suddenly the door opened, and Chandler rushed through it.

"Thank goodness you're dressed," he said, a harried look on his unshaven face. "I was climbing in the truck when I realized that I couldn't go off without you, but hurry, please."

Thrilled, Bethany got to her feet, tugging on the bottom of the rainbow-striped tunic top that she wore tied at the shoulders over an old blue T-shirt and a pair of matching leggings, both of which had faded to a pale denim shade.

"Wait just a minute, and I'll throw—"

"Now, Bethany, please," Chandler interrupted. "I'll explain on the way." Turning, he went out again.

Glancing toward the bedroom, she shrugged. She'd go without luggage if she had to. She would gladly dip into her savings to buy a change of clothes, she was that pleased to be going with her husband. Calling out a hasty farewell to her brother, Bethany grabbed her handbag from the desk beside the door and followed Chandler toward the stairs. He was halfway down the landing when she called out, "What's the hurry?"

"I have to be somewhere before seven-thirty."

"Oh. Okay."

"I'll bring the truck around front," he told her, sprinting ahead down the stairs.

Bethany kept a more sedate pace, aware that her center of gravity had shifted forward and that a fall could be catastrophic. The truck was waiting at the end of the brick walkway when she got there. She hurried around the front end and climbed into the passenger seat. They were off in an instant.

Chandler turned the truck right onto Chatam Avenue, as usual, but she didn't think a thing about it until he said, "I'll try to keep you from being late, but I promised I'd have money to someone early this morning."

"Late for what?"

"Work," he said, glancing at her in obvious confusion.

"But I don't have to go in to work today," Bethany pointed out, blinking.

The truck actually took a jerk sideways as he gaped at her. "You're not working today?"

"It's Friday."

He slapped a hand to his forehead. "Of all the insane… Tell me I didn't drag you out without any breakfast!"

She grimaced apologetically. "I only got up a few minutes before I heard you go out."

"Blast!" He whipped over to the side of the street and braked to a stop. "I'll take you back."

Torn between amusement and disappointment, she put on a smile and banished the other. At least he hadn't left without saying goodbye.

"No, it's okay. I'll eat later. I'm not even hungry yet. Go on. Keep your appointment."

"You're a sweetheart," he declared. Checking his mirrors, he started the truck moving again. "I'd take you back anyway, but Dovey was good enough to stable my horses at a very reasonable fee after Kreger sold the ranch out from under me, so I owe her. Her operation is always teetering on the edge of bankruptcy, though, and she called this morning to ask if I could pay early because she had a load of feed on its way. I just hopped out of bed and headed out. Then, I thought, oh, no, Bethany's got to get to work, so I ran back upstairs again."

"Sounds like Dovey woke you from a sound sleep."

"She did."

"She must need all the help she can get, then."

"She does," he admitted, "but I'm sorry about dragging you out like this. Guess my brain's not working yet."

"Aw, don't worry about it," Bethany told him, adding sheepishly, "I thought you were heading off to the rodeo without saying goodbye."

He slapped himself in the forehead again.

"I forgot! It's Friday!" Shaking his head, he huffed a disgusted breath. "Doesn't matter. I don't have to be there until three, and it's only a couple hours away. It'll be fine. In fact, tell you what, for being such a good sport about this, we'll stop off for breakfast somewhere on the way back from Dovey's. How does that work for you?"

"It works just fine," she said, smiling and settling in for the drive.

"I've done some stupid things," he said after a moment, "but this is one for the books." He started to chuckle, and soon they were both laughing.

She quite liked a man who could laugh at himself, Bethany decided. This one she could very easily love. In fact, she suspected that she already did.

It was a short trip. They exited the highway after only a couple of miles and traveled on the feeder road for some distance before turning to the right. Skirting a cookie-cutter-type neighborhood, they drove down a narrow lane. The pavement ended abruptly after perhaps half a mile, but Chandler never slowed. The truck barreled along, throwing up dust behind it, until even that dirt track ended at a barbed-wire fence. A hard left took them through a narrow, overgrown drive and into a yard of crinkly, sunburned grass.

As before, when they'd come out here to get the horses in the earliest hours of the morning on the day of their wedding—had it really been a mere week?—Chandler drove right past the modest frame house. Beyond it, cobbled together from a variety of materials, lay a maze of corrals, several small outbuildings and a pair of sizable barns. He brought the truck to a stop in a wide, dusty circle at the end of the drive and got out.

A thin, older woman in blue jeans and boots emerged from one of the outbuildings and lifted a hand in greeting. She started toward them, flanked by a pack of mutts ranging in size from knee-high to big-enough-to-saddle. One of them, a black, longhaired dog with a curled tail and a missing ear, loped ahead to yelp a greeting. As the welcoming party drew near, Bethany saw that one of the dogs was blind and another was horribly scarred.

Curious, Bethany got out of the truck. She'd always wanted a dog, but her stepfather and Jay both had refused to have one.

"Hey, y'all," the woman greeted them.

"Hey, yourself," Chandler said. Striding forward, he removed a wad of folded bills from his shirt pocket and offered it to her. "Here you go."

The woman smiled. Fiftyish and whipcord lean, she had a leathery look about her, aided in part by hair the color of tanned hides, which she had tied back with a dark ribbon. She took the cash from Chandler's hand, saying, "Thanks. This'll help."

"So will the sacks of feed I've got in the back," Chandler said, jerking a thumb toward the truck. He glanced that way and saw that Bethany had gotten out of the cab.

The woman tried to disguise her curiosity with a friendly smile, but Bethany felt it nonetheless.

Chandler waved her over and made the introduction. "This is Dovey Crawlick. My wife, Bethany."

The older woman goggled. "Wife!"

Chuckling, Chandler said, "The one and only."

"I had no… When did… Glory be!" She leaned

forward with an outstretched hand. "How do you do? Pleased to meet you."

"Fine. Thank you," Bethany replied, trying not to wince at the firm grasp.

Dovey lifted an eyebrow at Chandler, but he just rocked back on his heels, shrugging.

"You've been a busy boy," she said cheekily.

"Yes, ma'am." He lifted one foot and then another, pretending to examine them. "No moss on the soles of these boots."

He was enjoying this, Bethany realized, more pleased than she probably ought to be. Not wanting to betray herself, she went down on her haunches to pet the curly tailed dog. Chandler informed her that Dovey worked for a local vet, which abetted her inclination to rescue unwanted animals.

"Horses mostly," Dovey told her, waving toward the barns. "Costs a pretty penny, let me tell you." She looked around sharply and said, "There's the truck now."

"We'll let you get on about your business, then," Chandler said. "I need to feed my stock anyway. We're heading out to work in a couple hours."

"Good luck to you, then," Dovey said.

Chandler shook his head and pointed skyward. "It's all skill and the Man Upstairs."

Smiling, Dovey strode off toward the truck now idling in her yard. The dogs followed.

Chandler slid a hand beneath Bethany's arm, helping her to her feet. She wiped her hands on her leggings.

"Do you mind if I take time to feed my horses? I can take you home first if you want."

Bethany shook her head. "No, I don't mind."

Chandler smiled. "I appreciate that. Thanks."

"No problem." Actually, she was glad for the chance to spend more time with him.

They climbed back into the truck cab, and he drove it around to the nearest of the barns. After backing the vehicle inside, he went into a small room in the front corner and came out with a wheelbarrow. The rest of the barn was filled with two rows of stalls built of narrowly spaced metal pipes, one down each side of the building. Bethany got out and watched as Chandler heaved bags of feed from the bed of the truck and stacked them in the wheelbarrow. He pushed these into the small room and unloaded them, then returned for more. The final bag he wheeled down the center of the aisle to the very back of the barn, Bethany following on his heels.

*No wonder those shoulders are so wide,* she thought.

He finally stopped near the sliding gate of the final stall. Arroyo was a stocky, light brown horse with a smoky gray mane and tail, his broad back neatly bisected by a line of the same color. A lineback dun, Chandler had called him. He was the horse that Chandler used for steer wrestling.

Ginger Boy and Red Rover were a pair of matched bays with white blazes, reddish coats and black manes and tails. Each of them had bands of white, or stockings, on the lower front legs, and both were geldings. They were trained for team roping, and Chandler traded them off, using first one and then the other during competition.

The fourth animal, a beautiful black with black eyes, was a stallion. "His name is El Rey Ébano," Chandler told her. "It's Spanish for King Ebony. I call him Ébano for short." The horse tossed his head as if fully aware that they were talking about him. "He's full of himself, this fellow, but he has reason to be." He was no more proud of himself than Chandler was proud of him, though. That was obvious.

Bethany stood back while Chandler went about feeding and watering the animals. It was done within minutes, then he pushed the empty wheelbarrow back down the aisle. Bethany followed him, right into the little room. It was black as night in there and smelled of hay and oats. She looked around curiously, making out stacked bags of feed on a hay-covered floor, various cans and brooms and a pair of wide shovels as well as bales of something labeled "bedding." She assumed that was the shredded, spongy stuff on the stall floors. Chandler tilted the wheelbarrow up against one wall, turned and nearly mowed her down.

"Oops!" His big hands steadied her, grasping her by the upper arms.

She attempted to step back. But he didn't let her go.

She looked up, and for a long moment, they stood frozen. Bethany found that she couldn't quite breathe. His eyes gleamed in the darkness, and his head seemed to dip toward hers. She shifted her weight onto her toes, her heart slamming inside her chest. But then his hands dropped from her arms and she realized that she was staring at his cleft chin.

Clearing her throat, Bethany quickly turned away, embarrassed, and hurried to the truck. Chandler followed more slowly, and a few minutes later, the truck turned onto the dirt road. By the time they hit the pavement, Bethany's heartbeat had at last returned to normal. She hoped he hadn't noticed that she'd practically thrown herself at him back there.

They were almost to the highway when Chandler shifted in his seat and, without looking at her, said, "Thanks for your patience, especially after I hauled you out on your day off."

"I enjoyed it," Bethany said, and she had, very much. She'd have enjoyed it more if he'd actually kissed her. *Don't think about it,* she told herself. "I, ah, I've always liked animals."

He finally glanced her way. "Yeah? Me, too. Especially horses. I guess that's what drew me to Kreger to begin with. He lived on his grandparents' ranch and grew up around horses."

"The ranch you thought you'd invested in."

"The same."

"I'm sorry about how that turned out," she told him.

"Thanks. I'm trying to let that go, but it's not easy. Asher—that's my cousin, the lawyer—says I have no case because I had use of the property while I was giving Kreger money and no proof that it was anything but payment for use. The sale's final, so it's too late to file any sort of lien on the property anyway." He glanced at her as he guided the truck up the ramp onto the highway, saying, "Besides, what Kreger did to me is nothing compared to what that Jay character did to you. If you can survive that, I can survive this."

She propped her elbow on the edge of the door and laid her head on her upturned palm. "I thought he was saving me from the nightmare at home. And you know, I guess he did, even if it was all lies."

"I'd beg you to file charges on him, Bethany, if it wasn't for Matthew," Chandler told her.

She shook her head. "Like you, I have no proof."

"Even if you did," Chandler told her, "it would be

too dangerous. He'd be acknowledged as Matthew's father, so he'd have rights there. I asked Ash about it."

She shuddered and said, "It's better this way. Matthew has the father he needs."

Chandler smiled at her. "I hope so. I'll do my best, God as my witness."

"Don't you think I know that?" she asked him softly. "Do you believe, for one minute, that I'd trust my son to you if I didn't know that you are the best dad I could ever give him?"

He nodded and looked away, and she had the distinct impression that he was blinking.

After a moment, he cleared his throat and asked, "Want to stop by the waffle place? Or did you have something else in mind?"

Bethany smiled. "The waffle place suits me just fine."

*He* suited her just fine. Even if he never came to love her, he would always be the husband of her heart.

He seemed to make an effort to dispel the awkwardness, so much so that they wound up chatting like old friends. All through breakfast, they talked. He told her about his older brothers. One, a banker in Dallas, had a wife, grown daughters and two grandchildren of his own, but the other had never married. They had a different mother than Chandler and Kaylie; she had died long ago, and Hubner had married a second time, only to be widowed again.

Bethany talked about her own father's death and how hard it had been for her mom. It had been harder still after she'd married Doyle Benjamin.

It was good, sitting there talking with him, but that

moment back there in the barn hovered constantly in the back of Bethany's mind.

Had he really been tempted to kiss her? Or was her brain shrinking as her waistline expanded?

It had to be the latter.

She tried not to let that thought cast a pall on her enjoyment of the morning, and in truth, it did not, but when Chandler left for the rodeo a couple of hours after taking her back to Chatam House, Bethany silently wished that she was going with him. Apparently, the idea never even occurred to Chandler, and she wasn't brave enough to suggest it, so if she was disappointed, well, she had no right to be.

But she was.

She definitely was.

# Chapter Ten

Sighing, Bethany threw back the covers and sat up on the side of the bed. She'd called it a sleigh bed when she'd first seen it, but Magnolia had informed her that it was, "a French Empire burr chestnut with curved head- and footboards." Bethany had made the appropriately appreciative sounds, but in her opinion, its best attri- bute was the comfort of its mattress. Unfortunately, that comfy mattress made little difference tonight.

She knew that she would not be able to sleep until Chandler came home. It amazed her really. After Jay, she'd thought no man would ever be able to affect her again, but she was coming to realize that what she'd felt for Jay was a pale imitation of what she ought to have felt. In the end, all Jay had hurt was her pride. Chan- dler, she suspected, could break her heart without even knowing it.

Trying not to think about him, she'd kept herself busy by arranging the nursery and, this morning, at- tending church with the aunties. She'd happily gone to a Sunday school class for women her own age, where she'd sat with Cleo Ann, identified herself to the group at large as Bethany Chatam and explained that Chandler was competing in a rodeo in Louisiana that weekend. She had put his name on the prayer list, and they had prayed for his safety and success.

Cleo Ann had asked how she and Chandler had gotten together, and Bethany had answered truthfully, saying that he'd picked her up on the side of the road after her car had broken down. Thankfully, no one had asked when that first meeting had occurred. The subject of the baby shower had come up, but Bethany had discouraged the idea because Chandler's aunts had already been so generous.

The rest of the day had passed quietly. Bethany had eaten lunch with Garrett and dinner with the aunties, spending the hours between by puttering around in the baby's room. She supposed that she was "nesting" because she couldn't stay out of there. She decided that she'd just look in there now, be sure that all was as she remembered.

Before she could stand, a cramp tightened her abdominal muscles. She let it run its course, breathing evenly until it waned. The pains had gradually returned after her visit to the emergency room, but she calmed her fear with prayer and knowledge. Remembering what the doctor had told her about Braxton-Hicks and all that she'd been able to glean about the condition via the internet at work, she rose and pulled a big, misshapen T-shirt over the tank top that she wore with her usual loose-knit shorts.

Padding barefoot through the dark sitting room, she went straight to the nursery and turned on the colorful lamp that stood atop the highboy dresser. She wandered around, trailing her fingers across the furnishings, smiling at the color-blocked rug that softened the hardwood floor and matched the coverlet, which worked beautifully color-wise with the drapery. The bright yellow window coverings were somewhat more formal than Bethany would have chosen, but she wasn't about to complain, especially as they were permanent to the room.

Sweeping up a tiny stuffed horse with a pale blue saddle and soft yarn mane and tail, she sat down in the rocking chair that Chester had brought in from another room and pretended that she was cradling her son. Singing softly, she worked her way through every lullaby and baby song that she knew. She had just taken a breath when a sudden voice made her jump.

"What are you doing up at this hour?"

She looked around to find Chandler standing in the doorway, his boots in his hand. Her heart racing, she gasped, "You frightened me."

"Sorry." He set down the boots and walked across the floor in his stocking feet. "You didn't answer my question. Why aren't you asleep?"

She shrugged. "Just feeling kind of weird, I guess."

Frowning, he went down on his haunches beside her and lifted a hand to her forehead. "Maybe you're coming down with something."

"I'm fine." She smiled as she reached up to remove his hand from her brow. The baby suddenly moved. Bethany instinctively placed Chandler's hand on her abdomen, quipping, "I'm not the only one who can't sleep."

He stared at her belly as it rippled, little hillocks appearing here and there, only to smooth out again as the baby moved. Finally, Matthew subsided into stillness, and Chandler looked up at her with awe in his cinnamon eyes.

"Amazing," Chandler whispered.

Their gazes held for several long moments before he abruptly snatched his hand away and pushed up to his full height.

Bethany hurried to smooth over the sudden awkwardness, asking chattily, "So, how did it go this weekend?"

Chandler sent her a dark look and muttered, "Saw Kreger finally."

"Oh, dear."

"Would you believe that he actually wants to partner up again?"

Bethany sat up very straight. "You turned him down, of course. Didn't you?"

"Of course. He admitted to me that he sold the ranch because of gambling debts."

"Oh, Chandler, I'm so sorry."

He shook his head. "You know, it's probably for the best. I mean, it was wrong, but I sort of feel sorry for him."

"Why? He cheated you."

"Yeah, he did, but in the end, I came out of it better than he did. He says he's been living in his rig. His trailer's got one of those sleeping compartments in it. Thing's about the size of a coffin. I wouldn't want to try to sleep in there. Besides, if he hadn't done what he did, I wouldn't have met Drew. Might not have met you, either," he added softly. "I probably wouldn't even have been on that road then if Kreger had shown up at that rodeo." He waved a hand. "Anyway, the Bible says to forgive, and that's what I'm trying to do. Doesn't mean I want him hanging around, though."

He looked so dark that Bethany decided to change the subject. "Speaking of Drew and you, how did that go?"

Chandler brightened visibly. "We finished less than a tenth of a second out of first place."

"That's great!"

"It's in the money, anyway, but there's a lot more difference in first and second place than that fraction of a second."

"Financially, you mean."

He nodded. "And it doesn't help that I came in third in the tie-down and well out of it otherwise."

She sensed his frustration. "You'll find your stride," she told him encouragingly. "All you have to do is be patient."

"It's just that we're running out of time," Chandler groused. "It's August already. We're having a baby in little more than two months, in case you've forgotten."

Bethany hauled her belly up out of the chair, quipping, "You're kidding me, right? You've seen what I'm lugging around here."

His mouth twitched. "You say that all the time."

"What?"

"You're kidding me."

She frowned in puzzlement. "No, I'm not. How could I? Just look at me." She pressed down the fabric of her T-shirt, emphasizing the size of her belly.

Chandler grinned. "You say, 'You're kidding me' all the time. It's like your trademark phrase. Whatever anyone says, you come back with 'You're kidding me' or 'No kidding' or something to that effect."

Bethany blinked. "I guess I do. I hadn't realized. Sorry."

He chuckled. "It's not a complaint. I think it's cute."

Cute? She wrinkled her nose. Cute wasn't exactly how she wanted Chandler to think of her. Then again, for a woman shaped like a beached whale, it could be worse. She stepped closer and reached up to smooth back the lock of hair that had fallen forward over his brow.

"I just don't want to irritate you, not when you work so hard all the time," she said softly.

His sudden frown made her wonder what she'd said wrong. "I'm not the only one who works."

"I sit in a chair, answer the phone and smile at people all day," she pointed out drily. "You *work*." She tilted her head, studying his handsome face. "In fact, you look tired. You should go to bed and get a good night's sleep."

"That makes two of us."

She smiled. "I will if you will." A sharp, sudden pain made her gasp and grab her side.

Chandler clasped her protectively, one hand going to the small of her back and the other to her abdomen. "Is it a contraction?"

She shook her head, caught her breath and said, "Matthew just kicked me in the ribs."

Chandler breathed out a sigh. "So you haven't been having the cramps?"

She grimaced. "I have, but it's okay. I know what they are now, so it doesn't scare me so much anymore."

"So much?" he repeated, beetling his brow.

"I've learned to pray when I get frightened," she told him, patting his chest.

"Good idea," he said approvingly, covering her hand with his. "I find it helps me sleep sometimes, too."

Bethany smiled. "Yes, I've found that to be true. Maybe that's what we need right now."

Chandler pulled back slightly. "You mean that we should pray together?"

"Yes, please," she answered, closing her eyes before he could beg off.

After a long pause, Chandler began to softly speak. "We thank You, Lord, that little Matthew is so strong and active, and we trust You to keep him that way, but it understandably frightens his mom when those awful cramps come. Please spare her that pain and give us all peace and rest this night. Amen."

"Amen," she whispered. She looked up to find him smiling down at her. "Thank you for that," she said. He nodded. "Good night."

"Good night," he returned.

The kiss just seemed to happen, a natural consequence of all that had passed in the moments before she lifted her face and he lowered his head. The moment his lips met hers, she knew that this was what she wanted, needed from him, what she had been waiting for. She felt her hands slide around his neck, heard the soft sound that he made as he pulled her closer, his arms holding her tight. He was her husband, and she had never felt more like his wife than in this moment of sweet joining.

*If only,* she thought. *If only this was a true marriage.*

But how could she expect that of him? He didn't really want her any more than Jay had. How could he, fool that she was? Chandler had done his best to help her, but she and the baby were nothing more than burdens to him. All of which meant that this lovely kiss was a terrible mistake. Saddened, she made herself turn her head away.

He released her instantly, lurching back as if she'd thrown cold water on him. She quickly fled to the safety of her own bedroom. There she sat down on the side of the bed again, feeling foolish and scalded. After a time, she went to God, asking that He help her be satisfied with what He had given her—or help her make it all that she wanted it to be.

*So much for keeping emotional distance,* Chandler thought disgustedly. He'd managed for a time—if thinking about her every waking minute and missing her something awful when he was away could be termed "emotional distance." Still, he'd managed to keep from kissing her that day at Dovey's. Only to kiss her in their suite at Chatam House.

Mentally kicking himself all night long didn't do a bit of good. He couldn't take back that ill-advised kiss and he couldn't get it out of his mind. He dropped off, finally, thinking about it—and woke again on Monday morning with it playing vividly in his memory.

"Stupid, stupid, stupid," he chanted softly, dressing quickly in old jeans and a tan T-shirt.

He and Drew had agreed to practice three days a week, the same days that Bethany worked, Tuesday, Wednesday and Thursday. That left Monday and Friday for everything else, including traveling to and from weekend competition. The bigger rodeos ran two, even three weeks, but most were four or five days long. At this time of year, though, those venues were far from the hot South. He and Drew had reasons to stick closer to home, which meant that Chandler found himself with a rare day off, a day when he could have simply relaxed.

Chandler knew, however, that relaxation would be impossible this day. After pulling on his socks, he caught up his working boots and his sweat-stained straw hat and tiptoed out of the suite, thinking that Bethany would almost certainly still be asleep.

Pausing at the top of the stairs to pull on his boots, he balanced on first one foot and then another before trotting down in search of breakfast. His mood lightened considerably as he drew near the kitchen and caught the aroma of Hilda's cream biscuits. He could almost taste them. His stomach rumbling, he dropped his hat onto one of several pegs affixed to the wall before shoving through the swinging door. Hilda straightened and turned away from the big, old-fashioned stove, her rotund frame surprisingly agile. Beaming a welcome at him, she waved a large pan of golden-brown biscuits in one hand.

"Ah, he's up and about, is he? Well, come on and get your breakfast, then."

Inhaling appreciatively, he started to follow her to the small, sturdy, rectangular table situated before the brick fireplace, but then he halted. "Is that coffee I smell?"

The aunties were devoted to their tea. That being the case, Chandler had intended to pick up a can of coffee for himself, but he'd taken most of his breakfasts away from the house for one reason or another, so had never gotten around to stopping by the store.

Hilda nodded toward the table, saying, "You can thank your wife for that."

Surprised, Chandler leaned sideways a bit to look around Hilda, who was almost as wide as she was tall. Bethany sat at the table in baggy denim shorts and a blue sleeveless top, her face freshly scrubbed and heartbreakingly beautiful. As she tilted her pretty head, smiling shyly, her dark, sleek hair swung lushly about her slender shoulders. Chandler's breath caught in his throat.

"Good morning."

"Morning," he managed.

"You're too quick," Hilda told him, plunking the pan of biscuits onto a hot pad in the center of the table. "The missus here was going to bring you breakfast in bed."

Chandler froze, stunned to think of his pregnant wife serving him breakfast in bed. Hilda trundled off to take up a red enamel tray from the enormous metal work-table that took up a significant amount of floor space in the cavernous room. Carrying the tray to the table, she placed it in front of the chair across from Bethany's then forked up two tall, flaky biscuits.

"Tray was all ready," she said. "It was just waiting on this. You saved her the trip."

Hilda jerked her head, all but ordering Chandler to sit. He walked over and sat, deeply touched, and surveyed the contents of the tray: butter and Hilda's famous cinnamon fig preserves, cantaloupe and a cup of fragrant black coffee, plus those two high biscuits. His mouth watered.

"Y'all didn't have to go to so much trouble," he said, reaching for the butter knife.

"No trouble on my part," Hilda pointed out, waddling off toward the stove.

Chandler looked at Bethany. "Thank you, especially for the coffee. But you shouldn't be serving anyone breakfast in bed."

"The dumbwaiter comes up right outside our door," Bethany reminded him quietly, looking down at her own empty plate. She reached for a tall glass of milk beside it. "It's just that you looked so tired last night, and I…" She let the sentence dwindle away with a glance.

"She has an ulterior motive," Hilda announced loudly. "She wants to go with you today."

Chandler felt his eyebrows jump toward his hairline as Bethany tucked her chin, her cheeks pinkening. His pleasure at the request dismayed him. All the more reason, he told himself, to maintain some distance between the two of them. Pity he couldn't seem to do it. At least he managed to keep his tone level and noncommittal as he went about breaking open the hot biscuits. "That so? Not much of interest going on with me today. Thought I'd clean the horse stalls and trailer."

Bethany reached for the pan and transferred a biscuit to her own plate, keeping her gaze carefully averted. "I don't mind. I like it out at Dovey's place."

"Awful hot outside."

"I won't melt."

Chandler buttered his biscuits and slathered them with fig jelly, trying to marshal his defenses. "Wouldn't be much for you to do."

She looked up, hope softening her breathtaking blue eyes. "I can hold a water hose, you know."

Chandler tried to bolster his objections. "Horses can be dangerous. Given your condition, do you think it's wise to take such a chance?"

"Cindy's around horses all day every day," she argued gently.

He couldn't refute that. Besides, he had absolutely no defense against that pleading tone. He had no defenses against *her*. In truth, he didn't even know why he bothered resisting. She charmed him, had since he'd first laid eyes on her perched there on that stool in the diner. He gave up.

"Okay, come along, then."

Bethany beamed as brightly as if he'd given her a big, shiny diamond, which he'd have liked very much to do. Fat chance of that. Even if he could have afforded it, he doubted that Bethany would have taken it. She'd probably be happier with her freedom.

"I'll pack you a picnic lunch," Hilda announced, not even bothering to pretend that she hadn't been eavesdropping.

"That's wonderful!" Bethany exclaimed, spreading her smile around the room, from Chandler to Hilda and back again. "Thank you."

Still beaming, she smeared jam on half a biscuit and stuffed it into her mouth. Chandler shook his head. Who'd have thought watching a woman smile and eat a biscuit could be so fascinating?

He downed his own biscuits in two bites each, then reached for three more. Bethany finished a second biscuit and started to rise, saying she would help Hilda make their lunch, at which point Hilda pointed a butcher knife at her and ordered, "Sit yourself down and finish your milk and fruit, missy. You're growing a babe there."

"Yes, ma'am." Obviously tickled, Bethany shared a smile with Chandler and dutifully gobbled up her melon before gulping down her milk. Finished, she dabbed daintily at the corners of her mouth with her napkin and sedately rose.

She looked ridiculously gorgeous in her ragged,

knee-length denim shorts, form-fitting blue sleeveless top and tall red boots. Chandler remembered the way the baby had moved beneath his hand last night, and it was all he could do not to pull Bethany onto his lap and cradle them both. He knew that it was insane to take her with him. Keeping his distance would most assuredly be the safer, wiser course, but it was beyond him to deny her this or anything else she seemed to want. If only she wanted him.

*Oh, Lord, help me,* he prayed silently as he finished his breakfast and she went to help Hilda put up their lunch. *I'm finding that my father was right all along. I'm not a very wise man.*

Worse, he wasn't even sure that he wanted the wisdom that he so obviously lacked, for he had the sad suspicion that it would come at the price of a shattered heart.


"Can I ask you something?" Bethany said, sitting sideways on a saddle atop a low rack in the back of his pickup truck.

Chandler smiled to himself. She'd been asking questions all morning, while he forked out and swept the stalls, spread new bedding and fed, watered and groomed the horses. She'd helped in small ways, passing him pitchfork or broom, brushes or combs, pulling bedding from the bales. He'd made sure that he kept himself between her and the horses, but she couldn't resist reaching around him to dispense pats and rubs. Neither he nor the horses minded a bit.

He'd asked her if she'd ever thought about riding, and she'd replied that she'd always wanted to learn but had never had the chance. He'd blurted that he would teach her after the baby came, and she'd clapped her hands in glee. Praying that he'd have the chance to follow through, he spread an old blanket over the tailgate and bed of his truck, which he'd backed into the barn earlier.

His stomach growled like a surly wolf. Perching on the edge of the tailgate, he twisted around to reach into the cooler that Hilda had packed for them. After rummaging about for a moment, he came up with an apple and a bottle of water.

"Ask away," he said, biting into the apple.

"Don't you ever worry about getting hurt?"

He lowered the apple, the bottle of water in his other fist. "No, not really."

"Not even when you're leaping off a horse to grab a full-grown steer by the horns?"

"I don't *leap*," he said with a chuckle. "It's sort of a slide out of the saddle."

"Leap, slide, whatever. It's a full-grown animal and it has horns!"

He pushed back his hat with the cap end of the water bottle, touched that she seemed concerned for him. "Look, everyone gets hurt at some point. That's rodeo. That's sports in general. I couldn't compete at all if I wasn't willing to risk injury. That said, I do everything I can to protect myself, which is why I practice all the time, why I keep my gear in tip-top shape, why I concentrate and constantly work on my technique." He tapped the bottle against his knee and told her what he hadn't told anyone else, "That's why the last thing I do before I enter the arena is pray."

"I wouldn't have pegged you as a praying man when we first met," she commented gently.

He sighed. "Yeah, I know. But it's always been the

case. I—I guess I just thought I couldn't show my faith, that it made me…I don't know, less tough, maybe." He shook his head at his own stupidity. "And to be perfectly honest, I guess it has to do with my dad, too. You know, that PK thing."

"PK?"

"Preacher's kid."

"Ah. Yes, I can see that. I actually think that's part of the problem on your dad's end, too. He's a minister, so his kids should do more noble things than everyone else's."

Chandler sent her a surprised look. "You figured that out, did you?"

She shrugged and said, "Frankly, I think he's a little hurt that none of his children followed him into the ministry. I mean, he says and, I'm sure, believes that everyone has to be true to his or her own calling, but it would be a natural thing to secretly hope that someone would take up the mantle, so to speak."

Suddenly Chandler remembered talking with Drew about their sons one day roping together. He'd thought then how cool it would be if his son should follow in his footsteps. Why hadn't he realized that his own father might feel the same?

"Oh, wow," Chandler said. "I never thought of that. And he never said anything."

"He wouldn't," Bethany remarked. "He'd see it as putting himself in God's place. He always says everyone is called to something, but that we must be sure it's God's voice we hear and not our own or someone else's."

Chandler nodded at that. He'd heard the same all his life, and he'd always firmly believed that he was meant to rodeo, at least for now. Later, he hoped to be able to concentrate on raising and training horses. He'd tried to explain that to his father, but Hub hadn't understood.

"You're talking about occupation," he would say. "I'm talking about ministry. What is your *ministry*?"

Now, suddenly, Chandler wondered the same thing himself. If God meant him to compete in rodeo, and Chandler believed that He did, then what was the purpose? Where was his ministry in that?

He thought of Drew's openness about his own faith, and it hit Chandler that for years now his focus had been on winning and, if he were honest, rubbing his father's nose in it, not in living for God. Had he been half as out there as Drew, no telling who he might have encouraged or influenced. He might even have made a difference in Pat Kreger's life.

Sharply stung, Chandler bowed his head right then and there, without so much as a word of explanation to Bethany, and silently told God how sorry he was and how wrong he'd been.

*"I want to be the man You would have me be, Lord. I want to be the husband, the father, the son, the brother, even the cowboy You would have me be. So no more ignoring Your plans in favor of my own, no more living for that next win. Now I just want to live for You."*

That, he suddenly realized, meant doing something he had thus far avoided. He had admit to his father what had happened with Kreger and apologize for all those times he'd refused to listen. Only then could he really start getting right with God.

He looked up to find Bethany kneeling in front of him, concern drawing a line between her eyes.

"You okay?" she asked gently.

He cleared his throat. "Getting there."

She tilted her head as if thinking that through. He smiled, feeling lighter, brighter, and lifted the half-eaten apple.

"Aren't you hungry?"

She sat back on her heels. "I am, actually."

"Let's dig in."

She shifted around and reached into the cooler, coming up with chicken salad sandwiches, hardboiled eggs and crunchy slices of peppered cucumber, along with a wealth of tasty accompaniments. They feasted, rhapsodizing about the food.

It seemed to Chandler as if they were pretending to be what they wanted the world to think them to be, the average married couple, and he wondered what might have happened if they'd met the way people normally met. Would they have fallen in love and married? He doubted that he'd have done more than look her over, think her extremely attractive and turn away, intent on the next contest, never knowing what he'd lost. He was glad, heartbreakingly glad, that he hadn't missed knowing her, even if it was bound to end for him in disappointment and pain. Not that he had any right to ask more of her.

The woman was giving him a son, for pity's sake, literally *giving* him a son! He felt like an ungrateful fool for wanting more from her.

But he did.

Oh, he did.

Even so, he would humbly accept God's will for his life, whatever it might be. That lesson, at least, he had finally learned.

## Chapter Eleven

The newlyweds returned to the house late Monday afternoon filthy and exhausted. Magnolia regretted calling them into the parlor, but like her sisters, she had been eager to know if their outing together had gone well. Unfortunately it was impossible to tell under all that grime.

"Would you like tea, dears?" she asked, waving a hand at the tray on the table.

"Uh, no," Chandler replied, wiping perspiration from his brow with the back of his hand. He glanced at Bethany, adding, "Not for me, anyway."

The sisters were under no illusions about this marriage. They didn't know the details of Chandler and Bethany's relationship, but not even Odelia bought the notion that Chandler had actually fathered Bethany's baby. The aunts knew their nephew better than that and couldn't understand how his own father did not. She supposed it had to do with the dynamics of the parent-and-child relationship. Whatever the truth of Chandler and Bethany's situation, it was clear to all three of his aunts that Chandler had married Bethany for other reasons, reasons that had to do with that oily attorney Haddon.

Odelia insisted that Chandler had somehow rescued Bethany from "a fate worse than death." Magnolia scoffed, but secretly she wasn't sure that Odelia was entirely wrong.

Regardless of the reasons for the marriage, however, it was evident to all of them that things were not quite as they should be between the young couple. Carol had reported that they slept in separate bedrooms, and neither seemed particularly overjoyed with their situation. It was good to see them spending time together, though, even if the results were rather, well, fragrant. In fact, if she was not mistaken, Odelia was pinching her nose behind her hanky.

"No tea for me, either," Bethany said, holding out her hands to display streaks of dirt on her forearms. "All I want is a shower."

"Obi-usly, ewe two hab been busy," Odelia said from behind her hanky.

"You noticed," Chandler quipped. "We were cleaning the horse trailer. It was dirtier than I thought. Boots are clean, anyway. We hit them with the water hose. Otherwise, I think I have more stable than skin on me right now. So, see you later, if that's okay."

"Go, go," Hypatia said with a chuckle.

They went out into the foyer and up the stairs, taking their odor with them.

Odelia lowered her handkerchief, the tip of her nose bright pink in contrast to the bright orange pantsuit that she wore, complete with earrings of fake orange-slice candies. "I thought they went on a picnic," she said petulantly.

"Hilda only said that she'd packed them a picnic lunch," Magnolia pointed out.

"Well, picnic or cleaning a horse trailer, whatever they were doing, they were doing it together," Hypatia said.

Odelia brightened. "That's true."

"It doesn't mean that we don't still have praying to do," Magnolia warned.

Hypatia sighed. "I fear you're right. The marriage may have come before the romance in this case."

"Let's hope the baby doesn't, too," Odelia muttered.

Magnolia gasped. It was the most perceptive thing she'd heard her sister say yet.

"Thanks for taking me with you today," Bethany said. The day had been joy and agony for her, joy because they had worked together like a team and agony because she wanted so much more with him, so much that she feared she would never have.

"Thanks for the help," he returned. He climbed the stairs a step behind her, as if to catch her should she fall. Of course, that could be wishful thinking on her part. He might just be too tired to keep up. The man had worked like a Trojan today.

"I didn't do much."

"You did enough."

She smiled. "It was fun."

"Well, if that's your idea of fun," he drawled, "I'd hate to see your idea of hard work."

She laughed. He was the one who had worked hard, and she believed wholeheartedly that he'd enjoyed every minute of it.

Something, however, had changed after their conversation about his dad. She wasn't sure what, really, but she knew that Chandler seemed both more relaxed and more pensive afterward. He'd scrubbed the horse trailer with silent doggedness, yet she'd sensed that he was somewhat distracted.

Once in the suite they went their separate ways.

Bethany took a long, hot shower, dried her hair and managed a little nap before dinner. Chandler came to the table freshly scrubbed but very quiet. Even the aunties noticed.

"Chandler, dear," Hypatia asked at one point, "are you well?"

"Getting there," he replied with an absent smile.

It was the same answer that he'd given Bethany earlier in the day, and she could only wonder what exactly that meant. He disappeared into his room as soon as they returned to the suite after dinner, and she didn't see him again until the morning. Even then he seemed preoccupied, so she was surprised when, instead of dropping her off, he parked the truck and got out to walk up to the door of the Single Parent Ministry building with her.

It didn't end there, though. Not only did he open the door for her, he followed her inside. Glancing back warily, she carried her handbag to the reception desk and dropped it into a drawer. Chandler, meanwhile, stood watching…and waiting, it seemed.

Calling out a cheery "Good morning!" Hub appeared from the hallway. He froze when he saw Chandler there.

"Dad," Chandler said, shifting around to face the older man. "Got a minute? I need to talk to you."

Hubner looked to Bethany, who knew no more than

he did. Concerned, she started forward, ready to intervene if necessary. Chandler sent her a taut smile.

"It's okay, hon. No fireworks today, I promise. I just need a word in private with my dad."

Hubner opened his mouth as if to speak, but then he simply nodded, turned and walked back toward his office. Bethany rushed to Chandler.

"What's going on?"

He reached toward her, his hand landing in the vicinity of her waist. "It's time," he said. "Don't worry. I prayed about this for hours last night."

"You're going to tell him about us," she surmised softly.

He shook his head. "No. I wouldn't do that to you and Matthew. What's between us stays between us. This is about me and him."

She flashed back to the day before and their conversation in the back of the truck. Something warm and bright trickled through her. She wasn't sure why, but she knew that this was a special moment. As if to reinforce that feeling, Chandler leaned in and kissed her cheek before following his father into the hallway.

Bethany went back to her desk, sat down and bowed her head, praying that this might be the first step in a meeting of the hearts between father and son.

Oddly, he'd expected to feel like a child again about to face his father's disappointment and correction. Instead, Chandler felt strong and sure, even at peace, though he had not yet done what he'd come here to do. Hubner stood beside the door. Chandler stepped past him into the cramped office and glanced about as his father closed the door and moved around to sit behind his desk.

The room felt familiar, though Chandler had never been in here before. He recognized the carved cross hanging on one wall and the framed verse on a small easel on one of the bookshelves behind the desk. It was John 6:5-6.

Then Jesus lifted up His eyes, and seeing a great multitude coming toward Him, He said to Philip, "Where shall we buy bread, that these may eat?" But this He said to test him, for He Himself knew what He would do.

Smiling to himself, Chandler bowed his head. The aunties were right. God undoubtedly knew exactly what He was doing and why.

"I'm sorry, Dad," he said, unable to leave it for another moment. "You were right all along. I let Kreger drag me through dive after dive, and in the end, he cheated and ran out on me."

The chair creaked as Hubner sat forward. Glancing at his father's shocked face, Chandler stepped up and dropped down onto one of a pair of padded wooden chairs arranged in front of the desk.

"Don't misunderstand me," he rushed to say, folding his forearms against the desktop, "I believe—I *know*— that I'm called to rodeo. It's what I'm meant to do. But I'm also meant to use that as a way to witness, if only by proclaiming myself a Christian and living like it. I didn't get that until Kreger flaked out on me. Actually, I didn't get it until Bethany…" He shook his head. That was beside the point. "What I'm saying is, I'm sorry I didn't listen to you."

Hubner sat back again, lacing his fingers over his rounded belly. "Cheated and ran out, you say?"

"Yes, sir." Chandler briefly explained, ending with, "It's okay, though. I have a new partner now, and things are starting to happen for us. I just want you to know, it's not all about winning for me now. It's about being the man I'm supposed to be, the man God wants me to be."

His father stared at him for a long time, then he gripped the arms of his chair and sat up straight. "I don't know what to say, son. I truly did not want this disappointment for you, but I can't pretend I'm surprised or heartbroken. Frankly, I expect it's for the best. I always felt that Kreger pulled you away from us, away from your real purpose in life. Frankly, I thought that you were the one most likely to…rather, the one best suited for…" He grimaced, and Chandler smiled with wry understanding.

Pretty smart, that little wife of his.

"Dad, I'm not cut out for the pulpit. You know that."

Hubner steepled his hands. "I know it *now.* I admit that it took me a while to see it." He rubbed a hand over his face, sighing. "Took me a long time to see it. Hard to see what you don't want to."

"Amen," Chandler said to that. Then he caught sight of the decorative clock in the shape of a church on the corner of his father's desk and rose to his feet. "I've got to be going. Drew's expecting me in Stephenville. I just wanted…I just wanted to apologize."

He turned and moved swiftly toward the door, only to draw up short when his father spoke his name.

"Chandler."

His hand hovered over the doorknob. "Yes, sir?"

"Thank you."

Chandler nodded and went out, leaving his father with his head bowed in deep contemplation.

Neither father nor son offered any description of what had passed between them, and Bethany dared not ask. Hubner seemed as preoccupied as his son had the day before. Conversely, Chandler was in an expansive mood when he picked her up from work that afternoon. He chatted animatedly about the day's practice as they drove around town on errands, picking up his dry cleaning, gassing the truck, purchasing shaving cream and razor blades. They didn't get back to the house until dinnertime.

After the meal, they wound up in the sitting room of their suite, side by side on the sofa, watching TV on the screen mounted above the fireplace mantel. Happily, they liked the same program. When it was over, Chandler switched off the set.

"This is better than what we had out at the ranch," Chandler told her, aiming the remote at the screen. "I've gotta give it to the old dears, they may live in a hundred-and-fifty-year-old house, surrounded by antiques, but they do try to keep up."

Bethany chuckled and bumped her shoulder against his. "Do you know, I found Odelia on the computer in the study not long ago, surfing the internet in search of jewelry."

He laughed. "Is that where she finds her earrings?"

Bethany giggled. "I thought there was a crazy earring store around here somewhere."

He laughed even harder at that, until Bethany playfully scolded him. "We shouldn't make fun of her. She's such a darling."

"Oh, she is," he agreed. "They all are. I wouldn't change a hair on any of their heads. Or yours for that matter." His expression suddenly grew serious, and he skimmed a hair over her head. "You have beautiful hair."

"Thank you."

"And beautiful eyes."

"Thank you again."

"Beautiful everything."

She dropped her gaze, pleased and a little embarrassed. "I'm glad you think so."

"Sweetheart, I don't think it, I know it. It can't help but improve a man when he's got a woman like you on his arm."

"I don't think you need improving," she told him shyly.

"Yeah, I do," he said. "More than you know and in ways you can't see."

"What do you mean?" she asked, surprised he could think that about himself. As far as she could tell, he was the next thing to perfect.

He swallowed and shook his head, saying, "I think I better go now." He got up and headed for his bedroom, wishing her a good night.

Sighing, Bethany went to her own room, but she hadn't given up. She wanted this marriage, and she wanted this man. If only she could make him want her, too.

Watching TV, Chandler decided, could be a dangerous thing with a wife like his. She had no notion how tempting she was, and because he knew his limits, he'd figured that he better find something else to do tonight.

He flexed his hands inside the new gloves, feeling the lanoline with which he'd treated the leather ooze a bit. He was working them on an old rope so the emollient wouldn't destroy the stiffness of a new one. A limp rope wasn't good for anything more than tying bundles and tricks. He made a loop and tossed it at one of the standing plant holders scattered among the tables arranged around the softly chuckling fountain.

"You better not let Magnolia catch you roping her beautiful plants."

He smiled in the direction of his wife's amused voice, blinded by the light from a bulb mounted above the sunroom door. "Why do you think I missed?"

She laughed softly. What a beautiful sound it was, healing, almost, in its purity.

"Mind if I watch?"

He shrugged. "Nothing much to see."

"I think there is," she said, taking a seat on one of the chaises beside the fountain. "I find all these little jobs and the many tools of your trade fascinating."

"Yeah? Me, too," Chandler confessed. "Rodeo's pretty high-tech these days, but there's something comforting and powerful about doing things you know countless others have done before you, things that only a select few really appreciate now."

"I can understand that. When you get down to it, I suppose having a baby is the same way."

"I suppose it is at that," he said, pausing to think about it.

"One more thing we have in common," she said.

"What do you mean?"

"Well, we've both been betrayed by people we trust. We've both lost parents. We both love our remaining family. And we've both led fairly unconventional lives. Just look at what you do for a living. You make your own way. None of that nine-to-five stuff for you. I admire that. Wish my own lack of convention was as admirable. I mean, my so-called marriage to Jay was anything but normal."

"And look at us now," Chandler said, wincing at the edge of discontent in his own voice. "Ours isn't exactly a conventional marriage, either, Bethany," he couldn't help adding.

"No, it's not," she said, "but maybe we're not cut out for conventional."

"Maybe we're not," he agreed. "So, okay, my unconventional wife, let's rope us some chairs. Mags won't cut up at that. What do you say?"

Bethany laughed. "Rope all the chairs you want, cowboy. I'll even sit in them if you like."

"That won't be necessary," he told her. In truth, if he ever got a loop on her, he wasn't entirely sure he could let her go again.

It was nearly eleven when they finally turned in that night, but sleep eluded Bethany for hours afterward. She couldn't stop going over every moment that they had spent together lately. Funny how a few happy days could color a girl's world, she mused.

Cleaning stalls and eating a picnic lunch in the back of a truck hadn't been a romantic interlude by any means, and yet she had come away feeling as if she was a part of something real, one of a pair, half of a couple. The ensuing days had only reinforced that notion. The truth, of course, was that they were friends who happened to be legally wed, nothing more, and that only because Chandler was such a good man.

He had done so much for her. She wished that she could do something good for him in return. If only she could find a way to fully reconcile Chandler with his father. She felt they'd made a step in that direction, but it seemed a wary step at best. They were both such wonderful men, and each had been so very kind to her, despite the difficulties that she had added to their relationship, but they continued to circle each other like wary beasts, neither looking for a fight but neither coming closer. Lately she had been tempted to tell Hub the truth about her and Chandler so he would know what a truly fine man this son of his was, but she hadn't for two reasons.

One was entirely selfish. She wanted Chandler to be the father of this child and her husband for real, not just in the eyes of the world and his family. The second reason was simply that Chandler *was* her husband, at least in name, and she wouldn't go against his express wishes. Hub was *his* father. Marrying her had been *his* decision, his plan. In this case it was *his* truth to tell. Or not.

Chandler was set to leave Thursday morning for a rodeo in New Mexico. Why that should have Bethany feeling slightly panicked, she didn't know, but no sooner did her eyes open that morning than she threw on a robe and went to his room. Standing there in the doorway, she could feel her heart beating against her breastbone like a caged bird fluttering its wings.

"How long will you be gone?" she asked, trying to keep the tremor from her voice.

Chandler stuffed socks into his rolling duffel bag and looked up. "Probably be the wee hours of Monday morning before I get in."

Bethany nodded.

"I'll be done here in a minute, then I'll take you to work," Chandler went on. "Kaylie's going to give you a ride home this afternoon."

She managed a smile to let him know that she was appreciative, and then she took her courage in both hands and wrung it until the words she wanted came out. "If you could wait until then, I could go with you."

He froze in the act of zipping the bag.

"O-or I could ask Hub for the day off," she plunged on desperately.

Chandler slowly finished zipping the bag and straightened, turning slightly to face her. Her hopes plummeted. So sure was she that he was going to shoot her down, she began throwing up barriers herself.

"Oh, but…I—I do have a doctor's appointment on Monday afternoon, a-and I'm coming up on seven months, which means I won't be able to travel soon anyway, so…"

"So if you're going to go, it had better be now," Chandler said. He pursed his lips, looking thoughtful, and added, "I expect I could get you back in time for your appointment, and Kaylie will probably fill in for you today. I'll call her while you go pack." With that, he reached for his cell phone in his hip pocket.

Elated, Bethany was too stunned for a moment to do anything more than gape, but then Chandler made a shooing motion with one hand and began dialing his phone with the thumb of the other. Holding her belly with both hands, Bethany spun and ran back to her room, where she quickly threw things into her battered old suitcase. Her heart was beating double-time now, but for an entirely different reason. She was going with Chandler. They would be together for the whole, long weekend.

"Thank You," she whispered at the ceiling. "Thank You, thank You, thank You."

They drove away from Buffalo Creek Thursday at noon, heading for Lovington, New Mexico. It was a seven-hour trip that turned into nearly nine. Chandler didn't mind. Despite having to stop every hour so Bethany could make a dash for the ladies' room, he was thankful for the opportunity to get to know her better.

She finally told him all about Jay Carter, how he'd approached her at a football game during her senior year in high school. She'd known he was older, but she'd been flattered by the attention. He'd told her later that he didn't know why he'd stopped there that night, that it must have been fate. He'd claimed to have broken up with a long-term girlfriend and to be at loose ends. Chandler figured the creep had been trolling for a sweet young thing he could con. He'd hit the jackpot in Bethany. The brutality and hopelessness of her home life coupled with her youth had made her ripe pickings.

Carter, or Widener, had courted her assiduously but quietly over the next several months, aided by the travel supposedly required for his job. On the day of her high school graduation, they had eloped. The marriage, of course, had not been legal because the license had never been filed.

Chandler couldn't help being glad about that. If he could have, he'd have spared her the pain and trauma that Carter had perpetrated, but they might not have married otherwise. No matter how it turned out in the end, he was glad to be a part of her life now.

She was a good sport, fine company, a quick wit and a giggle box, seemingly ready to laugh at everything, even after all she'd been through. She was keen to learn all that he could tell her about rodeo. He hadn't talked so much in…well, he didn't think he'd ever talked so much. He hadn't realized just how much he knew about rodeo, either. She hadn't realized how complicated the business end of it all was.

"You need an accounting degree to figure it all out!"

"Or a lot of experience."

"Or a manager!"

"There are some. Right now, Cindy's kind of doing that for the team, and I'm piggybacking on her efforts for my individual events."

"Do a lot of wives do that?" Bethany asked.

"I imagine so."

He waited for her to say that someday maybe she could do it, but she just bit her lip and finally lapsed into silence. It didn't last. After a while she sent him a considering look and remarked, "I noticed that you have several saddles, more saddles than horses. Why so many?"

He chuckled and answered, "Different saddles for different purposes. Won some of them."

That sent them off into a discussion of prizes, which wound up with him promising to dig out some of his buckles, spurs and other whatnots. Most of it was pretty minor, but some of it was excellent stuff. Most of it was packed into the boxes in the attic.

"You need a display case," she decided, "a big one."

Shaking his head, he said, "I need to win some real money." Rolling his eyes upward, he added softly, "Please, God." If he could start winning regularly, then he might have something to offer her, something more than a last name for her son, some reason for her to consider making this marriage real.

## Chapter Twelve

He won nearly seventeen thousand dollars, coming in first in all three of his events. Seven thousand was his share of the team roping winnings, and for the first time in his career, Chandler picked up a sponsor. That meant that a portion of his entry fees would be covered for the next four months, until the national finals in mid-December.

Bethany actually hugged the half-dozen dark blue, long-sleeved shirts with the sponsor's logo on the sleeves before carefully packing them into his kit. Just seeing that was worth more to Chandler than the financial reward. He liked the feeling that she might be proud of him, liked it very much. It gave him hope.

They were both giddy with triumph, and let Drew and Cindy talk them into a celebratory dinner. The two couples had prayed together every evening before he and Drew went about their business. They had also attended worship services at the arena that Sunday morning before the last performance and were well on their way to becoming fast friends. After the leisurely meal, however, it became obvious to Chandler that Bethany was too tired to make the drive back to Buffalo Creek, so they waved goodbye to the Shaws and stayed one more night in Lovington.

They'd given up their room that morning, so they had to switch motels. That was no problem, even in a town of only 9,500 permanent residents. Until they ran into an unexpected fellow guest.

Chandler was lifting the bags out of the backseat of the cab while Bethany waited at the front of the truck when a car playing loud music pulled up and a door opened. Chandler groaned inwardly when Patrick Kreger practically fell out onto the pavement. Laughing uproariously, he lurched into a semi-upright position and sent his pals off with shouted instructions.

"You better be back here to get me by ten!"

Loose-jointed and lanky with a long, lean face and smiling gray eyes, Kreger somehow looked less substantial than he was, both physically and mentally. Whirling around, he started for the building, only to halt when he clapped eyes on Chandler.

"My man!" he crowed, throwing wide his arms. "Get your dancing boots on, boy. We're celebrating!"

"No, thanks," Chandler said, turning away with the bags. Obviously, the celebration had already been going on for some time.

"You got to!" Pat insisted, stumbling forward to throw a chummy arm about Chandler's shoulder. His dark hair fell haphazardly across his forehead, and Chandler wondered where the man had left his hat this time. "You did it, old son," he slurred. "You won big, and so did I!"

"Funny," Chandler said, stepping away to escape

the stench of alcohol, "I didn't realize you were even entered."

"Huh. There're other ways to make money on the rodeo," Kreger said, wagging a finger. "Bet on the big man, I told 'em. Not only has he got the goods, he's one of those blessed Chatams. And, brother, did you ever come through."

It made Chandler ill to think that his old partner had bet on him. It seemed that Kreger was quickly spiraling downward. Chandler was surprised to feel some responsibility. Not only was he no longer around to pull his old partner out of trouble, but he also had obviously made no impression on Kreger with his Christian witness. He'd thought he was showing Kreger how to live by following him around and rescuing him from one mess or another. Now he knew that he'd only abetted Kreger's downfall. He suddenly wondered how many opportunities he had squandered. Why hadn't he just *told* his friend about Christ? Oh, he'd laid out his beliefs more than once, and Kreger had even paid lip service to the idea of Christianity, but that had been long ago. Chandler was ashamed now that he'd settled for that.

"Pat," he said kindly, "you need to sober up and think about what you're doing."

"Good old Chandler," Kreger drawled, "still trying to be my conscience. It's a wonder I never knocked your block off."

Bethany stepped around the end of the truck then, saying nervously, "Chandler?"

"It's okay. Nothing to worry about," he assured her calmly.

Beside him, Kreger's smoke-gray eyes were bugging

out of his chiseled face. "Who's that with you? She's a looker even if she is knocked up."

Chandler dropped the bags and slammed Kreger against the truck before he realized what he was doing. He didn't know who was more surprised, him or Pat. Obviously, Chandler thought, he was having a little more trouble forgiving than he'd realized. Still, a point had to be made.

"That's my wife you're talking about," he said sharply, "so you watch your mouth."

Kreger's jaw dropped. "W-wife!"

"That's right. And don't you forget it."

Chandler stepped back, rolled his shoulders to ease the tension and picked up the bags again. Kreger was still plastered to the side of the truck when Chandler reached Bethany's side and glanced back.

She slid her arm through his, saying, "Let's go in. It's kind of chilly out here."

"Downright frosty," he agreed, though it was probably sixty degrees. The evening chill had less to do with the weather in the high desert than the company. He sent Kreger a hard look before picking up the bags and walking inside with Bethany, carrying their luggage and his regrets with him.

She wanted to talk about it as soon as they got into the room, but he didn't see what good that would do. Kreger was his past. She was his present. Matthew was his future. Besides, she was clearly exhausted, and they had to get up early in order to make it back to Buffalo Creek in time for Bethany's appointment with her obstetrician, which was scheduled for three o'clock in the afternoon.

"Let's just get some sleep," he told her.

Nodding, she went about her business in near silence and was out, so far as he could tell, almost as soon as her head hit the pillow. Chandler, however, spent a restless night, his delight at winning tempered by his run-in with Kreger.

He hated to see what his old friend had come to and hated the anger that still burned in his own heart, but change was a choice, one they each had to make for themselves. At least, Chandler thought, he had help. He had the awesome power and gentle—sometimes not-so-gentle—guidance of his Lord God.

Who, he wondered sadly, did Kreger have now?

Finally giving up the fight, Chandler rose before 5:00 a.m. and had them on the road within twenty minutes. Bethany, bless her, did her best not to hold up the process, but Chandler made sure to stop often. It was a near thing, though. They barely had time to drop off the horses at Dovey's before barreling across town to the doctor's office.

Chandler sat in the waiting room, one of only a pair of males in a building full of pregnant women, plugging numbers into his financial plan via his laptop. Seventeen thousand gave him a nice cushion, but it wouldn't pay for the upkeep of the horses, entry fees, even reduced, and travel expenses for very long, let alone rent and self-employment taxes. The cost of gasoline was eating him alive, what with his constant trips back and forth to Stephenville to practice with Drew. If he was careful, though, these winnings would see him through to the end of the year. If he was blessed with more winnings... That he could only leave in God's hands. At least he had a little breathing room now.

When Bethany came out after seeing the doctor, she

seemed a bit subdued, and that immediately concerned Chandler. So, as he was walking her up into the truck, he asked if everything was okay.

"Oh, yes. It's just that I have to register at the hospital soon."

He knew what that meant, and he couldn't imagine why he hadn't thought of it before. So much for his financial plan. "In other words, you have to start paying on the hospital bill."

"I've saved for it," she told him, smiling. He wasn't fooled a bit. She'd been paying the doctor on her own. She couldn't possibly have the funds for the hospital bill.

*Well, Lord,* he thought, *I guess when You give me money that means You're preparing me for what's coming. So be it. We'll use Your plan.*

He drove her straight to the hospital, wrote a two-thousand-dollar check as a down payment and signed a paper agreeing to pay the same for a period of months to cover the estimated costs. Bethany cried about it on their walk across the parking lot.

"This is so unfair. I never meant for this to happen to you. Why didn't I realize this would happen to you?"

"Here now," he told her, reaching around her to open the passenger door of the truck. "No reason for tears. This is what a husband and daddy does."

She turned and threw her arms around his waist, laying her cheek in the hollow of his shoulder. "Oh, Chandler! You're so good to me. That's why I—"

His heart stopped. Everything in him hoped, believed, that she was about to declare her love. Hovering on the very verge of elation, he stood poised to exult. Suddenly he understood what really mattered. Losing the ranch and all that money, having to live with his elderly aunties, burning up the highway between Buffalo Creek and Stephenville, winning, what anyone else thought—none of that mattered. Getting himself right with God, *that* mattered. This woman in his arms, *she* mattered. His family, especially Bethany and Matthew, *they* mattered. Nothing else.

*I finally understand, Lord,* he thought, holding his breath, waiting for the words that would make his world come right at last.

"I—I'm so grateful," she finally whispered.

The disappointment was crushing. It felt as if a six-hundred-pound steer had rolled over him. And then kicked him in the head, for good measure.

After a moment, Chandler realized that he was patting her awkwardly. Clearing his throat, he croaked, "No need for that."

He dried her tears with the tail of his shirt before driving her home to Chatam House and the separate bedrooms that summed up their marriage—and his foolishness—very neatly.

"Don't mean to be a wet blanket," Chandler said to his aunts at the dinner table that night. "But it's been a really busy few days."

Magnolia traded glances with her sisters before putting on a smile for their nephew. "Of course, dear."

"Congratulations, again, and sleep well," Hypatia said from her chair at the head of the dark, ornately carved dining table.

"Good night!" Odelia called gaily as Chandler disappeared into the hallway. Bethany had gone up perhaps half an hour earlier. She hadn't even waited for dessert to be served, though Hilda had baked her favorite butterscotch-glazed chocolate cake that day.

"The weekend seems to have taken a toll on our newlyweds," Hypatia murmured after a moment.

"Bethany did look a bit peaked," Odelia worried aloud. She seemed uncharacteristically subdued herself today, dressed in filmy pale gray with black bows, about a dozen of them, from the enormous one atop her head to those that dangled from her earlobes and ran down the front of her dress.

"Chandler will see to Bethany," Magnolia stated with absolute certainty. She did not doubt that her nephew and his wife cared for each other. Unfortunately, she wasn't sure that they realized that fact themselves.

"Humph." Garrett pushed back his chair just to the left of Magnolia and got to his feet, tossing his napkin down beside his plate. While Bethany and Chandler had been away, he'd taken his meals with the rest of the staff, but tonight his sister had wanted him at the table in the formal dining room when she'd announced Chandler's big win. Garrett had been as congratulatory as everyone else, but he obviously had an issue. "Ask me, she shouldn't have been dragged off to that rodeo."

"But she wanted to go, dear," Magnolia pointed out.

"No doubt she did," Garrett conceded. "That doesn't mean she should have."

Magnolia disagreed, but she didn't argue the point. Garrett's brotherly concern was entirely reasonable, if a bit shortsighted. He seemed to think that the marriage was set in stone. The sisters were not so sure.

Garrett left the room. The sisters sat in their places, calmly eating last bites and drinking last sips while his footsteps faded down the hallway. Finished with her meal, Hypatia placed her heavy cutlery just so atop her dessert plate, while Odelia fussily folded her napkin. Magnolia simply waited until she couldn't wait anymore.

"So, what do you think?"

Odelia looked up, shaking her head mournfully. The black bows swung from her earlobes like clock pendulums.

"Patience," Hypatia counseled. "They are acting more and more like a committed couple."

"They have been spending a good deal of time together," Odelia noted hopefully.

"And Chandler did say that he wants Bethany to give up her job now," Hypatia noted.

"Something she obviously has no intention of doing," Magnolia pointed out.

She suspected that they had not been told everything that had taken place that weekend, which was as it should be. Much of marriage was private, after all. More worrisome than that was the problem of Garrett and what he might feel compelled to do if this marriage did not "take." Oh, she didn't expect violence, per se, but Garrett's record implied that it wouldn't be pretty if Chandler and Bethany split and Bethany was less than happy about it.

Sighing, Hypatia said, "I just wish Chandler didn't have so much on his plate."

"Poor thing," Odelia opined. "His best friend cheats him, so he loses his home, his father thinks he got Bethany in a family way before he married her, and the marriage isn't even really a marriage."

"Yet," Magnolia put in. She had determined to remain doggedly optimistic on the subject. "It may not be a real marriage *yet*."

"But at least he won!" Odelia finished happily.

"Obviously," Hypatia said, with a decisive nod, "God is at work."

"We can only wait," Magnolia counseled, "to see what He will do." Meanwhile, she would continue to pray. Ah, well, prayer was always a good thing.

*One step forward, two steps back,* Bethany thought, sighing as she neatened the papers on her desk. It had been a busy day. Tuesdays always were, but that didn't keep her from dwelling on the lamentable state of her marriage.

Last week had been wonderful. Chandler had seemed relaxed, attentive, smiling, and he'd won! She was so happy for him and so proud to be his wife. The hospital bill still mortified her, but he had been so generous and good about it.

*"That is what a husband and daddy does."*

She closed her eyes, remembering the thrill of delight that had swept through her at those words. And then she'd gone and ruined it all by almost blurting that she loved him.

He had to have known. Why else would he have pulled back like this? She'd felt it at once, and though she'd tried to recover by saying that she was grateful instead, he had instantly put emotional distance between them. Oh, he'd been polite, solicitous, even, but it was as if they lived on opposite sides of a wall now. She'd tried to breach the barrier by bragging on him at dinner that night, but he had seemed uncomfortable with the praise.

Disheartened and exhausted, she'd excused herself early and gone up to their suite. He had come up a little later and gone straight to his room with only the barest, "Good night," and he'd hardly spoken a word to her since.

What could she conclude except that he didn't reciprocate her feelings?

A cramp suddenly tightened Bethany's abdominal muscles, making her gasp. Hub crossed the foyer, pointing a young mother with a toddler on her hip toward the provision room, where she would be allowed to pick up disposable diapers and clothing for the child, having finished her parenting class. As soon as the girl, for she couldn't have been more than seventeen, had passed out of earshot, he turned back to Bethany's desk.

"What's wrong?"

She shook her head, but the cramp was taking its time. She gripped the edge of her desk with both hands and tried to breathe until her abdominal muscles finally relaxed. "I-It's nothing."

Hub frowned. "It doesn't look like nothing."

"It's just the Braxton-Hicks," she assured him, taking a clean breath and offering him a wobbly smile.

Clearly not convinced, he asked, "Should I call someone? Your doctor? Your brother? Chandler?"

"I'm fine," she told him. "And Chandler's in Stephenville today."

Hub made a face. "A married man has no business being on the road like this all the time. Who is this Drew Shaw that he keeps running off to see, anyway? Another Pat Kreger, probably."

Bethany snorted at that. "Hardly. Drew and Cindy Shaw are sweet, Christian people. The four of us prayed together before every go-round last weekend. And Cindy's expecting a baby in early November, so we have a lot in common. I think they're wonderful."

Hub's expression had gradually eased as she'd spoken, but all he said was, "Hmm." Then, "What's a go-round?"

Smiling inwardly, Bethany told him. She told him a lot more after that, including details of the Cowboy Church service and how magnificently Chandler had performed that weekend. Hub tried to appear only mildly interested, but he didn't fool her. He was soaking it all up like a sponge. Amazed that father and son had never sat down together and discussed these things, she prayed that before this marriage ended, she would see them do it. That, at least, would be something good that Chandler could take from their time together as husband and wife.

Sitting on the tailgate of the truck on Thursday evening, Chandler watched the sun sink slowly in the west, painting the dusky-blue sky in shades of yellow-gold, orange and red. He was tired to the bone, worn to an absolute nub, and he had a rodeo to get to.

He didn't want to go. For the first time in memory, he just did not want to think about getting on the road. Yet, he couldn't stay. If he didn't get away from the very woman who drew him like a lodestone, he was going to shatter into tiny pieces. It hurt to be in a room with her, to breathe the same air that she breathed, and no matter how much he prayed, it didn't change.

The whole thing had him confused. It was as if God had made her just for him. What woman could be better suited to or more understanding of his lifestyle? Who else would be so sweet and patient with all his traveling? He supposed it was too much to ask that she love him, too, especially after all she'd been through, but that didn't keep it from hurting.

The door opened and closed behind him. Bethany came out onto the stoop beneath the porte cochere, her arms folded as if against a chill.

"Dinner in half an hour," she said hesitantly. "Stuffed pork chops."

Chandler slid off the tailgate and shoved it closed. "Sounds good, but I'll have to pass. Tell the aunties and Hilda that I said thanks and that I apologize for not staying."

"Can't you eat first?"

"I need to get on my way."

"You need dinner, too."

"I'll grab something later."

"And eat behind the wheel while driving," she said, frowning with disapproval.

"Nothing I haven't done many a time," he replied, checking again to make sure that everything in the bed was lashed down.

"But why do it when you don't have to?" she pressed.

He heard himself snap, "Stop nagging me, Bethany!" Instantly contrite, he squeezed his eyes shut.

"I just want you to be safe," she said in a small voice.

Knowing that he'd been unfair, he tried to make amends. "I'm sorry. I didn't mean that. You never nag."

"I would if I thought it would do any good," she admitted, shocking a bark of laughter out of him.

"I'll be fine," he assured her. "I've been doing this on my own for a long time."

"You're not on your own anymore, though, Chandler," she pointed out softly.

"Aren't I?" he asked, suddenly angry again. "Barely married. That's what we are, Bethany." He held up his thumb and forefinger, squinting through the tiny space between them. "Just barely married. We didn't even speak our vows in church because we knew we didn't mean them. How's that not on my own anymore?"

She shifted uncertainly, looking so sadly adorable in that same blue-and-white-flowered sundress in which he'd first seen her that he could have cried.

"What are you saying, Chandler?"

What was he saying? Nothing that he wanted to say. Nothing that he should say. He shook his head. "I'm not saying anything, Bethany. I'm just in a foul mood today, that's all."

"Because of the money," she said morosely.

"Money?"

"For the hospital."

He hadn't thought of that at all. In fact, he hadn't been able to think of much of anything lately except her.

"No," he said, "it's not the money. Well, it is. I mean, I have to make a living, but the hospital bill's just part of that."

"A big part," she said, twisting her hands together. "I'm so sorry. After the baby comes, I'll find a full-time job and pay it back to you, I promise."

"Pay it back!" he erupted, all but shouting at her. "You're going to pay me back for providing for my own son? He is my son, isn't he, Bethany? That's what we agreed."

She stood there staring at him with those big blue eyes without saying a word, and he felt like the biggest heel on earth. He had to get out of there before he did something even worse, like spill his guts and lay his heart at her feet.

"I'm sorry," he said, starting around the truck. "I can't talk to you about this now. I have to go."

She ran to meet him, skirting around the front end of the truck. "Chandler!"

He got the door open before she reached him, and they drew up with that hunk of metal and glass between them, that and so much more. It wasn't enough. He didn't think anything could be. There could be light-years and aeons between them, and he'd still want her.

"I'll pray for you," she promised breathlessly. "Please be safe, and come home soon."

He reached for her before he could stop himself, his hands cupping her head through the dark silk of her hair and pulling her toward him. She bumped up against the door, belly first, her blue, blue eyes plumbing his. If only he knew what those eyes were telling to him.

It took every ounce of willpower he possessed not to bend his head and kiss her until the rest of the world just disappeared. Somehow, he managed to let go. Ducking into the truck cab, he slammed the door shut and reached for the keys.

She stood with her hands fisted beneath her chin as he backed the truck out from beneath the porte cochere and around the corner of the house, and she was the last thing that he saw in his rearview mirror before he turned the truck toward Dovey's and the longest, loneliest, saddest drive of his life.

## Chapter Thirteen

Tears and prayer occupied Bethany's entire weekend. Even learning of Jay's lies had not frightened her like this. She'd been angry, yes, and hurt, but not afraid, not until he'd threatened to file for custody of the baby if she revealed his duplicity. She couldn't believe it had taken her so long to figure out his game.

Ironically, like Chandler, Jay had traveled for a living, supposedly as a paper goods salesman. She'd never known that, as Jason Widener, he possessed a controlling interest in the Houston paper goods distributor for which he supposedly worked. That was where he'd gotten the idea for his second persona, Jay Carter. Likewise, she was unaware that he owned a thriving real estate development business in Tulsa and had a second—or rather, a first—wife and family there.

The scam had been so simple, really. He carried two cell phones. One was supposedly for business use, the other for personal. She had called, used and answered the personal one many times over the years. She had never touched the other the phone, which he had kept on his person at all times, even carrying it into the bathroom with him when he showered.

Then she'd discovered that she was pregnant. He'd dragged his feet about having children, and she hadn't planned it, expecting that eventually his feelings would change, but suddenly they were going to have a baby. She was shocked by his anger. They argued about it incessantly every moment that he was there, which was less and less often. One morning he'd slammed out of the house in a rage over her determination to go through with the pregnancy, leaving his business phone behind. Almost at once, the thing had begun ringing insistently. Finally, concerned that it might be important or that it was him calling, Bethany had answered.

A woman on the other end of the line went berserk. Every word was permanently implanted in Bethany's brain.

*"Who are you? Where's my husband? I knew he was having an affair! I knew it! He's a married man, you hussy! Have you no shame? Do you even think about our children?"*

Stunned, she'd hung up without a word. She was throwing up when Jay returned, shocked into physical illness. It had taken her almost twenty-four hours to digest the full reality of her situation—and ten minutes to leave. Jay had first tried to convince her to "let things be," but as she'd packed her bags, he'd snarled that he would not let her ruin him and warned that no man would ever want her now.

"If you just hadn't insisted on having that kid!" he'd shouted.

Hours later she'd stumbled into Chandler's path. He had seemed God-given. She still believed it. He was the best thing that had ever happened to her, the best thing that could have happened for her son. And she was losing him. How could that be?

With that on her mind, when the phone rang in the suite late Sunday evening, Bethany literally recoiled. She never answered the phone at Chatam House, leaving that to the staff and the aunties. Besides, she'd never received a phone call there and didn't expect to, so she was surprised when Magnolia tapped on her door a few minutes later to ask her to pick up.

Hurrying to the desk, she reached for the wireless receiver, then paused in concern before carrying it to the sofa. An unexpected phone call had destroyed her world once before. Was history about to repeat itself?

Warily, she pushed the green button and held the receiver to her head. "Hello?"

A gusty sigh greeted her. "Sorry if I got you out of bed."

It was Chandler, and the sound of his voice both warmed and chilled her.

"No, no. I—I haven't gotten there yet."

"That's good," he said. Then, "No, actually, that's bad. You need your sleep."

"I'll sleep when you're home again," she said thoughtlessly.

A long silence followed, then softly Chandler said, "Honey, that's why I'm calling. I won't be in tonight. I broke an axle on the trailer, and it'll be tomorrow before I can find someone to repair it."

"Are you all right?" she asked shakily.

"I'm fine," he insisted. "Horses, too. But we aren't going anywhere until I get these wheels turning, and this is the back of beyond up here in Colorado. Drew's with me, though. Cindy didn't come this trip, either."

"Is there anything I can do?"

"Just keep praying. You must have some pull, girl. We did fine up here. Purse is not as large as last time, but what there was, we two walked away with. One of the fellas joked that we were in an all-fired hurry this weekend, and Drew said it was 'cause we couldn't wait to get home to our women." He laughed lightly, while Bethany's heart clutched. "He's right about that. Fact is, I miss you." Belatedly he added, "I-It's not half so fun without you and Cindy."

"Oh, Chandler, I miss you, too," she managed, her throat suddenly clogged.

"Bethany, I'm sorry about the way I left," he said, his entire tone changing. "I've got a bit of a temper, as you know. You've seen me and my dad go at it a couple times now. I didn't mean to take my frustration out on you. You've done nothing wrong, and you're more dear to me than you probably realize. It's just this lousy temper of mine."

She laughed as tears rolled down her cheeks. "If you call that a lousy temper, Chandler Chatam, then you know nothing of real anger. Now, my stepfather had a bad temper. A little moodiness now and again is a birthday party compared to that. Besides, you have a right to your frustration. I've complicated your life terribly."

"It's gotten real interesting, I admit," he told her, but there was a smile in his voice. "I was doing a good job of complicating things on my own before you came along, though. And I like your complications a whole lot better than mine."

She laughed again, then bit her lip as a painful

cramp hit her. They'd been coming every few hours, each seemingly more vicious than the last, and her back ached constantly these days. The former was no doubt a measure of her emotional stress, the latter a result of the extra weight she was carrying. She promised herself that she was going to stop worrying now and trust God to take care of things. That would surely take care of the cramps if not the backache.

"I'll call you tomorrow when I know what's what," Chandler promised. "You get some sleep now."

"I will," she said, trying not to let on as the cramp rolled through her. "C-congratulations on your wins. Wish I could have been there."

"Me, too," he whispered. "Night."

"Good night."

Breaking the connection, she laid her head back. As her muscles gradually relaxed, she dried her eyes and smiled. She had feared the unexpected call for no reason.

The most important bits played through her mind.

*You're more dear to me than you probably realize. I miss you.*

It was a start, she told herself. Good things could come at the end of a telephone line, too. Even with a broken axle to be mended and the necessary delay in his return, Chandler's call had given her more peace and hope than any other ever had.

"Keep praying," he'd said, and that was just what she was going to do. She'd pray her husband safely home and her way straight into his heart.

Chandler backed the trailer into the barn and killed the engine of the truck. Behind him, the horses bumped against the metal walls, eager to get out and chow down. He didn't blame them. What a rough few days it had been! He'd slept in his truck two nights in a row to safeguard his horses, sending Drew off home as soon as he'd found someone to replace the axle. That had taken an entire day, though, so here he was on a Tuesday afternoon just now getting back to Buffalo Creek.

Thankfully, he had won a good bit, enough so that the four hundred bucks he'd spent getting back on the road hadn't troubled him. In fact, he'd promised God and himself that he wasn't going to worry about the money anymore. They'd make do with whatever God provided.

He wasn't even going to worry anymore about moving out of Chatam House. When the timing was right, it would happen. Meanwhile, he could hardly complain about the accommodations. It was mostly a matter of pride with him, anyway. He was learning to swallow that when he had to. He'd swallowed a bit of it when he'd called Bethany, and he was glad he had.

As soon as he could work his courage up to it, he was going to tell her how he really felt and hope that it wasn't just her sweetness and misplaced guilt that had made her act as she had. He'd been thinking about the way she'd said that she missed him and other things— incessantly. It could be wishful thinking on his part, but it seemed to him that there was at least hope that her feelings had changed. And even if they had not, they still could. Maybe just letting her know that he wanted her to love him, that he wanted this marriage to work, would be enough to start the ball rolling. Whatever the outcome, though, he had to try.

The worst that could happen, after all, was what he

already had, a temporary marriage in name only. If that was what God willed, Chandler decided, then God would undoubtedly make a way for him to survive it.

He off-loaded the horses, walked them into their stalls and began hauling out the feed. He didn't bother with the wheelbarrow as the truck was in the way. His phone rang as he carried the heavy bag toward the stalls, balancing it on one shoulder. He fished the phone out of his shirt pocket with one hand and glanced at the caller ID. Frowning, he tried to remember the last time his father had called him. That had surely been the day Kaylie and Stephen had gotten engaged, though Hub's intent at the time had been to derail such a possibility by convincing her brothers to oppose the romance. Curious, Chandler answered the call.

"What's up, Dad?"

"Are you in town?"

"I'm just dropping off the horses."

"Thank God!"

Chandler's heart stopped. "Why? What's wrong?"

"Best come to the hospital, son. Bethany's in labor."

Chandler didn't wait to hear more. He dropped the bag of feed and sprinted for the rig, one hand clamped to the crown of his hat. He was in the cab before he remembered that he hadn't put up the ramp and locked down the trailer door. Barking questions at his dad, he hurriedly went about securing the trailer and jumped back into the truck.

According to Hub, Bethany had complained of cramps and nausea earlier in the day. He'd tried to convince her to go home, but she'd insisted on lying down on the sofa in the counseling room. When Hub had checked on her some time later, he'd found her holding her belly and moaning. He'd gotten her up and walked her to his car, intending to drive her to her doctor's office. She'd argued that she was merely suffering from Braxton-Hicks contractions—right up to the moment that she'd doubled over and screamed. Hub had rushed her to the emergency room. He had no idea what was happening with her now, as they wouldn't let him stay with her.

Lights flashing, Chandler raced through town, trailer and all, laying on his horn at intersections and praying fervently aloud.

"Oh, Lord, let it be another false alarm. It's too early, and she's all alone in there. Please just take care of them. Protect them both. Please don't let me lose either of them!"

He left the rig at the curb in a no-parking zone. Let them ticket him. Let them tow the whole kit and kaboodle! He didn't care. If his wife and son were not well, then nothing else mattered. Dashing inside to the elevators, he caught a car just as the door was closing on an elderly fellow carrying a pot plant. The old gentleman nodded, but Chandler was too overwrought to return the greeting. He poked the elevator button repeatedly, in the faint hope that it would somehow speed up the seemingly interminable ride.

At last, the elevator came to a halt and the door slid open. Chandler bolted for the nurses' station. A heavy-set, fortyish woman with a long, thin brown ponytail looked up and smiled at him.

"Where's my wife?" Chandler demanded.

The woman had obviously seen too many distraught husbands to pay much attention to them. "Name?"

"Bethany Chatam."

The nurse didn't even check her records before glancing up and saying, "They're on their way down with her now."

"Down?"

"Delivery is on the next floor."

"She's had the baby, then?"

"She has."

Stunned, Chandler babbled, "I-Is the baby okay?"

To his dismay, the nurse looked away, saying, "The doctor's with him now."

Chandler gulped and swept off his hat, remembering only then that it was still on his head. "I have to see Bethany."

The nurse gave him the room number and told him that he could wait there. He went straight to the room. The space contained a sitting area complete with sofa and recliner, as well as a private bath and flat-screen TV. It had everything except a bed. Tossing his hat onto the sofa, he paced the floor for several seconds before the door opened and his father walked in.

"Dad! Where is she?"

"She'll be along any minute."

"How is she?"

Hub hitched his pants up around his paunch, his frame otherwise so thin that he often joked that he looked like an olive on a toothpick. His expression lacked any hint of amusement, however. "Physically, she's fine. Doctor said she had a quick, easy time of it, though she's probably been in what he called slow labor for a couple days. It was obvious this morning that she didn't feel good. Still, she seemed to think it would pass until almost the very end."

"You said she's okay *physically*."

"Yes. Emotionally…" Hub shook his head.

"It's the baby, isn't it? What are they saying about him?"

Hub sighed. "I gather there are some problems. The doctor said something about babies losing weight during protracted labors like this and stress delaying development."

Feeling as if his legs might buckle, Chandler stumbled backward. "I—I don't know what I'll do if anything happens to either of them."

Hub reached out and clapped a supporting hand on Chandler's shoulder, saying, "Put your faith in God, son. He'll see you through."

Chandler nodded. "I know. I know. It's just…I should've been here! I've mucked up everything."

Placing both hands on Chandler's shoulders, Hub captured his gaze and held it for a long moment before softly saying, "No. No, you haven't. In fact, I'd say you've done very well. The fact is, I'm proud of you, Chandler."

Chandler shook his head. He'd waited a long time to hear that, but now that it had been said, it hurt more than it helped, for he knew the truth. "No, no. I—I've been holding out on God, Dad. It's not just that I refused to see what Kreger was doing. I enabled him. And I've been so angry, blaming him for everything, when the truth is that I'm as responsible for how it all turned out as he was. I didn't take care of my business, and I wasn't the man, the Christian, I should have been. You were right about that, too." He looked his father in the eye then, confessing all, "And the very worst part is that I never found a way to bring Pat around. I didn't even *try*. I never once told him, point-blank, what Christ did for him, for me."

Hub gulped, his chin trembling. "I may have been right about Patrick Kreger," he said, "but I was wrong about you, and neither case pleases me." Hub clamped his hands down hard on Chandler's shoulders, saying, "You're a better man than I realized. Bethany told me, you see. She didn't mean to. She was frightened and in pain, and she cried out that she wished you really were her baby's father."

"But I am!" Chandler insisted, alarmed. She wouldn't go back on that now, would she? He thought wildly that there had to be some way to keep that from happening.

"Of course you're his father," Hub agreed, nodding. "By choice. She told me everything. When the whole town, me included, I'm ashamed to say, just assumed you were the father, you could have denied it, but that would have exposed her to criticism, so you kept quiet. You could have walked away at any time and been fully justified in doing so, but you *chose* to give Bethany and Matthew your name and protection."

But he hadn't chosen to give them his heart. That had just happened.

The door swung open again, and Garrett rushed in. "How is she?"

"I called him after I called you," Hub explained. "Bethany asked me to, in case you were still on the road."

Chandler told him what little he knew. Garrett made a fist and smacked it into his other palm. "If I could get my hands on that Jay Carter…"

"You know?" Chandler said, surprised.

Garrett sent him a sideways look. "I figured it out.

What I'm not sure about is why you stepped into his shoes."

"I'll explain it for you, then," Chandler replied smartly, "right after I explain it to your sister."

The door opened once more. Chandler pushed past his father and brother-in-law as the head of a hospital bed appeared, only to step back again as the bed rolled into the room and a man in green scrubs maneuvered it into position. Bethany lay there, shivering and silently weeping.

The first words out of her mouth were, "I didn't get to see him! They wouldn't even let me see Matthew before they took him!"

"It'll be all right, sis," Garrett offered, but she ignored him, her gaze fixed on Chandler.

"I'm so glad you're here. I'm so frightened!"

Fear unlike anything Chandler had ever felt before swamped him, but he went to the bed smiling as brightly as he could manage and bent to smooth back her damp hair and kiss her clammy forehead. "Garrett's right, sweetheart. Everything's going to be okay."

"If I could just see him."

"We'll see our little Matthew soon, I promise."

Two nurses, the heavyset one and another who was quite young, swept into the room. Chandler took Bethany's hand, his thumb smoothing over the cool surface of her wedding band. He stayed at her side while the nurses did their thing, then before they left he asked, "Can you tell us about our son? When can we see him?"

"The doctor will be in," the heavyset one said tersely.

Bethany immediately began to sob.

Chandler looked at her crumpled face and made an instant decision. "Forget that." Bending, he scooped her up, bedcovers and all, and started for the door. "Where is he? We want to see our son right now."

The nurses went into a tizzy of scolding and urging, but he couldn't even hear them. "Right now," he repeated.

Garrett pulled open the door. Hub pointed the direction. With Bethany clinging to his neck, Chandler carried her out into the wide, gleaming hall, both nurses hot on his heels. The older one turned toward the nurses' desk. The other ran past them toward a solid metal door.

Behind him, Chandler heard his father whisper, "Gracious Lord God, please, I beg You…"

Chandler joined his prayers to his father's as he strode after the nurse. He couldn't bear the thought of losing little Matthew now, and neither could he bear the pain and fear of this woman who held his heart.

## Chapter Fourteen

The nurse turned to face them as if she would physically block their path. Chandler prepared to bully his way past her, if necessary, but then her brow beetled, and she swiped the ID card hanging about her neck through a card reader on the wall.

"Thank You," he whispered, knowing who had surely changed her mind.

The wide door swung open, the edge coming to rest next to a sign that detailed the nursery visiting hours. Chandler didn't even bother reading it. Instead, he strode through that door and followed the nurse, Bethany cradled against his chest.

The frantic nurse hurried past a pair of large windows with blinds drawn and went through a smaller door marked, "Medical Personnel Only." Chandler went after her, catching the heavy door before it swung closed.

Another woman in scrubs and a puffy cap rushed toward him. "Sir! Sir! You cannot come in here!"

"I can if my son's in here. Where is he?"

Chandler looked around, turning in a wide circle

in what was essentially a glass-walled hallway. The clear plastic cribs in the viewing room were all empty, though several showed signs of recent habitation. Those infants were probably with their mothers at that moment. In fact, so far as Chandler could see, there were only two infants currently in residence. One, a squalling girl, if the pink wristband was any indication, was being weighed. The other was ominously silent, a pale, tiny body in a closed, brightly lit incubator in a separate room. A young man with a dark complexion and a long lab coat came to the door and nodded them over. He introduced himself as the pediatrician and led them to the incubator.

Pulling a hard plastic chair forward, the doctor informed them, "He's small and jaundiced and his lungs are not fully developed."

Chandler stood for a moment with Bethany in his arms, staring at the tiny, wrinkled body covered with tubes and tape and a tiny diaper that seemed much too large. Chandler bit his lips, but still the tears trickled down his cheeks. Swallowing, he managed to say to Bethany, "He has your dark hair."

Bethany reached out a hand, touching the incubator. "Why are his eyes covered?"

"To protect them against the light." The doctor explained that phototherapy was used to help the bilirubin in the blood break down so the body could eliminate it. The feeding and hydration tubes would increase eliminations, as well as help the baby gain weight. At four pounds, he could use the help! A third tube was used to inject medication to help with the development of the lungs.

"Is he going to make it?" Bethany asked in a quivering voice.

"He'll make it," Chandler said, clutching her tighter.

"We'll know within twenty-four to forty-eight hours," the doctor answered honestly. "If he loses ground, we'll transfer him to an NICU in a larger hospital."

"He'll make it," Chandler decreed flatly.

"I've seen smaller, sicker babies pull through," the doctor went on, "but it depends on his organ development." Indicating the chair, he added, "If you'll wait thirty or forty minutes, you can hold him."

Chandler sat down in the chair with Bethany in his lap. She laid her head on his shoulder, and he kissed her temple. She closed her eyes, but Chandler knew that she wasn't resting; she was praying. He pressed his cheek to the crown of her head, closed his eyes and joined his heart to hers, as together they silently begged for the life and well-being of their son.

An hour later, Chandler followed as a floor nurse wheeled Bethany back to her room. He hadn't wanted to let her go, but the nurse had quietly insisted. Bethany had eased off Chandler's lap and into the wheelchair without a word, her gaze following little Matthew as the neonatal technician returned him to the incubator, reconnected his tubes, covered his eyes. He seemed lethargic and weak to Chandler, and the fear that had lodged itself in his chest would not ease.

Once they reached the room, Chandler lifted Bethany from the chair and tucked her safely into bed. "I had to see him," she whispered, clasping Chandler's hand.

She, too, seemed alarmingly weak, completely exhausted. "Of course. Rest now. Everything's going to be okay."

Bethany closed her eyes, and Chandler moved toward his father and Garrett, who sat side by side on the sofa. The nurse came in then, the young one who had opened the security door for them. Chandler caught her by the sleeve.

"Thank you," he said simply.

Nodding, she moved toward the bed and made Bethany swallow pills. Hub rose then. Garrett followed suit an instant later.

"We'll go so she can rest."

"Will you tell the aunties and everyone for us?"

"Spoke to them a while ago," Garrett said. "Everyone sends their love."

"Thanks."

"I'll be praying for you all, son."

"Never doubted it for a minute. Counting on it, in fact."

Hub patted Chandler's arm, then went to the bed and bent to kiss Bethany's brow. "Don't you worry now."

"I'll try not to," she murmured wearily.

Garrett took his turn, hugging her and kissing her cheek. "I'll check on you later. Call if you need anything."

Bethany nodded and closed her eyes.

"I'll take care of her," Chandler said.

Garrett smiled wanly. "I know you will." He shifted his weight and admitted, "I had my doubts, but not anymore." With that, he moved toward the door.

Hub followed, but then he paused and turned back. "I wasn't right about Kreger," he said. "To have been right, I'd have had to do everything in my power to win that boy to the Lord, but I was too busy blaming him for pulling you away from me."

"And I was too busy defending and using him," Chandler admitted. "This is a failure we share."

"Then it's one we'll have to rectify together," Hub said. "We'll pray, and when the time is right, we'll go together to speak to Kreger. He needs to know that God loves him."

Chandler nodded, his eyes swimming. "I'd like that."

Hub smiled and left them.

Chandler pulled the recliner around, took Bethany's limp hand in his and sat down at her side, where he wanted always to be.

Watching the nurse return Matthew to the incubator, Bethany wearily sat back in the chair. Most babies stayed in their mothers' rooms, but all through the night, she and Chandler had made the journey down the hallway to the nearly empty nursery to hold and talk to Matthew. They'd tried to doze between visits, but neither of them had gotten any real sleep, and it showed.

Chandler pushed away from the wall and reached for her hand, pulling her up to her feet. He looked like she felt, much the worse for wear. His hair was mussed and falling over his forehead, and he needed a shave, his beard glinting dark gold in the light. His clothing, a faded green, long-sleeved, button-down shirt and jeans, was rumpled and creased. She thought him the most handsome man she'd ever seen.

Sliding his arm about her shoulders, he urged her toward the door. Her head felt so heavy that she wouldn't have been surprised if it fell off and rolled across the floor, so she laid it on Chandler's shoulder, wrapping an arm around his waist. They walked out of the nursery and down the hall to her room, where someone named Kelli had signed her name with a smiley face in the place of the dot over the *i* on the whiteboard mounted on the wall. Apparently, the nursing shift had changed.

Bethany's breakfast tray sat upon the rolling bed table; the congealing food looked anything but appealing. Chandler announced that he would go down to the cafeteria for something more tasty. He took the tray with him.

Bethany made herself go into the bathroom to clean up. She brushed her teeth, then swiftly washed her hair by bending over the tub and using the handheld showerhead. Feeling better, she dressed in the frilly pink nightgown and flowered robe that Garrett had brought her the previous evening and sat on the edge of the bed to comb out her hair. She had just put away the comb and climbed into the bed when the mysterious Kelli came in with a laptop computer and a printer on a small rolling stand.

As she plugged in her equipment, the young nurse explained that, though the state required birth certificates be filed within five days, hospital policy dictated that the paperwork be done within twenty-four hours. She had already input the data required of the hospital. Once she got Bethany's information, she would print the form and witness Bethany's signature. After the doctor signed, the hospital would file with the state.

Bethany settled back and answered several questions, her own name, age, place of birth and address. Chandler returned then with hot coffee, cold milk, fresh fruit and quiche.

"Can't get that served on the floor," Kelli noted with

a wry smile before turning back to her business. "Father's full name?"

Bethany opened her mouth, but the words did not come out. All she could think was that the moment of no return had arrived. If Chandler's name went on that birth record, he would forever be committed to Matthew. It just didn't seem fair and at the very same time wasn't nearly enough to keep from breaking her heart. Helplessly, she looked to him, and found that he had frozen in the act of arranging their food on the bed table, an expression of wary disbelief on his face.

"Bethany," he urged softly.

The nurse spoke up. "I should have said, 'husband's full name.'"

"Hubner Chandler Chatam the third," Chandler said loudly.

"You'll have to spell that."

"H-u-b-n-e-r C-h-a-n-d-l-e-r C—"

"That's okay, I've got the Chatam part." She winked at Bethany, adding, "Everyone in Buffalo Creek can spell Chatam."

Gulping, Bethany asked, "What if the husband is n-not the f-father?"

"Bethany!" Chandler hissed.

She looked up, tears in her eyes. "It's just not fair for you to take on all this responsibility!"

"Honey, don't do this," Chandler urged softly. Glancing at the nurse, he reminded her, "HIPAA laws prevent you from revealing anything about your patients, right?"

"Absolutely." She cleared her throat and briskly informed them, "In Texas, the husband's name always goes on the birth certificate. If the mother is unmarried, she alone names the father. Anyone who disagrees has to file a paternity suit."

Bethany closed her eyes. So, it was already too late. She had unknowingly locked Chandler into fatherhood that day in the office of the Justice of the Peace in Oklahoma.

"What have I done?" she whispered. It would be different if he loved her, if the marriage was real, instead of the kind act of a truly caring and generous man.

"You've given me a son," Chandler answered softly.

"And me a grandson," said another familiar voice. Bethany opened her eyes to find a whole host of people filing into the room, Hub in the lead. He had his Bible in hand and a smile on his face.

"And us another nephew," Magnolia stated firmly, coming to stand between her sisters at the foot of the bed. She carried a vase full of flowers, naturally. Hypatia held a small, sturdy basket by the handle. Its contents, covered by a white cloth, gave off a mouth-watering aroma. Odelia, Bethany couldn't help noticing, was dressed in baby blue with little stick people dangling from her earlobes and a baby rattler corsage pinned to her chest. She held a blue-and-yellow gift bag, as if they hadn't already given her and Matthew enough! Kaylie carried another.

"Uh, I believe that's grandnephew," pointed out a dignified-looking man with twinkling eyes. Handsome and urbane, with streaks of gray at his temples, he had the Chatam chin, as did the older, rotund fellow in expensive pinstripes next to him.

"My brothers Morgan and Bayard," Chandler said, waving a hand between them. Bayard, a banker who lived in Dallas, had to be the heavy, older one. Morgan, as Chandler had told her, was a history professor at Buffalo Creek Bible College.

Morgan went on speaking to Magnolia, "Matthew Chandler would be your grand-nephew and *our* nephew."

A tall, grinning young man who was undoubtedly Kaylie's hockey-playing husband, Stephen, leaned forward and cheekily remarked, "I believe he's *my* nephew as well, if only by marriage."

"Well, *I'm* blood kin," Garrett said, pushing past him to the bedside.

"Good grief," Chandler said with obviously feigned disgust, "we've brought the whole family down on us."

"Hardly," Hypatia retorted with a chortle. "Just the immediate, as you well know."

The nurse wisely unplugged her equipment and beat a hasty retreat. Hub, too, slipped away, Bethany noticed.

"We apologize for interrupting your breakfast," Hypatia said.

"That's okay. We can eat later," Bethany told her.

"No, no." Morgan flipped back the cloth covering the contents of the basket in Hypatia's hands. "Go ahead and eat. We'll join you."

"Hilda's ginger muffins!" Stephen exclaimed, reaching over to snatch one.

Everyone began to help themselves. They all got comfortable, the aunties on the sofa, others leaning against the wall or sitting on the foot of the bed. Chandler sat down on the recliner next to the bed and wolfed down his own breakfast with his usual gusto, while Bethany worked on hers and listened to the chitchat. She recalled that Morgan and Bayard were the sons of Hub's first wife, who had been deceased many years now, whereas Kaylie and Chandler were the children of Hub's second wife, also deceased. That reminded Bethany that she'd seen Hub slip away.

Leaning toward Chandler, she asked, "Where's your father?"

He looked around. "Don't know."

Hypatia spoke up from the sofa. "I'm sure he'll return shortly."

Perhaps another quarter hour passed before Hub did so. He was not alone. A strange doctor followed carrying Matthew.

"Oh!" Bethany bolted straight up in the bed, holding out her arms. The doctor came over to place the baby in them.

"That's better," Hub said complacently, as everyone else "oohed" and "aahed" over Matthew.

Chandler shifted up to sit on the side of the bed next to Bethany, looking to the doctor. "I suppose you pulled rank on someone in order to manage this."

"Not at all. I just consulted with the neonatologist, at your father's request, and we made a decision based on the conditions and needs of both baby and mother."

"Thank you," Chandler said. He introduced the man to Bethany then, saying, "Honey, this is Brooks Leland, an old family friend."

"We spoke on the telephone," Bethany said, nodding to the newcomer.

Hub spoke up then. "All right, everyone, gather around. Gather around." The family all came to encircle the bed. "We're going to pray this new addition to our family home," Hub explained.

Holding her baby in her arms, Bethany looked around at them in amazement. These people weren't even really kin to her child, and she could see that they knew it, but here they all were on a Friday morning to pray over him just as if he truly did belong to them. Suddenly she knew that Matthew was exactly where he belonged. No matter who Matthew's biological father might be, His spiritual Father had brought them to his *true* father, to a true family. She would never question that again. Silently, she transferred Matthew into his father's arms.

Chandler jerked slightly in surprise, as he had not yet held his son. For a long moment, his gaze melded with hers. Then he tucked the tiny babe into the crook of one arm and looped his other about Bethany. Dressed in a tiny white gown, knit cap and blue blanket, Matthew stretched, mewled and turned his face into his father's chest. Beaming, Chandler glanced around the room.

Everyone shifted closer, laying hands on her or Chandler or little Matthew himself, and then they all bowed their heads as Hub began to pray aloud. He praised God for this new little family unit and thanked Him for the blessing of new beginnings. Finally, he beseeched God for Matthew's health, asking that the child thrive and grow and always be surrounded by the love of family and Christ Jesus. A chorus of Amens followed. Then Chandler dropped a delicate kiss on Matthew's cheek and smiled at Bethany.

"Well, that just leaves one other matter to attend," Hub announced, waving his Bible at Chandler and Bethany. "It's high time to bless this union properly. The legalities are one thing, but spiritualities are another." He lifted his sagging, cleft chin, adding, "And no child of mine is truly wed unless I officiate."

Bethany felt an instant of stomach-dropping panic,

but Chandler's arm tightened about her shoulders, prompting her to look at him. She was stunned by the openness in his eyes, by the softness of his expression.

"I want this," he said quietly. "It won't be forever until he says the words. And that's what I want with you, forever. I know I don't have a lot to offer you right now, but I love you, Bethany, you and Matthew, and I believe with all my heart that the same God who brought you to me will provide all our needs." He looked down at her with such tenderness, their child cradled against him, that she lifted a hand to stifle an exclamation.

He was, essentially, asking her to marry him, to really marry him. For always. It was exactly what she wanted, but how could he possibly love her? Jay's insidious voice whispered that no man would want her, but when Chandler looked at her with those warm brown eyes of his, she knew that Jay lied. Again. She didn't know whether to laugh or to cry, so she did both.

Wrapping her arms about Chandler's neck, she twisted against him and whispered into his ear, "I love you so much. I love you so much!"

He buried his face in the bend of her neck, and she felt him sigh, the air leaving him in a long exhalation of relief. Lifting his head, he pressed a fervent kiss to her lips.

"It's always the cart before the horse with this one!" Hub joked good-naturedly.

Everyone laughed at that, including Bethany.

"Well, get it done, then," Chandler retorted smartly.

"Right now?" Hub asked. "You don't want to shave or at least comb your hair first?"

"I don't want to wait another minute," Chandler said. He abruptly turned back to Bethany then. "Oh, but maybe you would prefer a ceremony with all the trimmings this time?"

She looked down at herself. Here she sat in a hospital bed, her hair still damp from a cursory scrubbing, as exhausted as she'd ever been in her life. She must look a fright. Moreover, she'd been through two wedding ceremonies already, both elopements. With Jay Carter, the whole thing had been a farce. The second time had been legal, at least, but she had never dared to think that the marriage was true, never expected it to be more than a temporary favor done her by a good man who had rescued her out of nothing more than necessity and Christian sensibility. Now that darling man had declared his love and offered her a genuine marriage, a forever marriage, witnessed by those dearest to them. Trimmings were nothing compared to that.

"You've got to be kidding," she said, squeezing Chandler's hand.

He planted a kiss in the middle of her forehead. Then he dropped a frown on Matthew, one brow arching, and muttered, "Better make it quick. I think I have a diaper to change."

Everyone laughed at that. But no one laughed minutes later when Chandler and Bethany repeated their vows, there in the midst of their extended family, and received the blessing that joined their hearts forever as husband and wife.

It had been a strange and unexpected journey from that little diner beside the road to home and family and the fulfillment of all her dreams, but looking back on it now, Bethany knew that God had directed her path from the very moment that she had placed herself in His hands. She wished she had been wise enough to understand what He was doing, but she found it difficult to have regrets now, sitting there in the bosom of her expanded family with her loving husband and beautiful son beside her. In fact, she would do it all again just to arrive here at this wonderful place. And she could hardly wait to see where God would take them next.

# Epilogue

Chandler crept into the bedroom, his boots in his hand. Bethany had left the light on in the bathroom and the door slightly ajar. He set the boots at the foot of the bed that had belonged to his grandparents and smiled down on his sleeping wife before tiptoeing to the cradle. Even after a month, Bethany preferred to keep Matthew close. Chandler preferred that, too. It had become more and more difficult to leave them both behind when he traveled to rodeos.

Drew felt the same way about Cindy, who was stuck at home awaiting the birth of their child, the slowpoke, as Chandler had taken to calling him, just to tease Drew, since Matt had made such an early entry. They were a pathetic pair, he and his partner, constantly thinking of those at home. Pathetic but successful, wildly so in the past few weeks, praise God!

No longer an infant scarecrow, Matthew had filled out well in the past few weeks. As Chandler stood there and marveled, Matt's plump little face scrunched up. His fists rose to bat about his head in the instant before he let out a full-throated wail. Chandler snatched him up, cradling him against his shoulder.

"Here, here," he whispered. "It's okay. Daddy's home."

Matthew crammed his fist into his mouth and continued to insist that he be fed. Chandler couldn't help chuckling. This was a boy in a hurry. Couldn't wait to be born, couldn't wait to get home from the hospital—a feat he'd managed only four days after Bethany—couldn't wait to grow, couldn't wait to eat, couldn't wait for clean britches. Just a sprinkle in his diaper was enough to set him off. Neither of his parents minded in the least.

Bethany groggily sat up and started to throw the covers off, but then she saw Chandler and smiled.

"Welcome home."

He bounced the fussing baby against his shoulder. "Glad to be here."

She held out her arms. "Let me have him before he wakes the whole household."

Chandler carried the little howler to the bed and watched in amazement as Bethany quieted him by holding him to her breast. She looked up, love shining in her bright blue eyes, and Chandler bent to kiss her, long and sweetly.

"I missed you, too," she said when he finally lifted his head. "How did it go?"

He fished a gold-plated buckle from his shirt pocket and tossed it on the bed, then pulled two more from his jeans and dropped those next to the first. Bethany gaped.

"Three?"

"Three events, three buckles," he said, grinning. "They'll fit better in a display case than three saddles."

She laughed and reached for his hand. "I'm so proud of you."

That meant more to him than anything else in the world. Chandler nudged her over with his hip and perched on the edge of the bed beside her.

"If we keep this up, Drew and I could make the national finals in December," he told her. "I might even qualify in steer wrestling. Tie-down's out of reach, though."

"This year," she said, and he smiled at her optimism. She glanced down at Matthew and commented, "We ought to be able to travel by December."

Chandler grinned. "Well, I'll see what I can do, then." They laughed together, then he sobered. "Speaking of December, I'd like us to be in our own place before the holidays."

She squeezed his hand. "Yes, I'd like that, too." It had been suggested that Chandler and Bethany move into Hub's house once he, Kaylie and Stephen moved out. "Your dad's house will be empty as soon as Kaylie finds something for them to lease." The house Kaylie was building with Stephen wouldn't be finished for at least another six months.

"I have another thought," Chandler said carefully. "What would you think about moving to Stephenville?"

Bethany lifted her eyebrows. "It would certainly make things a lot easier for you and Drew."

"We'd have more time to work, but more important I'd have more time to spend at home with you and Matthew," Chandler pointed out.

"A big plus."

He smiled, excitement welling up. "There's something else."

"Oh?"

"I had an offer on Ébano this weekend. Sixty-five thousand." She gasped. "I countered at eighty-five," he hurried on.

"And?"

"We split the difference at seventy-five thousand dollars."

"Chandler!"

"And I'm to train two other horses for the same fellow. If that works out, we might go into a partnership on the other end of things, so to speak. Then I'd be working with the horses most of the time instead of always running up and down the road chasing buckles."

"No kidding! That's wonderful! If…if that's what you want."

"That's exactly what I want," he told her emphatically. "It's the dream, sweetheart, the whole enchilada, everything I love, you, Matthew…" He stroked one hand over her cheek and the other across the baby's head, hurrying on, "having our own place, doing what I'm made to do and earning a good income at it, living the life. It's everything I've ever wanted."

"Oh, I'm so excited!" She bounced a little on the bed. Matthew grunted as if in agreement.

Shifting closer, Chandler quickly said, "I've had my eye on this little ranch east of Stephenville for some time now, and I've made a couple of phone calls. It's a pretty piece of land and in our price range. House isn't all that, but—"

She pressed a finger to his lips, stopping the flow of

his words. "If that's what God has in mind for us, I'm sure we can make it work. When can we go see it?"

He kissed that finger. "Soon."

She smiled and stroked his cheek. "Garrett and the aunties will miss us."

Garrett had proven to be an especially attentive uncle, and the aunties... Odelia was like a girl with a favorite new toy and Hypatia didn't even seem to mind the milk stains on her fine silks. Magnolia, however, was the big surprise. Her calmness and sturdy good sense had been a special blessing to these new parents.

Chandler nodded, so full of love and happiness that he thought he might pop like a balloon. "I'll miss them, too."

But this was best. No one could question that their family needed their own home or that God had made a way for them to have it.

"We'll visit often," Bethany said.

"Whenever we can," Chandler agreed, leaning forward to press his lips to hers.

He could barely believe how God had blessed him!

Back in July his life had been coming apart at the seams. Desperate, he'd fallen to his knees. Then God had lifted him up and set him on the right path, showering him with blessings that he could only have imagined a few short months ago. He'd said as much to Kreger just this past weekend when their paths had briefly crossed. To Chandler's surprise, his one-time partner had agreed to sit down and talk with Chandler and his father in the next couple of days.

That was a conversation Chandler intended to bathe in prayer. He was still hurt by his old friend's actions, but he was going to make one more effort to help Kre-

ger get his life right through Christ Jesus. After all, if
he didn't try, who would? Besides, Hub would be with
him. Together they would make an impassioned plea
and leave the rest to God. With his own life bathed in
blessings, Chandler figured it was the least he could
do. And the very best.

Matthew let out a contented sigh and blinked blear-
ily at his father. As his eyes drifted closed, his sweet
little mouth turned up at the corners.

"Look at that!" Bethany whispered. "He's smiling!"

"I know just how he feels," Chandler told her softly.
And, oh, he did.

Magnolia tiptoed away from the bedroom door, dab-
bing tears from her eyes with the sleeve of her bathrobe. She had awakened to the distant sound of the baby
wailing. Whenever they heard him cry, all the sisters
were eager to offer assistance, so much so that they'd
agreed to take turns. Magnolia was a tad miffed to find
that Chandler had arrived home and superseded her.
She was even more disappointed to hear Chandler and
Bethany speak of moving.

None of the sisters had ever believed that Chandler
and his little family would stay on at Chatam House
permanently. They had to make their own home sooner
or later, and God had obviously ordained the moment.
She never ceased marveling at the way God worked.

She supposed that she ought not to be so surprised
that He had used a baby to bring Chandler and Bethany
together. After all, He had used a babe to bring salva-
tion to a lost world. Still, an infant matchmaker!

Had Bethany not been pregnant and desperate, however, Chandler would never have been moved to marry

her. Then he would not have found the one true love
God had designed especially for him. It was only right
that they follow the path God had laid out for their little family.

But, Stephenville! Oh, how she would miss the little
scrap and his parents!

A sudden thought brought her to a halt at the door
to the suite. So, Chandler and Bethany and little Matthew would be leaving them soon. That must mean that
God was preparing Chatam House for someone new!

Who, she wondered, would God send to them next?

She moved quietly out onto the landing and patted
the wall with an approving hand as she trundled by.
Whomever God sent their way, Chatam House would
be ready. Obviously, He had appointed this place not
only as a haven for the lost and desperate, but as a gar-
den where love could take root and grow. And love,
Magnolia knew, was the sweetest, most beautiful blossom of all.

They were making quite a bouquet for themselves,
the Chatam sisters. Not bad for a trio of old spinsters.

She smiled contentedly as she made her way back to
her room, silently praising God in His infinite wisdom.

* * * * *

Dear Reader,

Have you ever feared that you were lost only to find yourself right where you needed to be? Life is like that sometimes. None of the landmarks feel familiar, and you can't seem to recall exactly how you got where you are. Then everything begins to make sense and you suddenly realize that you're right where you want to be.

We may not always know where we are going in this life or why, but as Christians we can trust that God is well aware of the paths we trod and has specific destinations in mind for each of us. Moreover, wherever God takes us, that's always the best place for us to be.

May you enjoy the trip as much as the destination!

God bless,

*Arlene James*

# AN UNLIKELY MATCH

You have granted him the desire of his heart
and have not withheld the request of his lips.
—*Psalms* 21:2

For Faith Itai Manase, adventuress, world traveler,
nurse, friend, daughter of my heart.
I am so proud of you!
Love always,
DAR

# Chapter One

Attorney Asher Chatam recognized a summons when he received one, though he could not imagine what legal advice his aunties needed so urgently that it would require his immediate presence. He shrugged out of his camel hair overcoat and surveyed the front parlor of Chatam House, the antebellum mansion where Chatams had resided for generations, including his maiden aunts, triplets in their seventies who had lived in the great house for their entire lives.

As always, Odelia first captured the eye. Wearing royal blue, she had anchored a crown of matching feathers in her fluffy white hair. Speckled, light blue beads the size of robin's eggs dangled by golden chains from her earlobes, completing the theme of her costume. Hypatia, her sister's polar opposite, in expensive bronze silk and a neat silver chignon, placed her delicate Limoges teacup on its matching saucer and graced him with a smile from her customary wingback chair. Meanwhile, Magnolia—known to her many nieces and nephews as Aunt Mags—garbed in her usual frumpy cardigan and shirtwaist dress, her iron-gray braid hanging over one shoulder, beamed her frank enjoyment of his surprise at the room's occupants.

Kent Monroe, a pharmacist well past the usual age of retirement, was Odelia's erstwhile fiancé from at least half a century ago. A barrel chest had long since given way to a serious paunch, now bisected by gray suspenders and shielded with a pale blue shirt, topped with a jaunty red bow tie that sat atop his jugular like a strangled cherry crowning a generous scoop of blueberry ice cream. After his failed romance with Odelia, it was generally assumed that Kent Monroe would forever keep a cordial, mannerly distance. And he most likely would have, in the normal course of events. But the normal course of events had been greatly altered.

Asher narrowed his eyes suspiciously at his baby sister. At twenty-three, a full fifteen years his junior, Dallas was as impulsive as her short, frothy hair was red. An inveterate romantic, she had sighed over Odelia's failed engagement since girlhood, even going so far as to strike up a friendship with Ellen Monroe, Kent's granddaughter.

"Dallas, I'm surprised to see you here." If he had been called in on a legal matter, then why was his baby sister here?

"It's Chatam House, Ash," she retorted. "They're my aunts, too."

"Of course we are, dear," Magnolia cooed in a placating fashion.

"And Ellie's my best friend," Dallas went on in a tone that a five-year-old would have punctuated by sticking out her tongue.

Ellie was the greatest surprise of all. Granted, he had last seen her on graduation day some two or three years earlier, but the pudgy, dark-haired baby doll of his memory had morphed into an astonishing beauty in that relatively short period of time. Next to his coltish sister, in her black jeans and white long-sleeved T-shirt, Ellie looked lush in a simple, navy blue sheath belted at the waist. Her chin-length hair curled and waved about her Kewpie doll face and violet eyes. Everything about her, even her smile, seemed luxuriant.

Abruptly aware of the streaks of gray in his own chestnut-brown hair and the subtle lines that creased his forehead, Asher felt suddenly self-conscious. He had previously thought those streaks entirely suitable for a successful attorney approaching forty years of age. He'd noticed the faint wrinkles without concern only days earlier. Now, suddenly, they seemed ominous declarations of the fact that he was aging. His aching knee called attention to itself at that moment, and he very nearly turned and walked out, mentally fabricating excuses for his aunts.

He did no such thing, of course. At thirty-eight, he was still in his prime. Plus, he *was* a Chatam, after all, as well as a very busy attorney, too busy to pay attention to old aches and pains. His sudden weariness could be attributed to this being Friday, the end of a long week, the third in the too-short, often dreary month of February.

"Asher, dear."

The sound of his aunt's voice recalled him to his duty. Dropping his coat over the seat of an armless side chair, he strode forward to leave a kiss against her soft cheek.

"Aunt Hypatia. It's good to see you. Is there an emergency?"

He could surely be excused for assuming such was the case. Though the aunties were a bit outdated in their mannerisms and sensibilities—Asher's father, Murdock, insisted that his older sisters had been born a hundred years too late—Asher had never before received a message from them. This one had arrived, written on ivory vellum and hand-delivered by the aunts' middle-aged factotum, Chester, only an hour earlier, requesting his presence at Chatam House as soon after five o'clock in the afternoon as possible. Naturally he had rearranged his schedule and appeared, as summoned, at barely a quarter past the appointed hour.

"Not an emergency, per se," Hypatia answered carefully.

"There is, however, a problem," Mags added, summoning him to her side. He craned around the piecrust table and bussed her leathery cheek, then repeated the process with Odelia's plump one.

For once, Odelia, who was seated next to Mags on the settee, did not giggle. In fact, she barely smiled, nor had she yet spoken. Lovingly referred to by her nieces and nephews as Auntie Od, the woman was usually effusive to the point of silliness, which made this uncharacteristic solemnity seem ominous at best.

"What's wrong?" Asher asked.

"It's the Monroes, dear," Hypatia informed him kindly, signaling the elder Monroe with a regal wave of her hand.

"Well, you see—" Kent Monroe began.

"Our house caught fire," Ellie interjected quickly.

Some things, Asher noted wryly, had not changed. Ellie had always exhibited an unfortunate tendency to interrupt. He raised his brows at her, as he always used to do, in silent rebuke—only to tumble headlong into her wide violet eyes. Surprised, he forced his attention back to the matter at hand.

"It's not a total loss by any means," she was going on blithely. "The smell is the worst of it, really, but that should prove no real problem. It's amazing how they have products now that can just take odors out of the air, isn't it?" She continued on about air fresheners and the unreasonable strictures of the fire department.

For an instant, Asher felt himself once more being pulled under by those dark-lashed eyes, and he realized that he was staring. He retreated swiftly to the fireplace. Parking himself there, he paused to take stock of the gathering in the huge gilt-framed mirror above the mantle.

The first face to jump out at him from that group reflection was, of course, Ellie's. Rounded and apple-cheeked, her face seemed made of sweetness, a disturbingly adult sweetness. Her unusual coloring—pale pink skin, dark hair and sparkling violet eyes—added a sense of the ethereal to a face that could only be described as…enchanting.

He felt a strange sense of alarm. This was Ellie, for goodness' sake, little Ellie Monroe, his baby sister's best friend.

She turned sideways on the edge of her seat, watching him with a wide, troubled gaze. He felt a sudden urge to bolt from the room. Instead, he turned and folded his arms, targeting Kent Monroe with a penetrating gaze.

"I'm sorry for your trouble. What exactly does this all mean?"

"The house is structurally sound but uninhabitable," Mr. Monroe said, glancing at Ellie apologetically.

"Which is why they are here," Magnolia put in.

Asher smiled. The aunties seemed to be making a habit of taking in strays. Over the past several months, they'd taken in no fewer than half a dozen needy souls, but he knew exactly who would be responsible for this particular state of affairs. He gave his sister a pointed, accusing glare, to which she immediately took exception.

"Don't look at me like that, Ash. Where else could they go?" She lifted her chin defiantly, tossing her short red curls. Like him and all the Chatams, she had a cleft in that proud little chin. Hers was nothing more than a gentle dip in the center; his was more pronounced.

"And, of course, they are most welcome," Hypatia hastily said, "but I'm sure that they would like the insurance matter settled sooner rather than later."

Kent inclined his round head, saying in a gravelly voice, "You are too kind, dear lady, you and your sisters. Believe me, we want nothing more than to go home as quickly as possible and would not impose a moment longer that necessary, but the insurance company—"

"—is so impersonal," Ellie finished for him, rushing on. "You know how they are. They don't return your phone calls when you think they should, let alone write the checks. It's infuriating for him, especially after all these years of paying premiums, which is why I've taken over the whole thing." She spread her hands as if to say that the matter was settled.

Asher looked to her grandfather. "I assume that you are the policyholder." Kent nodded. "Confidentiality rules would prevent the insurance company from discussing the matter with anyone but you or—"

"I'm sure they'll settle eventually," Ellie interrupted. "These things never move as swiftly as we'd like."

"—your appointed legal representative," Asher finished doggedly.

"Ah," Magnolia said in a voice of deep satisfaction. "I knew you would agree."

Agree? Asher noted at once the look of smug approval on his aunt's face and felt a jolt. All these years of avoiding legal pitfalls, and he'd been led into a trap by a trio of little old ladies with sweet smiles and teacups. And it was a very neatly sprung trap, too.

Arguments against the Monroes taking on legal counsel, his in particular, immediately formed. Legal representation could sometimes gum up the works when it came to routine claims, and an attorney too busy to devote adequate time to the issue could well delay, rather than expedite, matters. On the other hand, well-phrased and well-timed inquiries from a legal source could work wonders.

Asher glanced at Odelia, recognizing her shaky relief, and knew he would do what he could, if only for Auntie Od. Odelia, God bless her, seemed far less comfortable than Dallas at having the Monroes as guests at Chatam House. That alone was reason enough to help settle the insurance claim.

Besides, why spend time and energy on escape when compliance would free him sooner? In fact, if he hurried, he might still be able to make his meeting.

It was a routine matter, really, the usual gathering of regional youth soccer commissioners at the beginning of a new season. He had intended to argue, once again and most likely without results, for the formal training of volunteer coaches at every level of the system. But he didn't care if he lost the argument. Soccer was his great, overriding passion. It was his buffer against a crazy world. He couldn't wait to get the season started.

He checked his watch, pushing back his French cuff. If he hurried, he could make the last few minutes of the meeting and still press his point.

"I'll look into it," he announced, smiling as he stepped away from the fireplace. "Call my secretary Monday morning with the particulars," he instructed Mr. Monroe.

Ellie sat up straight. "Oh, but—"

"I'll get back to you in a few days," he went on, walking toward the door.

"Can't you stay long enough for tea?" his sister asked pointedly.

"Sorry. I have a meeting."

He didn't quite make it across the impressive foyer before the quick tap of footsteps on marble warned him of pursuit. Dallas, no doubt. Slinging on his coat, Asher cast a glance upward issuing a brief, silent plea for patience.

Of his three siblings, his baby sister had always tried him most, so naturally she had been the one to follow him from the family home in Waco to Buffalo Creek, where she had earned a teaching degree at Buffalo Creek Bible College and remained to teach second grade. Intending to make short work of any confrontation, he whirled—and nearly bowled over Ellen Monroe.

She bounced off him, pinwheeling her arms to keep from falling over backward. Instinctively, he reached out to grasp her forearms and steady her. A bright smile suddenly lit her face, and electricity shot up his arms. Jolted, he snatched his hands back.

"Sorry."

"No problem," she said, smoothing her skirt. "I—I just wanted to…uh, thank you."

"I haven't done anything yet," he pointed out, frowning.

"No, but you're going to," she said, "and I'm beyond grateful. But I hate for you to put yourself out over this. I know how busy you must be, and…" With a forced chuckle, she held out her arms in a broad shrug. "Well, I'm sure God will work it all out in His own good time."

Asher blinked, irritated by his odd response to Ellie, a response he couldn't quite characterize. "Is it not possible that God could use *me* to work it out?"

"Oh!" She clapped her hands to her chest just below her delicate collarbones. "I didn't mean—"

"Because I assure you that the insurance company will seek every means to mitigate their damages," he interrupted, "even if it's only delaying payment as long as possi—"

"But Dallas is always saying how busy you are, and I wouldn't want to impose."

He sighed. "You're not imposing. You're taking on legal representation." The attorney in him forced out a disclaimer. "Though, of course, I cannot guarantee that you and your grandfather will be entirely happy with the results of my actions."

Ellie flattened her lips as if disappointed. "I've found people are just about as happy as they make up their minds to be."

Life brought all sort of disappointments, as Asher

knew well, unhappy and tragic things, like death and divorce, injury, malfeasance, house fires… The list, in fact, seemed endless. But perhaps she was too young to understand the harsh realities of this life, while Asher, on the other hand, had seen far too much tragedy, animosity and downright dishonesty in the course of his practice to be so sanguine.

Recently, his cousin Chandler had been cheated of his investment in a ranch. Thankfully, all had turned out well. In short order, Chandler had married, become a father and purchased another ranch near Stephenville to the west. It had all happened, Asher mused, while Chandler and his now wife, Bethany, had been living in this very house.

Come to think of it, his cousins Kaylie and Reeves had also met their spouses while one or the other of them lived here, a fact that must surely have influenced his starry-eyed little sister to seek shelter for the Monroes in this place. Was Dallas trying to get Kent and Odelia together? And was Ellen also a part of that?

If so, shame on them.

Until a person had been disappointed in love, that person could not understand the depth of pain that accompanied such disappointment. Dallas and Ellie were still too young for that kind of experience.

Feeling sadly world-weary to the point of, well, old, Asher could have used a bit of Ellie Monroe's youthful naïveté and enthusiasm just then. Instead, he smiled and brought the conversation to an abrupt end.

"Have a good evening, Ellie."

He left her there, looking like the little girl she had been not so long ago, the little girl whom he, on some level that he definitely did not wish to examine too closely, needed her still to be. He pushed the image of her lovely violet eyes aside. He had no interest in romance. His one spectacular failure in that area had cured him permanently of any desire to meet, or date— let alone marry again.

Ellie sighed as the door closed behind Asher Chatam's back. She had always sighed upon first seeing him, and today had been no exception. For as long as she'd known his sister Dallas, some six or so years now, Ellie had thought the tall, lean attorney the finest-looking man she'd ever seen. Slim-hipped and broad-shouldered, with the build of an athlete, he seemed the very epitome of the successful barrister. She had always imagined him as a champion of the downtrodden and wrongly accused, but she knew little about his business. She adored the distinguished streaks of off-white at his temples, the warm amber of his eyes and the cleft in his strong chin.

Unfortunately, when he was around, she couldn't seem to think as clearly as usual. He made her nervous, and when she was nervous she blurted out things better left unsaid, interrupted others and often embarrassed herself. She had no reason to worry, though. He had never seemed to notice. Sadly, so far as she could tell, the man barely realized that she was alive. She was just his little sister's best friend, after all, a kindergarten teacher of limited experience. He, no doubt, fended off much more sophisticated women on a daily basis.

Nevertheless, Ellie found this turn of events intriguing. A dedicated attorney such as Ash Chatam would pay close attention to his clients, and she yearned for him to play close attention to her. But, she reminded herself, close attention could be disastrous. She had actually pleaded with the Chatam triplets not to impose on their nephew, but her entreaties had gone unheeded. In fact, the more she'd begged them not to involve Ash, the more determined they had seemed to do so, until finally they had dispatched Chester to enlist Asher's aid.

"He's definitely taking the case then?"

Ellie turned to find Dallas lounging against the staircase banister. Her friend's nonchalant pose and tone did not fool Ellie. Dallas was as concerned as Ellie herself. "Did you think he wouldn't?"

A small sigh escaped Dallas before she made a dramatic shrug. "I told you, if the aunties ask it, you might as well consider it done."

Ellie took a seat on the third step, smoothing her skirt neatly about her thighs. "Tell me again why you don't want Ash involved in this," she suggested as mildly as she could manage.

"You know perfectly well why," Dallas said, dropping down beside Ellie so she could pitch her voice low. "He'll have you and your grandfather out of Chatam House in no time, and the longer you're here, the more likely it is that your grandfather and Aunt Odelia will get back together."

"And that's the only reason?" Ellie pressed softly.

Dallas shifted her gaze away, springing to her feet. "Of course. What other reason could there be?" Dallas could never sit still, but Ellie suspected her restlessness had less to do with habit and more with…something else just now.

Ellie looked down at the marble floor.

"Gotta go, kiddo," Dallas said abruptly. She patted

Ellie's shoulder and whirled away to poke her head into the parlor and call out a farewell before setting off.

Ellie watched her go with a heavy heart. Frankly, she missed her friend. The two of them usually spent hours a day talking or just hanging out, but since the fire a distance had grown between them. The fire had left so many questions in Ellie's mind, questions for which Ash Chatam would surely demand answers.

"You're looking very pensive," her grandfather noted, as he trundled through the parlor doorway and across the foyer.

"Am I? Well, it's been a busy day."

"Keep you hopping, do they, all those five- and six-year-olds?"

"Do they ever!"

"You adore them, every one," he remarked.

Ellie smiled. "They're such fun."

"Have fun with what you're doing—" Kent began.

"—and you'll never want to do anything else," Ellie finished for him.

Ruffling her curls as he had done since she'd had curls to ruffle, he started up the steps, but then he paused, his gaze going back toward the parlor. Bending, he quietly asked, "Have you noticed how subdued she is?"

Ellie didn't have to ask which "she" he meant. "Umhm. But I wouldn't read too much into it."

Sighing, he straightened and began the long climb, muttering to himself, "A subdued Odelia is not the real Odelia."

Ellie pretended not to hear, her gaze on the bright yellow door that led out onto the front porch of the mansion, where Chatams had lived, according to Dallas, since the last brick had been laid. Even Asher had lived here for a short time long ago while his house was being built on the north side of town. She closed her eyes in dismay, once more seeking spiritual comfort.

Oh, if only the Chatam sisters had not called Ash into this mess!

It couldn't end well for any of them, not for Dallas, not for her grandfather, not even for the Chatam sisters, who had been so very kind, and certainly not for herself.

Broken hearts, she very much feared, were soon going to be the rule rather than the exception—her own among them.

# Chapter Two

Shifting in her customary seat on the antique settee, Odelia stifled a sigh. The room seemed strangely vacant now that Kent had excused himself. He'd stayed only long enough to be polite after Asher had gone, but then, Kent never lingered in her presence for a moment longer than necessary. She couldn't blame him.

Who would have imagined that her former fiancé would one day take sanctuary here at Chatam House? Odelia certainly would not have, not after what she'd done to him. Perhaps time had diminished the hurt she'd dealt him, but she was only too glad to provide him a kindness now or anytime. When Dallas had first explained the situation nearly two weeks ago, the first reaction of Odelia's sisters had been to gently refuse, but Odelia herself had argued fiercely that God had His reasons for bringing the Monroes to their doorstep, and she still believed that. She just hadn't counted on how having Kent in the house would affect her.

How could it be that after all these years, some small vestige of her original feelings for the man would still be rattling around inside this old heart of hers? Now, she longed continually for his company and, though he avoided her, dreaded the day when the Monroes would move back into their house. Why, oh, why had Hypatia and Magnolia insisted on calling in Asher? Their nephew was bound to get to the bottom of things and come to terms with the insurance company in short order, and then, before she knew it, Kent would be gone again. Well, perhaps it was for the best at that.

Blanching, she looked down at her hands, ringed fingers twining together anxiously. Once, she had wanted very much to marry Kent Monroe, and had nearly done so. Only at the last moment had she realized that she could never be happy living apart from her dear sisters. But when she had suggested to Kent that they live with her family, he hadn't taken it very well, claiming that a "real man" would make his own home. She had understood that perfectly, but it had still hurt.

The aftermath of the breakup had been quite difficult for her, but she had never regretted her decision not to marry. Kent had truly been the only man who had ever tempted her to do so. When Kent had married Deirdre Billups, Odelia had put away her secret longings, and she had been more than content over the years. She had actually been quite happy and genuinely glad for Kent and Deirdre when, after years of marriage, their son had been born. Likewise, she had grieved for Kent and Deirdre when their son had died in an accident at the age of forty-one and then again, over a decade ago now, for Kent when Deirdre had succumbed to an aneurysm.

Since that time, she and Kent had gradually renewed their friendship, always keeping a polite distance. She had found that arrangement very satisfactory and had imagined that they would end their lives as casual friends with their shared past unremarked but unforgotten, at least between the two of them. Instead, in thirteen short days she had somehow reverted to her old foolish self, longing for the kind of relationship that she had long since determined was not for her. How could she, at her age, feel such nonsensical, girlish emotions? She was simply astounded.

"Dearest, are you all right?" Hypatia asked, calling Odelia from her reverie.

Odelia looked up, glancing from one sister to the other. Both watched her with concern etched upon their faces.

"Who, me?"

"Certainly she means you," Magnolia said with a snort. "Who else? *I* certainly wasn't engaged to Kent Monroe."

Odelia forced herself to laugh brightly, hoping that it didn't sound as stilted as she feared. "I'm fine! Why wouldn't I be? It's not *our* house that caught fire."

"You just seem…not yourself lately," Hypatia observed gently.

"Not yourself," Magnolia agreed.

"If having Kent Monroe here is disturbing to you—" Hypatia began.

"It could be dyspepsia," Magnolia pointed out brusquely. "You remember how Mother suffered with dyspepsia. It put her all out of sorts."

"—we could always offer to put them up in a hotel," Hypatia went on, sending Magnolia a speaking glance.

"I'm not dyspeptic!" Odelia insisted, turning on Magnolia. "I've never had digestive difficulties in my life." As her waistline must surely demonstrate, she thought morosely.

"Well, of all of us, you're most like Mother," Magnolia argued defensively.

*Plump, she means,* Odelia thought. Perhaps she ought to pay a bit more attention to what she ate, she decided, mumbling, "My digestion is fine."

"It's certainly not unrequited love," Magnolia commented, chuckling. "Not at our age."

Odelia frowned and batted her eyelashes against a sudden welling of tears. She might be past the age of romance, but surely she should not be past the age of caring about her weight, if only as a matter of health. Abruptly, she wondered what Kent thought about her rounded figure. He had once declared her the very model of slender femininity, but what did he think now? Had age and indulgence robbed her of all appeal?

Closing her eyes, she told herself not to bring Kent into this, not even mentally. Obviously, to her shame, she needed to pray much more diligently about her personal lapses, and so she would. Meanwhile, she'd be boiled and peeled before she'd give in to this nonsensical emotional confusion.

Mentally centering herself, she heard Hypatia say, "I understand that new hotel out on the highway is quite comfortable and even offers kitchenettes. If we phrased it delicately and prepaid, say, a month's rent, I doubt that either Kent or Ellie would take offense. We could always—"

"Oh, for pity's sake, Hypatia!" Odelia snapped, popping open her eyes. "There is no polite way to turn someone out of your home when you have already offered them shelter and have more than ample accommodations for them."

Horrified at this uncharacteristic harshness, Hypatia drew back, her eyes wide.

Beside Odelia on the settee, Magnolia drawled, "I think she should see a doctor."

Embarrassed, Odelia considered placating her sisters by agreeing, but then she thought of Brooks Leland, the family physician, and knew that he was far too astute not to see that her problem was emotional and spiritual rather than physical.

Fighting for an even, melodic tone, she said, "I don't need a doctor. I just need…" she looked to the windows at the front of the long, rectangular room "…sunshine." Rising to her feet, she continued, "I need sunshine. And fresh air. Spring. I'm so very tired of winter. I need a dose of spring." Making a beeline for the foyer, she decided that she would take an overcoat from the cloakroom and let herself out the sunroom door. "If you need me, I'll be in the greenhouse," she told her sisters. *Praying,* she added silently.

Perhaps then she could put aside these ridiculous longings and dreams, for such foolishness should be the purview of the young. What need had she of love at this late date, after all? It wasn't as if they had time for children or growing old together. They were already old, she and Kent.

Too old.

Nothing promised such new possibilities as a Monday morning. At least, Ellie had always thought so. She loved the early-morning tranquility and neatness of her classroom, the moment of sublime peace before the children began to arrive, bringing their happy chaos with them, but Monday mornings were the best. As such, they always seemed ripe for prayer, but especially this particular Monday morning.

She'd mulled the problem of Asher Chatam all weekend without finding a solution, and now, as she read over her morning's devotional, she wondered why she had not simply taken the matter to God. As the author of the devotional reminded her, God knew everything to be known about the whole situation anyway, even more than she did. He was just waiting for her to ask Him for the solution. Really, she could be so foolish sometimes. It was a wonder, a testament to God's patience, that He didn't drop stones out of Heaven onto her head at such moments.

Spreading her hands over the pages of her devotional book, she closed her eyes and began as she always did, whispering the words in her mind.

*Holy Father, make me Your instrument this day. Help me to love and teach my students, to see and meet their needs as You would have me do. And, Lord, please show me how to deal with this mess I've gotten myself into. My grandfather deserves to be happy, really happy. He is the very soul of cheerful forbearance, as You know, and I know that Odelia would make him happy. I'm as convinced of it as Dallas is, only I would never have...*

She bit her lip, unwilling even to put into words what she feared. It wasn't as if she had any proof, after all. Besides, who was she to judge? And if Dallas had done something foolish to bring her aunt and Ellie's grandfather together, well, what sense did it make to waste an opportunity like this? Just because she wouldn't have done what she feared Dallas had done didn't mean that God couldn't use the situation for good. Did it?

If only the Chatam sisters hadn't brought Asher into

it! He could be a tad severe, and Dallas had always painted him as somewhat stodgy, but even she admitted that he was a very fine attorney, extremely intelligent and he could be trusted implicitly. Sadly, while Ellie admired those traits, they meant that he was bound to have the insurance company settling up in no time. Or worse yet, he might discover the truth of the fire—whatever that was—and then where would they be?

Would the insurance company even pay if the fire had been deliberately set? And what would happen to her dearest friend if… She turned off that line of thought, concentrating instead on her grandfather's happiness.

*Please, Lord, couldn't You intercede here, just delay things a bit, maybe? I mean, Ash is bound to be busy. He has that prosperous look about him that busy attorneys who make lots of money often—*

Her thoughts came to an abrupt stop. Money. That was the answer! All she had to do was tell Ash that she and her grandfather could not afford to pay him. Surely, that would put the brakes on things.

"Thank You," she said brightly.

"For what?" asked a child's voice.

Ellie's eyes popped open. Her gently arched brows shot upward as she took in the two former pupils who stood with their bellies pressed to the front of her desk. Students often did that, especially when they wanted something. One of their mothers, a woman by the name of Ilene Riddle, stood behind them at a short distance.

"Hello," Ellie said.

"Hello, Miss Monroe," the two girls replied in sync.

"We didn't want to disturb you," put in the mother, moving forward a step. "You seemed to be meditating."

An attractive platinum blonde with white-tipped nails and dark eye makeup, she had just been divorced for the second time when her daughter, Angie, had entered Ellie's kindergarten class about a year ago now. Angie and Shawna, the second girl, had quickly become best friends and apparently still were. Ellie noticed that in contrast to her mother's neat stylishness, Angie still looked as if she'd slept in her clothes, her short, dark-blond hair sticking out at odd angles.

"I like to start my day with a prayer," Ellie said, smiling. "Now, what can I do for you?"

"Please, Miss Monroe," Shawna pleaded, tilting her dark, sleek head, "we don't get a coach, and we 'membered that you can play."

"You played with us all those times at recess," Angie put in eagerly.

"Play?" Ellie echoed, puzzled. "Play what?"

"Soccer," Ms. Riddle clarified. "The girls have signed up for the spring soccer season, but there aren't enough coaches to go around. Unless we can find someone to help out, the girls won't get to play."

"Oh, dear," Ellie said, rising to her feet, her hands still planted atop the book on her desk.

"I've volunteered as team mother," Ilene went on, "but I know nothing at all about the sport. I mean, I can organize everything, but I just don't have any of the skills needed to teach the kids about the game, and the commissioner is apparently pretty strict about who is allowed to coach. We thought—hoped—you might be willing to help us."

Ellie stood speechless for a moment. She had never coached a sport in her life, but she did know the game, having played all through high school. Straightening, she folded her arms thoughtfully, one forefinger tapping her rounded chin.

"How many kids would I work with?"

"Nine is the minimum," Ilene answered. "We actually have seven right now and could use a few more. Twelve is the max at this age."

Twelve at most. Ellie looked around the room. She routinely corralled twenty-two in this small space and flattered herself that she actually taught them something worthwhile in the process. Twelve kids on an open field would be a piece of cake by comparison.

"How much time are we talking about?"

"It's nine games and twenty practices in ten weeks, so roughly twenty-five hours."

That was little more than a full day in total, spread out over more than two months. Besides, she'd always enjoyed soccer and could use the exercise. And hadn't she just asked God to show her the needs of her pupils and how to meet them?

"Sounds like fun," she decided. "Count me in."

The girls *hurrah*ed, bouncing up and down on their toes. Ilene Riddle reached past them to clasp Ellie's hands with hers, silver bracelets jangling.

"Thank you so much. I'll help every way I can, I promise. First practice is Wednesday afternoon at five-fifteen. Do you know where the field is?"

"I think so. Across the creek from the park, right?"

"Right. I'll bring all the supplies. You just bring the expertise."

"Deal," Ellie said, smiling broadly.

As the trio took their leave, Ellie dropped down onto her desk chair once more. Well, it looked like she had her work cut out for her, starting tomorrow afternoon.

She'd have to brush up on coaching tactics this evening. Thankfully, with all the information online, that shouldn't be too difficult. She'd see to it tonight.

That left this afternoon to convince Asher Chatam to drop her grandfather's case and turn his attention elsewhere.

Ellie smiled. Mondays really were her favorite day of the week.

Dropping the telephone receiver into its cradle, Asher stared at the leather-trimmed blotter on his desk. He hated Mondays. Just once, he wanted to get through a Monday without some unpleasant surprise. What, he wondered, had the aunties—and, by extension, he—gotten into? So much for settling this "routine" insurance matter and getting on with his life.

Unanswered questions about the fire at the Monroe house abounded, and Ellie Monroe had apparently done everything in her power to make certain that they remained that way. According to the adjuster, Ellie's cell phone number was the only contact information that the company now had, and she'd come up with every excuse imaginable to prevent the adjuster from speaking with her grandfather. Most troubling of all, the Monroes had recently increased their coverage and moved their most precious belongings into storage. The adjuster had even hinted at a financial incentive. Something smelled, and it wasn't smoke.

Asher was making notes on his computer when his secretary buzzed him. Without taking his eyes off the screen, he hit the intercom button.

"You heading home, Barb?" A fifty-something

grandmother raising a grandson, Barbara was adamant about leaving the office by five.

"In a minute. There's an Ellen Monroe here. She says it's important that she see you but promises she'll only take a few minutes of your time."

Asher sat back in his chair. Well, well. Ventured right into the lion's den, had she? Reaching forward, he shut down the computer and monitor.

"Send her in. Then get out of here and have a good evening."

"Will do. See you tomorrow."

He tightened the knot in his gold-striped tie, spun his tan leather chair to face the door and waited, hands folded. As the sound of footsteps on the polished oak floor in the hallway grew louder, Asher's heartbeat sped up. He told himself that it was his normal reaction, the old fire-in-the-belly response to a challenge. The instant Ellie appeared in the doorway, however, he knew that he was kidding himself.

Wearing a dark purple pantsuit over a rose-pink blouse, she looked absolutely lovely. She also looked distinctly uncomfortable. Intending to use that discomfort to his advantage, he found a smile and rose.

"Just who I wanted to see."

"Oh?" she said in surprise, her face lighting.

Nodding, he waved her over then watched as she folded down neatly into one of the chairs before his desk. She tucked a small handbag into the space beside her.

"Why did you want to see me?" she asked.

Sitting, he regarded her steadily. "Tell me why you're here fir—"

"You should know that we can't pay you," she

blurted, suddenly looking hopeful and somber at the same time.

Asher paused, concerned. He didn't like to think it, but this information could support the idea that the Monroes had a financial motive for setting fire to their house.

She sighed, gulped and sucked in a deep breath, all telltale signs of a less-than-truthful client. Which, he reminded himself, she technically was *not*; rather, her grandfather was his client.

"Even with the insurance money," she said, "I can't imagine how we'll pay for the repairs to the house. Granddad had already sunk every penny of his savings into the renovations before the fire. I don't know what we'll do now." She went on to list numerous expenses that must evidently come before his fee.

It might be true that the Monroes were strapped for cash, but he knew a convenient dodge when he saw one, and his curiosity was now piqued. Ellie Monroe was actively attempting to derail the insurance settlement, and he meant to find out why.

"My aunts have essentially asked this of me," he told her mildly, "and when I work for family I never take—"

"But we're not family," Ellie protested, "and you can't go around working for nothing! It wouldn't be fair. You have your own bills to pay, after all. I understand that." She bowed her head, the very picture of stoic acceptance. He didn't buy it for an instant.

Frowning, Asher leaned forward, bracing his elbows on the edge of his desk. "There's no need for you to worry about my bills, Ellie."

"So you're going to do this pro bono?" she demanded, sounding miffed. "Isn't that for charities and such?"

"Not necessarily."

While she sputtered about fairness and good faith and half a dozen other things he didn't follow, he mulled his options. He could throw her out—she wasn't his client and therefore had no say in his employment. On the other hand, her reasons for derailing the settlement could range from merely misguided to serious malfeasance. And, because she was not his client, he had no way to protect her in either case. He decided he would do his best to keep her out of trouble. She was his sister's friend and a tenant at Chatam House, which meant that he had represented her as well as her grandfather.

His decision made, he pulled open a side drawer, took out a receipt pad and flipped it open. "If it will make you feel better," he interrupted, "then by all means, pay me."

"But I just told you that—"

"How much cash do you have on you?"

For a long moment, she said nothing. Asher sat back in his chair, enjoying the moment. For once, he had reduced Ellie Monroe to speechlessness.

"What?" she finally squawked.

"How much cash do you have on you?" he repeated slowly.

Frowning, she pulled her purse into her lap. "Seven or eight dollars, maybe."

"Let's make it a buck, then," he said, leaning forward to scribble out the receipt. "No, two. One for you, one for your grandfather." He made certain to write both of their names on the correct line. After tearing the receipt out of the book, he tossed the pad back into the drawer and nudged it closed.

"You can't mean to represent us for two dollars."

"It's that or nothing," he retorted with a shrug. "You're the one who wanted to pay me. Call it a retainer, if it makes you feel better."

Frowning, she reluctantly laid two crumpled dollar bills on the desk. He swiftly traded the receipt for them and slipped them into his shirt pocket. "That takes care of that."

She made a face. "Look, even if your aunts did drag you into this, I don't expect you to knock yourself out settling our little insurance claim, not for two bucks."

He smiled. "I have a question for you." He folded his arms atop his desk blotter. "Why are you trying to get me off this case?"

Shock flashed across her face, followed swiftly by guilt. "I—I don't know what you mean."

"Tell me what you're hiding."

"What makes you think I'm h-hiding something?" she hedged, averting her gaze.

"This isn't my first day on the job," he pointed out, hardening himself against those suddenly woeful eyes. "And you're a terrible liar."

"I'm not lying!"

"You're stalling the insurance company," he accused in his most lawyerly voice. "Why?"

Biting her lip, she shook her head. "You don't understand."

"I'm trying to, because I can't help you if I don't know why you're doing this!" He leaned toward her. "Is it your goal to remain at Chatam House indefinitely?"

She broke, blurting, "I only want my grandfather and your aunt to have a chance to get together!" She quickly clapped her hand over her mouth.

"I knew it!" Asher cried, smacking a hand against

the desktop. The lawyer in him crowed, even while the annoyed nephew was exasperated.

But Asher Chatam, who had known Ellie for quite some time, was worried.

He now had at least a part of the truth.

He wasn't at all sure, though, that he wanted the rest of it. Because he wasn't sure that he could protect her—not if her foolishness was as great as he feared.

## Chapter Three

She had told him! She had told Asher of her deepest hope, despite Dallas having warned her that he would be appalled, even offended, at the very suggestion of Odelia and Kent rekindling their romance. Ellie suddenly feared what else she might tell him if he pressed hard enough.

"I need to know everything about the fire, Ellie," he said in a soothing voice that she dared not trust, not after the grilling she'd just endured. "Tell me about that night."

Dismay filled her, followed quickly by irritation that she'd let herself be cornered like that. She shifted in her seat, crossed her legs and hemmed and hawed before finally telling the story.

She and her grandfather had moved a quantity of furniture into storage to make room for the workmen who were renovating their seventy-year-old house. As the work progressed, they had replaced one room's furnishings with that of the next, swapping out contents as the necessary renovations were completed.

"They did the roof first, then moved inside, starting upstairs," she told him. "They were ready to move downstairs to the bedroom that had been my grandmother's, so we took her antique French Empire bed suite to storage that night. It's easily worth more than everything else in the house put together, and Grandpa takes good care of it, calls it part of my legacy."

Asher's brown eyes regarded her intensely. "Go on."

Ellie took a deep breath and explained that she and her grandfather were still trying to fit the bed suite into the rented space without damaging it when Dallas had arrived. Asher's brows rose as she repeated the story that Dallas had told her. Out jogging that evening, Dallas had stopped by the Monroe house on impulse to discuss a date Ellie had gone on the previous night. Dallas had ostensibly seen the fire through the front window. She waved down a passerby, who happened to be Garrett Willows, the gardener at Chatam House, as he drove down the street on his motorcycle.

Willows had called 911. The Fire Department had arrived within moments and put out the fire a short while later. That was apparently when Dallas remembered that Ellie and her grandfather were moving furniture into storage that night. Willows had offered to take her there so she could break the news in person. That was also when she'd called her aunts, who had immediately offered sanctuary.

"And that's all there is to it," Ellie said, not quite meeting his gaze.

"And how did the fire start?"

She gulped, then made herself look at him, noticing that as she did so his gaze dropped to her lips. "Apparently a can of paint remover spilled, then a hot lamp tipped over, the one we always left on when we were away from the house at night." She shrugged and looked down at her hands. "I don't know how it happened in an empty house. Someone said there was a loud noise, like a car backfiring nearby."

"And you think something like that could have knocked over a can of paint remover and a lamp?" he asked skeptically.

"There could have been a collision at the track yard," she insisted. "The switching lane is just a few hundred yards from the house. It isn't used much, but when it is, we can feel it, almost like the ground is moving."

"But if your theory is correct," he mused, "then the paint remover had to be open when it tipped."

"The workmen sometimes just set the cap on the neck and didn't screw it down until they were done," she told him. "They warned me about an open can more than once when I came into the room where they were."

Asher leaned back in his chair. "Plausible," he admitted, but his tone implied that he found it just barely so.

He stroked a fingertip over the cleft in his chin. "You, ah, mentioned going on a date the previous evening."

Ellie blinked at the change in subject. "What about it?"

"Just wondering if you've broken anyone's heart lately."

She scoffed, laughing. "Hardly."

"There hasn't been anyone special then?"

"I wish," she quipped. "What there have been are a lot of first dates, emphasis on the word *first*, as in not many *second* dates." She wrinkled her nose. "I just don't seem to find any keepers, if you take my meaning. Dallas says I'm too picky, but I notice that she doesn't have a steady boyfriend, either."

He smiled then abruptly sobered again. "By any chance, might one of those first dates have been with Garrett Willows?" he asked carefully.

Ellie blinked and frowned, shaking her head. "I never met him before that night. Why?"

"I'm just trying to understand the overall situation."

"But I've told you what happened."

"You put forward a supposition," he pointed out, "but you've as good as said that you don't really *know* what happened."

She slid to the edge of her seat and laid a hand on his desktop beseechingly. "Look, however it happened, it wasn't malicious."

Asher beetled his brow. "And how do you—"

"It just stands to reason," she said too quickly. "I mean, it's not as if we have enemies."

"Then who set the fire, Ellie?"

"I don't know!" she shot back. And she didn't. Not for sure. "No one! It was an accident."

"Did you arrange that fire to promote a romance between our relatives?" he demanded.

She gasped. He suspected her? Here she was trying to protect his beloved but harebrained sister, and he would put the blame on *her*? Indignant, she rose to place both hands on his desk. Leaning forward, she brought her face close to his, so close that she could smell the minty freshness of his breath. "I had absolutely nothing to do with that fire!"

"Nothing?" he asked skeptically.

"Zip," she declared flatly, punctuating her denial with taps of her forefinger against his blotter. "Nada. Nil. Zero. Zilch. I didn't set it! I didn't cause it! I didn't have anyone else do it! I didn't know it was going to happen. I still can't believe that it has!"

After a very long moment, Asher relaxed back in his chair. "I had to ask," he said, as if that excused all.

Sighing, Ellie dropped her head. He believed her. He believed that she had nothing to do with the fire, and in that moment, fool that she was, that was all that mattered.

Asher still had serious questions, but he felt sure that whatever had happened, Ellie had not purposefully caused the fire at the Monroe house. Deeply relieved, he smiled. She blinked and smiled back. For a long moment he couldn't look away. Then another thought came to mind. Though she might not have been responsible for the fire, she was certainly guilty of meddling in other people's lives.

"So you didn't start the fire, but you're not above using it for your own purposes," he accused, frowning.

She dropped down onto the edge of the chair again. "My grandfather taught me that God doesn't let anything into the lives of His children without a reason, and getting together two people who care about each other seems like a pretty good one to me."

"Please," Asher scoffed. "Odelia and your grandfather haven't had feelings for each other in fifty years."

"You don't know that."

"Even if they did have feelings for each another, I would discourage them from entering into a relationship at this late date. It isn't sensible."

Ellie gasped. "You can't be that cold!"

That, surprisingly, stung. Coldness was what his ex-wife, Samantha, had accused him of when her tears had not moved him. Perhaps if she had not employed them after making angry demands, he would have been more amenable. Perhaps she wouldn't have left him then. Perhaps his wouldn't have been the first divorce in his family. He blocked further thoughts on the matter.

"I'm simply pragmatic," he refuted, keeping his voice level. "Two people the age of your grandfather and my aunt ought not become entangled romantically. It's just not wise, fiscally, emotionally or in any other way."

Ellie narrowed her wide, violet eyes at him. "Just because they're older, you think they don't deserve to be happy? How hard-hearted can you be?"

Asher felt his temper begin to spike. "I never said they don't deserve to be happy."

"Just that they should ignore their feelings for each other!" Ellie exclaimed.

"You don't know that they have feelings for each other any more than I know they don't!" he pointed out.

"Well, we won't know whether they do or not if we don't give them a chance to find out, will we?"

"What difference does it make at this point?" he demanded. "They're past the point of contemplating children or building a financial future together."

"Love and marriage are about more than children and finances! It's about companionship and emotional support."

"Oh, please! It's not as if either of them is living a lonely, barren existence. Aunt Odelia has her sisters. Your grandfather has you."

"But what about tenderness, satisfaction, the fulfillment of a heart's desire?"

Asher rolled his eyes. "Believe me, it is entirely possible to live without those things. In some ways, it is even preferable."

Ellie fell back into her chair, staring at him with those breathtaking eyes. To his horror, tears welled up. "That's the saddest thing I've ever heard," she told him in a soft, trembling voice.

He gaped at her, his chest tightening, and felt the urge to rush around the desk, slip an arm about her shoulders and apologize. Then he realized that she'd manipulated him exactly as Samantha had always done. His anger abruptly turned outward again, though he did his best to subdue it with reason.

"Sad?" he echoed. "But that's just what I'm trying to tell you. Life without romance is not necessarily unhappy. In fact, it can be infinitely more comfortable. Believe me, I know."

"You poor thing," she whispered, her expression melting into compassion. "Who was she? Who was it who broke your heart?"

Asher's jaw dropped as his ex-wife's face flashed before his mind's eye. He saw her on their wedding day, resplendent in her white dress, even then, impatience and disappointment stamped on her face. He had ignored that, knowing that he had been less engaged in the planning and process of the wedding than she would have liked. He'd told himself that once he finished law school and passed the bar, things would settle down, but he'd soon realized that she expected more than he could ever deliver, more time, more attention, more emotion. He remembered the contempt on her face the day that she'd declared him hopeless and asked him to leave their apartment.

Quickly banishing the memories, Asher told himself yet again that the divorce had been the best thing. The marriage had been the mistake. At least he and Samantha had seen the error of their ways before they'd brought children into it. God had taught him a valuable lesson with the failure of his marriage—that his career and personality would leave him neither the time nor the inclination for love and romance.

He had since come to find that such things were not necessary. In fact, given all the acrimonious divorces that he'd seen, Asher did not understand why any mature person entertained notions of romance.

"You misunderstand," he began, reclaiming his composure, only to have Ellie interrupt.

"God can heal a broken heart, you know," she told him gently.

"Yes, of course, but—"

"But you must allow Him to do it," she counseled. "You must be willing."

Exasperated, Asher muttered, "It's not a matter of—"

"Because He surely has some lucky woman picked out for you," Ellie plowed on, not allowing him to complete so much as a sentence. "She's waiting right now, the one woman in the world who will treasure everything about you."

He lifted his eyebrows at that. "Oh, really?" he quipped with equal parts intrigue and ridicule.

She nodded, smiling. "She'll admire all your sterling qualities."

"Sterling," he mimicked, amused now. She was beginning to sound like his aunts. Obviously, the old girls were rubbing off on her. "I've always wondered. What exactly is a 'sterling quality'?"

She sat back in her chair as if surprised that he had to ask. "Well, in your case, confidence, kindness—"

"You told me I was hard-hearted a moment ago," he pointed out drily.

"I was wrong," she admitted with ease. "I said that without thinking, before I knew you'd been hurt."

He opened his mouth to tell her that he had not been hurt but he found he couldn't quite make the words come out.

"A hard-hearted man would not take on a case just because his aunts asked him to. Plus, you're intelligent and good at what you do, successful, respected, honest and you obviously value family. That's all very important to women, you know. And, of course, you're handsome."

"Handsome," he repeated, realizing only belatedly that he was starting to sound like a parrot.

"The graying at the temples is very distinguished," she went on, tilting her head. "Though it's not really gray, is it? It's more of a champagne color, I think. Very unique."

He suddenly couldn't think of anything sensible to say. "I, uh…" He shifted uncomfortably in his chair. "Um…thank you."

She beamed so brightly that her whole being seemed to shine. His lungs locked, refusing to allow air in or out. Then she ducked her head and confessed, "You have gorgeous eyes."

The reality of the situation slapped him fully in the face. She was flirting with him! His world tilted, leaving him clinging to the very edge of reason. Abruptly, he saw himself falling into that sanity-stealing violet gaze, and his every instinct demanded that he flee to safety. He was halfway to his feet when she bounced up, declaring that her grandfather was waiting for her at the pharmacy across the street.

"Ah." Not exactly an intelligent observation, but it would have to do. He threw an arm toward the door, wordlessly inviting Ellie to take her leave.

She rose smoothly and walked toward the door. He hung back, snatching his jacket from the rack and throwing it on. His overcoat followed that, yet he somehow managed to catch up with her in the doorway.

Pausing there, she turned and lifted a dainty hand to brush across his striped tie. "Just think about what I said," she whispered before moving off down the hallway.

Asher stared at her retreating figure for a long moment before he shut his eyes. No, no, he must not think about her...uh, about what she'd said. What had she said?

The door in the waiting area opened and closed, signaling that she had left the premises. He sagged against the door frame, shaking his head and sucking in huge drafts of air.

What on earth was going on? He had sworn off the fairer sex, and he'd been perfectly happy in his solitary existence. Besides, he couldn't be attracted to Ellie Monroe. Not only was she now officially a client, she was twenty-three, too impulsive, too talkative, too... everything!

Especially too pretty.

Why, the woman was downright dangerous. Oh, she might look as innocent as lambs and sweet enough to decay teeth, but that woman was poisonous to the male population, and henceforth, he told himself sternly, he would not forget that fact. He would be on his guard—stern, disciplined, wise—just as a man in his position ought to be.

But something told him that being on his guard might not be enough to combat the charms of Ellie Monroe.

Mentally kicking herself with every step, Ellie descended the stairs outside Asher's office to the ground floor below. She loved these old art deco buildings, but she saw nothing of her surroundings as recriminations piled on, crowding out everything else.

Could she have made a bigger fool of herself? She should have realized that Asher was not handling this case for the money. He was doing a favor for his aunts. Most likely, he would not have taken on the situation at all except at their behest. Informing him of her and her grandfather's limited means to pay had probably even insulted Asher, and that was the last thing she'd wanted.

To make matters even worse, she had shown her hand. He knew that she wanted him to drop or stall the settlement and why—or partly why. Hopefully, he would be satisfied with that.

The saddest revelation of all, though, had to do with Ash himself. The very idea that he had given up on romance broke her heart, for him and for all the women out there who begged God on their knees for such a man, herself included. As a Chatam, he would be a responsible, fiercely loyal and faithful Christian husband, much like her beloved grandfather. Ellie liked to think that her own father would have been such a man, too, but Chart Monroe had died in a helicopter crash while on a training mission with his military unit when she was only ten years old. His death had driven Ellie's unhappy grandmother into bitterness and her spoiled mother into paroxysms of self-pity.

Ellie had soon learned that just as she could not depend on her mother or grandmother to help her through her father's loss, neither could she make up for his absence, so she had clung to her good-natured grandfather. Not yet thirteen when her querulous grandmother had suddenly died, Ellie had naturally turned to him for support and comfort during their mutual time of grief, and that, her mother had declared before packing up and disappearing, was just where she belonged.

Her mother's abandonment had hurt, but leaving Ellie with her grandfather was perhaps the greatest kindness that Sonia had ever given her daughter. Ellie owed so much to that wonderful old man. For years, he had bravely smiled in the face of criticism and coldness from his wife. He had been as devastated as she by their son's passing, perhaps more so, but somewhere along the way, Kent Monroe had learned to make his own happiness. He had taught Ellie to do the same. Just once, though, Ellie wanted her grandfather to actually have his heart's desire, and she wasn't about to apologize for that, not even to Ash, who had obviously allowed his own disappointment to warp his judgment about such things.

Pushing through a heavy glass door, Ellie stepped out onto the sidewalk of the downtown square that framed the Buffalo Creek courthouse. Pausing to toss on her jacket, she spied Lance Ripley coming toward her.

She had done her best to avoid Lance after their date on Valentine's Day. It was not an easy task. As coworkers, they taught in the same building, but while she loved teaching and enjoyed children, Lance, she had discovered, despised both. He had told her bluntly that he would continue to teach only until one of his unlikely inventions sold, the latest of which was a backpack containing an air bag. Ellie shuddered at the idea of school hallways filled with exploding air bags as children did what came naturally, bumping, shoving and jabbing each other.

Lance called out to her even as she quickly turned in the opposite direction. "Ellie!"

Sighing inwardly, she resigned herself and put on a smile before slowly facing him. He strode up to her, hunching inside his rumpled trench coat. His tall frame seemed to fold in upon itself as if unable to support the shock of wheat-blond hair that sprouted from his scalp, too thick to part or comb down without a proper styling. One of those men who could have been truly handsome with just a bit of attention to the details of grooming, he had once struck her as a bundle of possibilities. Now, he represented every dating disappointment she'd ever experienced.

"I've been wanting to talk to you." The pale blue eyes that pinned her from beneath the line of a shaggy unibrow seemed oddly calculating, but she forced a tight smile anyway.

"Hello, Lance. I've been, um, busy."

"Not too busy for me, though, I'm sure," he insisted, sliding an arm across her shoulders.

Ellie stepped aside, frowning at his familiarity. They'd shared a single date, for pity's sake, and she'd regretted it long before their dinners had arrived. He'd asked her out a full week in advance, and she'd been happy to accept. She'd dressed carefully, twisting up her hair and donning one of her favorite dresses, only to find that he hadn't even bothered to make reservations. After driving all over town, they'd wound up eating burgers in a joint frequented primarily by loud teenagers while he droned on and on about his invention. She'd avoided his good-night kiss after that and his calls ever since.

"Actually," she told him, "this is not a good time. I've got to run. Sorry." She attempted to step away, but his hand shot out and fastened around her arm.

"Now, hang on," he said, frowning.

Ellie glanced around meaningfully, but Lance seemed not to realize that they were on the verge of a very public scene. "Please let go of me."

"You've been avoiding me for the past week or more," he accused, as if she had not realized that fact, "and I want to talk."

"Lance, I don't have time for this," she began firmly, but he cut her off.

"Those old ladies you live with, the Chatams, they might be interested in investing in my safety pack. I didn't get a chance to meet them last time, so I thought I could come by sometime soon and do that."

He'd picked her up at Chatam House for their date. Thankfully, the Chatam sisters had been out at the time; otherwise, he might have hit them up for investment funds right then and there! Alarmed to think that he would try to use their tenuous connection to importune the Chatams, Ellie glared up at him.

"Absolutely not! My grandfather and I are just guests at Chatam House. We've only been here for a couple of weeks. I wouldn't feel comfortable having my own company come over."

"Huh," he said, as if the niceties of such things had never occurred to him. "But I'm not really company. We're dating."

"No, Lance, we're not," she stated flatly, drawing herself up straight. "And I really have to go."

Scowling, he gave her arm a shake. At that precise moment, Asher pushed through the door of the building and stepped out onto the sidewalk. Barely glancing at Lance Ripley, he walked over, calmly took Ellie's arm in his, breaking Lance's grasp, and turned her toward her grandfather's pharmacy.

"Excuse us," he said over his shoulder, propelling her down the sidewalk. "Mr. Monroe is waiting."

Stunned, Ellie glanced back at Lance. He brought his hands to his hips and glowered but did not seem inclined to follow. "I'll phone you," he called, as if that alone would prompt her to take his calls when she had not done so thus far.

"You can try," she muttered, swinging her smile up at Asher. She couldn't help a tiny thrill of appreciation. It really was rather gallant, the way he had swooped in and swept her away.

*My hero,* she thought with a melodramatic, inward sigh. If only she could believe he'd meant something personal by it. But of course, given his feelings about romance, that was out of the question. Entirely.

# Chapter Four

*Of all the stupid, ill-advised things to do!* Asher scolded himself sternly, all but shoving Ellie Monroe along at his side. He glanced down at her worshipful gaze and inwardly groaned. If he was not mistaken, the girl had a crush on him already, and he had just added fuel to that fire. Nothing could come of it, of course. He was old enough to be…well, fifteen years her senior.

A decade and a half.

Good grief, he'd been learning to drive when she was born! But did that stop him from riding to her rescue like a knight of old? Nooo.

Yet what else could he have done? He had come down the stairs intending to turn to the back of the building and walk right out into the alley where, as usual, he had parked his SUV. Then he'd caught sight of Ellie and that man through the front glass. Within moments, Asher had realized that the idiot had put his hands on her and that she was not particularly welcoming the familiarity. He hadn't really thought at all after that. Before he'd even known what he intended to do, he was doing it.

"One of your 'first dates,' I assume?" Asher muttered.

"A first and *only* date," she answered.

"He seemed anxious for a repeat performance."

"But not for the reason you may think."

"Oh?"

"He wants your aunts to invest in one of his inventions."

Asher stopped short of the corner and looked down at her. "Inventions?"

"A backpack with an air bag." He blinked slowly at that. She made an expression somewhere between a grimace and a grin. "To guard against pedestrian accidents."

"Pedestrian accidents," he muttered, shaking his head. Glancing back over his shoulder, he ushered her forward once more. "Doesn't exactly take a hint, does he?"

"He's still there?"

"Afraid so."

Thankfully, the light changed before they reached the corner. Asher all but pushed her across the street, and they wound up in front of the door to her grandfather's pharmacy. The lettering on the front window read, "Monroe's Modern Pharmacy and Old-Fashioned Soda Fountain."

"Thank you," she said.

Nodding, he glanced back down the street, frowning. "Maybe I'd better have a word with our inventor."

She caught him by the arm before he could turn away. "Uh, why don't I treat you to a root beer float, instead. He'll leave after we go inside."

Asher lifted his eyebrows. "A root beer float? I

haven't had a root beer float since…actually, I'm not sure I've ever had a root beer float."

"Well, it's about time you did, then," she told him, pulling him through the door with her.

He went along because, really, what else was he going to do? Dig in his heels like a recalcitrant four-year-old?

Redolent of peppermint, the shop spread out in a straightforward manner, with a single cash register and short counter at the front perpendicular to the door. Rows of products ran horizontally through the center of the store, providing a clear line of vision from the glassed-in prescription counter at the back.

"Hey, sugar! Be with you in a minute," Kent Monroe's gravelly voice called out.

"It's okay, Grandpa," Ellie answered, tugging Asher toward the candy-striped counter along the far wall. "We're going to have a treat."

"Help yourselves."

It had been ages since Asher had parked himself on one of those small, round stools at the soda bar. He usually visited one of the specialty coffee shops on the square these days. Something about those red vinyl-covered seats edged in chrome and fixed atop a stationary metal pole made him feel silly. Still, he sat when Ellie motioned him to it. She rounded the corner and slid behind the counter.

"Now, let's see," she said, looking around her, "maybe you'd prefer something other than a float. Say, a cream fizz or a sarsaparilla?"

"Really?" he said, leaning his elbows on the counter. "A sarsaparilla? No, I don't think so."

"Well, then?"

"Maybe you'd better choose."

She smiled. "A float it is, but a very special one."

He watched doubtfully as she squirted a measure of dark syrup into a tall metal cup, added a firm scoop of vanilla ice cream, blended the ingredients and then divided the resulting sludge between two tall fluted goblets. She flooded the goblets with cola from one of the fountain taps, forming an impressive lather on each. Plucking two straws from a container, she shoved them into the goblets and carried both around the counter, where she took a seat next to Asher, facing backward.

"A cappuccino root beer float," she announced, plunking his down in front of him. Hanging her elbow on the counter, she took a long pull on her straw then drawled in a thick, syrupy voice, "For the sophisticated palate."

Asher didn't know whether to be amused or wary. He took a careful sip and arched his eyebrows, surprised by the rich flavor. "Mmm, that's good."

"It is," she agreed, spinning around on the stool so that they faced the same direction, "and terribly addicting. I limit myself strictly to five a week."

He sputtered a chuckle around his straw. "You're kidding."

"I couldn't get through that door back there if I had five of these a week. A girl can dream, though, can't she?"

"Is that what you dream of?" Asher asked offhandedly, helping himself to a napkin from a dispenser.

"No, not really," she answered, suddenly serious. She stirred the drink with her straw, drawing languid circles in the thick foam. "I dream of what every woman dreams of. Husband, home, children. Romance."

"Romance," he echoed sourly, with a shake of his head. "Romance will wreck the other three, if you're not careful."

"Is that what happened to your marriage?" she asked softly. "She wanted romance to go along with the home and husband?"

That came surprisingly close to the truth—so close, in fact, that Asher heard himself say, "Life is not romance. It's a lot of hard work and, if you're very blessed, part pleasure."

"And that's it?"

"That's all I've ever had time for."

"But what about other things, like children?"

"We didn't get that far," he said tersely, "but I can't imagine that adding kids to the mix would make room for romance."

"I think your definition of romance is too narrow," she told him. "You're talking about grand gestures of the flowers-and-mood-music sort. Sometimes romance is just knowing that you'll be together at the end of the day. It's *wanting* to be together even when the demands of life necessarily separate you."

"According to her, the 'demands of life,' as you put it, was the only part that I was any good at."

"Maybe she wasn't any good at some of her parts, either."

"What makes you say that?" he asked, shooting Ellie a surprised look. "She seems to have done okay the second time around."

"Maybe she has more in common with her husband this time, or maybe he doesn't have to work as hard as most. A wife has to be supportive of a hardworking husband."

"Even if it means giving up what she wants and needs?"

"Why would it?"

"Maybe he just doesn't have time for her. What then?"

"Then he doesn't really care for her."

He stared at Ellie, his worst fear laid bare.

"Look," Ellie said, shifting closer and lowering her voice, "every couple has to learn to make time for each other. Sometimes, one or both has to give up something, but normally they do it through shared interests and goals."

Asher stared at his drink. He could have given up soccer. At the time, it had seemed like the only thing keeping him sane, the only way he could get through law school and come home to Samantha with anything less than a snarl on his face. When they'd been dating, Samantha had often come out to watch and cheer him on when he'd played, but after the wedding, she had lost interest and come to resent every moment that he'd spent playing. But he hadn't been willing to give it up. It had seemed unthinkable, frankly. What did that say about him as a person, let alone a husband?

"Do you still love her?" Ellie asked, watching him closely.

He wasn't entirely sure now that he had ever loved Samantha, but he simply shook his head and went with the short answer. "No."

"Then it's the failure that destroys you," Ellie surmised.

Astonished, Asher set his glass down with a plunk. He stared at her for a long moment, wondering just exactly what it was that he saw in her eyes. Understanding? Sadness? Wisdom? Hope? Something more, something from which he instinctively shied.

"I expect Mr. Inventor has gone on his way by now," he said, injecting just the right note of avuncular humor into his tone. "Gotta run." He took a last drag on his straw—the drink really was quite good—spun his stool and left, leaving her with a smile and a nod of thanks.

He didn't pretend that he wasn't running away, because he was. And he counted it among the wisest things he'd ever done.

*Lord, heal that man,* Ellie prayed, as Asher walked away. It wasn't as simple as a broken heart; she saw that now. The poor man had chosen the wrong woman, and he'd taken on the full blame for the failure of the marriage, but his ex had chosen wrong, too. It wasn't all his fault. Somehow, he had to learn to forgive and trust himself again. *Open his eyes, Lord,* she whispered in her heart, and then, because she couldn't stop herself, *Let him see what's right in front of him.*

Her grandfather trundled up to her. His footsteps were no longer as quick or sure as they had once been, and his belly strained against the buttons of his white lab coat, but he was still himself—a man with a huge, loving heart. She smiled in gratitude for all he was to her, all he'd taught her.

"Asher didn't stay long," he remarked.

"He's a busy man."

"The best ones are." She said nothing to that, just smiled. "Ready?" he asked.

She popped up off the stool. "Just let me wash these glasses first."

He squeezed in behind the counter and helped her.

Seconds later, they left the building together. Relieved to find that Lance had, indeed, gone away, she happily allowed her grandfather to escort her to her red truck. His old sedan was constantly being serviced or repaired, so she often gave him a ride to or from the shop.

Ten minutes later, Ellie turned her pickup between the thick brick pillars at the foot of the drive, passing by the wrought-iron gate with a tall golden *C* at its center. As she downshifted to make the slight incline, a sense of peace enveloped her. This wasn't home, and it didn't feel like home, but it did feel like sanctuary.

About halfway up the hill, the drive curved into a broad circle, with the graceful mansion standing at its apex. It was a beautiful old house, flanked by a rose arbor on the east and an enormous magnolia tree on the west. Everything about the place evoked a sense of permanence, continuity and hope.

Parking at the foot of the broad redbrick walkway, Ellie paused to silently thank God for the safety, comfort and peace that she and her grandfather had found in this place.

"It's a special house, isn't it?" Kent remarked. "It always has been a special place because the people in it are special. Funny how we imbue a place with our essence. I think that's why there is nothing sadder than an empty house." He shifted in his seat, looking at her. "Have you ever noticed how quickly an empty house deteriorates? You can sit there for decades and do little to nothing to maintain the place, and it will eventually fall down around your ears. But walk away, leave it empty, and it'll go to pot in a matter of months, weeks sometimes."

"I hope this house is never empty," she said.

"Not until Jesus comes again and makes all things new. And even then I hope there will be Chatams here."

It was a sweet thought, one that humbled her. How silly she was to try to handle every little problem herself when the God of Creation and the Savior of Souls was in charge. From now on, she decided, she would let Him handle things and confine her own involvement to prayer. If Dallas had done what Ellie had feared she had, Ellie didn't even want to know because she didn't want to lie, even if it meant protecting her well-meaning but foolish friend. Besides, Ellie could not change anything that had happened or convince Asher to give her grandfather and his aunt time to search their hearts for long-buried feelings. Only God could do that.

Besides, being in Asher's company awoke foolish dreams. Why embarrass herself and feed her foolishness? He was not the man who could give her what she wanted, needed and deserved. He didn't even believe himself capable of being a good husband, and didn't want to try.

Perhaps it wasn't even about Asher, though. Perhaps it was all about her.

Perhaps no man was right for her. Perhaps God intended her to remain single.

Better that than married to the wrong man.

It was only later, as she settled into her comfortable bed there in Chatam House, that a thought struck her. Asher had not always thought himself a poor candidate for marriage. Obviously he had wanted to marry at one time. Otherwise he would not have done so. No, it was just as she'd thought earlier. He had chosen the wrong woman, and that had changed his outlook entirely. Might the right woman change it once again?

*There you go,* she scolded herself, punching her pillow into a more comfortable shape, *asking for trouble. Imagining yourself with Asher will only set you up for disappointment.*

It would definitely be better to avoid the temptation of spinning dreams around Asher Chatam, which meant avoiding the man himself. God would bring the right man to her in His own good time. He had never failed to provide her with anything else, after all. She could trust Him for her own happiness, as well as her grandfather's.

It was past time that she acted like it.

"Asher, dear!" Hypatia tilted her head to receive his kiss on her cheek. "We weren't expecting to see you again so soon."

Glancing meaningfully at his sister on the settee next to their Aunt Magnolia in the front parlor of Chatam House, Asher fixed a smile in place. "Well, I was told that I could find my sister here." Run her to ground, more like.

She had dodged him repeatedly over the past twenty-four hours. He'd been forced to go by the elementary school where she taught, only to be told by a coworker of hers that she'd mentioned having dinner with her aunts. He'd decided to drop by Chatam House and corner her here. Besides, he wanted a chance to get the story from Garrett Willows, the aunties' gardener.

"You'll stay for dinner, of course," Magnolia stated, exactly as Asher expected.

"Oh, say you will," Hypatia urged before he could respond.

"Absolutely," he agreed, noticing his little sister's frown.

He had to judge for himself whether Dallas knew something that Ellie wasn't telling him about the fire at the Monroe house. After all, he could not in good conscience hand off the case to another attorney until he knew what he might be handing off.

He had determined in the midst of a long, restless night that he definitely had to shed the case. And Ellie. Even if it meant paying the costs himself, though he'd make sure no one ever realized that.

The whole idea smacked of skullduggery, but he just didn't see any other way to handle things since Ellie had made him that root beer cappuccino float and effectively laid bare his soul. He just needed enough information to make sure that he picked the right attorney to take over. Otherwise the aunts would carve out his heart with their dainty silver teaspoons.

That wasn't the only reason he needed to see Dallas, though. The matter of his sister's meddling had to be addressed.

"Dallas, dear, will you tell Hilda that we need an extra plate laid at the dinner table?" Hypatia asked sweetly.

"Sure." Leaping to her feet, Dallas tossed Asher a sour look, her short red curls bouncing.

As she left the room, he took her seat next to Magnolia, asking, "Where is everyone?"

Magnolia revealed that Odelia had taken a walk and the Monroes had gone back to their house to put out food for their cat. "They rarely come down until dinner is on the table, anyway," she said.

Asher felt a bit of relief. He wanted to judge their reactions to his last conversation with Ellie, but he didn't want to spend any more time with her than necessary.

"They try so hard not to impose," Hypatia told him softly.

"And Aunt Odelia? Is she well?"

"Well enough," Hypatia replied, glancing away.

"She's dieting," Mags hissed, her disapproval clear.

"You're kidding!" he blurted out.

"Won't even take a decent tea," Mags told him in a low tone of voice.

Asher frowned. Could it be because of Kent Monroe? He shook his head. A younger woman might seek to lose weight in order to impress a man, but a woman of Odelia's age? He couldn't believe it. On the other hand, she had grown rather round in the past few years. Perhaps it was a simple matter of ill-fitting clothes.

He suddenly remembered an old photograph of Odelia in a strapless ball gown. Her chestnut hair swept up in an elegant style, diamonds at her earlobes and throat, she had worn a corsage tied about one wrist and a beaming smile. Beside her, Hypatia might have traded places with the queen of England, while Mags had resembled nothing so much as a farm girl in her mother's Sunday best. Odelia, however, could have been a movie star to rival the likes of Ginger Rogers.

Perhaps having a young woman in the house—a woman as lovely as Ellie Monroe—had inspired Odelia to reclaim her figure.

He cleared his throat and tried to get his thoughts off Ellie, asking, "Is Garrett Willows around?"

Magnolia raised her eyebrows at him. "I expect he's in the greenhouse. Why do you ask?"

Asher served up as much truth as he was willing to

at this point. "I've never had the opportunity to talk to him. Just thought we might be able to connect over the dinner table."

"Oh, no, dear. Garrett doesn't eat with us very often now that his sister has moved out of the house," Hypatia told him.

"I don't know why," Mags groused. "The boy's not just staff now. He's practically family!"

"Young men need time to themselves," Hypatia told her.

Mags merely *humphed* at that. Her fondness for the fellow spoke well of him, but Asher believed in forming his own opinions, and Willows had more than the usual number of variables to assess. He forgot for the moment that Willows and the Monroes would soon be someone else's problem.

Hypatia changed the subject to Asher's parents, and they chatted about his father's plans to retire at last from his practice. Surgery, Asher pointed out, was a complex matter requiring constant reeducation, and his dad had just turned sixty-nine. At sixty-one, his mother intended to continue seeing pediatric patients several days a week, but she had recently taken on a much younger partner.

"Do you think they'll move home when your mother fully retires?" Hypatia asked hopefully.

Asher smiled. "I wouldn't count on it."

His parents had lived in Waco for thirty years. Though their ties to Buffalo Creek were strong, he didn't see them moving back here anytime soon. His mother had hinted that the advent of grandchildren in their lives could change that, but Asher had told her in no uncertain terms to look to his younger siblings, none of whom were married yet. Phillip, thirty-one, lived in Seattle and pretty much kept to himself, answering phone messages with texts and the occasional email, often weeks after the fact. No one was even entirely sure what he did for a living, though one thing was certain: like the rest of the siblings, it was not connected to the field of medicine. Petra, at twenty-five, still lived with their parents while finishing her master's degree in hotel management. That left Dallas, who was in her second year of teaching—and her twenty-third year of meddling, which was why the Monroes were now ensconced in Chatam House and disrupting his life.

In fact, if Dallas had not purposefully set out to make the acquaintance of Kent Monroe's granddaughter, she would not even be friends with Ellie and he would have been spared the inconvenience of…an unwanted attraction. Dallas had announced her intention to introduce herself to the Monroes on the very day that she had first arrived on campus at Buffalo Creek Bible College. As her much older brother, Asher had always taken a rather parental role with Dallas, so he hadn't hesitated to caution his sister not to interfere in something that did not concern her, but as usual she had not listened.

Over time, Asher had relaxed about the situation somewhat. For one thing, she and Ellie seemed to have developed a genuine friendship. For another, Dallas obviously had not made much progress in her campaign to rekindle a romance that had been dead for nearly half a century. He'd known from the beginning that Dallas's romantic obsession with their aunt's failed engagement was going to prove catastrophic in the end; he just hadn't anticipated that the catastrophe would somehow involve him.

Laughter suddenly echoed in the foyer. Recognition shivered through Asher. Though he was quite certain that he had never heard Ellie laugh like that, he knew it was her. He recognized her on a visceral level, as if some part of her had invaded his subconscious. Staying where he was took every iota of his willpower. But he didn't know if his impulse was to run away—or run toward her.

## Chapter Five

"You make fun," Kent Monroe said, trudging into the parlor, "but I've always wanted a tree house, and now seems a good time to go for it."

"I don't think Grandmother's French Empire bedroom suite will fit up in a tree," Ellie noted wryly, following behind him.

Kent stopped in his tracks, sighed dramatically and slumped his shoulders. "Well, so much for that. Another dream bites the dust."

Coming up beside him, Ellie looped her arms about his shoulders, counseling softly, "Never give up your dreams, Grandpa. It's not too late."

Kent smiled, patted her forearm and quoted, "Where there's life, there's hope."

"Exactly."

A throat cleared, and Ellie looked around just as Asher rose to his feet. Kent smiled and boomed a hearty welcome, but Ellie's first feeling was dismay. How was she to keep her distance from Asher when he could pop up at Chatam House at any moment? She quickly smoothed her features and nodded in greeting.

"Any news?" Kent asked of Asher.

"Uh, no. Sorry. I'm simply here to have dinner with my aunts."

"I thought you wanted to speak to Dallas," Mags said.

"That, too." He looked at Ellie. She quickly glanced away. Kent sent her toward an armless side chair before plodding over to drop down into the empty armchair next to the settee.

"And how is your pet?" Hypatia asked him as soon as he was seated.

Asher waited until Ellie sat before resuming his own seat. She smoothed the skirt of the royal blue mini-dress that she wore over matching leggings and flat ankle boots.

"Still haven't seen old Curly," Kent said, "but at least he's eating."

"Or something is," Ellie put in. "We really have no way of knowing if it's the cat or something else. We just put out the feed, and it disappears."

"An opossum could be eating it," Magnolia commented, "or a skunk. "

"Mice even, maybe," Ellie said. "We keep the cat food bag on the enclosed mud porch, and something has torn a hole in it."

"Guess I'll have to do a thorough search for my poor old tom," Kent said. "He must be traumatized by all that's happened, and it can't help that we're not around for him to come home to."

Ellie sent her grandfather a sympathetic smile. "I'm sure he's fine. He always did like to roam, you know."

Kent nodded. Dallas appeared in the wide doorway

between the foyer and the parlor just then, announcing, "Hilda says to come to the table."

"Oh, but Odelia isn't here," Kent protested, glancing around the room as if making certain that he hadn't missed her.

"Yes, she is," Dallas said, flashing a smile at him. "She's waiting in the dining room."

Kent hauled himself to his feet and swiftly lumbered into the foyer. Dallas stepped aside to let him pass, targeting Asher with a self-satisfied look. He flashed her an irritated glance, then smoothly came to his feet as Ellie and his aunts did. Ellie brushed her hands over her skirt and swiftly moved forward. It was going to be an interesting evening. She meant to keep her head down and her mouth shut; she could only hope that Dallas would do the same.

Asher stepped toward the door, hot on Ellie's heels, only to feel a hand catch at his elbow. He looked down to find Magnolia gazing up at him, her gray braid lying upon her shoulder and brushing against the notched collar of her shirtwaist dress. Of course. How could he have forgotten, as Kent obviously had, that his very proper aunts would expect a gentleman to provide them escort to the table?

Dutifully, he offered one arm to her and the other to Hypatia. Smiling graciously, his dear old aunties flanked him, and they began a stately progression. Ahead of them, Ellie and Dallas walked close together, their heads bent in quiet conversation. As they moved toward the dining room, Asher couldn't help comparing his sister and her friend.

Dallas looked boyish in her slender jeans and skinny

black turtleneck sweater, while Ellie…well, even in her heyday Ginger Rogers had had nothing on Ellie Monroe.

Asher admitted to himself that he might have misstepped by coming here like this. He'd had little opportunity to speak with his sister in private thus far, and Garrett Willows seemed likewise unavailable, so all he'd really accomplished by getting himself invited to dinner was to throw himself into company with Ellie Monroe, which was the last thing he should have been doing.

Determined afresh to concentrate on the matter at hand, he glanced down at his aunties, only to find them sharing a knowing look. Asher felt his face heat. He had just been caught staring at Ellie Monroe. And for that he was going to rip his little sister to shreds. Just as soon as he managed to corner her. If she had just cooperated…but then, when had Dallas ever? Well, he could be stubborn, too.

Biding his time throughout dinner, Asher struggled to observe his sister and ignore Ellie, with little success. Though she sat on the opposite side of the long table and several seats farther down than he did, Asher couldn't help noticing the gusto with which Ellie enjoyed her meal. And the way she constantly smiled. At everyone but him. That rankled more than it should have, and despite his better judgment he found himself purposefully engaging her.

"So, how did you find the odor at the house today, Ellie? Still overpowering?"

"We didn't go into the house itself," she reported with a frown. "The firemen blocked the doors."

"Though what the holdup is on getting the blocks

taken down, I can't imagine," Kent put in from his seat at the foot of the table. "Ah, well, makes little difference. It's not like anything is going to change until the insurance company ponies up." Smiling, he looked to Odelia as if expecting confirmation of his assessment. Odelia, however, was staring at her plate with a woebegone expression.

Troubled by what her sisters had told him earlier, Asher asked, "Don't you like the pasta, Aunt Odelia?"

She looked up in surprise. "What?"

"You're not eating," he pointed out. "Is the pasta not to your liking?"

"Of course it is," she said, giving him that sweet smile before quickly forking a bite into her mouth. "Delicious."

"It is," Asher agreed. "One of Hilda's best dishes, which is saying something." He meant to let the matter end there, but instead he heard himself saying, "Ellie certainly likes it."

She instantly dropped her fork, her face coloring. Too late, he realized how that must have sounded, as if he thought she was eating too much. And he couldn't think of a way to smooth it over. Everything that came to mind would only make it worse.

*I don't think you're a pig.*

*I like a woman with a hearty appetite.*

*You look great to me, so don't even think about going on a diet.*

Ellie turned to Hypatia, saying quietly, "Hilda is an excellent cook."

"We're very blessed to have her," Hypatia agreed.

"This is so good that I'm quite full already," Ellie went on softly, "so if you'll excuse me…"

"Oh, of course, dear." Hypatia smiled politely then glanced at Asher.

Ellie pushed her chair away from the table, stood and left the room.

Obviously, his thoughtless comment had driven her away. Mortified, Asher bent his head and continued to eat, only to discover that his own appetite had gone with her. He put down his fork and picked up his glass of iced tea, telling himself that he should be glad she'd left the room. But he didn't feel that way at all. Frustrated, he fought not to follow Ellie, bouncing his knee beneath the table, an old habit he'd thought mastered long ago.

Dallas stood next, saying, "No dessert for me, either. I'll just pop into the kitchen and thank Hilda before I head out." She started off but Magnolia hailed her.

"Dallas, dear, would you mind running out to the greenhouse? If Garrett is still there, tell him to stop what he's doing and come in to dinner."

Dallas smiled. "I'll see to it."

Doubly frustrated now, Asher once more watched Dallas leave on an errand for his aunties, while Magnolia muttered about Garrett working too hard and being stubborn. Quickly, Asher, too, excused himself.

"Isn't anyone staying for dessert?" Hypatia asked in an exasperated tone.

"Maybe I'll have some later," Asher told her with an apologetic smile.

As he made for the door, Asher heard Kent declare that he was looking forward to dessert. Asher didn't linger to hear more. Instead, he hurried after his sister, down the hall and into the sunroom at the back of the house. Weaving his way through the wicker furnishings, he let himself out the French doors onto the patio.

The greenhouse stood in the distance. The glass-paned walls of the sizable structure, though lit from inside, were fogged. Still, he could see a shadowy figure moving about at the rear of the building.

Asher sprinted across the yard, dodging mulched flowerbeds devoid of blossoms and the occasional strategically placed bench. The cold of winter had yielded to a gradual warming in past days, inspiring Asher to leave his coat in his office. The evenings remained crisp, however, leaving him grateful for the lack of wind and even the insufficient weight of his suit jacket.

Before he could reach the greenhouse door, a tall, muscular man stepped out. Wearing comfortable jeans, heavy work boots and a dark T-shirt under a denim jacket, he brushed something from his coal-black hair, hunched his shoulders and started toward the carriage house behind the mansion where the staff—Chester and his wife, Hilda, her sister, Carol, and the gardener—lived. This, then, had to be the latter.

"Willows, is it?" Asher said, picking up his speed and putting out his hand.

The man stopped, his expression inscrutable in the deep shadows of night. "And you are?" He kept his hands in his jacket pocket.

"Asher Chatam. Nephew."

Willows withdrew a hand from a pocket and offered it for a shake, saying, "The lawyer." The tone of his voice made it clear what he thought of that particular breed, so Asher didn't make polite conversation but instead got straight to the point.

"I have some questions about the fire at the Monroe house and your involvement in it."

The hand went back into the pocket. "Didn't have

any involvement in the fire. I was riding down the street on my motorcycle when this redhead in a jogging suit dashed out in front of me, waving her arms like a crazy woman. I managed not to run her down. She pointed out the fire, I phoned 911 and, since she said no one was inside, waited until they got there and put the thing out. Whole thing didn't take twenty minutes. Then, when I realized she was a Chatam, I gave her a ride to the storage unit. She stayed with the Monroes. I came back here. Then later, they all wound up here. No surprise in that, I guess. Every stray in town seems to wind up here sooner or later. Myself included. Most of this is in my statement to the authorities, by the way."

Asher frowned, uncertain whether he liked or trusted this fellow. He seemed awfully flip for a convicted felon on parole. Everyone in town knew the story of how he'd gone to prison for beating his stepfather, who by all accounts had been a brutal man and murdered Garrett's mother. No one in the family had been especially pleased when Magnolia had hired Garrett. Deciding to ignore that last statement, Asher went back to the beginning.

"So you were just riding down Charter Street, on your way where exactly?"

He felt, rather than saw, the fellow's smirk. "Church."

*On Thursday?* Asher thought. The fire had happened on the first Thursday in February. "Which church?"

"Downtown Bible. Same as you, I imagine, though I haven't seen you, not at the late service and not at the monthly men's Bible study."

Asher tried not to let his irritation show. "And you're a regular attendee of that Bible study, are you?"

"Not yet. It just started in January, and I missed February. For obvious reasons."

"How long have you known the Monroes?"

"Since the night of the fire."

"And Dallas?"

"Since the night of the fire."

"But you stopped for her anyway?"

"It was that or run over her. I almost laid down the bike as it was."

"So you're just the Good Samaritan in all this?"

Willows said nothing to that, just stood there, a big, silent shadow in the dark. Asher's frown deepened. They stood about the same height, but the other man's bulk made him seem larger, tougher—and somehow not particularly trustworthy. Still, his story pretty much jibed with Ellie's. So far. Cold prickled Asher's skin, but he'd have turned into a human Popsicle before he'd have let on.

"Okay. Thanks. I know where to find you if I have any more questions."

Willows nodded but before he started off again, Asher jerked his head toward the greenhouse. "My sister in there?"

"Your sister?"

"Dallas."

That came as an obvious surprise to the man. He took a half step back, his hands sinking farther into his pockets. "No. Ellie is, though."

It was Asher's turn to be surprised. "I thought my sister was supposed to be coming out here to remind you that it's time to eat."

"Don't know about that," Willows said, walking off

toward the carriage house, "but like I told Ellie, I'll eat as soon as I wash up."

Asher stood staring at the door to the greenhouse. He warred with himself, torn between running after Dallas, who had obviously sent Ellie out here in her place, and finding out just how well Ellie Monroe had gotten to know Garrett Willows since coming to Chatam House. Or maybe they were both lying and they had known each other for some time—long enough to plan an arson, say. Asher didn't really believe that. Then again, he didn't know what he believed anymore.

Striding forward, he wrenched open the door. Moist, welcome warmth flowed over him. Rows of rough wooden tables stacked with tiered shelves of potted plants in various stages of bloom lined both long walls. Larger plants, some that would decorate the patio in more sultry weather, filled the interior of the long, narrow building, including a number of small trees that seemed about to outgrow their space.

Asher came to a space enclosed in heavy plastic sheeting, split down the middle to allow access. Slipping through, he glanced around at tables laden with tiny pots of seedlings basking beneath the benevolent light of long, hooded lamps. A figure turned from a shadowy corner, a figure he would know anywhere.

"Ellie."

At the same time she asked, "Garrett?"

"Where's Dallas?" he asked, not bothering to correct her because her recoil at the sound of his voice had signaled her recognition.

"She said she had to leave and asked me to deliver a message to Garrett for Magnolia."

Asher snorted at that. "Did you tell her that I know

about your little plot to embroil my aunt in a romance with your grandfather?"

"Yes, of course."

Of course. So, Dallas knew that the jig was up, and she was making herself scarce to avoid a scolding. No doubt she was gone by now. Pushing back the sides of his jacket, he parked his hands at his hips and shook his head.

Well, this need not be a wasted opportunity. In this private setting, he could tell Ellie that he had decided to hand off the case. He could say that he didn't have time to give the matter the attention that it needed or even that another attorney had more experience with insurance companies, which would be true as soon as he found someone like that.

A little voice inside his head asked if he really wanted to hand off the case, and he had to admit that he did not. What he really wanted was to get to the bottom of this situation and see it resolved happily for all involved. Looking at Ellie standing there in the soft light of those heat lamps, he wondered if that was even possible, especially for him. Whatever happened, no matter how this turned out, he was going to come away from this with a sense of discontent.

He didn't precisely know why that was so. He only knew that nothing would ever quite be the same again.

Fidgeting nervously, Ellie considered her options. She had promised herself that she would avoid Asher. He had to know that she admired him, but he obviously did not return the sentiment. He'd implied, in fact, that she was an overeater, and he'd done it in the same tone that she'd heard him take with Dallas—a light, brotherly voice seasoned with a pinch of patronization and a dash of criticism, not that she could blame him. She was a little round, and she did enjoy a good meal. Since coming to Chatam House, she'd enjoyed far too many of them, in fact, and he had obviously noticed.

"I'm sorry if I upset you earlier. I didn't mean to imply...that is, I wouldn't want you to think that I think you're too—"

"It's all right. I know I'm chunky."

He looked up sharply. "You're not chunky. You're..."

She wasn't about to argue the point. "Okay, I'm too curvy then."

"No, Ellie, you're perfect. That is, your shape is perfect. Not that you aren't personally. I—I mean, I wouldn't know that, but I can see..." He winced, lifting a hand to the back of his neck.

Swamped with delight, Ellie stood there with her mouth open for several seconds.

He looked up at the glass ceiling. "Surely," he said through his teeth, "I don't have to tell you that you're very attractive."

"Really?"

Sighing, he bent his head and pressed the fingertips of his left hand to the space between his eyes, as if his head hurt.

"Are you okay?" she asked after a moment, concerned even though she couldn't seem to stop smiling.

"Fine," he croaked. "I'm fine." He waved his hand without looking at her, turned and said, "I should be going."

"Wait." Emboldened by his compliment, she stepped forward to lay a hand upon his arm. He froze. "I should apologize to you, too."

He finally looked at her. "For what?"

"Yesterday. I snapped at you."

"Well, I essentially cross-examined you."

She blinked. "That's what you do, cross-examine people. That's to be expected, but I called you cold and hard-hearted."

"Believe me, I've been called worse," he said with a lopsided smile.

She frowned, hating to think of him being called ugly names, but then she remembered something more important. Looking deeply into his eyes, she lifted her free hand to his shoulder. "Have you thought about what I said?"

"Uh…"

"You can't give up!" she exclaimed.

He shook his head as if confused. "Give up on what?"

"Romance! Love." He groaned, but she barreled on, "God is just waiting to heal your broken heart, and I know that love is out there for you. No one understands better than I do how difficult it is to have faith about this. I've been looking for the right guy my whole life, with zero results thus far. But I know that God will bring him to me when He's ready, when I'm ready."

He rolled his eyes, frowning. "You're too young to even be thinking about settling down—"

"This isn't about me. It's about you. Don't you want children?"

"I—"

"You must. Think what a wonderful father you'd be."

His brows drew together in a pained expression. "You don't know that."

"Yes, I do. Why wouldn't you be?"

He shook his head. "You have to be a good husband

before you can be a good father, and I'm not husband material."

"Don't be silly!"

"Listen, I tried marriage, and I wasn't any good at it."

"Then she wasn't the right woman for you," Ellie insisted. "You just need the right woman."

He stared at her for so long that she began to feel foolish. When his gaze dropped to her lips, her heart started to thunder. For one insane moment, she thought he was about to kiss her. She tilted her head and was on the very verge of going up on tiptoe when the door to the greenhouse thumped open.

Asher jerked back as if she'd suddenly burst into flame, shock contorting his face.

She had been right in what she'd said. All he needed was the right woman.

But that woman was not—and could never be—her.

## Chapter Six

Following quietly as Asher slid through the heavy plastic sheet dividing the building, Ellie tried to quell her disappointment. This was precisely why she should avoid him. When she was around the man, she imagined all sorts of improbable scenarios! He was hazardous to her sanity, and now that she'd said her piece, she would definitely keep her distance.

That shouldn't be too difficult after tonight. She was sure he'd want to avoid her now for fear that she'd read too much into his compliment. She understood now, of course, that it was just part and parcel of his apology.

Still, she would treasure his words.

"That's Odelia," Asher muttered, parting the branches of a small tree. He angled his shoulders as if about to push through the potted forest toward his aunt, but just then the door opened again and Kent came inside.

Quickly, Ellie grabbed Asher by the arm and tugged him back. Maybe her time hadn't come yet, but she believed with all her heart that her grandfather's had.

When Asher looked at her, confused, she lifted a finger to her lips.

"Are you all right, Odelia? You don't seem well."

Odelia twittered, but the laughter sounded forced to Ellie's ears. "Thank you for asking, but I'm fine. Just needed a breath of fresh air."

"You came out without your coat," he pointed out.

"Oh, but it's wonderfully warm in here, don't you think?"

"I suppose it is."

She laughed again, that nervous, birdlike twitter that could not have sounded more uncomfortable. Kent sighed audibly.

"Odelia," he said, "I wouldn't willingly cause you a single moment of distress. Perhaps Ellie and I should find somewhere else to go."

"Don't be silly!" Odelia retorted, much too brightly. "Why would your being here distress me? I'm just feeling my age this winter."

"Pish-posh," Kent refuted heartily. "You are ageless, my dear, as beautiful, vivacious and adorable as ever."

"Oh!" Odelia squeaked. "Oh, my!" With that, she fled the greenhouse.

Kent sighed once more. Ellie gently parted the limbs in time to see him follow Odelia out, sadly shaking his head. She turned at once to Asher.

"See? There's still something between them."

"That's not how it seems to me. He may be carrying a torch for her, but she obviously wants nothing to do with him," he said.

"Of course she does! How could she not?"

Asher folded his arms. "Look, I'm sure your grandfather's a great guy, but Odelia declined to marry him once, and she doesn't seem too keen on a flirt—"

"My grandpa's not a flirt!" Ellie protested, insulted on his behalf.

Asher pinched the bridge of his nose. "Just once, could you not interrupt?"

Ellie recoiled. "I didn't realize that I was. I don't usually."

"Not only do you interrupt, you finish other people's sentences."

Wounded, Ellie concentrated on breathing steadily. Blinking her eyelashes to keep the tears at bay, she gulped. "I—I never mean to do that, and it's only when y-you're around." Suddenly realizing what she'd just said, she couldn't bear another moment in his presence. "Excuse me," she whispered, plowing through the trees toward the door.

"Ellie!" he called, crashing behind her.

She pushed through the door and ran for the house, barely feeling the sting of the February chill. The door of the greenhouse slammed but she didn't slow or look back.

"Ellie!" he called again. Then, just as she reached the house, he muttered. "Oh, what's the use? I'm wasting my time."

The words carried clearly over the cold night air. Wasting his time. He thought her a waste of time.

Ellie pulled open the French door and rushed into the sunroom. Dashing her hands across her eyes, she pulled herself together, lifted her chin and crossed the room to step into the hallway, which was mercifully empty. Despite her best efforts, however, tears were rolling from her eyes by the time she reached the privacy of her room.

"Of all the idiotic, ill-advised, inept…" Asher grit his teeth against further invective, mentally kicking himself as he strode around the great house. He'd be hanged if he'd follow her inside and try to apologize—again— in front of his aunts. Not after almost kissing the girl!

What on earth had possessed him to stay in that shadowy, private space with her anyway? He couldn't even make a sensible, decent apology when she was around.

*Surely, I don't have to tell you that you're very attractive.*

Surely, he should have his head examined for saying such a thing! Except, she honestly hadn't seemed to know.

What was that about anyway? Hadn't any of those clods she'd dated told her?

He picked up his pace, only to nearly mow down someone hiding in the shadows, someone small and plump and wearing too much flowery perfume.

"Aunt Odelia," he gasped, clasping his arms about her to steady her.

"Oh. Asher," she said, trying to hide her sniffling.

"What are you doing out here?" he asked.

"J-just taking a walk," she warbled.

But they both knew it was too cold for a walk. That was why she'd gone to the greenhouse to begin with.

"What's wrong?" he asked.

"What m-makes you think there's anything wr-wrong?"

"You're crying!" he exclaimed. "Is this about the

Monroes? If it is, I'll have them out of here by dark tomorrow."

"No!" Odelia gasped, her hands clamping onto his forearm. "You mustn't!"

"But if Mr. Monroe's presence here is—"

"Don't you see?" she wailed. "This may be all I ever have! When he goes again, he may never come back."

Asher's jaw dropped. Then she shivered, and he quickly slipped out of his suit coat to drape it about her shoulders. As she murmured thanks, he turned her and walked her toward the front of the house. Gathering his thoughts, he ushered her across the thick brown cushion of grass to the redbrick walkway, then turned her toward the front porch.

"Let me get this straight," he said, climbing the few steps beside her. They walked to the trio of wrought-iron chairs placed to one side of the bright yellow door. With their cushions stored away for the winter, the chairs were stiff and cold, but Odelia sank right down onto the nearest one. Asher took the chair beside her, clasping her frail hand in his. "You don't want the Monroes to leave?"

She shook her head then nodded and finally sighed. "That's right. I don't want them to leave."

"Especially not Kent Monroe," Asher probed gently.

She parked her elbow on the arm of the chair and dropped her forehead into her palm. "I never stopped caring for him, you know. I just couldn't leave my sisters." She looked up at him then with wide, liquid eyes, adding woefully, "No matter how handsome and charming he is."

*Good grief,* Asher thought, dumbfounded. *Ellie and Dallas are right.*

"You won't tell, will you?" Odelia asked urgently. "I know he doesn't feel the same way, and I don't want my sisters to think they're responsible for anything. Because I chose them, I mean."

"I won't tell," Asher promised. Still, he hated to see his sweet auntie so bereft. "But what makes you think he doesn't feel the same?"

"Well, he married, didn't he?"

Surely, she hadn't expected the man to pine for fifty years. On the other hand, perhaps she had. And perhaps he did. "He seems pretty smitten to me," Asher muttered beneath his breath.

"Oh, no," Odelia refuted firmly. "That's just his way. So charming."

Asher opened his mouth to ask what she meant by that, but then he thought of the unanswered questions about the fire. Odelia didn't deserve to get caught up in that. Besides, what were the chances that anything would come of this? The Monroes would eventually move out and the aunties would go on as always. Wouldn't they? Patting her hand, he mumbled, "I'm sure it'll all work out."

"Yes, of course," she agreed, nodding her head decisively. "God will take care of everything in time. In truth, I'm grateful to Him. I never thought to have these weeks, you know."

Asher didn't know what to say to that. A chill raced across his shoulders then, and he rose, drawing his aunt up with him. "It's too cold for you out here. I want you to go inside and ask for a nice hot cup of tea."

Odelia smiled. "Excellent idea. You always know what's best to do, dear."

He wished. Her confidence in him humbled him,

however. He walked her to the door, received his coat, kissed her cheek and saw her inside before turning toward his SUV, wishing heartily that he had never come here this evening.

How had he let himself get dragged into this mess? Henceforth, he decided, he would limit his involvement to pressuring the insurance company and keep his distance from Chatam House and the Monroes. With the spring soccer season about to start, that shouldn't be too difficult, since his time would be at a premium.

Why that thought didn't comfort him, he didn't even want to know. Meanwhile, he would ask his cousin Chandler about Garrett Willows and get a better read on the fellow that way. Beyond that, he didn't know what else to do.

*Poor Odelia,* he thought. She was deluded about not one but two men—Kent Monroe and him.

Why, Asher wondered, gripping his cell phone almost hard enough to crush it, had he thought that his cousin Chandler would be impartial when it came to Garrett Willows? The man was Chandler's brother-in-law, for pity's sake. Of course he would have only good things to say about his wife's brother.

Chandler had quite a bit to say about Kent Monroe and Ellie, too. Had Asher realized how well Chandler knew them, he'd have been more careful about his own comments, but no, he'd had to shoot off his mouth about Ellie's ridiculous romanticism. At least he had enough sense to keep mum about the scheme to get Odelia and Kent together, but that didn't keep Chandler from laughing at the notion that either of the Monroes or Garrett Willows might have had anything to do with the fire, and wondering aloud if Asher had more than a "professional" interest in Ellie.

"The girl is fifteen years younger than me!" Asher protested.

"So what?" Chandler retorted. "You're both adults."

"Not to mention," Asher ground out, "that we're total opposites."

"You know what they say about opposites attracting."

"Plus, she's a client," Asher pointed out incredulously.

"You're entirely too rigid about that stuff," Chandler chided. "You need to loosen up. Smiling Ellie might be good for you."

"Smiling Ellie?"

"Sure. Haven't you noticed? She's always smiling. Kent, too. It's one of the things I like best about them."

*Always smiling,* Asher thought sourly, pinching the bridge of his nose, *except around me.* That might have to do with the fact that he continually found ways to insult her.

He wasn't usually so ham-handed with people. He'd walked that fine line for years, the line between probing and speculating, implying and accusing. Yet with Ellie he always seemed to say the wrong thing. Shame dogging him, he remembered the look in her eyes before she'd run away the night before. He should have followed her, but how could he when he obviously couldn't trust himself around her? Really, he had no choice but to stay away.

He changed the subject to Chandler's family and listened to Chandler gush happily about the joys of marriage and fatherhood. Though he was glad to know that his cousin was so happy, the conversation did nothing to help Asher with the Monroe case. He felt a bit depressed when the call finally ended.

*What a perfect waste of a Wednesday afternoon,* Asher thought in disgust. He pulled his office door closed behind him as went out, pausing only to lock up. The weather had turned unseasonably warm, with temperatures rising into the sixties. A good day for soccer, then, even if not for him.

Today was the deadline for coaching assignments, which meant that he would have to disappoint at least one team. He didn't look forward to telling a group of eager first graders that they didn't have the adult volunteers or players to qualify for competition, but he really had no choice. Rules were rules, after all, and while they might yet recruit enough players to field a team, the team couldn't play without a qualified coach, no matter how much they or he might wish otherwise.

Ten minutes later, he parked his SUV, shrugged off his suit jacket and surveyed the athletic field. Green was beginning to sprout in the carpet of winter-brown grass.

Three teams were milling around in front of three different goals. A few parents in lawn chairs had taken up seats on the sidelines. He recognized two coaches, one of whom balanced a soccer ball against one hip. The other team was scattered, with kids running around flinging dirt and grass clippings at one another while a blonde woman in jeans and a brown jacket sat watching from a rough bench, a bright orange cooler on the ground beside her. This, he assumed, was Ilene Riddle, the team mother who had vowed to find a coach, without success, apparently. They had spoken on the telephone but had not yet met.

As Asher strode toward her, he pulled his black referee's cap from his rear pocket and fitted it to his head.

Only the letters "BCYSA" emblazoned on the front in yellow-gold letters, the acronym for Buffalo Creek Youth Soccer Association, set him apart from the other referees, who wore plain black. The blonde woman turned her head as he drew near, and he put out his hand as he heard a vehicle pull into the graveled parking area behind him.

"Ms. Riddle?"

"Yes."

"Asher Chatam, soccer commissioner."

She hopped to her feet and slid her hand into his, her white-tipped nails lightly scoring his wrist. "Nice to meet you." They shook before he parked his hands at his waist.

"I see that you haven't found a coach."

"Oh, we have."

Asher lifted his brows. "Really? That's good news. Where is he?"

"She," Ilene Riddle corrected, pointing, "is right there."

Asher turned. And couldn't believe his eyes.

Ellie Monroe closed the door of a pickup driven by her grandfather. Wearing pink shorts and an overlarge, black, long-sleeved T-shirt, she had pulled back her curly hair in a short, jaunty ponytail. Waving goodbye to her grandfather, she turned toward the field and started forward at a jog, only to falter when she met his gaze.

"Asher?" she asked, coming to stop before him. "What are you doing here?"

Try as he might, he could not help but admire those violet eyes again. "You're the coach?"

Nodding, she answered, "Yes, but why are you here?"

"I'm the commissioner," he said, not sure whether to laugh or yell in frustration.

She gawked for a moment, then threw out her hands. "Dallas mentioned that you played soccer in college, but I had no idea you were still involved in the game."

He'd hardly viewed what he was doing as being "involved in the game." It wasn't the way he'd hoped to be involved, anyway, but that was beside the point. Her involvement was the issue here. "Have you ever played?"

"Fourteen seasons," she told him proudly, "from the time I was four years old straight through high school."

*Well, that's just wonderful,* he thought sardonically, wanting to tear out his hair. How was he supposed to keep his distance from her now? Desperate, he began shooting questions at her, testing her acumen. She didn't miss a beat. Her violet eyes sparkled so brightly that Asher had to look away. When she started arguing for the Dutch Model, which focuses on foot drills, he all but gave up, despite his own conviction that the physical education class mode worked best for young children who didn't take instruction particularly well or possess sufficient dexterity for skill-based coaching.

"That doesn't mean it shouldn't be fun, of course," she babbled on enthusiastically, "and I've got some ideas about that, too."

"You'll have to pass a background check," he growled, already resigned to the fact his plans to stay away from her had failed, plain and simple.

"I'm a schoolteacher," she reminded him cheerfully.

"I've already passed a background check. It's an unfortunate necessity for anyone who works with children."

"The time commitment is significant," he ground out.

"Nineteen more practices and nine games over ten weeks," she acknowledged with a dismissive wave of one hand.

"You understand that the team could still be disbanded if you don't meet the league minimum of nine players within the next week?"

"I've put the word out at school that we're looking for kids who want to play."

Asher sighed. "I'll get the forms you need to sign."

"Great!"

"Great," he muttered, trudging toward his vehicle for his clipboard and papers.

Ellie called together her team and introduced herself, though most already knew her—and, judging by the hugs she got from her players, liked her.

She put them in two facing rows and started them kicking balls to each other up and down the line. They missed more than they connected, but they kept at it even while she stepped aside to look over and sign the forms.

"I'll leave a few recruitment forms with Ms. Riddle, but you can download and print others if you need—"

"I already have," she told him cheerfully.

He slid the forms beneath the spring clip, feeling that she had somehow gotten a step ahead of him. "I'll get a copy of your background check from the school and make sure it doesn't need updating. There's a meeting on Saturday morning that you are required to—"

"Just tell me when and where."

He grit his teeth and forced out the words. "Nine. My house."

She smiled. "Can I bring anything? Doughnuts, maybe?"

He stared at her stupidly. It had never occurred to him to serve anything more than coffee at these meetings.

A child shrieked with laughter, and Ellie glanced over her shoulder, saying, "I'd better get back to the team." She turned away, calling, "See you Saturday."

"Saturday," he acknowledged.

The first of many in the coming weeks, apparently.

"Lord, help me," he whispered fervently.

Ellie's racing heart made her feel slightly light-headed. The thought that Ash was the soccer commissioner circled round and round inside her mind even as she went through the motions of drilling the kids. What did it mean? She had prayed and prayed about conquering these inconvenient feelings that she had for him, and avoiding his company had seemed the natural first step, but that idea had just been shot out the window. Asher was the soccer commissioner!

Should she back out of coaching?

Nope, she decided. Not an option. She'd given her word. Besides, this had come to her out of the blue. God had to have a purpose for that.

She would not dare to hope that His purpose had anything to do with romance—not hers, anyway.

Ah. There it was. This obviously had to do with her grandfather and Odelia. And Asher himself, of course. What a joy it would be to bring her grandfather and

Odelia together! But to see Asher once more embrace the possibility of love and marriage…

She ignored the pang in her chest and lifted her thoughts Heavenward, falling back on a familiar phrase. *Holy Father, make me Your instrument. In this and in all else. I want what You want, and I trust You to bring me what is best, even if that's not what I imagine it to be. Change my heart to comply with Your will. And heal Ash's heart so that he might say the same. In the name of Christ Jesus, I pray.*

Feeling a little calmer, she did her best to concentrate on the task at hand, but it was difficult, since she had developed a kind of radar where Asher Chatam was concerned. She seemed to know just where he was at all times, even when he was across the field talking to another coach.

It was all she could do not to follow him with her eyes everywhere that he went.

# *Chapter Seven*

While Ellie went about drilling her players, Asher spoke to the other two coaches, reminding them of the mandatory Saturday meeting. He noted quite a few envious glances tossed toward Ellie's players, who were laughing and chasing down balls like the neophytes they were. Asher figured he'd better stick around in case she needed a few tips. He could always use the time to return phone calls that he hadn't gotten to that afternoon.

He strolled along the sidelines, one eye on Ellie and her team, his cell phone held to his ear. Despite the giggles and general air of fun, she had good control of her bunch. True, there were only seven of them, but at least they were routinely connecting with the ball and each other. He was less certain about the little jig she had them doing at the end. Then he realized that Ellie herself was dancing with the ball, dribbling in place. She let the kids try, none with success, but they were keen to work at it, and that, he had to admit, was half the battle.

As the practice wound down, cars began arriving with parents picking up their children. Asher made one more phone call, this one to his sister, Petra, in Waco, who just needed an opportunity to vent. The things she saw, working the night shift at an upscale Waco hotel, made her question her career choice, but as she was in the final semester of earning her degree, he, of course, counseled her to stick with it. She had known that he would; she just needed to hear someone say it.

With their brother Phillip basically unreachable and Dallas unsympathetic, Petra had no one else to whom she could turn. Their parents would only tell her that she should have opted for med school. Asher suspected that they were hurt because none of their offspring had followed in their footsteps. They were wonderful Christian people and good parents, but they lived and breathed medicine to the point that little else existed for them. That attitude had prejudiced their children against medicine as a career.

He finished his call and looked around. Ellie sat sideways on a rough bench, her cell phone in her hand. Asher wondered where her ride was, but he waited until everyone else had gone before approaching her.

"Kent running late?"

"Yeah, he's stuck in traffic. He had to run into Dallas to pick up a drug for some sick kid, and you know how that traffic is, especially at this time of day."

"Doesn't he have his own car?"

"He does, but it's been in the shop. Again. I'm sure it's ready to be picked up by now."

"Kind of like you."

She laughed, but he noticed that she had yet to look at him. "I thought about asking Ilene for a ride, but she already had a car full of kids. She really wants this team to make it, you know, so her daughter can play. She's recruited half the kids herself, and I have to say they're pretty enthusiastic. There will be a lot of disappointed kiddos if we're shut down."

Asher said nothing to that. She seemed to be implying that he should bend the rules, but he couldn't. Nevertheless, he felt a bit like an ogre.

She seemed uncomfortable now that everyone else had gone, and he couldn't really blame her. Their private meetings never seemed to go very well, but he couldn't drive away and leave her there on her own, so he sat down on the bench. For a long moment, neither of them spoke. Finally, he took it upon himself to make conversation.

"Can I ask you some—"

"Ask away. I've got nothing to hide."

He knew that was a reference to the fire and his grilling her that day in his office, but he didn't want to go there, not now.

"Sorry," she muttered. "Didn't mean to interrupt."

"I was just wondering why you didn't play soccer in college. You obviously know your way around the game."

She shrugged. "I only wanted to go to BCBC, but so did nearly everyone else on my team, and some of them were better soccer players than me. Besides, I had other options."

"Such as?"

"An academic scholarship. Couple of grants." He was impressed. After a brief pause, she spoke again in a wistful voice. "When you don't have parents willing to take responsibility for you, you can sometimes get a little extra help."

He was sorry he'd asked. Despite their dedication

to medicine, his parents had never shirked the smallest responsibility, especially not when it came to their children. He'd attended one of the best universities in the country, and even though they'd been disappointed in his field of study, they'd paid every nickel that his soccer scholarship hadn't covered. He'd been that rare graduate who hadn't owed a penny in loans, and his siblings had followed in his footsteps. Maybe it was time that he stopped resenting his parents for wishing he'd become a doctor.

"Can I ask *you* a question?" she said after a moment.

He quailed at the thought, but he'd started this. "Okay."

"I've been thinking about something Dallas said a long time ago. She said that the law was your second choice. It's none of my business, but I can't help wondering what she meant by that."

He crossed his legs at the ankles. "She meant that I wanted to play professional soccer."

Ellie swiveled around on the bench. "Really? Why didn't you?"

"Blew out my knee in the middle of my junior year," he said, rubbing the scar that ran alongside his kneecap. "They yanked my scholarship when the rehab didn't go well."

"That stinks."

"The team gave me another shot my senior year, but I knew I wasn't going to get picked up, so I enrolled in—"

"How could you know that?" she interrupted, and this time he found himself smiling at the interruption.

"I just did. I prayed about it, and deep down I knew that God was telling me to give up my dream."

"That can't be!"

"We all eventually give up our dreams, Ellie. It's part of growing up."

"I don't believe that. The way I see it, if God doesn't change your heart's desire then He just brings it to you in another way or at another time. Look at David in the Old Testament. In his youth, he obviously aspired to music and poetry, but God called him to be king. And yet we have the Psalms as proof that David realized his dream of composing music and praise lyrics."

"We also have Job as an example," Asher pointed out. "He said it himself. 'My days have passed, my plans are shattered, and so are the desires of my heart.'"

"Yes, but God gave it all back to him. He even doubled Job's wealth because Job remained faithful and sought righteousness."

"You're thinking of your grandfather now, aren't you?" Asher said, his tone sounding accusatory even to his own ears.

"I am, and why not? He's a good man, a godly man, and he's waited patiently and faithfully for what he wants."

"And you're not above 'helping' God to see that he gets it, are—"

"Yes!" she erupted, launching onto her feet. "I admit it. I tried to stall the insurance settlement so Grandpa could have time with Odelia, but I see now that was a lack of faith on *my* part. My faith doesn't figure into it, though. It's Grandpa's faith that counts, his and Odelia's."

Asher felt a surprising urge to tell her what Odelia had revealed the night before, but he decided not to get involved. It was not his grand scheme. He looked at Ellie and felt a momentary rush of warmth for her, this woman who believed so strongly in romantic love.

"Come on. I'll drive you home," he said, getting to his feet.

She folded her arms mulishly, but she followed him to the SUV. While they drove toward Chatam House, she called her grandfather to tell him not to come to the soccer field, then gave him a glowing report of her first practice. The SUV swung through the gate and tooled up the hill. Asher brought it to a stop right in front of the walkway.

"Hilda probably has dinner ready. I'm sure your aunts would be happy to have you at their table again," she said.

He shook his head even though she was perfectly correct about his generous aunties. He just didn't think he could sit across a table from Ellie tonight—he needed some recovery time, so to speak. "Best get on. Give my love to my aunties for me."

"I will," Ellie promised, sliding down to the ground. "Thanks for the ride."

Nodding, he drove away, knowing that skipping dinner was a pointless gesture. He was already thinking about when he was going to see her again.

What could God possibly be doing? Was He allowing Asher to be beset by unfathomable events meant to test faith and resolve? Or was He making a point that this lowly attorney could not seem to grasp?

As he watched Ellie disappear into the house, he had a feeling it was the latter.

"My sister's husband was a brutal man," Hilda said, tucking a thick stack of paper napkins into the basket that she had filled with three dozen plump, fragrant ginger muffins still warm from the oven. She had insisted on providing them when Ellie had mentioned wanting to pick up some ready-made variety for the meeting at Asher's house. "I feared he'd kill her before she could get away from him," Hilda confessed bluntly, "but the Misses called Mr. Ash, and he took care of it."

A large woman with thin, straight, gray hair cropped bluntly just below her ears, Hilda ruled the kitchen at Chatam House with a stern but indulgent hand. Covering the basket with a crisp, white cloth, she pushed it across the chrome worktable toward Ellie, saying, "It's the least I can do after Mr. Ash handled Carol's divorce free of charge." That, apparently, had been years ago, and Carol had since joined the staff at Chatam House as a maid.

Ellie thanked Hilda and carried the basket out to her truck, belting it into the passenger seat. She couldn't help smiling at this new information about Asher. Apparently, he'd always been willing to help anyone his aunties brought to him. She wondered if that was the limit of his largesse and somehow doubted that it was. He volunteered as youth soccer commissioner, after all, and that had to be a big job. She felt a certain pride in that, even though she knew she had no right to such pride.

Everything told her that she had zero chance with Asher Chatam. Even this beautiful, modern home made that clear. It was the exact opposite of the aging, modest Victorian house that she so loved. Asher was serious and confident; she preferred a sunnier outlook but constantly doubted herself. He projected a maturity far beyond his years; she still often felt like a mercurial teen.

He was successful and ambitious; she loved teaching and had no plans beyond that.

She had to face facts. As much as she admired Asher, she wasn't cut out for a man like him. So why would God put her in the way of a broken heart like this—unless it was for Asher's sake? Perhaps her purpose was to help Asher see the possibilities, even if she herself was not intended to be his. Well, so be it—she'd do what she could.

Squaring her shoulders, she pressed the doorbell and stepped back, grasping the handle of the basket with both hands. While she waited, she glanced around at the tall, arching entryway. Built of creamy white stone, it contrasted nicely with the rough brown brick and mossy green trim. She was not so admiring of the landscaping. Even with the arched drive crowded with vehicles, the plantings seemed rigid and unnatural. Ellie couldn't help musing that Asher could use the assistance and expertise of his Aunt Magnolia and her gardener.

The door opened abruptly, signaling the impatience of her greeter. Asher stood there in faded jeans with a simple sweater over a plain white T-shirt, the sleeves pushed up to expose strong forearms lightly sprinkled with cinnamon-brown hair. Ellie couldn't help but smile.

"You're late," he barked.

Ellie's smile abruptly faded. "I am not. It's four minutes 'til nine."

"Everyone else got here ten minutes ago."

"Good morning to you, too, Asher. I brought some muffins," she said, wondering what she'd done to deserve such a greeting.

He glanced at the basket then turned and waved, indicating that she should follow.

Ellie stepped across the threshold.

A raised dining area at the rear of a sunken living room hosted a long rectangular table and armless, tan leather side chairs. A wall of glass looked out over a stone-rimmed swimming pool and several wood benches flanked by empty planter boxes. At least a dozen people, mostly men, sat or stood around the table. Nearly all held stiff paper cups of coffee. Each was dressed casually in some type of athletic clothing. And every one of them stared at her as she stood there in black flats, black leggings and an electric blue, long-sleeved tunic.

Ellie knew instantly that she had overdressed. Without even realizing it, she had dressed to impress. She had instinctively dressed for Asher without a single thought to who else might be in the room—or the actual purpose of the meeting. Her face heated.

Asher walked to the table and pulled out an empty chair before continuing on to another space at the far end.

"This is Ellen Monroe, team two-sixteen."

"There are two hundred and sixteen teams?" Ellie asked, surprised at the large number.

"Uh, that's sixteen teams in tier two," a man explained. "We're all tier two here today."

Ellie nodded to the group and set the basket on the table just as someone else said, "I didn't know that team made it."

"It hasn't," Asher announced, pushing around some papers on the table. "They have a coach now but not the minimum number of players."

"Yet," Ellie said with a smile.

At the same time, the buff, fortyish man next to Ellie

commented pointedly that "something" smelled good. A tall, slender woman with long, light brown hair reached across the table and lifted the corner of the crisp white cloth covering the basket.

"Muffins. Mmm."

"From the cook at Chatam House," Ellie confirmed, removing the cloth. "Help yourselves."

A muscle flexed in Asher's jaw as everyone surged toward the basket. Several minutes filled with happy chatter and appreciative noises as the assembled company enjoyed Hilda's muffins—everyone but Asher, who stood at the end of the table with his arms folded, watching Ellie with an expression she couldn't read. Reminding herself that she had done nothing wrong, she sat and nibbled at her own delicious treat while someone farther down the table poured coffee from an insulated carafe into a paper cup and passed it to her. After her second sip, Asher called the meeting back to order.

The group immediately quieted. Asher began speaking, noting alternate schedules, outstanding fee payments, issued equipment, even team colors. Ellie learned that her own team had been assigned the color yellow and that Ilene Riddle had turned in all the necessary funds, with the exception of Ellie's own fifteen-dollar payment for her coach's jersey.

"I'll have to get it from my car later," she said, realizing only belatedly that she'd interrupted him. He didn't so much as glance in Ellie's direction before picking up where he'd left off in midsentence.

Ellie mentally bit her tongue. Obviously, Asher Chatam was a harsh taskmaster. His volunteer coaches came ten minutes early for meetings and sat in silence as he spoke. More proof that she did not fit his model of acceptability. A few moments later, she realized that everyone was staring at her.

"What?"

Asher pinched the bridge of his nose and spoke, obviously repeating himself: "In the event that your team makes it before the deadline, you'll need to decide on a team name."

Thinking of yellow-and-black team uniforms, she almost said, "Bumblebees," but at the last moment, she realized that probably wouldn't sound fierce enough. "Yellow Jackets," she offered.

Asher nodded curtly. "Now, the scheduling. Since we have a questionable team, I've had to draw up two schedules for this tier. The first requires each team to play two games in one day at some point during the season. The other..."

Ellie listened intently, hearing some muted grumbles as Asher laid out the entire scheme. The brown-haired woman leaned forward and spoke to Ellie out of the corner of her mouth, "Übercompetitive."

"They're six- and seven-year-olds, for pity's sake," Ellie muttered back. "How competitive can they be?"

"Not the team, the coach."

"Ah."

"Any questions?" Asher asked, looking directly at Ellie.

Embarrassed and irritated, Ellie snapped, "Yes, as a matter of fact, I do have a question. Since we're playing 'small-sided,' I don't understand why I have to field a minimum of nine players."

"It's true we only field five players on each side at this age, but you must have substitutes," one of the other coaches pointed out.

"And you hardly ever get all the kids there at one time," someone else put in.

Ellie shrugged. "If enough kids don't show up to play, you forfeit the game."

"It's the rule," Asher said flatly, obviously intending to close the subject.

But Ellie wasn't ready to let it go, and why should she? It wasn't as if giving in would change anything. "Why should seven kids not get to play for lack of two?" she asked.

"Let's not take up everyone else's time discussing it right now. Anything else?" he asked, looking at the others.

Ellie leaned back in her chair, folded her arms and fumed until the meeting ended a few minutes later.

As everyone else filed out, Asher parked one hip on the edge of the table and helped himself to a muffin.

"There are reasons for rules, Ellie," he said quietly, "and we all have to follow them."

"You don't have to tell me that. I'm a kindergarten teacher. But what about fun? Soccer's a game. Games are supposed to be fun."

He shook his head. "I can't make an exception, Ellie, no matter how much I might want to. The other coaches would be all over me. Surely you can see that."

She decided to try another tack. "You've obviously forgotten how important having a little fun is."

"I have lots of fun," he said, looking slightly startled.

"Oh, yeah? Name one fun thing that you do."

He shrugged. "Being soccer commissioner is fun for me."

She rolled her eyes. "So you enjoy long hours, meetings and laying down the law."

"Okay, I admit, that part's more about the kids, but I like soccer. I watch it on TV all the time, and I make every live game that I can. Besides, I'm not just the commissioner. I'm a referee, too, and I even coach."

"It's a proven fact that kids learn best when they're having fun. Now, if you want to see some real fun and how it impacts learning, just drop by my classroom sometime. I'll be glad to demonstrate."

He looked directly at her. "I don't have time for that."

"Well, you'll be at church tomorrow, won't you? I teach a pre-K class. Stop by during the Sunday School hour. We have a blast, and the kids learn plenty."

"I have to finalize upper-tier schedules tomorrow. I usually leave after the early service, anyway."

They stared at each for a long moment. Then Ellie conceded, swallowing back further comment. Obviously he was letting her know that he intended to keep her at arm's length. She told herself that it was better this way.

*Okay, Lord,* she prayed silently. *Lesson number one. Don't push.*

Ellie began removing the remaining four or five muffins from the basket. "Hilda said you were to get any leftovers."

Asher nodded. "Thank her for me."

"I will. Think about coming by tomorrow. Everyone could use a little reminder of what real fun is from time to time, including you, Asher."

Papers in one hand, basket in the other, she turned and hurried toward the front door.

# Chapter Eight

Sunday morning found Odelia unaccountably depressed. Stepping down into the foyer, Odelia walked slowly across the marble floor toward the front parlor, tugging at the white cuffs on the long sleeves of her navy blue dress. She'd bought this garment years ago for a funeral, but in the end she hadn't been able to bring herself to wear it. The thing was just too severe and depressing. Today, however, it somehow seemed appropriate, as did the small pearl earrings and simple gold chain that she had chosen for accessories. She usually went for much more gay attire, but this morning she'd looked at her colorful closet and collection of fun jewelry, and absolutely everything had felt wrong. Only this suited her current mood, and it would certainly do for church.

She meandered into the parlor to find Hypatia standing next to her customary wingback chair, a frown on her face as she stared down at the settee, where Kent Monroe sat with a cup and saucer balanced on one knee.

"Don't trouble yourself," Kent was saying. "I really

don't need the sugar in my diet, anyway, and I wouldn't want to make you late for Sunday services."

"No, no, it will only take a minute," Hypatia replied. "My sisters haven't even come down yet." She tapped her cleft chin with the tip of one finger. "I just can't remember the last time that Hilda forgot the sugar bowl." She dropped her hand. "Well, no matter."

She turned, saw Odelia and did a mild double take before exclaiming, "Odelia, how fine you look! Very elegant." She moved toward the door, patting Odelia's shoulder as she passed. "Excuse me for one moment. Hilda has forgotten the sugar bowl."

Odelia stood uncertainly in the center of the floor, torn between fleeing the room and allowing herself just a few moments of Kent's company. The latter desire won out over the self-protective impulse, and she walked, head down, to the armless side chair at one end of the occasional table.

"May I pour you some tea?" Kent asked solicitously.

"Oh. No. Thank you. I'm not in the mood just now."

Kent's cup and saucer clattered as he set them back on the tray. He slid across the settee to the corner nearest her and leaned forward, speaking in a soft voice. "My dear, I'm concerned by your subdued manner. This isn't like you."

Forcing a smile, Odelia said, "It's just the end-of-winter doldrums. You know how it is. The promise of sunshine one minute, gray skies the next, and the thermometer can't make up its mind whether it's on the way up or down."

"Well," Kent said in a dubious tone, "I look forward to your spring magnificence, then. I must say, I miss your more colorful self."

Delight brought roses to Odelia's cheeks. The next moment, dismay leeched it away. Clearing her throat, she changed the subject.

"Have you found your cat? I know you were looking for it again yesterday."

Kent sighed. "I suppose I shouldn't be concerned. He's just a stray tom, and you know how they are, but I guess I got used to seeing him around. He certainly kept the vermin out of the garage. I just can't help wondering where he is now. The fire must have traumatized the poor old thing."

"I could organize a search if it would make you feel better," Odelia offered automatically.

Smiling, Kent reached over and squeezed her hand. "I've always admired that huge heart of yours."

Odelia gasped. "How can you say that? You, of all people!"

He seemed surprised. "Odelia," he said quietly, "I've always understood why you refused to go through with it."

"You have?"

"Absolutely. Triplets share an unusual bond. I know why you can't leave your sisters to live with me."

"But you were so wounded at the time."

"Well, of course, I was! The beautiful girl who had stolen my heart was not going to be mine. I admit I was bitterly disappointed, but even then I understood why it had to be that way."

She shook her head. "I—I don't know what to say."

"You don't have to say anything," he told her kindly. "And you're still that beautiful girl who stole my heart."

She laughed stiltedly at that, telling herself that he was just being his usual charming self. He couldn't help it really. She'd always loved that about him. Correction. She had always *appreciated* his natural charm.

Closing her eyes at the lie, she sent up a silent prayer. *Father God, help me overcome these foolish feelings. I know it's too late for romantic love, especially as nothing has changed. Even if Kent could care for me again, how could I possibly leave my sisters now? Forgive me for not being properly grateful for the life that You've given me and the many blessings that I've known. Amen.*

She felt a little better afterward. Whatever was she doing, anyway? Eating her heart out at her age. Ridiculous!

Ridiculous and so very depressing.

"Something is definitely wrong with Odelia," Kent observed softly as Ellie slid behind the wheel of her truck.

Glancing over at him, she shifted in order to straighten the slim skirt of her cherry-red dress. He sat slumped down in the passenger seat, craning his head to watch the long, storm-gray town car carrying the Chatam sisters turn out of the drive and onto the street. Anxious not to be late for Sunday school, Ellie quickly buckled her seat belt, started up the engine and engaged the transmission.

"What makes you say that, Grandpa?"

He sat up a little straighter as the truck moved forward on the gravel drive. "She's wearing navy blue."

"Navy blue what?"

He shrugged. "Just…navy blue. A dress, I guess. Nothing spectacular. I'm not sure she's even wearing earrings."

That did sound serious. Ellie could not remember

a time when she had seen Odelia Chatam without big, wild earrings.

"This is all my fault," Kent growled.

"How is it your fault?" Ellie asked, glancing at him worriedly.

"She was fine before I moved into Chatam House," he rumbled.

"You don't know what she was like day-to-day before we came to Chatam House," Ellie pointed out.

"I sense that she is disturbed!" Kent argued, shaking his hands in frustration. "I feel it!"

"Why don't you talk to her about it?"

"I've tried."

"Try again."

He rubbed a thick, heavy hand over his face. "I don't know. If my presence is upsetting her—"

"Pray about it first, then."

"I pray about it every day," he murmured. "I pray for her every day. I have for the majority of my life."

That was so sweet that Ellie blinked back tears as she drove toward the Downtown Bible Church. She felt a great yearning for worship today. She hadn't felt such need to be in God's house in a very long time. Perhaps because deep down she knew that she would have to accept disappointment for her grandfather as well as herself.

They spoke no more as she parked the truck at the curb in front of the pharmacy and they got out to walk around the square to the stately old church. A few steps later, Kent headed off to a senior men's class, and Ellie hurried to the children's wing.

"Sorry I'm late," she called as she reached the pre-kindergarten play space.

Her coteachers, Sherry Hansen and Anna Burdett Chatam, who was married to Asher's cousin Reeves, paused while laying out supplies in the craft area to greet her with smiles.

"No problem," Sherry said. "We've still got a few minutes."

Ellie pulled the appropriate posters and props from the cabinet mounted on the wall and prepared the scene while bantering with Sherry and Anna, the latter of whom was well known for her wit. Anna's stepdaughter, Gilli, kept up a steady stream of chatter as she helped distribute cotton balls.

The other children began to arrive, in ones and twos at first, then in flurries of a half dozen or more, until some forty-plus were climbing over the large plastic play gym or sitting down to tables to create pastoral scenes with cotton balls, cutouts and glue. Ellie sat down in the middle of the gym set and allowed the children gathered there to climb over and around her as they played.

At the proper time, she gathered them up and herded them to the story station. Taking her place on a small, low chair, with the children arranged in a semicircle on the floor around her, Ellie guided the children through a short prayer. When she looked up again, she saw Asher standing outside the hallway. He had an oddly wistful look on his face and a little half smile.

Ellie's heart clunked. When she'd invited him to stop by this morning, she'd just been trying to make a point about how children learn best through fun. She hadn't really thought that he would take her up on the invitation. Indeed, he'd indicated that he would not. Now she wondered how long he had been standing there and why he had come. She couldn't quite believe that he meant to take instruction from her. At any rate, she didn't have time to deal with him now, as the child tugging on her skirt reminded her.

"Miss Ellie? Miss Ellie!"

She dropped a quick smile on the impatient boy, but when she glanced back to the window, Asher had gone.

"All aboard the Homebound Train! Woo-woo!"

For the second time in three days, Asher watched Ellie in action, this time through her classroom door. Hopping around to present her back to the class, she pretended to pull the string of a horn then crouched slightly and moved her bent arms in a churning motion.

"Chugga-chugga-chugga, chugga-chugga-chugga. Remember your tickets! How do you get your tickets?"

"Put away your stuff!" a child called.

"And get your backpack!" someone else yelled.

One by one, children tucked away their toys and art projects and ran to grab their backpacks from hooks on the wall. Laughing and giggling, they fell in behind her and clamped their hands onto the shoulders of the person ahead.

"Chugga-chugga-chugga. Here we go!"

*She's right,* Asher thought, watching her rock back and forth as she pretended to build up enough steam to pull away from the station. *I really don't know much about fun.*

He'd watched her two days earlier in the Sunday School classroom when she'd all but become a part of the indoor gym set. She'd looked so happy, and the kids all obviously adored her. He'd felt a strange pang, wondering if he had ever been that happy. His work certainly didn't lend itself to her kind of gaiety, and he couldn't remember now when soccer or anything else had really been fun for him.

He didn't know what had compelled him to stop by her Sunday School classroom that day; he hadn't even intended to go to church last Sunday, but somehow he couldn't stay home. Then, after the early service, when he usually slipped out, he'd found himself walking the maze of halls until he'd come to the pre-K unit. He didn't know what he'd expected to see, but he couldn't seem to help himself. Not then. Not now.

A call to the school on Monday morning had told him that he could not gain access to Ellie's background check without her. He could have asked the school staff to have the form signed, but instead he'd said he would take care of it himself. Now here he stood on a Tuesday afternoon, watching her at work and wishing he hadn't been quite so hard on her lately.

Happily *chug*ging, the line of children followed Ellie on a snaking trail through the room, winding in and out of low tables and miniature chairs, finally coming to a stop at the door. An electronic bell sounded just then, and utter chaos erupted. Up and down the hall, doors flew open, spilling children and teachers out in a noisy rush. Inside Ellie's room, however, the children waited patiently, smiles on their faces, while she traded places with her assistant.

Asher backed up as Ellie swung open the door and stepped out, facing away from him. "Bye. See you tomorrow. Have a good evening, everyone."

Ellie's class followed the assistant down the center of the hall and through the chaos to an outside door, beyond which waited parents and buses. Asher started forward to make himself known, only to jerk back again as several older children dashed past him and through the door into Ellie's classroom.

"Hold on!" she called, laughing. "I haven't booted it up yet. Give me a sec."

Leaving the doorway, she walked across the room to a computer station. Asher, as yet unnoticed, followed.

"Hurry, hurry," one little girl urged. "My mom will be here any minute."

"You can go first to show Donnie how it's done," Ellie said, as music swelled from the computer. "But then you have to let him play."

"It's a soccer game," Asher said, unaware that he'd spoken aloud until Ellie whirled to face him.

She smoothed the surprise from her face, backing up a step. "Yes, it is. This particular game is designed to teach the rules of the game."

"Really?"

"It gives you a scenario and several options for how to play it. Choose correctly and your play succeeds. Choose the wrong option and your opponent, in this case the computer, gets the ball, but only after the computer shows you the correct play. You go on until someone gets a goal scenario. Choose correctly then and you score."

"That's marvelous," Asher said. And fun, obviously.

A cry of jubilation went up from the kids gathered around the computer.

"You didn't come here to watch computer games," Ellie said to him.

"I did not," he acknowledged, presenting the form in his hand. "I need your permission in order to get a copy of your background check for the league records."

"No problem." She took the paper from him and carried it to her desk, where she picked up a pen and signed her name.

Meanwhile, a little boy at the computer was hitting buttons with lightning speed. Suddenly, everyone cheered, and the boy began to jump up and down.

"I won! I won!"

"And very quickly, too," Ellie praised. Moving forward, she bent at the waist to bring her face level with his and asked, "So what do you think? Would you like to play real soccer?"

"Uh-huh, yes! I wanna play!"

Reaching back, Ellie whipped a sheet of paper off her desk and presented it to him with a flourish. "Take this to your parents. If they have any questions, they can call me."

"Okay." Clutching his paper, the boy turned back to the computer, where another child was taking a turn.

"An effective recruiting tool, too." Asher smiled.

"It certainly is." Picking up some papers from her desk, she handed them to Asher.

He glanced over them, his eyebrows rising. "You've already signed up three new players. You've made your team in a single day."

Ilene Riddle stuck her head in the door just then. "Let's go, kids. I'm double-parked." Three of the children trooped to the door, protesting as they went. "You, too, Donnie, your mom's waiting outside. Ellie, Commissioner, see you tomorrow."

"See you!" Ellie called as the group disappeared. The boy raced after the others, waving his enlistment form.

Asher shook his head. "You never cease to amaze me."

She smiled and said, "I'll take that as a compliment. Thank you."

"You're welcome."

"Wanna play? The upper levels are pretty challenging."

"Oh, no," he said, shaking his head. "I shouldn't."

"I dare you."

"No, really, I should—"

"Coward," she said with such a daredevil grin that he couldn't quite manage to be offended. "I'll go easy on you, I promise."

He was surprised by how much he wanted to play that silly game with her. And why not? What would it hurt?

He shrugged out of his coat. "Now I'm going have to beat you at your own game. Literally."

"Ha!"

He pulled up two chairs while she plugged in the controllers and programmed the game. All those toggles and buttons were confusing at first, but before long he was giving her a challenge. It became evident quickly that they were fairly evenly matched, but Asher wasn't about to push his luck, so the moment that he tied up the game, he called it.

"I could beat you if I had time, but I'll settle for a tie in the interest of my schedule."

"In your dreams, bub. I admit that I probably couldn't keep up with you on a real field but—"

"Probably?" he scoffed playfully.

"But I've got this sewed up," she bragged, grinning. "I was going easy on you, remember?"

"Now who's dreaming?"

"Hang around and find out."

"Wish I could," he said, "but I have to change and get to the soccer field." He hauled himself to his feet and turned to see a tall, thin, familiar young man wearing a wrinkled shirt and a frown in the doorway.

"Ellie," the man said abruptly, "we need to talk."

Behind Asher, Ellie groaned. "Not now, Lance."

Ignoring her, he stepped forward and put his hand out to Asher, introducing himself. "Lance Ripley. We didn't meet last time."

Asher slid into his coat, avoiding shaking hands with the man, whom he disliked instinctively, having witnessed him lay his hands on Ellie over a week ago. "Asher Chatam."

The fellow flushed, his ears turning red. Abruptly, he switched his attention back to Ellie. "It's been too long since we went out. We'll have dinner together tonight."

"Uh, no," Ellie said flatly.

Smiling to himself, Asher glanced over his shoulder. As he'd expected, she'd folded her arms. He almost wished she hadn't. That was *his* pose, the one he so often elicited from her. Lance Ripley had no right to it. Or to her, no matter what he thought.

"Now, Ellie," Lance said, "you know you don't mean that."

"Lance, I am *not* going out with you again."

"We'll have a nice dinner and talk this over," he said reasonably.

"No. We won't."

"I'm afraid I can't accept that."

"I'm afraid you have no choice," said Asher, unable to stay quiet any longer.

Hostile, ice-blue eyes swung his way. "I don't see what you have to say about it."

"Oh, I have quite a lot to say about it, actually. I'm Miss Monroe's attorney, the one who will be filing the restraining order if you don't leave her alone."

Watching the tumblers fall into place in Lance's mind, Asher felt a greater sense of satisfaction than he had known in some time.

"You're *that* Chatam."

"Indeed I am. And you are not welcome. Remember that the next time you approach my client. She doesn't want to see you, not here, not on the street, not at Chatam House. I trust I've made our position clear."

Eyes wild, Lance Ripley glared at Asher, his mouth working silently around unspoken words. Then he blinked, visibly calming himself, and lifted his chin before spinning away and disappearing.

Asher smiled, only to feel a hand snatch angrily at his elbow and turn him about. "What are you doing? He's going to think I'm suing him for harassment!"

"Maybe you should. He has harassed you, hasn't he?" Asher was puzzled by her anger.

"That depends on your definition of harassment."

"Mine happens to be the legal one," Asher told her. "I'd like to hear yours."

Sighing, she dropped down onto the corner of her desk. "Okay. Maybe he has been a bit persistent."

"Well, I don't imagine he'll be coming around here anymore."

"Oh, yes, he will," she retorted. "That's the problem. He works here. I can't help running into him from time to time."

Asher literally gnashed his teeth over the thought. "I'll speak to him again."

"No!"

"You told him no. That should be the end of it."

"I just told you no, too."

He ignored that, another thought occurring. "I still can't believe you went out with that jerk on Valentine's Day."

"No one wants to sit home alone on the most romantic night of the year."

Asher had, for a long time. He'd proposed to Samantha on Valentine's Day, and he'd spent every one alone since they'd divorced. That seemed pointless now, a silly excuse to ignore the "most romantic night of the year," as Ellie put it. Apparently, she hadn't found this past Valentine's Day date quite so romantic, though.

"Look, Ellie, are you sure that you haven't rebuffed some other guy who might have taken it out on your house?" he asked roughly, trying to get his mind off Valentine's Day.

She shook her head, laughing in a forlorn way. "Look, I'm just not the sort to inspire that kind of passion."

"Oh, yes, you are," he replied. Ellie's jaw dropped. Scurrying to recover, he babbled, "I—I mean, according to the insurance company, *someone* set that fire. If not one of your, ah, disappointed boyfriends, then who?"

She looked positively stricken. Coming to her feet, she glanced around as if looking for threats in the shadows, her full lower lip clamped firmly between her teeth. Asher realized suddenly that she was trembling. Because of him. Because he had frightened her with his rash words.

"It's all right," he promised, stepping forward to take her into his arms. "You're safe. No one's going to hurt you. I promise."

She nodded, resting against him. "I know."

"I mean it," he told her, tightening his hold. He couldn't help noticing that she fit neatly into his arms. He barely had to lift his chin to accommodate the top of her head. "Don't be afraid. I'll take care of everything."

"H-how can you?"

"I'll just do my job."

She shook her head, asking softly, "So, the insurance company thinks the fire was intentionally set?"

"They've implied as much. So I don't want you or your grandfather talking to anyone about the fire without me there. Understand?"

Gulping, she nodded and turned her face into the hollow of his shoulder. Somehow his hand found its way into her silky, springy hair.

"If anyone contacts you, refer them to me," he instructed softly. "No interviews unless I okay them."

"All right," she said huskily. "Thank you." She tilted her head back, her lovely violet eyes holding his. "You were right about me not being in favor of you handling this."

"No. Really?" he quipped with a lopsided grin.

"But I'm really glad now that you are."

"Me, too," he said. It seemed appropriate to cup her face in his hands then. Until he realized he was about to kiss her!

Mentally recoiling, he derailed himself in time to land the kiss in the middle of her forehead, as if she were a child.

She stepped back, her head bowed. His hands drifted down to his sides. She cleared her throat and turned away. "Will I see you at practice tomorrow?"

He jammed his hands into his coat pockets. "Um,

maybe. Probably not. I don't know," he stammered, confusion clouding his mind.

"Okay," she said lightly.

He pretended to check his watch, saying, "Gotta run." He managed a single step.

"Ash."

The sound of her speaking his name stopped him right in his tracks. Cautiously, he turned back and saw that she held out the signed form.

"Oh. Right." Slipping forward, he gingerly took it from her. "Thanks."

She sent him away with a single nod.

He couldn't wait to get out of there. And at the very same time, he could hardly bear to go.

Which was reason enough to run for his life.

## Chapter Nine

It didn't take a sledgehammer to penetrate her thick skull—a brotherly kiss to the forehead managed that just fine. That kiss in her classroom yesterday had made it abundantly clear that Asher was not attracted to her, no matter what her runaway imagination wanted to say about it. Oh, she had thought for a moment that he had meant to give her another kind of kiss entirely, but reality could not be denied. She simply did not draw men like him. No, she attracted the kooks and goofballs.

Ellie turned away from the parking area where Asher, dressed in a black warm-up suit, was exiting his SUV. He had been so ambivalent about being at practice today that she had not expected to see him here, and for once she wished that he had stayed away. Looking down at herself, she sighed. This had seemed like such a fun, clever idea last night, but she could just imagine how Asher would see it. Too late to worry about that now. Determined to make the best of it, she put on a smile and ran toward her gaping team, her arms full of yellow tulle and caps. The wings on her head flapped and the tutu that she wore over her athletic gear fluttered as she moved.

Dredging up as much enthusiasm as she could, Ellie passed out the tutus to the girls, who slipped them on over their workout shorts as instructed, giggling uncertainly. The boys got bright yellow caps decorated with black felt wings like hers. Partially stiffened, the wings flapped as the wearer's head moved. Once the laughing kids had donned their respective costuming, Ellie broke out the black cotton gloves. She'd sewn the fingertips of both hands together to remind the children not to use their hands.

"Okay, let's line up for drills." She demonstrated the proper technique of handling the ball, showing them how still her tutu and wings remained when she did it right.

The kids worked at it uncertainly at first but with increasing progress as the practice went on. Ellie was aware that the other teams on the field had stopped to gawk. She even heard one little girl run to her mother and whine, "I wanna soccer tutu!" Ellie smiled. Not only were her players the envy of their counterparts, they were developing greater dexterity and finer technique, too.

Blowing her whistle, Ellie signaled the start of a scrimmage. She rotated a different kid into the net every few minutes, reasoning that they all needed to know what they were up against on both sides of the ball. Before long, they were all pretending to be goalies making heroic saves. Ellie called them back to their purpose by reminding them that goalies did not score goals. She then pulled aside her best two goalie prospects and told them that goalies helped win games by keeping the other team from scoring. She rotated those two in and out of the goal while allowing the other kids to take one-on-one kicks before starting a new scrimmage.

By the end of the practice, Ellie could feel that the team was coming together, and she had almost forgotten that Asher was watching from the sidelines. Almost, but not quite.

Deciding that the tutus and winged caps had served their twin purpose, she took back only the gloves before removing her own "learning aids" and turning to face Asher. The kids ran to grab juice boxes and pretzels from Ilene before racing off to their respective parents, tutus fluttering and wings flying.

Asher stood with his hands clasped behind his back. Determined to take her medicine without flinching, she walked over to him, tutu and cap in hand.

"Your technique is stellar. Your methods, though…" He shook his head.

She folded her arms, and his lips twitched. Then an instant later, he burst out laughing in great, wrenching guffaws. Sighing, she waited out his attack of hilarity, waving from time to time as players or their parents called out farewells.

"Sorry," he gasped. "Can't help it. Never seen…such a thing…in my life!"

She tapped a toe impatiently while he got himself under control. "It worked, didn't it?"

Wiping his eyes with both hands, he nodded. "Quite possibly. They're certainly the most enthusiastic team in the league, I'll give you that. But you understand that they have to play in regulation uniforms."

"Of course I understand that they have to play in regulation uniforms," she retorted, glancing at her cleats.

"They don't have to *practice* in regulation uniforms, though, do they?"

Asher shook his head, still grinning. "There's no rule about practice gear," he began, "so long as they wear knee and elbow guards and rubber cleats, but—"

"It's just a bit of fun," she argued, "and they're learning. You saw that for yourself."

"Fun, again." He shook his head in disbelief. "Yeah, okay, fine. It's your team. I'm not going to interfere."

Relieved, Ellie pressed her hands together in an attitude of prayer. "Thank you. That's wonderful, because I have an idea about—"

He raised a hand, palm out. "Don't tell me! I don't want to know."

"Why not?"

"Because," he said, "there is a principle known as plausible deniability." He gave her a lopsided grin. "And the way things are going, sweetheart, I have a feeling I'm going to need it."

Throwing up his hands, he turned and walked back to his vehicle, chuckling and muttering that he'd be lucky if he wasn't asked to resign his position. She dismissed that concern immediately. What she could not dismiss—what she would think about time and time again—was that he had called her *sweetheart*.

Still grinning and shaking his head, Asher drove away. The sight of Ellie in a tutu and winged cap had made his eyes water with laughter. What amazed him, however, was the way her tutued and cap-winged team had caught on to her technique. The woman had a true gift for teaching kids, as well as a talent for making life bright and—he had to admit it—fun. More fun than he'd had in eons.

She also had a way of banishing his good sense. So why was it, he wondered, that he couldn't manage to keep away from her?

Even if she wasn't his client, she was still too young, too naive, too…*exuberant.* And the only commonality he could point to, really, was a mutual regard for family. Okay, so they both liked soccer, but her approach couldn't have been more different than his. It was like comparing Roman gladiators to Keystone Kops.

They were both Christians, too, of course, but her "brand" of Christianity seemed to be a kind of feel-good, pie-in-the-sky, God-is-going-to-take-care-of-everything hope, while his was… He had to think about that. His interpretation of Christianity was responsibility and righteousness, he decided, endurance, sober self-knowledge and acceptance of certain facts without complaint. This, after all, was not Heaven, he reminded himself, so naturally it lacked…what? Happiness?

Verses from the fifth chapter of Galatians ran through his mind.

*But the fruit of the Spirit is love, joy, peace, patience, kindness, goodness, faithfulness, gentleness and self-control.*

Frowning, he examined that list of qualities. He had love, lots of it, the love of God and the love of family and friends. He could do without the romantic kind, which was why—he congratulated himself on this— he had peace. Although sometimes it actually felt as if he had too much peace, but then perhaps he was equating peace.

Patience he had in abundance. Mostly. About most things. He tried to be kind and others were, often enough, kind to him. Goodness brought to mind the aunties, which made him smile. As for faithfulness, no one, absolutely no one, could say that he was not faithful. Gentleness? Well, when it was called for, he supposed. And self-control was something upon which he prided himself.

Did that, he wondered, make it a sin instead of a blessing? He frankly didn't know.

That left only…joy. Which was not, Asher reminded himself, the same as happiness, though he had both. Didn't he?

Certainly, he enjoyed many things. But that was not the same, was it?

How, he wondered, could he enjoy so much in his life and yet not know for sure if he had joy? Had he missed something? He thought of Ellie, who had essentially lost both of her parents and was now effectively homeless, with no assurance that she would ever regain what she had lost. Yet, somehow, he sensed that she knew a kind of joy that he lacked. Maybe his "theology" was wrong or incomplete.

Good grief, she had him doubting his core beliefs. Why was it, then, that he couldn't seem to hold her in anything but the highest esteem?

That question remained in the forefront of his mind as he arrived at the high school athletic field. The schools were good about sharing assets with the Buffalo Creek Youth Soccer League because so many of their middle and high school players came up through the system. He wondered if they'd be quite so cooperative, however, if the coaches and athletic directors ever got a load of a certain BCYSL coach's teaching technique.

After parking the truck, he grabbed his black cap and cleats from the passenger seat. Skirting the home stands, he threw his legs over a rail to reach the grass. Several teenage boys were already involved in a scrum. Two more came loping across the field from another direction. One of them, Rob Holloway, was a fairly new recruit. He had lots of promise. Try as he might, though, Asher couldn't seem to get the switch to flip inside that kid's head.

An image of Ellie dribbling and booting the ball in her tutu and floppy-winged cap flickered in Asher's mind. His hand went automatically to the yellow flags he had in his pocket, and an idea was born. Or rather, reborn, since it was Ellie's to begin with.

He tore a flag into four somewhat equal sections, pinning one to the top of his cap with a safety pin from the stash he kept to repair the nets. He left the ends to drape down on either side of his ears. Gesturing to Rob, who wore a hooded sweatshirt, and two other boys who had caps, Asher took out his cell phone and handed it to one of the more trustworthy kids with instructions to film what was about to happen.

He helped the boys pin on the floppy cloths, then appropriated the ball and led them out onto the field to start a vigorous short-sided scrimmage. One of the boys comically tossed his head as if the scrap of fabric were actually a mane of luxurious hair. After a few minutes of play, Asher called a halt and had the boys follow him to the sideline, where he reclaimed his phone and took a look at the video.

"Here," he said, tapping the tiny screen. "And here. Do you see what I'm talking about, Rob?"

"My head's all over the place!" the boy exclaimed, watching his yellow cloth flop and flutter while the others remained somewhat stable.

"That's what I mean by 'core discipline,'" Asher explained, enjoying seeing the light go on in Rob's mind.

He heard a lot of laughter on the field that day, and a good deal of it was his own. As they left the field at the end of practice and called out their farewells, they no longer addressed him as "Mr. Chatam." He was "Coach" now. Maybe for the first time.

And he knew exactly whom he had to thank for that.

"I don't suppose my granddaughter has put in an appearance yet?"

Odelia looked past Hypatia to find Kent standing in the doorway. He looked tired. In Odelia's opinion, he ought not to be working at all. Yes, he went in to the pharmacy late and came home early, limiting himself to four days per week, but at his age he should have been enjoying a life of leisure and looking after his health, not counting pills and mixing syrups. He certainly shouldn't have been dealing with house fires and insurance companies, which was why Asher had been called in.

"As we've just told Dallas, we haven't seen Ellie this evening," Magnolia told Kent, passing a cup of tea to their niece, who occupied the gold-striped wingchair.

Dallas had practically become a fixture at Chatam House since the Monroes had moved in. Odelia appreciated the frequent visits, though probably not for the same reasons as her sisters. She loved having family around, of course, just as they did, but these days she appreciated the distraction even more. Despite her best efforts, her gaze wandered back to Kent, who openly stared at her.

"What a lovely ensemble, a harbinger of the bright spring days ahead."

Knowing that her mood had affected her appearance, Odelia had made a concerted effort to punch up her appearance that morning, choosing a grass-green skirt and flowered blouse, along with a headband sporting a pink daisy and yellow daisy-chain earrings that hung almost to her shoulders. Kent noticed, even if no one else seemed to have done so.

Her cheeks heating with ridiculous pleasure, Odelia thanked him while pretending a great interest in the hem of her full skirt. What a goose she was to let a simple, polite comment set her heart racing!

After a moment, Kent excused himself and went upstairs, remarking that he needed a nap before dinner. Odelia let herself relax a bit, only to note a wry, knowing smile curling one corner of her niece's lips. Dallas sipped her tea and ate a cinnamon cookie, obviously biding her time. Blessedly, before she could comment on Kent's compliment, Ellie came in.

"Sorry I'm late. It was an eventful practice." She crossed the room, wearing shorts with knee socks and a vibrant yellow T-shirt, the only portion of her outfit that Odelia could truly approve. The yellow cap was fun, too, though. Its black wings flopped forward and back, like a pair of clapping hands, as Ellie collapsed onto the chair before the fireplace. "I am so out of shape!"

"Interesting hat," Dallas remarked, amber eyes dancing.

Ellie groaned and swept the thing off, leaving her curly hair in disarray. "Teaching aid," she explained tersely, tucking it beneath her.

"Oh?" Hypatia said brightly. "What subject, dear?"

"Soccer, Miss H. Didn't I say? I'm coaching a soccer team for six- and seven-year-olds now."

Dallas plunked down her cup and saucer, jostling the other contents of the tray. "Get out of here! You never mentioned that."

Ellie grimaced. "Didn't I? It came up unexpectedly not long ago."

"Puh-leze," Dallas drawled. Grinning at her aunts, Dallas added meaningfully, "And I suppose the fact that Ash is the soccer commissioner has nothing to do with anything."

Odelia immediately brightened at that reminder. Trading looks with Magnolia, she smiled. "So he is. Well, well. I had forgotten all about that."

Hypatia lifted her eyebrows, and Odelia knew that the sisters were all thinking the same thing: whenever anyone came to stay at Chatam House, a romance inevitably followed. But Ellie and Asher?

"Who'd have thought it?" Odelia chirped happily, distracted for the moment from her own problems.

"Who'd have thought what?" Ellie asked.

Hypatia shrugged. "I suppose it was inevitable."

"What was inevitable?"

"That a romance would be brewing," Magnolia declared jovially.

Smiling over the rim of her cup, Dallas leaned back into the corner of the armchair and crossed her long slender legs.

Ellie glanced at Odelia, smiling slightly. "O-kaay. And the 'brewing romance' that we are discussing is..."

"Why, yours, dear," Odelia answered brightly.

"Mine?" Ellie yelped, sitting forward. "Whatever gave you the idea that I'm having a romance?"

"Oh, just the facts," Dallas said nonchalantly. "First, you were alone out in the greenhouse with Ash the other evening—"

"*You* arranged that!"

"So? I was told by someone who would know that it was a lengthy tryst."

Ellie glanced from Dallas to Odelia and back. "Who would that be?"

"Garrett Willows, as it happens." She slid a look at Odelia from beneath her lashes, adding, "In fact, I heard there was quite a bit of traffic in the greenhouse that night."

Odelia felt hot spots blossom high on her cheekbones. They had been spotted, she and Kent! Oh, no, no. It couldn't be.

"I don't care what you heard," Ellie said emphatically. "There was no 'tryst,' as you put it." Odelia allowed herself the tiniest bit of relief.

"No?" Dallas scoffed. "And I suppose it's just a coincidence that you've now gone from client to coach in my brother's soccer association?"

"Yes! That's exactly what it is, a coincidence."

"Oh, my dear," Hypatia said with an indulgent shake of her head. "There are no coincidences for God's children."

"It's a concept young people seem not to grasp anymore," Magnolia said, tsking.

"Wow," Dallas exclaimed, sitting up straight as if an idea had struck her. "A twofer."

Odelia blinked at that, horrified. "A what?"

"A twofer. You know, it means two for the price of one."

"I'm sorry, dear. I don't understand," Hypatia said.

"If there are no coincidences," Dallas explained, "then it can't be a coincidence that Mr. Monroe is in residence here at Chatam House, either."

Hypatia shrugged in confusion, while Odelia's face flamed hot. "I suppose."

"Well, then," Dallas went on, nodding at Odelia as if encouraging her to confess all.

Odelia felt the color drain from her face. "Y-you can't possibly mean…"

Dallas glanced around the gathering. "Oh, come now," she said with some exasperation. "Ellie isn't the only Monroe staying here."

"What does that have to do with anything?" Hypatia demanded.

"All I'm saying is that if Ash can fall in love, anyone can, even…" She looked pointedly to Odelia.

Gasping—squeaking, really—Odelia lurched to her feet. Only belatedly, as she was juggling them, did she realize that she still held her teacup and saucer. Somehow, she managed to get them safely onto the tray, but by that time, everyone was gaping at her.

"Excuse me," she said, lifting her chin. "I have to…"

The thought trailed off. She couldn't think of a single thing that she had to do just then. Except escape. Which was exactly what she did. She quite literally turned tail and ran, and she didn't stop until she was locked safely in her room in the suite that she shared with her sisters.

Whatever could Dallas be thinking? she wondered, wringing her hands as she paced the floor. Obviously, Garrett had seen Kent follow her to the greenhouse that night, or perhaps Asher had mentioned something about their discussion afterward. No, no, she couldn't accept that. Ash was the soul of discretion. Yet what Dallas had said could not be entirely dismissed.

"No coincidence," she muttered. "No coincidence."

But no romance, either.

Not for her.

Not for a foolish old lady who had missed her chance long ago.

## Chapter Ten

Glancing at her sister's rapidly retreating back, Magnolia frowned at her niece. "Whatever has gotten into you, Dallas Chatam?"

"Surely you've noticed—" Dallas began, only to break off at the sound of the door knocker.

"Who might that be?" Hypatia murmured, casting a curious look over one shoulder.

"Whoever it is," Magnolia said, setting aside her teacup with a huff, "you'll have to entertain without me. I don't have time for any more nonsense today. Spring will not wait for my repotting." Casting a frown at Dallas, she rose and hurried away, leaving Hypatia to reluctantly answer the door.

Ellie seized the moment to hiss at her friend. "I agree with Magnolia. What is wrong with you?"

"Just stating the obvious," Dallas retorted defensively.

"The obvious, my foot! Making them believe there's something between your brother and me."

"Well, isn't there?"

"No! Besides," Ellie went on, realizing that she ought

not to dwell on the subject of her own nonexistent romance, "you practically had Odelia in tears."

"Oh, please," Dallas protested in a harsh whisper. "Auntie Od in tears? I may have embarrassed her a little, but—"

"A little? You think that was *a little* embarrassing? Sometimes I think you're certifiably insane."

"That's harsh," Dallas muttered with a frown.

"Not harsh enough," Ellie scolded hotly, "not if you—" She broke off as Hypatia reentered the room. Hypatia, however, was not alone.

Behind her strode an attractive, boyish-looking fellow with neatly groomed nut-brown hair. Dressed in a dark blue button-up shirt with a somehow familiar logo embroidered in white above the breast pocket, he smiled benignly, his sharp gaze tracking from Dallas to Ellie and back again. Not much taller than Hypatia, he carried a simple dark blue folder in his left hand. In other words, he seemed utterly harmless—until Hypatia pointedly said, "Ellie, dear, this gentleman would like to speak to you and your grandfather."

Ellie stared hard at that logo and gulped. "I…h-he…"

"I've explained that Mr. Monroe is taking a much-needed nap," Hypatia went on helpfully.

At that point, the fellow dodged around Hypatia and went straight to Ellie, putting out his right hand. "Jared Lawrence, Miss Monroe, with Insurance Nation."

"In-insurance. I see."

He seemed unconcerned when she failed to immediately take his hand. "I have some questions about the fire at 1001 Charter. But first…" He plucked a sheet of paper from the folder. "I'll need you to sign this interview document. It's just to fix the time and date of our conversation and attest to the validity of your stateme—"

"Y-you've caught me at an in-inconvenient moment," Ellie interrupted, sliding sideways out of her chair. "Please excuse me." Her gaze followed his as he looked down at the crushed, winged cap that she had left behind on the seat of her chair. "While I change," she improvised quickly, snatching up the thing and tucking it beneath one arm.

With a sharp nod, she bolted for the door. Behind her, she heard Hypatia stiltedly offer Jared Lawrence a cup of tea. Ellie didn't catch his reply as she hurried across the foyer to the gear bag that she'd left on the floor. Dropping down onto her haunches, she reached into the bag for her cell phone before darting up the stairs.

By the time she'd made the turn in the broad, sweeping staircase, she'd located Asher's phone number and hit Send. She hurried into the small apartment that the Chatam sisters referred to as the East Suite. Seeing that her grandfather's bedroom door was closed, she crossed the sitting room to stand before the fireplace.

"Answer. Answer," she pleaded as the phone rang on the other end.

Just when she thought all hope was lost, she heard a click, then a cautious, "Hello, Ellie."

She didn't bother with a greeting, just blurted, "You said not to talk to anyone unless you were here, but he's downstairs in the parlor right now!"

"Who?"

"Jared Lawrence. From Insurance Nation. He wants me to sign a paper and talk to him."

"Sign nothing, say nothing," Asher instructed sternly. "I'll be right there."

He ended the call before he could hear her say, "Thank God!"

Glancing gratefully toward her grandfather's closed door, she hurried toward her own bedroom at the opposite end of the suite. Without waiting for the water to heat, she quickly rinsed off beneath a cold shower, managing to keep her head mostly dry in the process, then changed into jeans and a sweater. After stepping barefoot into leather clogs, she dragged a brush through her unruly hair and headed back downstairs. Asher was shaking hands with Lawrence when she reached the parlor.

"I believe we spoke on the phone not long ago," Asher said, looking as if he, too, had just stepped out of a shower, his chestnut-and-champagne hair plastered sleekly to his head.

"I believe we did," Lawrence confirmed genially.

"And I thought it was understood that I would serve as point of contact for the Monroes," Asher went on.

"Ah," was the noncommittal reply.

"I don't appreciate the end run," Asher stated flatly.

Jared Lawrence just smiled. "Noted." Taking an ink pen from his shirt pocket, he flipped open the folder in his hand and asked, "So when and where exactly would you like me to conduct the interviews?"

Obviously, this man was not going to be put off indefinitely. Ellie chewed her lip and caught Asher's eye as he glanced in her direction.

"Perhaps," Asher said slowly, "it would best serve everyone's purpose if the interviews were to take place at the Monroe house."

Jared Lawrence nodded his agreement. "Very well. Visuals are always appreciated."

"I'll arrange to have the house opened and let you know when we can meet."

Lawrence closed his folder and pocketed his pen, saying, "I look forward to hearing from you soon." Lawrence smiled at Ellie. "Give my best to your grandfather when he wakes."

"Yes. Thank you," she returned softly.

Nodding deeply to Hypatia, he said, "I appreciate the hospitality."

"Our pleasure," Hypatia murmured.

Dallas, who had observed all in silence, rose then. "I'll see you out."

Still smiling, Lawrence followed her from the room.

Ellie immediately crossed to her customary chair and collapsed upon it with a gusty sigh.

"Not so fast, my girl," Asher said, pulling her up by the arm again. "I'd like a word with you in private."

"Use the library, why don't you, dear?" Hypatia suggested, sounding weary.

"Excellent idea," Asher said, striding off in that direction with Ellie in tow. Dallas turned from the door just as they crossed the foyer. Her eyes widened, a speculative gleam lighting them.

Ellie groaned, but Asher did not slow down until he'd closed the library door behind them.

"We are out of time," he stated flatly. "I need straight answers."

Ellie glanced away. "I've given you straight answers." To those questions he had asked, anyway.

"Do not be fooled by that man's mild manner! He may be young and all smiles, but he knows exactly what he's doing, and today's little stunt tells me that he's clever. Beyond that, if I were a betting man, I'd lay odds that he knows something that I do not. So spill it, Ellie!"

"Spill what?"

"You're holding something back."

She threw up her hands. "I've given you the facts exactly as I know them!"

He stared at her for several moments, one hand moving agitatedly against his thigh until he clapped it to the back of his neck. "Something is missing from this picture, and if you can't supply it, then I need to speak to your grandfather." He looked up suddenly. "Is your grandfather having financial difficulties?"

"No! We may not be wealthy, but the Monroes have always been solvent. I don't make much money, of course, and I do have student loans, but to my knowledge, Grandpa has no major debts."

"What about a mortgage?"

"The house was inherited. I don't think it has ever carried a mortgage. The drugstore is free and clear and brings in a steady income."

"How were you paying for the renovations?"

Ellie shrugged. "Grandpa said there was money. I suppose it has to do with the drugstore. He took in a young partner a few years ago and recently struck a deal to sell. Not immediately, but over time. I assume there was a substantial down payment, and there had to be savings, too. Of course, it's all gone now. Grandpa paid off the contractor after the fire."

"That may have been a mistake," Asher mused. "It's possible the contractor or subcontractor was negligent."

Sighing, Ellie felt tears well up. It was all such a mess. She was tired and hungry and overwhelmed with worries about Dallas and Odelia and, especially just then, her grandfather. She had tried so hard to take the burden from him and protect Dallas in the process, but nothing was going as she'd hoped. The more immediate concern, however, was one she'd pushed to the back of her mind.

"We're never going to get back into our house, are we? But where are we going to go?"

"Hey," Asher said, "it's not like you're going to be out on the street."

"But we can't stay here indefinitely, and if we can't get the house back into shape…" She sniffed and tried to swallow back the lump thickening in her throat, but she could not keep the tears from falling. "G-Grandpa should be r-retiring and t-taking it easy, but I don't know if that will be p-possible now."

Asher patted her shoulder awkwardly. "Don't cry. That won't help."

"D-don't you understand? I can't p-pay rent for the two of us, but it's not fair for him to have to c-continue to work. He deserves better than this!"

Against his better judgment, Asher reached out and pulled her into his arms. "It's going to be okay."

She sniffed and closed her eyes, her head upon his shoulder. "You don't know that."

"I promise you." Pushing her away a little, he framed her face with his hands, tilting it upward. "Just work with me, sweetheart. We can't be at odds here. We have to be a team. Okay?"

"Okay," she echoed, smiling softly as she gazed into his amber eyes. "A team."

"That's my girl," he said, and then he set his lips to hers.

It was a completely natural gesture, a light, comforting kiss, but it quite literally curled Ellie's toes.

Suddenly, Asher wrenched away, leaping back so far that he bumped up against the door. Her hand lifted to her lips in wonder. He abruptly spun about, wrenched open the door and strode through it without a word.

Ellie ran forward, intending to call him back, but before she could get out a word, Dallas appeared. Ellie jerked to the side to look over her friend's shoulder, only to see Asher pulling the front door closed behind him. Deflated, she glowered at her friend.

Squealing like a teenager, Dallas grabbed Ellie by the shoulders and walked her backward into the room. "He called you 'sweetheart'! I heard it!"

"You were eavesdropping," Ellie accused.

"Duh. Did he kiss you? It sounded to me like he kissed you."

Oh, he had kissed her, and it hadn't been a brotherly affair this time, either. Ellie felt a smile tugging at her lips, but the memory of what had followed changed everything. That kiss had been an accident. Obviously, he hadn't intended to do it. There had been nothing romantic about it, not on Asher's end, anyway. He'd simply meant to comfort her and gotten carried away.

The thought brought fresh tears to her eyes. Suddenly, she couldn't help feeling that Dallas was very likely responsible for the train wreck that her life had become. If not for that fire, she'd never have been thrown into Asher's path. She'd never have let her girlish crush burgeon into something so desperate, and her grandfather and Odelia wouldn't be tiptoeing around the house like scalded cats. No matter how lofty Dallas's motives might have been, Ellie just could not feel in charity with her best friend at that moment.

"I am not listening to your nonsense, Dallas Chatam, not now. I'm facing a major problem here, in case you've forgotten."

In typical fashion, Dallas waved that away with the flop of her wrist. "Ash will take care of that."

"He's not a magician, Dallas. I have no doubt that he'll do what he can, but even he can't predict what the insurance company will do."

"Oh, come on. They'll pay. Besides," she said, waggling her eyebrows, "I'm less interested in how Ash is handling the insurance company than how he's handling you."

"Stop it!" Ellie hissed. "You don't know what you're talking about."

"So tell me."

"There is nothing *to* tell. And I don't want to talk about it anymore."

Huffing, Dallas parked her hands at her waist. "Well, that's no fun. You always tell me everything."

"What part of *nothing* do you not get?"

Dallas rolled her eyes. "Fine. So let's talk about your grandfather and my aunt Odelia."

Ellie wasn't much in the mood for their usual confab, but she parked herself on the edge of the large, rectangular table in the center of the floor. "I'm not sure there's anything to discuss there, either."

"Are you kidding? After the way she behaved earlier? No, I'm telling you, this is working. Getting them together under the same roof is the smartest thing we've ever done."

"We?" Ellie shook her head. "This wasn't my idea, Dallas. I'd never have thought of moving in here."

"Too true," Dallas admitted. Winking, she added, "I take every bit of credit for that particular stroke of genius." She reached around and patted herself on the back, grinning widely. "I cannot wait to tell my know-it-all big brother that I was right about Odelia and Kent!" With that, she whirled away and made for the door, saying, "Gotta run. I have a PTA meeting tonight. We'll talk more later." She paused to wag a finger at Ellie, adding, "And don't think you can spare the details indefinitely just because he's my brother."

She all but skipped through the door, leaving Ellie to wonder glumly just how far her friend would go to achieve her ends—and just how much longer she could go without asking Dallas for the truth.

Wincing at the slam of the door behind him, Asher paused on the deep porch of Chatam House. The guilt he'd been trying to outrun slammed into him, dealing a full body blow that made him stagger and moan.

He had done it. Good grief, he had actually kissed her! He hadn't just thought about it. He hadn't just anticipated it. He'd actually done it.

*Dear Lord, what's wrong with me?* he mentally howled, but before he could pursue that prayer to any satisfactory conclusion, a familiar voice called to him.

"Asher? Dear boy, whatever is the matter?"

He spun on one heel to find Odelia sitting in the same position where he'd last seen her, except this time she was swathed from head to knee in white faux fur. She appeared, in fact, to be wearing a hooded cape, which on anyone else would have been an oddity.

"Is something wrong?" Odelia pressed, obviously alarmed by his silence.

"Uh. No. That is, there was an insurance investigator here, and I was called in to run a little interference."

"Oh. I didn't realize. I only saw your car pull up in front of the house from my bedroom window, but by the time I made my way down here to wait for you, there was no one else about."

"He didn't stay long," Asher said, moving on to the more salient point. "You wanted to see me?"

Odelia smiled, but her gaze remained troubled. "Oddly enough, you seem to be the only one I can talk to about my situation."

Asher was almost relieved, and the irony of that was not lost on him. Just days ago he'd rather have taken a blow to the head than talk about his old auntie's crush on a past beau. Now, it seemed a much-needed distraction from his own tortured feelings. He would not think of *that* as a crush. No, no, a mature man did not form a crush on a woman young enough to be his... okay, daughter was a stretch. Still, she was too young.

Shaking his head, he walked over and took a seat next to his aunt. "How can I help you, Aunt Odelia?"

"I'm not sure you can, dear," she admitted, looking down at her lap. "I'm not sure anyone can. It's just that I'm so confused."

"About what exactly?"

She bit her lip, her capped teeth making significant indentations in the thick layer of bright pink lipstick that she wore. The sight made Asher smile despite everything. It struck him suddenly that despite the fact they'd been born on the same day, Odelia had somehow managed to stay younger than her sisters. He hadn't realized it before because their looks, if not their styles, were so similar. Something vibrant shone from Odelia's countenance, something that made her seem strangely innocent.

"Do you think it's possible," she finally began, "to find love at my age? Romantic love, I mean?"

*No* sprang to the tip of his tongue. It was the wisest answer he could give her, the surest. But he couldn't say it. He looked at that sweet face and those sad, yet expectant eyes, and he couldn't find the strength to crush her dreams.

"There is much to consider for someone in your position," he began carefully, only to feel the words he wanted to say dwindle away. Several awkward moments passed, during which he felt uncharacteristically unsure of himself. Gulping, he finally said, "I have to answer with a qualified yes. Anything's possible, after all…" He paused again, struck by the hope that had kindled in her eyes. Realizing suddenly that he couldn't argue his way out of this with logic alone, he stopped trying and gave her what she obviously needed to hear. "Yes. I think it's possible for someone your age to find love and romance."

She stared off into the distance. "Well," she said finally, "it's a moot point. Even if Kent should harbor some true feeling for me after all this time, nothing has changed. I still can't contemplate leaving my sisters, you know, not that I would expect to have the opportunity, mind you." She shook her head. "No. Regardless of what Dallas says, it's not my romance that God has ordained this time."

"This time?" He tilted his head, feeling that he'd missed something important.

She reached across and patted his knee. "I'm so very glad for you," Odelia told him warmly.

He had definitely missed something important. "I don't understand."

"Now, don't be coy. We've come to expect it, you know."

"Expect what?"

Odelia giggled. "Surely you've noticed. Every time someone seeks sanctuary in this house, a romance soon follows. Yours is no exception."

"Mine!" he yelped, jerking sideways in his chair.

"Well, yours and Ellie's. Tell me," she went on curiously, "when did you first notice her that way?"

Notice her? Notice Ellie? *That way?*

The truth blindsided him, knocking him out of his chair and onto his feet.

He had noticed Ellie the first moment that he'd laid eyes on her, when she'd been nothing more than another incoming freshman at BCBC. He'd instinctively buried the attraction beneath the knowledge that she was his baby sister's friend and, therefore, too young and off-limits. She was *still* too young.

Wasn't she?

*Client,* he reminded himself desperately. Baby sister's best friend. Fifteen years his junior. Client. Plus, he had no intention of ever remarrying. He did not want to get married again. Period. End of discussion.

Apparently not, however, so far as his aunt was concerned.

"I wouldn't have put you and Ellie together," Odelia was musing, tapping the cleft in her chin, "but God always knows best about these things."

Asher searched for the words that would lay to rest her romantic expectations on his behalf once and for all. "I fear you've misconstrued the situation, Aunt Odelia.

Ellie is not…my type." Unless not being able to stop thinking about her said otherwise.

"No?"

"I mean, she's a delightful wo…er, girl." He couldn't quite remember when he'd started thinking of her as a woman.

"Such a sunny nature," Odelia confirmed with a smile, "and you know what they say about opposites attracting. Oh, not that you're dour by any means, just so very…serious," she finished apologetically.

Asher stared at her for a full five seconds, no idea what to do or say. In the end, he took the coward's way out. Shivering, he clapped his arms about himself. "Brr. Chilly out here. Easy to forget it's still technically winter until the sun sets, isn't it?" He got up and sidled toward the steps at the edge of the porch, babbling, "But you didn't forget, did you? Nice and toasty in that lovely cape, I imagine. Me, I am…" *The world's greatest idiot.* "In a hurry. Sorry." He darted forward and smacked a kiss on her cheek then rushed to the steps, calling, "Stay warm. See you later."

"Bye-bye, dear," Odelia returned, lifting a hand in a tentative wave.

Asher fled as if someone had set the hounds on him. It was not, he reflected later, his finest moment, but it paled in comparison to what he'd done there in the library with Ellie, and it did not haunt his dreams that night.

Ah, no.

When at last he turned out the lamp on his bedside table that night, he dreamed, not of flight, but of kisses and violet eyes that seemed to look straight into his shabby soul.

## Chapter Eleven

"The house is Ellie's inheritance," Kent Monroe said, laying an arm on the edge of Asher's desk as he leaned forward in earnestness. "It's all I have to leave her, you see. My young partner at the pharmacy is making semiannual payments on the buy-in, but upon my death, everything having to do with the business goes to him."

Asher nodded. It was standard practice for partnerships, particularly if one of the partners carried a heavier load in conducting the business, as Asher assumed Monroe's younger partner did. Certainly the man had made no complaint when Asher had stepped into the pharmacy Friday morning to ask Kent for a word in the privacy of his office down the street.

"So the renovations were in aid of assuring the integrity of your granddaughter's inheritance," he said, intentionally suggesting a valid argument in support of their case.

"Just so," Mr. Monroe confirmed.

"And you paid for those renovations with the funds from the buy-in?" Asher asked hopefully.

Monroe shifted back in his chair, letting his hands fall onto his knees. "Not entirely. I had other funds."

"Savings."

"Some." Monroe sighed. "It's all gone now, of course, with very little to show for it, I'm afraid. Oh, the upstairs was not damaged by the fire, so technically what I paid for remains, with minimal smoke and water damage, but what difference does it make with the downstairs unlivable? I suppose I should be thankful that it wasn't the renovated portion that burned."

Asher tapped a finger against the arm of his chair, considering. Kent's version of events dovetailed neatly with Ellie's, and yet he could not escape the feeling that something was amiss.

"Can you think of anything else that I should know about this matter?" he asked.

Kent Monroe shook his balding head, but Asher noted that he averted his gaze. "Of course, I'm no lawyer."

Asher studied the man for a moment longer, trying to see him as Odelia and Ellie did, but his lawyer's sense told him that like his granddaughter, the old fellow was not being entirely forthcoming. Stymied, Asher decided not to press the matter further—for the moment.

"All right. Thank you for your time, Mr. Monroe."

Looking greatly relieved, the older man said, "Kent, please."

Asher rose to his feet. "Well, then, Kent, I'll see you on Monday afternoon at three-thirty."

Kent took several seconds to hoist his bulk to a standing position, but his handshake was strong when he grasped Asher's hand in farewell. "Oh, ah, Ellie says a quarter of four is about the best she can do. Something about bus duty."

Asher sighed. Ellie hadn't been out of his head for ten minutes at a stretch in the past forty-eight hours. Just the mention of her name drove him to distraction, and he couldn't afford to be distracted—not with the insurance adjuster about to return to the scene.

After seeing Kent out, Asher returned to his desk, but his disquiet would not yield to the usual panacea of work, and he eventually turned away from the computer screen to pray.

"Lord," he whispered, "I don't know what I ought to do now, but all I ask is that You please somehow help me protect Ellie."

Only after the words had left his mouth did he realize exactly what he'd said or what it was that weighed so heavily upon his heart. It was no surprise, really, that he hadn't recognized it earlier. In his lifetime, Asher rarely had known real fear. Bitter disappointment, yes. Heartbreak, even. Loss. Failure. Shame, too, once or twice…the entire gamut of negative human emotion.

But this was the first time he'd felt such fear for someone who had become so important to him.

On the following Monday afternoon, Ellie turned the truck into the familiar narrow drive and got out to walk around to the front, where she huddled inside her hooded raincoat, waiting for her grandfather to join her. Asher stood on the front porch of the house, his luxury SUV at the curb. The day had taken on a gray cast and sputtered intermittently with a cold, brittle mist that would have coated the ground with a slick sheet of ice only a couple weeks earlier. Today, it produced only gloom, which seemed sadly appropriate.

Dreading what was to come, Ellie surveyed the beloved old Victorian house. As always, its white, pink and pale gray gingerbread exterior, complete with a turret, elaborate trim, shutters and tall brick chimneys, evoked thoughts of horse-drawn carriages and courtly manners, of young girls in wide-skirted ball gowns and prosperous gentlemen in swallowtail coats. However, it no longer quite felt like home.

How odd. She still felt very much a guest at Chatam House, and this place had always been home to her, even when she'd lived elsewhere with her parents. Yet that somehow seemed in the past to her now.

Asher walked down the three broad, wooden steps to the cobblestone walkway that bisected the shallow front yard and stood impatiently, his hands brushing back the sides of his suit jacket to lightly bracket his waist. Ellie hung back enough to let her grandfather take the lead. He traded words of greeting with the younger man and trudged up the steps. Asher met her gaze grimly before holding out an arm in welcome or perhaps encouragement. She walked ahead of him up the steps and into the deeper gloom of the porch, wishing she could have a moment to speak to him. But now was not the time.

The X-shaped metal bar that the fire department had bolted across the front door had been removed and now lay to one side. Without preamble, her grandfather opened the door and went inside. Ellie followed, the scent of burnt wood and fabrics assailing her nose.

Gray streaked the flocked green-and-white wallpaper in the entry; brown water stains mottled it into a garish mess. The red oak hardwood floor had been scorched in a wavy pattern right up to the edge of the narrow staircase with its delicate hand-turned spindles. Soot covered everything, including the small but elaborate chandelier overhead.

Down the hall, she could see the remains of the kitchen with its warped cabinets and soggy, molding linens. Only the tin ceiling panels had kept the ceiling from falling down in that room. They had not been so fortunate in other parts of the house.

Turning left, they took in the parlor. It looked like nothing so much as a garbage heap. The heavy velvet curtains had burned right to the rods, one of which had fallen down. Chunks of ceiling plaster hung down like spooky, ragged flags and covered what sodden furniture still existed in great gray clumps and fine white spatters. The carpet had melted to what was left of the floor, and the far wall had burned to the studs.

The only truly intact section of the room was the fireplace, which shared a sturdy brick wall with the dining room. The brick and mortar would need a great deal of scrubbing, but at least the ornately carved wooden mantle remained untouched.

After looking around for a few minutes, Asher nodded at a burned-out section of the parlor floor where the couch had stood. "Is that where it started?"

Some oblong lumps of charcoal were all that was left of the sofa, which had sat facing the doorway, and the tall, narrow table that had stood behind it. A rusty-looking tin can, a small, twisted rod and a few shattered pieces of milky, grayish glass showed where the lamp had fallen.

Her grandfather nodded. "Yes, that's it. The lamp stood on a table at the back of the couch, and the workmen had placed some tools and supplies behind there so they'd be out of sight. It was a tall lamp on a tall, narrow table. Gave good light, that lamp."

There were no overhead lights in the parlor, and the large glass shade on that lamp had provided ample illumination, which was why they'd kept it despite its top-heavy proportions. Ellie suspected that her grandmother had added the wide, domed, cobalt-blue glass shade herself years earlier.

They talked through what information they'd been given and their own actions of that day several times before the insurance company rep arrived. To their surprise, before he asked a single question, he walked them through what he knew, and by the time he was done, it had become abundantly clear to Ellie and everyone else that the paint remover had been turned over *before* the lamp had fallen.

"I just assumed that the lamp had to fall and knock over the can," her grandfather said, shaking his head. "The lamp was top-heavy, after all, and the plastic bucket with the paint thinner inside was on the floor."

Lawrence made a noncommittal sound at that and walked over to the window. "The other window on this wall has a storm unit affixed to the outside. This one does not. Why?"

"Cross ventilation," Ellie supplied. "My grandmother hated the central air unit after it was installed and often preferred to open a window, but she had a difficult time with the storm windows, which is why we removed one on each side of the house for her. We just never replaced them."

"But it was cold that night, wasn't it?"

"Yes."

"So why open the window?"

"Paint fumes," her grandfather answered. "The house reeked of them, and since we were busy moving things around, we were warm enough."

"I notice that it has no screen," Lawrence pointed out.

Kent grimaced. "I put a hoe handle through it while raking leaves last fall. I wasn't in any hurry to fix it. No insects in winter even if the window does have to be opened."

Again, Lawrence made that noise, which was beginning to sound skeptical to Ellie. "So you left the house open while you moved furniture into storage?"

"Not intentionally," Ellie told him. "I meant to close the window before we left." Actually, she'd thought she had, but she'd opened and closed that window so many times since the renovations had started that she couldn't remember one instance from another.

"Don't suppose it would have mattered," Lawrence said lightly, "since the fire department reported that they'd found the front door unlocked when they arrived."

Ellie's jaw dropped. At the same time, an expression of horror came over Kent's face.

"That...that was my fault." He looked to Ellie apologetically. "I know I said I'd take care of it, but when you mentioned locking the front door, that reminded me that I needed to look up the code to open the storage unit. Once I'd done that, well, I forgot about the front door."

"Then anyone could have come into the house af-ter you'd left," Asher quickly pointed out. "Isn't that right?"

Ellie gulped and nodded worriedly. "I suppose." Anyone could have—but Dallas had been the one on the scene. Which was the last thing she wanted to point out to Asher.

Lawrence just smiled and asked who might have had reason to set the fire. Who, he meant, besides the owners of the house. Ellie said nothing. All her words and thoughts from that point on were reserved for God.

Asher had to give the young investigator credit for not blustering and pressing for answers. Then again, it was to the insurance company's benefit to delay making a ruling on the case. By denying the claim without overwhelming evidence of wrongdoing on the part of their insured, they opened themselves up to a lawsuit. On the other hand, they could delay settlement via patient investigation. They had some very reasonable questions, after all. The problem was that in at least a couple of instances, the Monroes had no reasonable answers.

When he returned to the house after seeing Mr. Lawrence off, he found Ellie perched on the porch swing.

"Grandpa's looking around out back for his cat," she said, sliding to make room for Asher. Feeling unaccountably weary, he sat down. A number of issues clamored for attention, but he couldn't seem to organize his thoughts just then. The gray of the day mirrored his gloomy mood perfectly.

"Think you'll have to cancel soccer practice?" Ellie asked.

"Already have."

"What about tomorrow?" she asked.

He shrugged. "We'll have to see."

Nodding, she used her feet to put the swing in motion, pushing against the floor of the porch. Asher let himself settle back and enjoy the lulling sway of the hard bench seat beneath him. Seconds later, however, he realized that he had to say something. He locked his knees, halting the movement of the swing.

"Ellie, I apologize for the other day. That kiss never should have happened."

She made a small sound of distress, but when he looked at her, her gaze was trained woodenly on her lap.

He plodded on doggedly. "I don't usually do that sort of thing. Especially not with clients. Especially not with young clients who could misunderstand how these things can—"

She got up and leaned a shoulder against a slender post supporting the porch roof, her back to him. "I'm not stupid, you know."

"I never thought you were."

Putting her spine to the post, she folded her arms and glanced at him before dropping her gaze to the floor. "Your aunts and sister think we're having a romance."

"I know." Asher sighed and leaned forward to prop his elbows against his knees. "But they're wrong," he added softly.

"Are they, Asher?" she asked. Not waiting for an answer, she sent him an unreadable look then pushed away from the post, turned and calmly walked down the steps, putting her hood up. He watched her go to her truck and slide in behind the steering wheel. An instant later, she started up the engine. After a few moments, Kent trudged around the house and got in.

Asher sat where he was until the little truck had backed out and gone on its way. Finally, he pulled out his phone and called the fire department, asking for someone to come and put up the door blocks again.

* * *

Asher sat behind his desk and stared at the computer screen, trying to bully his mind into cooperation. He had a case coming up on the local docket and needed to prepare, but he couldn't focus. The gray weather seemed disinclined to lighten, spitting chilly rain for another day. He'd had to call off soccer practice again, and he itched to do something besides sit and brood.

On pure impulse, he got up and tossed on his overcoat before heading down the stairs and out onto the sidewalk. He crossed the street and walked to the corner. Shoving through the heavy glass door, he entered the pharmacy and went to the soda counter, realizing only then that he'd hoped to find Ellie or even Kent Monroe there. Instead, he found a teenage girl with too much eye makeup and pink streaks in her hair doing homework at the counter.

She got up off her stool and moved behind the counter. "What can I get you?"

"I'll have a cappuccino root beer float."

Nodding, she went to work. He took a seat two stools down from her textbook. Moments later, she set the tall fluted glass in front of him, a long spoon and a straw poking up through the foam. He paid the two and a half bucks that she asked for and set about demolishing his treat. By the time he was done, he felt pleasantly full—and had reached a decision of sorts.

Perhaps, he thought, he had been mistaken. Perhaps what he sensed in the Monroes was guilt for having failed to secure the house. Or perhaps he was making excuses for them because he wanted it to be that way. Regardless, he had to get to the bottom of this thing before the insurance company did. Rising, he left the pharmacy and drove straight to Chatam House.

It was pitch-black out, the gloom of the day having carried over into the evening to effectively block even the faint light of the moon and stars. Asher approached the yellow door, its brass lamps burning softly on either side.

To his surprise, Ellie answered the door. The wide, deeply cuffed neck of her oversize sweater had slipped off one smoothly rounded shoulder. She tilted her head, curls bouncing.

"Hello, Ellie. Do you have a few minutes?"

Nodding, she backed out of the doorway. "Come in. Your aunts are in their suite watching TV, I think. Grandpa and I are enjoying the fire in the front parlor."

He followed her across the foyer. Kent sat in the armchair across from the fire, staring at the dancing flames. He looked up only as Asher folded himself down into the seat next to Ellie on the settee. The older gentleman nodded.

"Asher. Didn't expect to see you again so soon."

Sighing, Asher leaned forward, his elbows braced against his knees, and clasped his hands together. "I want you to know, I've prayed about this at length and—"

"You think we set the fire," Ellie said.

Asher dropped his head. "I didn't say that. But I'm concerned about what I've heard. And about what I haven't heard from the two of you."

Ellie and her grandfather traded looks. Kent cleared his throat before saying, "I don't understand."

"Don't you? Every instinct I possess is screaming that you haven't told me everything."

"I—I can't imagine what else there is to say," Kent sputtered.

Odelia barreled into the room at that moment, wearing a blue-green-and-gold-paisley caftan. "Did I hear the door? Ah. Asher. Hello, dear."

"Aunt Odelia."

She looked from one grim face to another before asking shakily, "Is everything all right?"

Kent twisted sideways in his chair. "Asher is concerned," he pronounced gravely.

"Oh. Oh, my." Eyes widening, she stepped forward. "Not about…" She glanced at Kent before bearing down on Asher. "You wouldn't…you certainly don't have to…"

"It's about the fire," Asher said in an effort to put her mind at ease.

A muscle twitched below her left eye. Gulping, she nodded. "Well, I'm sure it's none of my business, then. I'll leave you to talk. Excuse me please." Her hands fluttered at her sides. "Always blundering in where I'm not wanted," she muttered, turning away.

Kent sent Asher an accusatory glare, heaved himself up to his feet and went after her.

Asher sighed and lifted a hand to his forehead. So much for getting to the bottom of things. He couldn't press the matter now if he wanted to—and he did not, not after seeing the worry on Odelia's face and the affront on Ellie's. Neither of them would ever forgive him if he forced Kent to confess to arson, not that he'd intended to do any such thing. He couldn't reconcile the notion with what he knew of Kent Monroe. Still, something was not right, and Asher couldn't help feeling trapped between that proverbial rock and hard place, especially given his aunt's feelings for Monroe—and his feelings for Ellie.

Sitting back, he stretched an arm along the cushioned back of the settee and conceded at least part of the battle. "You're right about those two."

She relaxed, brightening visibly. "You think so? What changed your mind?"

He wouldn't break a confidence, but he didn't have to. "Did you see the way they looked at each other just now?"

She favored him with a soft smile. "I did, but I didn't think you would."

"Now don't get your hopes up," he warned, even though he was absurdly glad to have given her even that little bit of joy. "Odelia has made it clear that she has no intention of leaving her sisters, now or ever."

"She's talked to you about him then?"

Asher nodded. "I can't betray a confidence, of course, but we have spoken about it."

"Have you counseled her not to get romantically involved?"

He looked her straight in the eye. "No, actually, I haven't."

Ellie's violet gaze studied his face for a long moment. "What are you going to do?"

"What I've been doing," he said. "Pray."

She smiled again. "Can't argue with that. I've been doing a good bit of it myself." She scrunched up her nose. "You don't suppose we're praying at cross-purposes, do you?"

"I hope not," he said sincerely. Then, strictly on impulse, he offered her his hand. "We could make sure by praying together."

Her visage softened. Eyes glowing, she slid close and put her hand in his. This, Asher knew, was right. He might not know what else to do, but this, at least, was exactly the right thing at this moment. Bowing his head and closing his eyes, he began to speak softly.

"Father God, You work all things to our good, even if sometimes it doesn't seem that way. We may not understand what is going on or why, but deep down we know that You always have our best interests at heart. Keep us mindful of that, Lord, and whatever happens, whatever comes, help us trust You to protect those we love." Ellie squeezed his hand, and he whispered, "Amen."

He looked up to find Hypatia and Magnolia standing before him, twin smiles upon their dear old faces. Magnolia wore a rumpled housecoat over a voluminous nightgown and soft corduroy slippers, her thick iron-gray braid curving across one shoulder. Hypatia was her usual tailored self in black silk pajamas, matching wrapper and foam-lined house shoes. It had been years since he'd seen her silver hair down. Caught at her nape with a band, it hung down her back between her shoulder blades.

"Do you mind if we join you?" Hypatia asked.

"Of course not," Ellie said, loosening her hand from his and sitting back.

"Please," Asher put in, standing.

"We thought we'd enjoy a cup of tea in front of the fire," Hypatia said, stepping around the wing chair opposite them to sit down. "Doesn't seem wise to build a fire in our suite at this hour when this one's already toasty warm. Won't you join us in some refreshments?"

"I'm sure there are sandwiches," Magnolia said, moving toward the door.

"And cookies," Hypatia called, hunching her shoulders in an expression of girlish delight, her amber eyes sparkling.

Asher smiled and lifted his arm to rest loosely about Ellie's shoulders. It wasn't wise, especially with the aunties already speculating about a possible romance between the two of them. Yet he could not stop himself.

He still had to get to the bottom of the fire at the Monroes' house, but worries and questions could wait for another day. With no small sense of contentment, he noted that Ellie relaxed beside him, her shoulder tucked into his side.

At that moment, all seemed exactly as it should, and he was in no mood to turn away that gift.

For the first time in a very long while, Asher pushed aside his concerns and simply let himself be at ease.

# Chapter Twelve

Kent caught up to her in the sunroom. His Odelia was
surprisingly spry, he noted, breathing heavily. No, not
*his* Odelia. Not any longer, not for a very long time.
And never again.

"Wait," he called. "Please."

Aiming for the door to the outside, she halted in mid-
step and, after a moment, turned cautiously, her beautiful eyes wide. Kent felt a kick in his chest. She was
still the dearest and most beautiful woman he'd ever
known—and he was obviously hurting her. He drew a
deep breath, pulling in his stomach as he did so.

"I cannot bear this, Odelia," he said, his voice even
more gravelly than usual. She flinched. "I cannot bear
to see you so unhappy," he went on, moving closer so
that he could lower his voice.

She frowned at that. "What makes you think I'm
unhappy?"

He sent her a wry look. "My dear, how long have we
known each other?"

"Oh, sixty years or so, I imagine," she muttered,
blinking.

"Sixty-two," he corrected wistfully. "Sixty-two years, two months and three days."

He remembered it like it was yesterday, that evening when, a reluctant teenager, he had accompanied his parents to a Christmas dinner at Chatam House. Odelia and her sisters had been dressed in matching rose-red frocks heavily embroidered with holly green, their lustrous brown hair brushed and pulled back from their almost identical faces by pearl clips, the ends crimped into curls that brushed their slender shoulders. They were as alike as peas in a pod, yet it had been Odelia who had fascinated him, Odelia whom he had sought out, Odelia who had earned his heart by evening's end with her sparkling smiles, sweetness and fun spirit. Years had passed before he'd worked up the courage to try to be more than her friend and years after that before he'd gone down on his knee to her. He still could not believe that she'd agreed to marry him that day.

For a time afterward, his world had been golden and bright. When she had broken it off, he was not really surprised—she had always been too far above him— but he was almost mortally wounded. He had eventually pulled himself together and gone on with his life, marrying, becoming a father and grandfather. If not for the latter, he might now question his choices, frankly, but Ellie, dear Ellie, had been his solace and delight since the day of her birth. Not even she, however, could replace this lady in his heart, and as before, he could bear his own pain more easily than Odelia's.

"I will leave immediately, dear lady," he announced, "rather than continue to upset you with my presence and my unrequited love."

Her hands flew to her face. "Did you say…you cannot mean…after everything, can you really l-love me?"

It was his turn to be astonished. He stepped closer, reveling in her proximity. "My darling, I have loved you since I was thirteen years old. I will love you until the day I die. But I would rather love you from afar if that would make you happy again."

"Oh!" she squeaked, gazing up at him. Her warm amber eyes filled with tears. "I never dreamed that you might still care."

He bowed his head. "I have asked God so many times to take away these feelings, but for some reason He has chosen not to. And I cannot honestly say that I regret them, except for the pain they may cause you." He would have stepped away then if she had not reached out her dainty hand and grasped him by the shirtsleeve.

"I, too, have prayed and prayed," she warbled, "trying to quiet my own feelings, but I cannot help caring for you."

"Odelia!" Kent whispered, covering her hand with his. "I don't understand. Are you saying that I must g-go…or…stay?"

"I'm saying that you will break my heart if you leave this house," she told him, leaning into his chest.

He clapped his arms around her, a familiar elation puffing up his chest. It was the same as that day he'd slipped his ring on her finger. How could it be? She even felt as she had that day, as if she fit perfectly against him. Only one thing was different: he could not quite imagine a future for them this time.

Realizing suddenly that it was the future that he had envisioned for them before that had spelled their end, he pulled himself straight, the top of her head tucked beneath his chin. Had he not been so set on living in the Monroe family home, would things have gone differently for them? The thought of being here at Chatam House, with her and her sisters and parents, had seemed unthinkable back then. He was an only child, after all, and it had always been understood that the family home would go to him. As a young man eager to begin a family of his own, he had been looking forward to setting up his household. Living with her family had seemed less than manly, but when she had said that she could never leave her sisters, he had thought that she was really saying that she could not be with him. Had he been wrong about that? If so, what did that mean for them now?

"We will pray through this together, my love," he decided, "and then we shall see what God may have in store for us."

She nodded and turned her face up to him, a smile trembling upon her lips. "Yes. Yes, let's do that."

Turning her toward one of the colorful chaises, he kept her close. It seemed to him that his feet barely touched the floor as they walked side by side toward an uncertain but hopeful future.

The house was quiet as Ellie walked Asher to the front door, the sisters having retired some time before.

"The weatherman says the front will lift tomorrow," she told him. They'd sat for long minutes in companionable silence before the fire, but now for some reason she felt compelled to speak.

"That's good." He shrugged into his overcoat. "Maybe everyone can get in a practice tomorrow."

"If we can't practice, do we still play on Saturday?"

"Depends on the fields. I'll take a look tomorrow and let everyone know by lunchtime."

She nodded. "Will I see you at the soccer field?"

He looked at the floor, thumbing the cleft in his strong chin. "I don't know." He grimaced. "Maybe."

Obviously, he was greatly conflicted about seeing her again. Still, he had come over tonight, and he hadn't, after all, pressed her about the fire. Instead, he'd prayed with her and sat with her. That was something, she supposed. It wasn't his fault that she wanted more. She backed up a step.

"Sleep well."

"For a change, you mean?" he quipped lightly. She tilted her head at that. He made a dismissive face. "Soccer season is always a busy time for me, so many details and tons of paperwork. I have a case coming up for trial soon, too."

"And now us," she said apologetically.

"And now *you*," he said, tapping the tip of her nose with his forefinger. "You worry me, Ellen Monroe. You worry me."

She didn't know what to say to that. He slipped away before she could decide, leaving her with the bittersweet feeling that he did care for her. But would he ever care in the way she cared for him? She was beginning to believe that he could—if he would allow himself to do so.

"Nervous?"

Ellie whirled away from the soccer field where her team was loping back and forth to warm up before facing their first opponents. Many of them had worn their tutus and winged caps, to the disdain of the other team, but Asher noted that her kids were laughing and grinning while the other coach and team mother were trying to stop the rude jeers of their own players. Ellie shook her head in answer to his question.

"You came," she said, sounding so pleased that he smiled.

He'd tried not to. He really had. And he'd managed to stay away from practice, at least, but he just couldn't miss this, her first game on this bright first Saturday of March.

"No reason to be nervous," he told her.

"I know. Win or lose, what matters most to me personally is that my kids have fun."

He smiled ruefully. "They might enjoy winning."

"Better that they enjoy playing soccer," she countered.

The referee, a tall, thin, teenage boy, blew his whistle and tapped his wristwatch before holding up five fingers. Ellie called her team in and stripped them down to their regulation uniforms, handing off the tutus and caps to a bemused Asher while the team mother passed around small bottles of water. Dropping down into a crouch, Ellie engaged every eye.

"Game faces," she instructed, demonstrating her own. She held the fierce, wooden expression for several heartbeats before breaking into a wide grin. The children followed suit, sitting solemnly then breaking into laughter. "Okay, listen to me. Just play your positions as you've learned them and don't worry about the outcome. I want you forwards taking shots on goal and not just passing to each other, and you defenders need to keep track of the ball all the time. Remember, you're in the play even if the ball isn't close to you, so be ready. Now, let's have some fun." Rising to her feet, she called out positions and names. Players popped up one by one and hit the field, high-fiving each other enthusiastically as they took their places.

"You know the other team has been playing together for a couple years now, don't you?" Asher asked softly. Despite her bravado, he desperately did not want to see her disappointed.

"I do. I also know that they don't have the skills our players do," she told him confidently.

He said nothing to that. The game would tell if she was right about that or not.

Ellie's team won the coin toss. The ref blew the whistle, and her team made a running kickoff. What followed was twenty-five minutes of chaos that somehow resolved itself into a competition.

The second half proved more settled than the first. With the score one to one, Ellie's team seemed to sense that they could win. It looked as if the contest would end in a tie, but at the last moment, a girl on Ellie's team booted a ball right into the corner of the goal. The stunned goalie of the other team stood there with his hands on his hips, glaring in disbelief while Ellie's Yellow Jackets erupted in cheers. An instant later, the ref blew his whistle. Ellie looked to Asher in astonishment.

"Did we win? Did we win?" one of the bench sitters demanded.

Asher's lips curved into a lopsided grin. "You did," he confirmed.

"We actually did!" Ellie threw her arms around Asher's neck with joy. His own arm automatically banded her waist. For a single heartbeat, they stood in an embrace, and then she straightened.

"Well done, coach," he muttered.

At almost the same moment, Ilene announced, "Ice cream sandwiches!"

Ellie's team tugged her away, but she glanced back at him. "You're right. Winning is fun!"

He bent his head to hide his grin, which grew wider with every moment. "Ellie, Ellie," he whispered. "What am I going to do with you?"

Ellie certainly hadn't expected to see Asher here today, not after he'd failed to show at practice, but she could still feel that strong arm snug about her waist even as parents overwhelmed her with their delight.

Somehow, despite the celebratory ice cream sandwiches, Ellie managed to get everyone packed up and the area vacated so that the next team could access the field. All the while, Ellie accepted a steady stream of congratulations while keeping an eye on Asher. He hung about, just a little apart from everyone else. By the time the last kid had piled into his parents' vehicle, Asher had moved to Ellie's side, his hands in his pockets. She waved until there was no one to wave at before turning to him.

"That went well, I think," she said, trying to be modest.

He laughed. "You think? I commend you on your strategy. Fun wins."

Ellie grinned. "My kids had a blast, didn't they?"

"And would have if they'd lost," he conceded.

She grinned so widely that her cheeks hurt. But then his expression sobered, and he looked down.

"Ellie, I think we should talk. Do you have a few minutes now?" Torn between hope and dread, she nodded. "Come sit in my car then," he suggested.

She followed him across the parking lot and allowed

him to hand her up into the passenger-side seat before he moved around to slide beneath the steering wheel.

"Ellie," he began, reaching for her hand. For a moment he said nothing more, just smoothed the pad of his thumb across her knuckles. Her heart beat so loudly that she could barely hear him when he said, "This can't go any further."

Her heart clunked inside her chest. Had he guessed her feelings, somehow divined her dreams?

"You have to tell me what you've been holding back about the fire," he said. "I *have* to know."

Relief swamped her, followed swiftly by…guilt. She squeezed her eyes closed, praying for guidance. On one hand, she felt the need to protect her friend. On the other, she *had* omitted information. Then again, Dallas was his sister. Surely, she could trust him to help her protect her friend from any foolish behavior.

Taking a deep breath, she looked up and softly confessed, "I told Dallas we would be gone that night."

Asher's expression did not change. "Okay."

"She knew we would be at the storage unit."

He just stared at her. "And your point is?"

Ellie gulped and lost her nerve. "I—I just remembered, that's all. Thought you'd want to know."

He dropped her hand, clapping his to the nape of his neck. "Ellie, I need significant facts. You must know that you can trust me with the complete truth. I'm not just your attorney, I am also your friend. Whatever happened, whatever you or your grandfather might have done, I'll help you."

She tilted her head, telling herself that his failure to grasp the significance of what she'd told him didn't mean what she feared it did, but she would not directly accuse her friend. She'd told him what she'd kept back, and that was as far as she was prepared to go.

"You wanted to know what I hadn't told you. Now you do."

"That can't be all there is to it. Someone *arranged* that fire."

She waited for him to make the connection, but it gradually became obvious that he'd already come to a conclusion and it didn't have anything to do with what she'd told him. "You suspect Grandpa and me of setting our house on fire."

"I'm just trying to get to the truth."

"I've given you the truth."

"Ellie, you have to face facts. If you didn't set that fire—"

"I didn't!"

"Then someone else must have."

"Yes, someone else!"

"I know it's difficult, but you are a Christian woman," he began warmly. "You know that once the truth, the full truth, is out, you'll not only feel much better, but you'll be able to tap into the comfort that God is standing ready to give."

"I have told you the 'full truth'!" she snapped. "And don't you dare question my Christian ethics!"

He bowed his head and visibly, deliberately relaxed. When he looked up again, he was wearing a patently phony smile. Clapping a hand upon her shoulder, he said cajolingly, "You're too young to fully understand the situation. There are remedies, *legal* remedies, that you can't be aware of. Trust me to—"

"Trust you?" she snapped, blazingly angry now. "You discount me, disparage me, belittle me and my grandfather…you don't even listen to me! But I should *trust* you?" She yanked open the door, pivoted on her seat and slid down to the ground, whirling back to face him.

He sat stony-faced, his jaw grating. "You're behaving foolishly."

"Am I? Like a child, do you think? Well, I may be little more than a child in your book, and I may not understand as much as I think I do, but I know this—I can't trust a man who doesn't trust me."

"I'm trying to trust you," he said quietly.

"Are you? I think you're trying *not* to trust me, because that might mean that you actually care about me. Personally. But that's the one thing you won't do, isn't it? You won't care. I've got that now. And you've got the truth, whether you believe it or not, so I don't think there's any more to be said."

She slammed the door closed, turned and strode to her truck without so much as a backward glance. She dared not look back. She couldn't let him see the tears streaming down her cheeks. She couldn't let him or anyone see what it cost her to walk away from the one man she had dared to dream she might actually love.

Staring at the tall, arched, mission-style doors of the inner sanctum of the Downtown Bible Church, where Chatams had been members since its founding, Asher again considered his options and deemed them just as limited as they'd been in the middle of the previous night. He hadn't been able to sleep thinking about how horribly he'd blown it with Ellie yesterday. He couldn't forget how hurt she'd seemed, and the longer he'd thought about it, the more he'd feared that she would never speak to him again.

The idea had seemed wise at the time. He'd thought that after meeting her at the soccer field, where they obviously had something in common, he could take on the manner of a fond uncle and inspire her to tell him what he needed to know. He'd thought, too, that maintaining an avuncular attitude would help him keep his feelings in perspective.

Wrong on both counts. All he'd done was ruin her first win, insult her and drive her away—and he hadn't exactly felt like her wiser, older relative in the process. Why couldn't he have just let her enjoy her first coaching success? Because, he admitted to himself, that hug on the sideline had knocked him for a loop. Everything about Ellie seemed to knock him for a loop. The worst part of all, though, was the deep, roiling panic that he felt at the thought of never speaking to her again.

That panic astonished, humbled and troubled him. Yes, it had to do with the case. Ellie's cooperation was vital to keeping her and her grandfather out of trouble. But it was more than that. It was more than her being a family friend, too, more than her being *his* friend, so much more that he'd eat crow to mend the rift, which explained why he was here now. If he had to grovel, he might as well do it on hallowed ground.

Squaring his shoulders, Asher stepped forward and pulled open the door far enough to slip inside. The minister of education was announcing the start of a new Bible study. Asher stood at the back, oddly aware of the soaring arches, gleaming brass fixtures, stuccoed walls and stained-glass windows that surrounded him.

He had known the crowd would be large at the main service, but he hadn't expected to see the backs of quite so many heads. An usher approached him then, silently offering to help him find a seat. Smiling, Asher shook his head and returned to his survey. Finally, he spied her, more than halfway down. She sat three people in from the end of the pew, her grandfather on her left, Asher's uncle Hub on her right, with his cousin Kaylie and her husband, Stephan, on the outside.

As Asher made his way down the side of the church, he noted that Kent sat next to Odelia, who wore an enormous pink feathered hat. A pair of bluebirds almost large enough to be real swung from her earlobes as if attempting to land on her yellow-clad shoulders. He smiled, despite his disquiet. It looked as if his dear old auntie was back to her eccentric self. Glancing at Kent, who leaned in to whisper something in her ear, Asher felt a spurt of alarm on her behalf. What would happen to his sweet aunt if it turned out that her old beau was responsible for the fire at his house? Telling himself that he had enough worries of his own at the moment, Asher stopped at the end of the pew, sent Stephan Gallow an apologetic glance and stepped over the big man's enormous feet.

A professional hockey player, Stephan sent a glower his way, then smiled as if to say that it was nothing more than habit before shifting aside. Asher nodded at Kaylie then jerked his head sideways to suggest that she move down. She sent a bemused glance toward the other end of the crowded pew and snuggled up next to her husband. It occurred to Asher as he struggled past his surprised uncle that Kaylie couldn't be much older than Ellie. Yet there she sat, happily married. He wondered just how old Stephan was. Not as old as him, surely, he thought, placing a hand on his uncle's arm to let him know that he wanted to squeeze in next to Ellie, who only then looked his way.

A frown turned down the corners of her mouth, and she moved as far from him as possible, all but turning her back on him. He wedged himself into the small space, stretching his arm out along the back of the pew in order to give himself more room, and leaned in close to whisper pleadingly, "Ellie."

She twisted slightly, jabbing her elbow into his ribs. "I don't want to talk to you," she whispered, "now that I know you're not on our side."

"I am," he softly insisted.

Suddenly she launched herself to her feet. Music erupted, and he realized that somehow, he had missed the call to worship as well as the announcement of the first song. Rising belatedly, he allowed himself to really gaze at Ellie. He almost wished he hadn't indulged the impulse.

She looked achingly beautiful in a strawberry-red sheath. She'd caught her hair up on top of her head somehow, leaving curly little tendrils to fall about her face and nape. Tiny ruby studs adorned her delicate earlobes.

"I'm sorry," he whispered in her ear.

She ignored him.

"I only want to help you," he said.

Nothing.

"Please don't be mad at me."

She sent him a speaking glance, her eyes so sad that it was all he could do not to take her in his arms right then. Instead, he lifted a hand to help her support the hymnal that she held and listened as she began to sing. She had a credible alto voice. After a moment, he joined his own limited baritone to hers, singing as much in supplication as praise.

## Chapter Thirteen

Ellie did her dead-level best not to so much as glance in Asher's direction again throughout the remainder of the service, but she sensed that he was as aware of her as she was of him. She resented that he had cornered her, literally, in church. Maybe he really did feel bad about offending her, but that didn't change the fact that he suspected her of arson. He had to know that if he'd approached her elsewhere, she'd have told him to get lost, but she couldn't do that in the midst of a worship service. She didn't have to acknowledge him, though, and spent most of the time talking silently to God.

*Lord, I don't want to be angry, but he thinks I started that fire! Do I have to spell it out for him? And what about Grandpa? How could he suspect my grandpa of something like that? Especially now, especially after Asher kissed me.*

Oh, it was best not to go there. That kiss had meant nothing, less than nothing. Why, it had been downright insulting. He had apologized for it, for pity's sake. How much more proof did she need that... Wait a minute. Had that kiss been about softening her up so she'd confess? Was that why he'd sat by the fireside with her, casting her those poignant looks and holding her hand while he'd prayed?

Suddenly incensed, she shifted to sit on one hip in order to present her back to him as much as possible.

"Ellie," he whispered pleadingly.

She stared straight ahead, but she didn't hear one word that the pastor said. Later, when the congregation rose for the closing hymn, she was among the last to get to her feet. Immediately, she shifted to her left, intent on putting as much distance between them as possible, only to feel his arm slip around her waist and pull her close to his side. Stiffening, she pretended not to notice.

As they filed out into the central aisle behind his aunties and her grandfather a few minutes later, she did her best to move away from him, but Asher made certain to stay close, his hand curled around the curve of her waist. She attempted to walk ahead of him, but his hand went with her and the rest of him caught up.

Eventually they made it to the cavernous foyer, and she slipped free. The Chatam sisters were there ahead of them, of course, along with her grandfather and Asher's uncle and cousin and her husband. It felt very much as if they were waiting for her and Asher. She saw the curiosity and speculation in their eyes, but before she could escape, Odelia stepped forward.

"Asher, dear, what a delight to see you here this morning. You'll take lunch with us at Chatam House, of course. Won't you?" Surprised because the aunties usually "ate simple" on Sundays so the household staff could have the day off, Ellie blinked. Then Odelia turned a worshipful gaze on Ellie's grandfather and crooned, "Kent grilled for us yesterday. Isn't that lovely?"

Asher's eyebrows rose. He cleared his throat and said, "That sounds great."

"Chicken and pineapple kebabs," Kent announced proudly. "Warming in the kitchen even as we speak."

Ellie targeted her gaze on her shoes to keep from glaring at him. She hadn't told her grandfather about Asher's suspicions because she hadn't wanted to upset him, so naturally he thought everything was fine. Well, that didn't mean she had to be welcoming of Asher. Let the others do that. She edged toward the exit, but Asher's hand shot out and fastened about her wrist. She either had to fight him for it or stand still. Fuming, she stood still.

"I'd love to join you for lunch," Asher said formally.

Nodding with approval, the aunties extended the luncheon invitation to Hub, Kaylie and Stephan. "Oh, no, thank you," Hub refused for them all. "Kaylie has a pot roast in the slow cooker."

The sisters took their leave of their brother and his daughter and son-in-law with hugs and pats.

"We'll see you at the house then, Asher," Magnolia called as they trundled away. Her grandfather went with them. He'd driven the town car that morning so Chester, the Chatams' houseman and driver, who had a mild cold, could stay in. Ellie could have gone along, but she'd preferred to make the short trip alone. She hadn't been in the mood for company since she'd spoken with Asher the day before. Silently, she jerked on her arm, but he held fast.

"Ride with me."

She shook free. "I drove my truck."

"Your grandfather could—"

"He's driving the town car," she said dismissively, very aware of Asher's surprise. She didn't wait around for his response. Instead, she walked away without another word, leaving Asher to figure things out for himself.

"Well, that's a first," Asher muttered, watching Ellie walk away.

"It's been a morning of firsts," his cousin Kaylie said.

Asher turned to find her, her husband and his uncle staring at him as if he'd grown a second head. Kaylie's eyes twinkled merrily as she glanced at Ellie's retreating figure and then at him. "What?"

Hub cleared his throat. "First, Kent is driving the town car."

"Chester has a cold," Kaylie supplied helpfully.

"Then we learn that the Monroes have been staying at Chatam House for weeks!" Hub declared.

"I'm afraid we've neglected the aunts a bit," Kaylie said apologetically. "It's just been so busy, finally moving into the new house, traveling to hockey games…"

"It's the middle of the season," Stephan explained.

"And now this," Kaylie said, waving a dainty hand to indicate Asher's presence. "Do I detect a ro—"

"Don't say it," Asher growled, striding past her.

"What?" he heard Hub ask.

"The *R* word," Stephan muttered.

"What *R* word?"

*"Romance,"* Kaylie answered succinctly, her laughter tinkling like chimes in the soaring space as Asher strode across the foyer. "It's what happens at Chatam House."

Wincing, Asher hurried out into the cool, cloudy day to his vehicle. Kaylie was right. And wrong. There was a romance afoot. It just wasn't his. He imagined the family's shock if Odelia and Kent did marry.

He felt a pang at the idea, and not because Odelia was his aunt or they were older. He thought of how Kaylie had fallen in love with Stephan while he was recovering from an accident at Chatam House and of how happy they seemed together. For the first time in his life, he knew the bereft, sinking bite of envy.

That didn't mean that he and Ellie were destined to follow suit. He cared about Ellie. She was a bright, beautiful, creative, unique woman, but even if he had been convinced that he should try marriage again— and he wasn't—she was a client and too young for him. Those were the facts, plain and simple. His personal ethic demanded that he keep those facts in mind. Even if he had kissed her.

So what, he asked himself, was doing? What compelled him to pursue Ellie like a lion running down a gazelle? He had apologized. For perfectly reasonable behavior, given the circumstances. Shouldn't that be the end of it? Why couldn't he leave it at that?

He asked himself those questions throughout the midday meal—an odd affair, to say the least. Ellie could not have been more uncomfortable. But Hypatia and Magnolia seemed as oblivious to that fact as they were to the way that Odelia blossomed beneath the fawning attention that Kent poured over her. Asher watched in astonishment as his old auntie twinkled, giggled, fluttered her eyelashes, laughed and teased. Perhaps her behavior wasn't so different from normal—she was known for her ebullience, after all—but it had been weeks since she'd been her old self.

Kent had attention only for Odelia and so did not seem to notice that Ellie ate in withdrawn silence. More accurately, she pushed her food around on her plate without ever glancing up or speaking a word, when she should have been smugly happy at the byplay going on between her grandfather and Odelia.

When, at length, Odelia pushed back her chair and announced that she was going to help Kent look for his cat, her sisters seemed almost relieved, perhaps even eager, to get her and everyone else out of the way.

"I'll help you clean up," Ellie murmured, speaking for the first time.

"Oh, no," Magnolia objected, rising to her feet. Asher dropped his fork and shot up in an attempt to maintain the aunties' exacting standard of polite behavior.

"We'll just carry everything into the kitchen, put away the leftovers and stack the dishes in the washer," Hypatia said. "It won't take long."

"In that case," Ellie said, getting up, "I'd like a private word with Asher."

Surprised but pleased by that turn of events, Asher gladly followed her from the large, dark dining room into the library.

"Thank you," he began before she even turned from closing the door. "I want to apologize again for—"

"Your services are no longer needed," she interrupted bluntly.

Stunned into silence, he could only stand there gawking while she folded her arms, strode farther into the room and parked herself on the edge of the mahogany library table.

"I haven't spoken to my grandfather yet," she went on, "but I'll have to tell him what you said yesterday."

Asher clapped a hand to the back of his neck, trying to think. "A-about that, you misunderstood what I was trying to say. Whatever you might think, I am on your side, and I do care ab—"

"Goodbye, Asher." She abruptly launched herself toward the door.

Before he knew what he was doing, he'd grabbed her by the arm and spun her around. "You can't fire me!"

"I just did."

"For yourself, maybe, but not for your grandfather!"

"Fine. I'll let Grandpa fire you himself, but you no longer represent me!"

"Is that right?"

"That's right."

"Good enough!" he exclaimed, angered beyond reason. What did she want, for pity's sake? He'd apologized. Repeatedly. For perfectly logical behavior. He'd turned himself inside out trying to protect her. And she fired him? Well, that changed everything. "If you're no longer my client, then I can do this." He yanked her to him and pressed a kiss onto her lips.

A heartbeat later, they sprang apart, both gasping, each trying to gauge the reaction of the other. After a moment, she tugged her jacket into place and lifted her chin before leisurely turning to stroll toward the door once more. But then she paused to look back at him.

"You're still fired, by the way."

With that, she walked out the door.

Being fired, he thought, watching the door close behind her, was the least of his problems!

* * *

If she'd had any idea how he'd react, Ellie mused, she'd have fired Ash long ago. She had not dared hope that he felt as drawn to her as she did to him, and then yesterday after the game, when he'd seemed intent on squeezing a confession out of her, she'd been angry and hurt. Now she wondered if perhaps he *needed* to suspect her of culpability in the fire in order to protect himself from his own feelings. She was still miffed about that, but somehow, after this latest kiss, it seemed much easier to forgive him. Besides, wasn't she as guilty of assigning guilt to Dallas for that fire as Asher was of suspecting her and her grandfather?

Up in her room, curled around a pillow on her bed, Ellie relived that kiss repeatedly. In the process, she talked the situation over with God. Being with Asher seemed so right to her, so entirely what she was supposed to do. On the other hand, she could very well be building castles in the air. It was so easy to mistake one's own desires for God's will, and she earnestly wanted what God wanted for her. What good was getting her own way if it was going to make her unhappy in the end?

She'd learned that lesson from her grandmother, God rest her. Deirdre Billups Monroe had set her cap for her husband long before he'd ever looked her way and only after he'd given up hope of marrying his first love, Odelia. According to Deirdre herself, Kent had been blatant about his feelings, but Deirdre had been determined to have him. Eventually she had convinced him that they were each other's only chance at making a family, or so Kent had told her. Sadly, though, over time the knowledge that he'd loved another had eaten up Deirdre's love for him. Deirdre had gotten her way, but she'd been unhappy with the results. Ellie was determined not to be so foolish.

It still surprised Ellie that her father had married a woman so like his own mother. It seemed that he had learned how to love from his own dad and how to *be* loved from his mother. Ellie hoped that she had learned better. Her dad and grandpa had shown her what sort of man she wanted to love her, and her mother and grandmother had shown her what sort of wife and mother she did *not* want to be.

But what if she could not be better than them and God knew it? What if this was all just history repeating itself? What if she was hung up on a man who couldn't truly care for her because he couldn't get past the failure of his first attempt at love?

These things went around and around in her thoughts until a remembered bit of favorite Scripture, Psalm 20:4, brought clarity.

*May He give you the desire of your heart and make all your plans succeed.*

That was what she had prayed for her grandfather for years now, for if the fulfillment of one's heart's desire came from God, rather than simply from one's self, then it was the right, best thing.

Finding a measure of peace at last, Ellie sat up. She had no idea what would happen next, but it was all in God's hands, just as it should be. If that kiss meant anything at all, then surely Asher would act upon it. If not, well, she wouldn't be any worse off than before, would she? At least she had finally unburdened herself about Dallas. If Asher hadn't made the connection, well, then perhaps, please God, there weren't any connections to be made.

She scrambled off the bed and went to brush her hair, knowing that the Chatam sisters would expect her to show up in the common areas of the house looking her best. Just as she laid the brush atop the dresser, she heard a bustle in the sitting room.

"Careful. Careful!" came Odelia's voice.

Curious and surprised, Ellie went to the door of her room. Her grandfather was gingerly placing a cardboard box on the coffee table standing in front of the cream-white sofa. Glancing up, he motioned her closer.

"We found him, Ellie. We found old Curly!"

"You found the cat?" She rushed forward.

"Odelia found him," Kent said, carefully beginning to fold back the flaps on the box. "He was upstairs in my room."

"Upstairs!"

"In my room," Kent confirmed, folding back the last flap.

"All this time?"

Ellie peered into the box. A rag-and-bones Curly lay atop a soiled towel, his dark eyes rolling. Not only had he lost weight, patches of charred black and raw red marred his mottled yellow fur.

"Don't touch him," Kent warned. "He's been injured, poor old thing."

Ellie studied the cat's hide. "Grandpa, that cat's been burned!"

"Yes, that's what I figure, too."

"Don't you see what this could mean?"

"Yes, of course. It's very serious. Though if he's lived this long, I expect he'll make it."

Ellie clapped a hand down onto her grandfather's shoulder. "It means that the cat was in the house when the fire started. Grandpa, it means that Curly could have started the fire!"

Kent reared back. "But…how?"

"He must've come through the open window," Ellie theorized. "He could've knocked over the bucket while using it to jump up onto the sofa table."

"And then knocked over the lamp," Kent mused.

"It wouldn't be the first time he'd done that," Ellie pointed out excitedly. "But it would be the first time for the paint thinner."

Kent dropped down onto the sofa. "Good grief, that's the answer."

"We must tell Asher," Odelia pointed out, patting Kent's shoulder.

"Yes, yes, you're right." He looked to Ellie. "You'll take care of it, won't you, dear?"

Ellie rocked back on her heels. "Oh, um, you should talk to Asher about this. He's *your* attorney, and this is official business, so to speak."

"Ah. Well, if you think that best."

He traded a look with Odelia, who said brightly, "I'll just call my nephew Reeves and find out which veterinarian he uses for his daughter's cat." After patting Kent's shoulder again, she hurried away, leaving Ellie to smile serenely at her grandfather.

"I'm sure Curly will recover. It's been a while already, as you said, and he's still with us, after all."

"So he is," Kent acknowledged, nodding. He leaned over the box and crooned, "I think this warrants a dish of cream, old man. Don't you?"

"Well, I'll just let Dallas know the news," Ellie said, moving toward her bedroom.

Closing the box, her grandfather rose. He smiled at Ellie, a look of compassion in his eyes. "You do that, sweet girl, and I'll take care of her brother."

It appeared that he understood only too well that she was avoiding Asher. He couldn't know why, of course, but he had to realize that a rift had opened between them. What no one but God Almighty could know was whether that kiss had served to bridge that fracture in any way.

"Thank you, Grandpa," Ellie answered softly. *May He give you the desire of your heart and make all your plans succeed,* she thought. *Even if He doesn't do the same for me.*

## Chapter Fourteen

Bowing his head over his desk, Asher pressed the fin-gertips of both hands to his aching temples. He had not slept well. Again. Every time he'd closed his eyes, that kiss had played through his mind. To make mat-ters worse, he'd repeatedly confessed his foolishness in instigating the event but had never quite felt absolved. It felt, in fact, as if God was laughing at him. Well, chuckling, anyway, as if to say that he was old enough to know better than to get himself into this mess. In desperation, Asher had resorted to enumerating all the reasons why a romance with Ellie Monroe was a bad idea. He felt the need to run down the list again now.

One, he'd already tried and failed at being half of a couple. Two, she was not the sort of woman he'd ever envisioned pairing up with—not that he'd envisioned pairing up with anyone in a very long time. Three, quirky was not a trait he'd ever valued. Four, he hardly even knew the girl, really! Even if he somehow felt that he did. Five, she interrupted everyone. Six, she was too young. Seven, she could be an arsonist. Okay, he didn't really believe that, but no lawyer worth his salt would entirely discount the possibility. Eight, she was almost painfully beautiful, and why he hadn't realized that before he couldn't understand.

No, wait. Scratch that last.

Frowning, Asher bludgeoned his mind for the remainder of the list. At times he'd gotten as far as twelve, but somehow during the night he'd lost a few of those reasons. What really troubled him, though, was that he could feel his will to keep Ellie at arm's length going the same way.

When Barb buzzed him to say that Kent Monroe had "dropped by for a word," Asher figured that he need not worry about keeping Ellie at a distance any longer. He fully expected that Kent would walk in, fire him and walk out again. He told himself that he was relieved, but the way his gut roiled put the lie to that. The last thing he expected was the beaming bonhomie with which the older man greeted him.

"Asher, my boy, great news! Great news!"

Surprised, Asher didn't even make it all the way to his feet. Kent bustled across the room and dropped down into the armchair in front of the desk, grinning broadly.

"It was the cat," he said the instant that Asher's behind touched the chair seat again.

"Pardon?"

"We found him, my old tom, Curly, holed up licking his wounds. Burns," he clarified significantly, crossing his thick legs. "Vet says he'll mend, though he probably won't have hair in places." Kent waved that away, explaining all that he'd discovered.

Listening, Asher's understanding grew. He smacked

himself in the forehead with the heel of his hand. "That's it. That's the answer."

Kent made a wiping motion across his own forehead. "Whew! That's a relief, I don't mind telling you." He shifted in his chair, adding, "Fact is, I can't rightly remember turning on the lamp that night. Then again, I forgot to lock the front door, didn't I? Odelia says the shock of the fire has confounded my brain."

Asher thought it best not to comment on that statement. Instead, he glanced at the clock and reached for his electronic address book. "I'll call the insurance company today."

"Yes, yes. The sooner the better. Again, I can't tell you how relieved I am. To tell you the truth, I haven't been entirely forthcoming with you."

Asher set aside the handheld gadget, his senses pricking. "No. Really?"

If Kent suspected sarcasm, he didn't signal as much. Grimacing, he said, "I took out a private mortgage."

Asher sat back in his chair. "Ah." No wonder the insurance adjustor had hinted at financial impropriety.

"Just a small one," Kent went on. "Less than fifteen thousand. I didn't have the cash to finish the renovations, you see, but I didn't want Ellie to know. It's all for her, for her inheritance, but she never thinks of herself and wouldn't have wanted me to go into debt." He tilted his head, saying in his gravelly voice, "I hope you won't tell her."

Asher shook his head. "Let's just leave Ellie out of this, shall we? She fired me, anyway."

Kent's bushy eyebrows leaped upward. "What?"

"We, um, had a difference of opinion," Asher confessed, feeling the burn of guilt. "Actually, I offended her, and she fired me. I no longer represent her."

"I'm sure it's just a misunderstanding," Kent murmured, obviously troubled.

"I'll understand if you'd prefer to let someone else handle things from here on out," Asher offered carefully. To his relief, Kent shook his head.

"No, no, no. I'm sure you'll work out your differences between you. Besides, we could be family soon, you and I."

Asher reared back in shock. Kent couldn't really expect him to marry Ellie. Could he? They hadn't even been out on a date! "What makes you say that?"

Kent Monroe squared his shoulders and set both feet flat on the floor. "I should tell you bluntly that I intend, very soon, to…again…ask your dear aunt to marry me."

Asher worked hard at keeping his expression placid. Of course. He should have expected that. "I see. Well, since we're being blunt, I feel I should warn you that Aunt Odelia has told me, quite recently, that she has no intention of ever leaving her sisters."

Kent waved that away with a swipe of his hand. "I'm not a man who makes the same mistake twice. If she doesn't want to leave Chatam House, then we won't. My house is going to Ellie anyway." Kent shifted in his seat and added, "I had thought to give it to the two of you."

Nothing Asher could do would keep his jaw in place. "I beg your p-pardon?"

Kent leaned forward. "I admit I've been distracted, but a blind man could see that the two of you have feelings for each other."

Asher rubbed his ear in an effort to hide his embarrassment. That obvious, was it? What was just as obvious was that Kent Monroe approved.

"You should hear the way she speaks of you," Kent told him. "I don't think she even realizes she's doing it. 'Ash will take care everything.' 'Ash is so generous.' 'Ash says this, Ash says that.' I've never heard the like from her."

She called him "Ash" in private, did she? Only his closest friends and family called him that. It thrilled him to know that she thought of him that way. But that didn't really change anything, did it?

He met Kent Monroe's frank gaze. "You don't think I'm too old for her?"

Kent looked surprised. "I've always thought that an adult is an adult."

Clearly, in Kent's mind, his granddaughter was an adult. That made it difficult for Asher to hold on to the idea that Ellie was too young for him. And she wasn't his client anymore, either. That meant that the only thing standing between them was...

*What shall we call this, Lord?* he asked silently. *Caution? Fear? My own stiff-necked stupidity?* Whatever it was, maybe it was time to get it out of the way.

For Kent Monroe, he had only a smile and a wish. "May you know every happiness, sir, and my aunt along with you."

They both got to their feet and shook hands before Asher walked the older man to the door. As soon as Kent had gone, Asher turned back to his desk and picked up the phone. He had plans to make.

*Three days,* Ellie thought. Three days since that kiss. She'd hoped that he would show up at the Monday practice, but he'd been conspicuously absent, and she hadn't seen any sign of him on this Wednesday afternoon, either. If he was going to come see her, he'd have done so by now. No, she had to face facts.

Two of her kids were hip-bumping when they should have been paying attention to the ball.

"Chuck, Miguel, eyes on the prize!" she called.

Asher might be attracted to her, but he was apparently able to put her out of mind easily enough, while she couldn't seem to stop thinking about him. Well, what had she expected? Hadn't she known all along that she wasn't the sort of woman to inspire devotion in a man like him? Or perhaps any man?

Keeping the kids on task seemed to require a huge effort of will, but Ellie managed to stumble through the lengthy scrimmage.

"Good job!" she praised when it was time to pack it in. "I'll see y'all on Friday," she called, as the kids ran off the field.

"Turned out to be a pretty day," Ilene commented, shoving balls into a net bag while Ellie swigged down a bottle of water Ilene had handed her.

"Um-hm."

She hadn't really noticed, but the sun was out and the sky was clear on a day so mild that the temperature didn't even register with her. Hadn't it been gray earlier? She couldn't remember. Her mood was so gray that it probably colored everything around her. Sighing, she turned to help Ilene carry the cooler to the trunk of her car. They were halfway there when she saw him.

Dressed in a brown suit and a white shirt with an open collar, Asher stood next to his SUV in the distance, ankles crossed as he leaned against the fender.

Ellie stumbled, and in the instant required to right herself, he pushed away from the vehicle, starting toward her with a long, loose-limbed stride.

They reached the rear of Ilene's car and lifted the cooler into the trunk. Ellie turned away as Ilene started loading kids into the backseat.

"See you Friday."

"See you."

Walking over to her truck, Ellie pulled her keys from the pocket of her shorts and unlocked the driver's door. Then she simply stood there and waited for him.

"What's up?" she asked as he drew near, determined to show him that she had maintained an even keel despite that kiss.

He reached inside his coat and pulled out a dollar bill. "I came to return this," he told her, holding it out.

Frowning, she shook her head. "I don't understand."

"It's your retainer. Now that we've ended our professional relationship, I need to return it."

She rolled her eyes. "I think we can agree that you've earned your retainer."

"Take it, Ellie. To ease my mind."

"To ease your mind?" she said angrily. "Is that what this is about? Well, let me do that by telling you that the cat did it. The stupid cat started the fire." The slightest of smiles curved his lips, but he just waved the dollar bill. "You already knew, didn't you?" she realized.

Reaching for her hand, he turned it palm up and plopped the bill into it. She curled her fingers around it, eyeing him as he smoothly told her, "I am ethically constrained from discussing cases with anyone but my clients." He leaned forward slightly and reminded her, "You are no longer my client."

"Fine," she snapped, clasping the top of the truck door in preparation for sliding into the cab.

He covered her hand with his, halting her in midaction. "I'd be happy to discuss the ethics of my profession with you."

Like she needed a lecture on why he regretted kissing her and wanted to keep his distance. "Sorry," she told him. "I happen to be really hungry at the moment."

"That actually works well for me," he said. "We'll have dinner."

"Dinner," Ellie echoed stupidly. She glanced down at herself. "I don't think so. I'm not exactly dressed to go out for dinner. Unless you intend to do a drive-through."

"Actually, I have something else in mind. And you're perfectly dressed for it."

Ellie blinked. So, this had to do with soccer after all. "Okay. Where are we going?"

"Why don't you just ride along with me," he suggested, taking her by the arm. "I'll bring you back to your truck later."

She glanced around at the busy parking lot. There were a few empty spaces, so she supposed she wouldn't be putting anyone out by leaving her truck here for an hour or so. Shrugging, she backed out of the truck and locked the door.

He walked her to his SUV and handed her up inside before taking his place behind the steering wheel.

"So how did practice go?"

"Pretty well," she said, not interested in providing further details. Asher got the message.

They drove in silence until Ellie realized that they had left the business district behind and were instead driving through his neighborhood.

"Where is this restaurant we're going to?"

"Who said anything about a restaurant?" Asher asked lightly, making the turn into the drive. She realized that they'd pulled up behind his house when he hit a button overhead and the garage door started to go up.

"So it's a dinner meeting at your place?"

"That's right."

He pulled the truck into the garage, killed the engine and got out. Ellie slipped out on her side before he could come around to open the door. He went to the door that led into the house. She glanced around her, noting that his garage was neater than most people's living rooms.

She followed him into a dark, narrow hallway that led past a sizable laundry and a small powder room to the kitchen. Backtracking to the laundry, she quickly stepped out of her cleats, returning to the kitchen in her stocking feet. He stood peering into the refrigerator when she got back.

"How do you feel about an omelet?" he asked. "It's that or a sandwich, and I can't vouch for how long this sliced turkey's been here."

Ellie froze in the act of sliding up onto a tall chair placed at the kitchen bar. "What had you planned to fix?"

"I hadn't planned anything," he told her, taking out a tray of eggs.

Now, wasn't that just like a man! "Well, how many are you expecting?"

He cast her a dry look. "We're all here."

Ellie hopped down off the chair she'd just settled on. "You mean it's just the two of us?"

Asher placed the eggs on the counter, then braced his

hands against it. "Listen, Ellie. Let's just scramble up some eggs and see where that takes us. Okay?"

Her heart fluttered and began slamming inside her chest. "Yeah. Okay. I can go with that."

He took down a bowl and started cracking eggs into it. "There's a game on TV if you want to go into the other room and turn on the set."

"Oh, ah, why don't you handle that and let me take care of the eggs?"

Smiling, he dropped the eggshells as if they were hot rocks. "Look around for whatever you need. I'll be right back."

His shoulder brushed hers as he passed by on his way into the living room. Ellie stayed where she was for a moment, then carefully moved around the bar to the island countertop where the eggs awaited her.

No promises, Asher had said, but maybe some answered prayer.

They ate eggs scrambled with green onions, black olives, bits of ham and sour cream that she'd found in the refrigerator. Asher got down plates that they filled and carried into the living room, where they watched a South American match, sitting side by side on his sofa.

She was having such a good time that she forgot completely about those at Chatam House until her grandfather called her cell phone. He brushed aside her apologies and didn't seem at all surprised when she told him that she was with Asher.

"At any rate, I'll be home by nine," she promised.

"I won't wait up if you're later," he said, unconcerned.

"I won't be. Tomorrow's a school day."

"Aw, but you're the teacher, not the student."

"Which means that I have to be there earlier than anyone else."

After she'd hung up, Asher asked, "Has your grandfather spoken to you about Odelia?"

"Not really. They're spending a lot of time together, though, and he seems happy."

Asher just nodded at that.

Once the game ended, they carried their plates back into the kitchen and loaded them into the dishwasher, which was half-full. Explaining that he normally only ran the appliance once a week, Asher scrubbed out the skillet that she'd used.

When that was done, he glanced at his wristwatch. "Better scoot if we're going to get you home by curfew."

She rolled her eyes. Then she saw that he was grinning. She went to the laundry room, thoroughly confused, to get into her shoes. He waited in the hallway then followed her out to the garage. This time he insisted on opening the car door for her.

What was going on here?

They drove back to the soccer field, which was dark and deserted. He got out and walked her to her truck. Opening the door, she started to slide into the cab.

"Not so fast," he said. Lifting her hand from the truck door, he stepped to the side, drawing her out from behind it. "I want to be clear about something. Tonight was not a date."

Ellie tamped down her disappointment, saying lightly, "Believe me, Asher, you've made it clear for some time now that our spending time together is not 'a date.' But I enjoyed myself anyway."

"Excellent. Enough to try the real thing?"

"The real thing," she echoed uncertainly, standing at arm's length.

"Dinner," he said. "In a restaurant this time. Oh, and a movie." A slow smile stretched his lips. "Not on the same night, mind you. Thought I'd nail down the second date now."

Elation swept through Ellie as she allowed him to reel her in. "You're asking me out on a real date?"

"Two dates," he corrected. "I refuse to be a one-date discard, and for the record, I'd like several more dates after that."

Tears gathered in Ellie's eyes. "Seriously?"

"Seriously. Now, what do you say?"

Stepping close, she wrapped her arms around him and laid her head on his shoulder. "Dinner. Movie. Every date after that. I accept them all."

He chuckled and shifted so that her head was tucked neatly beneath his chin. "I've been alone a long time, Ellie, and I wasn't any good at being with someone before."

"Maybe it was the wrong someone."

"Maybe. And maybe I was the wrong someone. I don't know. But I want to try to be the right someone for you, Ellie."

She slipped her arms around him. "I think you can do anything you want to do."

He laughed. "From your lips to God's ears, sweetheart. From your lips to God's ears."

She closed her eyes and smiled. That was one thing he didn't have to worry about. God would continue to hear from her regularly—she had much to be thankful for.

\* \* \*

They went to dinners. Plural. They went to movies. Again, plural. They went to soccer games and soccer meetings and soccer practices. They even went to church together.

At times, Asher felt sure he'd lost his mind, but those times were invariably when he was away from Ellie. When they were together, all seemed just as it should be. He noticed that she didn't interrupt him anymore. He also noticed that he seemed to smile more often. And eventually he noticed that his little sister seemed rather subdued.

Being with Ellie had given him a new perspective on Dallas, and he began to think that he might have sold Dallas short, so to speak. Consequently, when the opportunity arose to engage her in meaningful conversation, he took it gladly.

They met on the front porch of Chatam House at the very end of March. He was coming; she was going.

"No romance going on under this roof," she quipped drily, and would have swept right by him, but he snagged her by the arm and turned her back to face him.

"Where are you off to?"

She shrugged. "Nowhere in particular. But Ellie has a date. With you. Again. And Odelia's gone off somewhere. Mags is working out in the greenhouse, so Hypatia is catching up on some paperwork having to do with the BCBC scholarship fund or something like that. No reason to hang around here."

He tugged her toward the chairs where he'd sat with Odelia one dark night a few weeks ago. "Sit down a minute. I have something to say."

Sighing gustily, she stomped over and dropped down

onto the seat of one chair. Asher folded himself down into the chair next to her and leaned forward.

"I think I owe you an apology."

Her jaw dropped, which made him laugh. She pointed a finger at him. "You are apologizing to me?" She shook her head. "Well, that's one for the books. What exactly are you apologizing for? No, wait. Doesn't matter. This is still a red-letter day. I'm going to go home and write it on my calendar with a red marker. 'Ash apologized to me today.'"

Chuckling, he patted her on the knee. "I've discounted you, sis," he said. "Put you down as an overgrown teenager. I've mocked your romantic ideals and dismissed your ambitions. I was wrong to do that. In my defense, all I can say is that you're my baby sister and maybe I've wanted to keep you that way. I haven't wanted to let you grow up. But, of course, you have, anyhow."

"Is there a camera crew hiding around here somewhere?" she joked, glancing around suspiciously. "I'm going to see this on TV next week, aren't I?"

"Only if you're filming it yourself," he said, getting to his feet. "Now get out of here. You're making me late for my date, you know."

He turned toward the door, only to turn back at the sound of his name.

"Ash."

"Yeah?"

"Thanks."

He just smiled and started to turn away again.

"She loves you, Ash."

His heart stopped, then stuttered and took off again.

Sucking in a deep breath, he looked his sister in the eye. "I believe she does."

"And?"

"And," he said, reaching for the doorknob, "I'll get back to you on that."

She made a disappointed sound, dropping her shoulders and lightly stomping one foot. He just laughed at her and opened the door. There were some things that a baby sister ought not to be the first to know.

On the other hand…

Standing there in the foyer of the ancestral Chatam family home, the staid attorney discovered that he might be something of a romantic, after all.

# Chapter Fifteen

Sitting on the edge of the porch at Chatam House, Ellie tucked her A-line skirt around her thighs and crossed her legs at the ankles on the step below. She'd donned the skirt over her shorts because it feminized the silky, red polo-style top that she'd bought to match the colors of Ash's select team. Adjusting the thin, red elastic band that held back her curly hair, she sighed happily.

Her team had won again that morning for the third Saturday in a row, despite a stiff early April wind that had played havoc with the ball. Asher had been on hand to see it. Now she waited for him to pick her up for an evening match between his select team and another club in Dallas.

Smiling to herself, she braced her elbows atop her knees and parked her chin in her upturned palms, enjoying the colorful sunset as she anticipated Ash's arrival. They'd been in each other's company a good deal these past several weeks, and she was hopelessly, unabashedly in love, though she dared not say it. He was much more fun and lighthearted than anyone else knew, yet also steady, careful and responsible—maybe too much so to commit himself permanently to a zany woman like her.

Her smile faltered.

Despite all the "second dates," as Ash called them, she still worked against getting her hopes up. Even if nothing ever came of the time they'd spent together, though, she knew that she would never regret it. Ash was everything she'd ever wanted, but she couldn't quite imagine that he would feel the same way about her. It could be, likely would be, that he'd move on soon to some woman nearer his own age, someone who had more in common with him than kids' soccer. If so, then at least she could take joy in having proved to him that the possibility of love remained a reality. She could say, if only to herself, that God had used her to reawaken the heart of a good man.

The familiar white SUV turned into the drive and accelerated up the slope. When it reached the circle, it veered right. Straightening, Ellie lifted a hand to wave in welcome. As the vehicle came to an abrupt halt, she rose and nervously adjusted the line of her skirt.

Asher practically leaped out and came loping around the front bumper. Taking the steps in one long stride, he snagged her hand and towed her toward the front door.

"What's going on?"

"I have news," he said, amber eyes twinkling, "good news."

"About what?" she asked, laughing as he opened the door and pulled her through it into the foyer.

He towed her into the front parlor, where the Chatam sisters lingered over their ubiquitous cups of tea. All three rose to their feet, Hypatia turning, as the newcomers burst into the room.

"Asher, dear." She switched her gaze back and forth between him and Ellie, pressing her hands together. "I sense an announcement."

"The insurance company has settled." He looked down at Ellie, adding, "They've offered a generous amount, very generous."

Obviously disappointed, the sisters traded looks. Ellie put on a bright smile, determined to be happy with this news.

"That's wonderful," Odelia said in a subdued manner.

Asher made a face. "I should have told Kent first," Asher suddenly said. "He *is* my client."

"No worries, my boy," Kent's hearty voice said, preceding his appearance by a mere heartbeat. "And it's about time, I say."

"Grandpa," Ellie said, rushing to his side. "Think what this means. We can go home as soon as the repairs are complete."

"I'll call the contractor," he said, smiling down at her. His gaze went then to Odelia. "But I have no intention of leaving this house. Ever. Unless my darling Odelia herself throws me out."

"Oh!" Odelia squeaked, her hands going to her cheeks. The next instant she launched herself forward, neatly avoiding the table and armchair as she ran toward him with outstretched arms. She'd produced a hanky from somewhere and waved it wildly. "Kent, do you mean it?"

He caught her hands in his. "I was foolish enough to try to take you from your sisters once before, my love. I'll do anything I must to never lose you again. I've just been waiting for this, so there would be no confusion as to my motives." He went down on one knee, to the gasps of several in the room—everyone, perhaps, except Asher. "Odelia, my heart, will you, at long last, make me the happiest of men and marry me?"

Hypatia staggered backward, while Magnolia plopped down on the settee behind her. Odelia hurled herself into Kent's arms.

"Yes! Yes! Yes! Yes!" she cried between pecking kisses that left vivid pink imprints on Kent's beaming face.

Delighted, Ellie clapped her hands and laughed. A grinning Asher stepped over and helped the happy couple rise, one hand clamped firmly under each of their arms.

"I don't believe it!" Hypatia breathed. "*You two* are the romance?"

"And what's wrong with that?" Odelia demanded, edging closer to Kent, who looped an arm protectively about her shoulders.

Magnolia cleared her throat and got to her feet once more. "Odelia, are you sure about this?"

"I'm going to marry Kent," Odelia insisted firmly, "and if you don't want us here, we will move to Charter Street." She lifted her chin, which Ellie noted was trembling.

"Of course we want you here," Hypatia said in a mollifying, slightly exasperated tone. "We're just…stunned by this…unexpected event."

"Unexpected?" Odelia echoed, snapping her hanky as if it were a whip. "It's been coming for fifty years!"

"So it has," Kent chuckled. "No rash actions for us, eh, my darling?"

Odelia cooed at him as if he'd just uttered the most

clever, romantic words in history. Ellie blinked back
tears at a dream realized.

Hypatia glanced pointedly at Magnolia, swallowed,
tilted her head regally and said, "Quite right. Welcome
to the f-family, Kent."

He made a courtly bow. "Thank you, dear sister,
from the bottom of my heart."

Asher moved to Ellie's side and slipped an arm about
her waist, smiling down at her as the chatter around
them rose in volume. Magnolia demanded details of
Odelia and Kent's "clandestine" romance, and they happily told the tale. Ellie dashed away tears, so very happy
for her grandfather. Gazing up at Asher, she mouthed
the words *Thank you.*

He shook his head, asking softly, "For what?"

She went up on tiptoe to whisper in his ear, "For not
advising her against him."

"I am going to recommend a prenup," Asher muttered.

Ellie just smiled at him. "I'm on to you, Asher Chatam. You're as much of a sappy romantic as the rest
of us."

"You think so?"

"I do."

"We'll see."

"I suppose you'll want a proper wedding," Hypatia
was saying.

"Oh, yes!" Odelia exclaimed before glancing up at
Kent. "That is, we haven't discussed it."

"Whatever you want, my love," he told her, "but first
things first, I always say. We haven't even purchased
an engagement ring yet. I thought you'd like to choose
your own this time."

Odelia squealed and clapped her hands around her hanky, while Hypatia muttered something about "gaudy bits" and Magnolia bit her lip.

"We'll be needing flowers," she said, launching to her feet and bustling toward the door. "*Lots* of flowers."

Hypatia turned and sat down heavily in her customary chair. Ellie almost felt sorry for her. Major change had finally come to Chatam House. For her grandfather and Odelia, Ellie couldn't have been happier, but the sisters had some huge adjustments in store.

She couldn't quite believe that her grandfather hadn't shared his feelings and details of the growing romance with her before this. Oh, she'd had clues, of course, but she had assumed that the older couple were taking it slowly. It had even occurred to her that they might have achieved all they really wanted, relationship-wise. At their ages, a deep friendship might have seemed as important as romance. It had never occurred to her that her grandfather might be waiting to pop the question until the matter of the insurance settlement was resolved.

"We have to go," Asher said, urging her toward the doorway. Ellie nodded somewhat reluctantly and moved with him in that direction.

It was a measure of Hypatia's distraction that she did not even note their departure. Odelia and Kent happily waved them on their way with wishes for a successful outcome to the game and went back to celebrating their engagement. Chuckling, Asher hurried Ellie out of the house and into his car.

On the drive to Dallas, Asher admitted to having known for some time that Kent intended to propose and had surmised that the old boy was just waiting for the insurance company to settle before doing so. He just hadn't expected a proposal on the spot. Ellie detailed her own suspicions about a burgeoning romance but confessed that she was taken off guard by this evening's events.

"Well, at any rate, you and Dallas have gotten your way," he told her. "I may even have to admit to her that she was right about the two of them all along."

"Oh, the horrors!" Ellie teased.

He laughed, guiding the vehicle off the highway, and she reflected silently how relaxed and pleased he seemed. Might he one day realize that she had played a part in that and hope to secure such for his future? On the other hand, why should he? Perhaps this was all he ever wanted, someone with whom to laugh and tease and spend time. Their kisses, while sweet, had certainly been few and far between.

She thought of her grandfather and Odelia and could not squelch a pang of envy.

*Forgive me, Lord,* she thought, as Ash drove through the busy streets of University Park. *Grandpa deserves his happiness, and it's been a long time coming. Thank You for answering my prayers on his behalf.*

Psalm 21:2 rolled through her mind. *You have granted him the desire of his heart and have not withheld the request of his lips.*

That followed the verse in the previous chapter that she had been praying for so long. Suddenly she felt compelled to pray that verse for herself, paraphrasing as needed.

*May You give me the desire of my heart and make all my plans succeed.*

It seemed selfish to pray on her own behalf in that

manner, but hadn't Jabez asked for what he wanted? Hadn't David and Solomon and even Christ?

*Not my will, Lord, but Yours. You know best. You always know best.*

They reached the lighted soccer field. A small stadium, really, it boasted elevated seats and a concession stand offering peanuts, popcorn, nachos and pizza, along with sodas and water.

The team had already assembled. The team manager had already unloaded the equipment and started warm-ups, but Asher did not go to the bench. Instead, he walked Ellie to the stands and suggested that she take a vacant space next to his sister on the third row up.

"Dallas!" she exclaimed, surprised. "I didn't know you were going to be here. Why didn't you ride with us?"

Her friend just shrugged and patted the metal bench next to her. As Ellie climbed over the bottom two rows, she noticed more familiar faces.

"Ilene. Angie. Shawna. What are you guys doing here?"

"It's a learning experience," Ilene told her. "We figured the kids could learn a thing or two by watching an older, select team."

"Good idea! Don't know why I didn't think of it myself." A glance around before she took her seat showed her other parents and kids from her team. Apparently, when Ilene said "we," she really meant "we."

"You won't believe what's happened," she said to Dallas, as she made herself comfortable on the bench. "Odelia and Kent are engaged!"

Dallas grabbed her hand, squealed and stomped her feet. "That's fabulous! That's fabulous! I knew it would work. I knew it!" Hopping up, she cupped her hands around her mouth and bawled at her brother, "I told you so!"

To the laughter of those around them, Asher turned, shrugged and lifted both arms in a gesture of acceptance. Dallas dropped back down and begged for details, which Ellie eagerly furnished. As they chortled over Asher's having to help the happy couple to their feet after Kent's dramatic proposal, the ref trotted to the center of the field and blew his whistle to start the game.

It was an exciting match. Ellie couldn't resist the opportunity to instruct those of her players present, and she continually pointed out good moves and explained strategies. With four minutes left to play, Asher's team was down by a single goal.

"Still time, still time," Ellie chanted, twisting her hands together.

With two minutes left, she started rooting for a tie and overtime. But the other team's defense just proved too strong. Ash's goalie hung his head as he made his way to the sideline, but Asher went out to meet him and brought him in with an arm looped about his shoulders.

As the team huddled up, people started leaving the stands, but when Ellie rose, Dallas yanked her right back down again.

"Ow!"

"Just hang on," her friend counseled. "Give Ash a minute with his team."

Ellie sat again, noticing that they weren't the only ones staying put. Suddenly a whistle blew, and Asher's team jogged back onto the field. Confused, Ellie was just about to ask Dallas what was going on. Just then, the team split apart and ran in opposite directions, un-rolling a banner between them.

"What on…"

Her words died away as the banner came into view. It read, "Ellie, will you marry me?" And there in front of the stands, Asher spread his arms wide, staring up at her with a question in his eyes.

For a long moment Ellie didn't move. She'd clapped a hand over her mouth and just sat there staring at him. Only when Dallas shoved her did she stumble to her feet and start climbing down to the field. As she did so, people began applauding. Asher didn't think she even heard. By the time her feet met the tarmac on the path in front of the stands, she was crying.

"Are you serious?" she squeaked at him.

In response, Asher dropped down onto one knee and reached into the pocket of his jacket for the ring box he'd stashed there. He tried to joke, saying, "Kent stole a bit of my thunder." With his heart in his throat, it came out sounding pretty strangled.

This had all seemed like such a good idea when he'd discussed it with Dallas earlier. He'd wanted to do something fun, something that his exuberant Ellie would love. But maybe she didn't love him after all. Maybe he'd rushed her. Maybe he'd been so sensible and so stoic for so long that he just couldn't pull off something this wild.

She stood there with her hands over her mouth, and he started to feel like a fool. What now? Get up and walk away? Try to live the rest of his life without her? He couldn't even imagine such a thing. Not now.

Clearing his throat, he tried to remember all the eloquent words he'd practiced, but they came only slug-gishly to his mind. "You were right. I had let failure mark me, and I wouldn't let God take it away. Instead, I clung to it, used it like a shield against any possibility of…romance." There. He'd said it. Silly word, *romance.* Silly, essential, wonderful word. "Then you came. I think I should more rightly say that God sent you. I've learned so much from you, Ellie. Mostly, I think, I've learned to love."

"Ash."

"I love you, Ellie. I love you."

Apparently, he got it all right because she dropped her hands, sniffed and said, "I love you, too!"

He breathed a tiny sigh of relief and got to his feet at last. "Without even knowing it, I've been waiting for you, waiting for you to grow up. Waiting for God to bring us together." She stood there staring at him with the world in her watery violet eyes and a smile on her ruby lips, and he couldn't resist a quip. "Waiting for you to say yes."

She burst out laughing. "Yes!"

"Whew!" He started to open the ring box, but sud-denly she threw herself at him, her arms encircling his neck. Laughing, he swung her around in a circle to the applause and laughter of their secretly invited audience.

When he sat her on her feet again, she gazed up at him with love in her eyes and exclaimed, "I can't be-lieve you're serious!"

"Sweetheart," he said, keeping a straight face. "I'm always serious. Everyone knows that."

They laughed again, and he finally got that little box open and the ring on her finger. Every woman within shouting distance ran to see the rock he'd picked out.

By the way she kept looking at it and him, he knew he'd chosen well.

Asher shook his head at the wonder of it all as his back was clapped and congratulations rang in his ears. He'd once thought himself too busy for love, but now he realized that he'd kept busy because his life was so empty that he'd had to fill it up. Now that God had brought the right woman to him, his life and his heart were full to overflowing.

Who would have guessed that it would be Ellie, though? Young, exuberant, absolutely perfect Ellie.

When the crowd dwindled to a select few, Asher couldn't wait any longer to pull her into his arms and kiss her. He lifted his head a few moments later, happiness swelling his heart, and noticed Dallas standing nearby in tears. He hadn't expected that from his headstrong little sister, but she was the unrepentant romantic. She surprised him again when she said, "I'm sorry your team lost." As if that mattered!

"Did they?" he quipped. "Hadn't noticed. Must've had something else on my mind." Ellie giggled and slid her arms around his waist.

Suddenly, Dallas's face crumpled and noisy sobs grated out of her. Ellie slipped out of his arms to go to her.

"Dallas?"

"I have to tell you something," she gasped, holding up a hand as if to hold off Ellie's comfort. "I did it. The fire. It was my fault."

"What?" Asher blurted, stunned.

She turned her tear-filled eyes on Ellie. "You told me you were going to be at the storage unit, right after you told me how awful the fumes were in the house, and that if they didn't get better you might have to move out for a few days." She gulped and went on. "I was going to go by while you were gone and make sure all the windows were closed so the fumes wouldn't dissipate, then wait for you to come in and suggest that you stay at Chatam House for a couple of days."

When she'd found that the door was open, however, she'd gone in, and on her way to check the window, she'd turned on the lamp. That was when she'd seen the bucket with the can of paint remover and come up with the idea of removing the cap, but she'd dropped the can and spilled the liquid. The fumes had been so awful that she'd opened the window after finding it already closed. The cat had jumped into the room, and when she'd chased him, he'd jumped up onto the table and knocked over the lamp.

"There was nothing I could do!" she wailed in a small voice. "I ran out the front door in a panic and into the street. Garrett nearly ran me over on his motorcycle. The rest you know."

Asher stood there dumbfounded while Ellie sighed. "I knew I'd shut that window."

The truth hit Asher like a ton of bricks. "And you knew that she shouldn't have been at the house. You were protecting her!"

Ellie grimaced and nodded. "In the end, I did try to tell you."

"And I all but accused you of setting the fire."

"You didn't accuse me. You rightly suspected that I hadn't told you everything." She looked at Dallas. "Just as I suspected that Dallas had had something to do with it."

"I'm so sorry, Ellie!" Dallas exclaimed. "I should've

told you right away, but then you'd have known I was scheming, and I didn't want you to think badly of me."

Ellie turned an agonized look on Asher. "The insurance company."

"We have to tell them," he said quietly, "but I don't think it will make any difference. Ultimately, it was all an accident."

"Now I have to say something," Ellie told him, stepping close again. "You suspected that my grandfather and I were involved with the fire, and I took great offense at that, but all the time I was guilty of the same thing with Dallas." She looked at her friend and admitted, "I actually thought you might have done it on purpose."

Dallas parked her hands at her waist and threw out one hip. "Well, thank you very much."

"It wasn't that unreasonable of an assumption," Asher told her. She rolled her eyes, but her teeth worried her bottom lip.

"You're sure this isn't going to set back things with the insurance company?"

"Don't worry about it," he said. "I'll take care of everything."

She laughed, that incorrigible redhead, and wiped her eyes. "Don't you always? Boy, that's a load off my shoulders."

Ellie turned her gaze up at him then. "You do, you know, always take care of everything. That's why you wouldn't let up about the fire. You knew I'd held back information."

"And I was afraid for you," he admitted softly.

She brushed a hand across his chest. "I want you to know that I wasn't angry so much as I was hurt that day," she said. "I was hurt because I so desperately wanted you to care about me."

"I care," he said, wrapping his arms around her. "I cared then. I was just so bound up in the armor I'd created to make myself impervious to love that I couldn't admit it, even to myself. But you'd already worked your way into my heart. I think you've been there all along. I couldn't let you go." He pulled her closer. "I won't let you go."

Squaring her slender shoulders, Dallas exclaimed, "Wow! I'm even better than I thought I was at this matchmaking thing."

His sister the matchmaker. Asher shuddered at the thought, but then he looked down at Ellie and smiled. Maybe she did have a kind of instinct for the job.

"Just think," Dallas went on. "The aunties have two weddings to plan now!"

"Let them have at it," he said, gazing down at his Ellie. "So long as they do it quickly," he amended.

Laughing, she lifted up on tiptoe and pressed her lips to his.

Odelia and Kent might have had fifty years to fool around, he thought, but he was a busy man, a man in a hurry to claim all the joy that God allowed.

\* \* \* \* \*

Dear Reader,

You've surely met those with whom you seem to have "everything" in common. Conversely, you must've met those to whom you could barely relate. Background, age, ethnicity, language, social status, politics, religion...so many things can come between us. Often, however, if we give ourselves an opportunity to get to know someone with whom we seemingly have little in common, we find that a very special relationship forms.

Such is the case with a young lady who wrote me from her native Zimbabwe as a twelve-year-old. After years of correspondence, we were able to meet in person. I still marvel that a girl born and raised in another culture on another continent could come to occupy such a large place in my heart! I pray that you will give yourself a chance, like Asher and Ellie, to know such "unlikely" joy.

God bless,

*Arlene James*

We hope you enjoyed reading
this special collection.

If you liked reading these stories,
then you will love **Love Inspired®** books!

You believe hearts can heal. **Love Inspired**
stories show that faith, forgiveness and hope
have the power to lift spirits and change
lives—always.

Enjoy six new stories from
**Love Inspired** every month!

Available wherever books and
ebooks are sold.

*Love Inspired*

**Uplifting romances of faith,
forgiveness and hope.**

STEPLI

# Get 2 Free Books,

## Plus 2 Free Gifts —

### just for trying the Reader Service!

*Love Inspired®*

**YES!** Please send me 2 FREE Love Inspired® Romance novels and my 2 FREE mystery gifts (gifts are worth about $10 retail). After receiving them, if I don't wish to receive any more books, I can return the shipping statement marked "cancel." If I don't cancel, I will receive 6 brand-new novels every month and be billed just $5.24 for the regular-print edition or $5.74 each for the larger-print edition in the U.S., or $5.74 each for the regular-print edition or $6.24 each for the larger-print edition in Canada. That's a saving of at least 13% off the cover price. It's quite a bargain! Shipping and handling is just 50¢ per book in the U.S. and 75¢ per book in Canada.* I understand that accepting the 2 free books and gifts places me under no obligation to buy anything. I can always return a shipment and cancel at any time. The free books and gifts are mine to keep no matter what I decide.

Please check one:
- ☐ Love Inspired Romance Regular-Print (105/305 IDN GLWW)
- ☐ Love Inspired Romance Larger-Print (122/322 IDN GLWW)

| | |
|---|---|
| Name | (PLEASE PRINT) |

| | |
|---|---|
| Address | Apt. # |

| | | |
|---|---|---|
| City | State/Province | Zip/Postal Code |

Signature (if under 18, a parent or guardian must sign)

Mail to the **Reader Service:**
**IN U.S.A.**: P.O. Box 1341, Buffalo, NY 14240-8531
**IN CANADA**: P.O. Box 603, Fort Erie, Ontario L2A 5X3

**Want to try two free books from another line?**
**Call 1-800-873-8635 today or visit www.ReaderService.com.**

*Terms and prices subject to change without notice. Prices do not include applicable taxes. Sales tax applicable in N.Y. Canadian residents will be charged applicable taxes. Offer not valid in Quebec. This offer is limited to one order per household. Books received may not be as shown. Not valid for current subscribers to Love Inspired Romance books. All orders subject to approval. Credit or debit balances in a customer's account(s) may be offset by any other outstanding balance owed by or to the customer. Please allow 4 to 6 weeks for delivery. Offer available while quantities last.

**Your Privacy**—The Reader Service is committed to protecting your privacy. Our Privacy Policy is available online at www.ReaderService.com or upon request from the Reader Service.

We make a portion of our mailing list available to reputable third parties that offer products we believe may interest you. If you prefer that we not exchange your name with third parties, or if you wish to clarify or modify your communication preferences, please visit us at www.ReaderService.com/consumerschoice or write to us at Reader Service Preference Service, P.O. Box 9062, Buffalo, NY 14240-9062. Include your complete name and address.

LI17R2

## SPECIAL EXCERPT FROM

*Love Inspired®*

*Widower Caleb King is set on raising his two small children without assistance from anyone—especially a relative of the wife who'd abandoned them. When Caleb is injured, Jessie Miller is just as determined to help her late cousin's family—never imagining that coming into their lives would lead to her own happily-ever-after.*

*Read on for a sneak preview of*
*SECOND CHANCE AMISH BRIDE by* **Marta Perry,**
*available September 2017 from Love Inspired!*

Caleb darted a quick look at Jessie, and then his gaze dropped. "You never told me about your business out in Ohio."

It took a moment for Jessie to process the unexpected words. Finally she shrugged. "There didn't seem to be a reason to."

"Or an opportunity?"

She shook her head slightly, but it was probably true. They hadn't had many casual conversations, and she tended to pick her words carefully with him.

"Zeb told me about it. He said you gave it up to come and help us."

"I couldn't be there and here, could I? It seemed more important to be here."

"Why?" His eyes met hers, challenging. "Why was this important to you?"

Jessie hesitated. She glanced at the *kinder*, but they didn't seem to be paying any attention to the adults' conversation. "I grew up being responsible for my cousin. I guess I still feel responsible. If I can do something to right a wrong, then I want to do it. I need to do it."

Jessie couldn't bring herself to look at his face, afraid of what she'd read there. He reached out suddenly to grab her wrist, covering her hand on the wheelchair, and her breath caught.

"You aren't…" he began.

But she wasn't to know what he might have said. Becky gave the chair a big shove. "We can take it the rest of the way. We don't need any help."

Jessie let go and watched the children struggle to get the chair into the barn. She wanted to assist, but not at the cost of upsetting Becky.

What had brought on that sudden reaction on the child's part? The fact that Caleb had been momentarily occupied with Jessie? She wasn't sure. But each time she took a step forward with Becky, it seemed to be followed by a plunge backward.

As for where she stood with Caleb… She didn't even want to think about that problem.

*Don't miss*
*SECOND CHANCE AMISH BRIDE*
*by Marta Perry, available September 2017 wherever*
*Love Inspired® books and ebooks are sold.*

www.LoveInspired.com